The Tusitala

by

Terence F. Moss

Dedicated to absent friends.

To everybody who helped in the creation of this book, including all at Trafalgar Publishing, to Danny Moss for all his help on the day-to-day issues, to Wendy Moss for her inspiration and support, to Chris Schüler for editing the book and anybody else who I may have missed... Thank you.

Works by the author
Stage musicals
Angels and Kings 2007
Soul Traders 2008

Television
The Inglish Civil War 2009 (pilot comedy)
Closing Time 2010 (pilot comedy)
Dave 2011 (pilot comedy-drama)

Stage plays.
Better by Far 2015
Ali's Bar 2017
All Those Years Ago 2018

Novels
The Prospect of Redemption 2012
The Killing Plan 2013
The Tusitala 2015
Be Happy with my Life 2018.

Contacts
Terence F. Moss can be contacted at
butchmoss@OUTLOOK.COM
Terence F. Moss on Facebook

Table of Contents

The Tusitala

By

Terence F. Moss

He walks softly by your side or tiptoes in your shadow, and you give him not a second glance... and then one day, he clears his throat, and you are startled by his presence...

Mesopotamia 1915

Tell me, am I dead?
Why do you ask?
I am not sure.
So how will you know for sure?
If I answer, I could tell you a lie...
I will trust you.
But if you would trust me, why not trust yourself?
Because I do not know for sure that I am alive.
You could lie to yourself.
I could, but that is why I am asking you.
Why?
Because I need to be sure.
But can you be sure of anything?

Can I ask you another question?
Of course,
Are you dead?
Not dead, not as you would understand.
So, what is your name?
My name. Ah well, my name it means nothing,
for it comes in many tongues and on many tides,
and is infinite.

Why do you talk in riddles?
Because all life is a riddle.
Have you not yet realised that?
No. So, am I dead?

It was a cold, grey Sunday morning, Valentine's Day, February 14th, 1915, and the pitiless overnight bombing of the Allied positions had been remorseless. Hopelessness and despair, two inseparable allies, permeated opposing trenches. Their constant companion and the last haven of respite, oblivion, now beckoned. Everybody was welcome to the party to end all parties. But even death, the occasional welcome friend, could not arrest the anguish and the pain.

The ethereal glowing end of a cigarette appeared suspended in mid-air just moments before Captain Phillips emerged from the gloom. A foreboding, melancholic expression hovered over his face. Fortunately, there was insufficient illumination for Drew to fully appreciate the significance. There was no moon that night, only pale illumination from the oil lamps hanging on the trench walls, a glistening whimper of golden light onto the duckboards and soldiers' faces.

There was a sudden splash of daylight, a starburst shell exploded overhead, and the solitary crack of a sniper's rifle in the distance. Another soul was leaving the jamboree.

A giant black rat scampered past, pausing to glance up, wondering who might be for lunch tomorrow.

'Evening, sir,' said Sergeant Drew, coming swiftly to attention. The rich, mellifluous tone of his voice - a hint of Wales in there somewhere - brought half a smile to Captain Phillips's face. He could remember…

'At ease, sergeant,' replied Phillips.

'What are they up to, sir,' enquired Drew? 'They haven't stopped tonight.'

'I'm not sure,' replied Phillips thoughtfully. 'I think maybe Johnny Turk intends to keep us awake as long as possible so we don't have time to prepare ourselves for our next attack. In that respect, they are undeniably succeeding in their objective.'

'We'll fuck 'em, sir, excuse my French,' replied Drew, 'They're only bloody oiks.'

Phillips half smiled with dutiful resignation - the English way - took another long draw on his cigarette and gazed into space. *Take your punishment like gentlemen, his form teacher had always sermonised. No matter what the circumstances and especially in the presence of oiks.* He glanced momentarily at Drew and half-smiled again, this time in ironic admiration. They were side by side in the same shithole now. It mattered not where they originally came from; they would probably die here together today.

'No doubt their intelligence reports have advised them we intend to launch an attack later this morning. They always seem to know when we are coming.'

'So, they are giving us a good pounding first to try to soften us up a bit,' suggested Drew, 'in readiness?'

As Sergeant Drew had correctly assessed, the Turks had taken advantage of the heavy overnight rain. Their goal was to ensure the patch of barren wasteland between them, the ground that was being so bitterly fought over, was as inhospitable as possible for the assault that would soon begin. The earth had been turned into a raging quagmire of mud and dismembered parts of unrecovered decaying bodies. The greyed eyes now gazing with bewilderment to heaven. Delicacies for the crows to peck out; the remains of the soldiers' bodies sustenance for the rats and foxes. They, too, wished to survive another day.

'Correct,' replied Phillips.

'What time do we go over, sir?' asked Drew.

'Eight o'clock sharp... don't be late. Can't start the show without you.' He smiled briefly at Drew to make sure he understood his sardonic quip. Drew smiled back.

'I'll be here, sir, no problem. I've got nothing else in the diary today.' Captain Phillips glanced at Drew for a second and smiled again; he could not help but admire somebody who cared even less about dying than he did.

The murky swamp of human detritus that spread out before them was eighteen inches deep in places. That alone would severely impede any significant movement towards the enemy's position. The foetid stench of degeneration was always there in the air, the bittersweet aroma of death that would linger in your memory. Its essence, trapped deep within the nasal passages for your lifetime... if you were destined to have a lifetime, however long that might be.

'So, what did you do before you washed up in this hellhole?' asked Phillips, not really expecting Drew to reply with anything out of the ordinary.

'I was a writer and a carpenter.'

'A writer of what?' asked Phillips sounding surprised.

'Books. Novels mainly, well, a couple, and some poetry.'

'Are you famous, like Brooke and Kipling?' he asked curiously. 'I've read some of their stories, even met Brooke once, nice chap.'

'No, not at all. Never even had a book published, to be honest,' he replied poignantly. He paused momentarily as his thoughts drifted back to his wife and son, both now dead. Both would probably still be alive had he been published and earned some money, but he had not, and they had perished.

'Are you still writing?'

'Not really. Something happened, and I stopped and never started again. There didn't seem to be any point. That's why I'm here.'

'There's plenty to write about here,' remarked Phillips. 'All this death and destruction. I could write a few pages about it, so I'm sure you could write something half decent.'

Drew thought about Phillips's words, and slowly a story began to form in his mind...

Creeping stealthily over the sides of trenches and rolling along the walkways, the mist of putrefaction would have deterred any sane person from venturing one yard into this cesspit of hell. This fiery furnace of gases, flames, disorder, chaos, and noise... the sound of failure and death. If the foetor, the sulphurous anal halitosis of decay, did not make you wretch, then the thought of certain death just moments away certainly would. Worse still, the ever-present threat of partial dismemberment, the final insult that you should linger on, to survive, to tell the tale of how you had ceased to be that which you once were. That boy, that bloodied perfect body delivered from his mother's womb in a moment of sublime exultation, held high in praise to a God. Now he was transformed by another perfect body into something that you could never, in your maddest hallucinations, your worst nightmare ever have imagined.

The visions and memories gently torment your mind as you crawl back through the detritus of failure, with maybe only one leg or arm. The batsman who once scored a tireless century, cheered on by his team, friends, and lover... Never again. His talent won the day, but no more. The Cambridge blue could no longer pull an oar as before, one arm now a withered, blackened stub. No longer trailing fingers in the Cam, just empty sleeves.

Although hopelessly dying, the soldier clings desperately to the vain belief that he might survive if he could only return to the safety of his own lines. That place of protection he left only a few minutes earlier, even back to his mother's womb, he prays - when he might be born again on a different day. Then he might live a little longer... but probably he would not...

'I'm beginning to think this is all absolute madness,' said Phillips, interrupting Drew's meanderings.

'Madness?' said Drew. 'I don't understand.'

'All this killing, fighting over a bit of land, but to what end?'

'We have to stop them,' said Drew innocently, unaware of the real reason they were standing, soaked to the skin, in a trench full of mud in Mesopotamia.

'But it is their land. We are only here because of the oil. If there was no oil, we would be gone. It's all about money in the end, and we are just here to make somebody else rich.'

Drew did not reply but quietly pondered over Phillips's accusatory words before drifting back...

With the Turks holding the higher position, the blood-stained rain blatantly refused to soak further into the saturated ground. Slowly it began trickling back into the potholes and the English trenches. Seeping down the sides of the mud and sandbag walls, darkened umber rivulets of blood and mud, the final remnants of life.

Today's assignment was an impossible manoeuvre: uphill, over treacherous ground, through barbed wire. The enemy's position was heavily fortified; the attackers were outgunned. Their chance of success was minimal. The probability of survival past the first five minutes was virtually non-existent. However, their instructions were explicit and unambiguous, without room for discretion or debate.

'We must take their trench at any cost; this could be a turning point in the war!' This mindless rhetoric would be cracked out by the sergeants and corporals to embolden the enlisted men before they went over the top.

'This could be the battle that sees the beginning of the end of this conflict,' barked the captains and majors. But they were oblivious to the insanity of their commanders. There would be no end to this conflict today or for many years, just the end of more lives, thousands of young lives, all squandered in a foreign land. Fodder for the foxes, eyes for the crows.

The English guns stopped pounding the Turkish position at five minutes to eight; even the English weren't stupid enough to bomb their own infantry, hopefully. A pallid, misty cloud crept slowly over the field of play between the lines.

The protocols of engagement clearly "stated" that surprising the enemy was terribly bad form – and definitely 'not cricket.' The English had effectively given the Turks a very respectable five-minute warning. Time enough to prepare themselves for another easy slaughter of the virgin soldiers.

'Are the lads ready,' asked Phillips?'

'Ready as they will ever be,' replied Drew, suddenly snapping back from his daydream.

'Right.'

The whistles started to blow. Captain Phillips, with his Webley pistol held firmly in his hand, and Sergeant Drew at his side, marshalled his platoon of thirty-three men up the rickety wooden duck ladders and out of the trench. Sergeant Drew ran swiftly, ever diligently, to his right, encouraging the men to keep in a straight line. The flames of hell leapt out from the Turkish guns, decimating half the platoon within seconds. The grim reaper rode merrily among them, waving his sword and laughing at the idiocy of it all. Today's takings would be good, and his thirst would be quenched in full. He would have no need to make any further calls for a while.

Artillery shells landed everywhere, separating men from their extremities; heads disappeared, and men disappeared, vaporised by the heat and shrapnel of exploding shells. Captain Phillips was still leading his men from the front when the ratchet of machine-gun fire instantly severed his right leg. He stood precariously for a few moments, a solitary dazed figure on a single stump, the other clean bowled… and then fell. The machine guns swept the ground around him, throwing up large terpsichorean clusters of mud and water like twirling ballerinas, and he was lost in the quagmire. Two soldiers ran valiantly to where he had fallen, a shell exploded close by, and they were instantly gone. A red mist slowly descended to earth, the only evidence they were ever there or that they had ever existed.

Sergeant Drew had been drawn to the left of his position to avoid a large bomb crater, but seeing Phillips drop to his right, he turned and made his way back around the hole to where his captain had fallen. As he ran, the machine guns followed his path, peppering the ground with dancing pirouettes of death, close but not close enough to harm. Defying them to do their worst, Drew arrived where Phillips was lying face down in the mud. Turning him over, Drew saw he was still breathing but severely wounded.

The machine gunners continued to fire mercilessly at Drew. They were obviously concerned that one man trying to save another man's life might endanger them or even change the outcome of the battle. No time for honourable intentions, mercy, or compassion; these would be left for another day.

For whatever reason, the gunners could not find their mark today. Drew, seemingly impervious to all the butchery around him, slowly dragged Captain Phillips backwards towards the bomb crater he had just passed. They both fell into the relative safety of an area just below ground level. Drew cautiously peered over the edge of the bomb crater to see how the rest of his men were faring. He was unsure whether to resume his platoon leader duties and guide his men or try to save Captain Phillips's life. But they were all gone. The half dozen that had made it to the barbed-wire defence had been shot to pieces, now hanging like unloved rag dolls on a washing line.

The battle raged on above, but he knew he could do no more. Drew slowly slipped back into the crater and looked across at Phillips, unconscious and bleeding badly from where his knee used to be. He removed his belt and tunic and ripped the tunic in half with his bayonet. He slipped this over the tattered remains of Captain Phillips's leg just above the knee, wrapping it around his thigh. He then tied his belt tightly around the thigh to staunch the bleeding.

It was at this moment that he became aware of somebody else in the crater. He turned quickly to see an elegant man shrouded in a grey cloak, sitting on the other side of the pothole, smoking a cigarette. Was this the Reaper? thought Drew. He looked up at the sky, expecting death at any moment, but there was nothing. He grabbed his captain's pistol and pointed it at the figure.

'Who the hell are you?' demanded Drew.

The figure appeared utterly indifferent to the battle raging above them. Even less so by the pistol now pointed directly at his face.

'I am intrigued by your wanton disregard for your safety and unstinting heroism,' the figure replied, 'I thought you might require my services.'

'Who are you,' repeated Drew? 'Are you a doctor?'

'I am many things: the darkness in your soul, the fear you cannot hide, the you that you would rather never know. I am your revenge and strength to smite your enemy and those who have betrayed you.'

'I have no time for your riddles,' shouted Drew. 'Tell me who you are, or I will shoot you where you stand.'

'I am sitting,' replied the man, looking at Drew with a curious expression.

'Sitting, standing, it makes no difference,' replied Drew, stunned by the man's stunningly inappropriate flippancy. 'Tell me who you are or...'

The man smiled and blew out some smoke. 'I am your friend, and I choose my friends very carefully. My name is Mephisto.'

'Mephisto? What kind of name is that? Are you a fucking Turk?'

'No, I am not,' replied the man indignantly. 'Mephisto is the name I travel under today. I am a man of the world, with many names, but not from any country.'

'You speak in conundrums and puzzles, and you make no sense. But if you are a friend, you will help me carry Captain Phillips back to our lines,' pleaded Drew.

'I will help you, my friend. All in good time,' replied Mephisto.

'There is no time. He's dying,' exclaimed Drew, frustrated by the stranger's apparent inability to comprehend the magnitude of Captain Phillips's wounds.

'He will not die,' replied Mephisto.

'What?' exclaimed Drew abruptly, astounded by the man's arrogant declaration.

'I told you - he will not die. Whatever the outcome of our discussion, he will not die today or any day for that matter. Not from this wound, anyway. He will die eventually, as must we all, but not for many years.'

Drew felt a strange sensation begin to engorge his body, a sense of immense well-being, something he had briefly felt when he was much younger but not since. His immediate fears and concerns for Captain Phillips began to abate. It felt as if he were taking a Holy Communion and all his sins were about to be forgiven. Drew lowered his gun and rendered himself up to this man who called himself Mephisto.

'All right,' said Drew. 'What do you want?'

'Can you feel anything,' asked the man?

'Yes, yes, I can,' replied Drew suspiciously.

'Do you know what that is,' he asked?

'I'm not certain,' said Drew.

'Yes, you are. You know exactly what it is,' replied Mephisto. He smiled and moved his head around in a small circle as if he had a neck ache. Then he took another draw on his cigarette before dropping it in the mud.

'You tell me, if you know everything, you tell me what it is,' said Drew with challenging belligerence.

'Immortality – that is what you feel right now, and that is what I can offer you. The infinity of life.'

'To live forever,' asked Drew?

'No, not forever, but an exceptionally long time for you. But I cannot wait forever.'

Drew wondered what he meant. 'Who are you to tender such a gift?'

'Whoever you want me to be,' said Mephisto.

'Only the devil can offer such a prize; as I remember, there is always a price. Someone always has to pay the Tillerman,' replied Drew cautiously.

'Of course, there is a cost: I want your soul… eventually, but not just yet, in a few years, when you are finished with it, and our contract is concluded. No man wants to live forever, to outlive all his friends and children… What benefit is immortality if a man has no one with whom to share it? So, you will only be trading something in the future for which you will have no further use, for something far more valuable now.'

'But I have already lost everything that meant anything to me, so what good is that to me? That would just be one more kind of purgatory in exchange for another,' said Drew.

'Not quite,' replied Mephisto. 'I will grant you immortality until you have recovered everything that rightfully belonged to you, everything you once had. But on that day, when you retake possession of all that was once yours, I will take your soul, and it will become mine forever. Agreed?

Drew laid back against the mud wall, the crater slowly filling with water. He looked across at Captain Phillips, quietly moaning as he drifted in and out of consciousness. He noticed the bleeding had stopped, which was unusual in his experience. He looked back at this stranger but said nothing as he considered the proposal.

'What do you have to lose,' asked Mephisto? 'Your life was over anyway. Your novel was stolen by your publishers. All the money that should have been yours has been taken. Your wife and son died in agony because you were too poor to pay for a doctor, and now maybe your friend will die. Oh, and your platoon are all dead…'
He popped his head over the side of the foxhole and quickly looked around. 'Except that is for a few mumblers and grumblers, and they will be dead soon enough when they eventually concede that it is time to take my hand.'

'You said he wouldn't die, no matter what,' exclaimed Drew, pointing at Captain Phillips, who was now mumbling incoherently.

'So, I did. Fair enough, he lives, but you must carry him back.'

'How did you know about…' But Drew stopped, for he now knew who he was talking to. This was no delusion. 'Why me,' he asked, 'and why today?'

'I embrace tragedy. It satisfies a desire,' replied Mephisto. 'It's very much the same as comedy. Two sides of the same coin, you might say.' He smiled and casually leaned back. 'Life and theatre are all about timing, and good timing can intrigue and entertain an audience…' He took out a packet of cigarettes, lit two and offered one to Drew. 'And this entertains me.'

Drew took the cigarette. 'You think this is funny?'

'On the contrary, Gideon, I did not say that… In fact, I think this is all an absolute tragedy. I prefer to choose my moments for the best dramatic effect.' Mephisto smirked again.

'You know my name,' exclaimed Drew sounding mystified?

'Of course I do. I know everybody's name.'

Drew said nothing at first, deliberating over a decision that could change his life forever. But, as Mephisto had said - what did he have to lose?

'I want him to live!' exclaimed Drew suddenly, pointing at Captain Phillips.

'I have already agreed to that. You can have him as a gift... whether you trade or not. I'm feeling generous today.'

'I wouldn't need to trade if we both got back,' said Drew.

'I didn't say you would both get back alive.'

'Oh,' said Drew. 'I thought that...'

'You thought wrong. You would carry him safely back to your lines and then, at the very last moment, just as you thought you had made it... Bang! Lucky shot in the back of your head, and you're dead. Bloody sniper.'

'That's unfair!' exclaimed Drew.

Mephisto laughed. 'Of course it's unfair. That's life. Have you not worked that one out yet? It is all one outrageously offensive joke – but then maybe not. Who knows?' He laughed again, pulled a sword from a scabbard, and waved it in the air. The sun began to shine with intense brilliance.

'So here we are, decision time,' said Mephisto. He was now eating a banana, something that Drew had only seen once before in his life. Mephisto offered half the banana to Drew, but he declined, more out of disbelief than any other reason.

'So, what do I do?' said Drew, still confused but now yielding to the offer.

'Nothing much,' replied Mephisto, taking another drag on his cigarette and blowing smoke rings into the air. 'Just climb out of here and carry your captain back home. If you have not declined my offer by the time you get back into your trench, you will both arrive safely, but if you utter the words *You may never take my soul*" between here and there, you may be shot. I do not know. It depends, but that would have happened anyway; it's nothing to do with me. My partner deals with fate. It's a sort of job-share arrangement we have.'

Drew sat for a moment, gazing at Mephisto, who was finishing his banana. Then he turned to pick up Captain Phillips. As he struggled to pull him over the edge of the shell hole, he found he could not gain purchase on the muddy sides and kept slipping back.

'Can you give me a hand,' asked Drew?

Mephisto laughed, 'Absolutely not. I have already given you his life. What more do you deserve? You will manage.'

At that moment, Drew found the inner strength to haul the almost lifeless body of Captain Phillips out of the shell hole. Half lifting the captain onto his shoulder, he pulled him upright and began to carry him back to his lines. The Turkish machine guns immediately began raking the ground around him, but once again, they could not find their mark. Drew made it back to the trench and carefully lowered Captain Phillips to the waiting hands. He was impervious to the pirouettes of death, playing out one last performance just for him. He heeded not their empty threats.

He turned to face the crater where they had been hiding. As he did so, a shell landed on the very spot, and their temporary shelter erupted in another enormous explosion. Drew said nothing as he slipped over the sandbags into the waterlogged trench to the cheers of his fellow warriors.

The devil's supply of souls needs to be continuously replenished; without them, he cannot inhabit the earth. Today, Gideon had made a bargain, and another soul was lost, but at what cost to his very being?

Chapter 1
1984

This story starts long before it begins and finishes long after it ends. In fact, the end is the beginning, in a manner of speaking. You must decide where and when it reaches its conclusion and from where it could have begun. This is only one small episode of a much larger story...

Blake Thornton sat in his study, leaning back in his tattered, green leather captain's chair, gazing at the photograph of his wife Catherine and their two children, Max and Claudia. The antique silver picture frame had been a present from Catherine on his thirty-fourth birthday back in 1981, along with the portrait she had commissioned from a professional photographer. Receiving that gift had been one of the happiest moments in his life, although he didn't realise that at the time.

'Something to inspire your wearisome days,' she had whispered as she gave him the present. 'Something to look at daily, to remind you that no matter what happens, we will always love you.' Then she gently kissed him. It was a declaration of love, unlike anything he had experienced before. Thornton was enraptured by its intensity. But he had failed to notice the tiny hint of dark foreboding deeply couched within the words.

Catherine then took hold of his hands and eased him slowly out of the chair. 'Dance with me, Thornton,' she whispered forcefully. 'Show me how much you love me.' She wrapped her arms around his body, and he slipped his arms around her tiny waist. Thornton smiled demurely, for he could not resist her – he never could.

He was not a particularly good dancer and had always been self-conscious about his awkwardness, but it felt different with Catherine. It was as if nothing else in the world mattered - it was just the two of them. 'Dance as though no one can see you' – that was what Catherine always told him. She touched the play button on the stereo system, Billy Joel started to play, and they began...

'By the way,' whispered Catherine, looking up at Blake. 'I have another birthday present for you.'

'What?' asked Blake.

'I'm pregnant.' Blake smiled and kissed her again before they slowly fell back onto the sofa, kissing and caressing each other, eventually sliding to the floor, where they made love. The children were fast asleep in bed...

Catherine's plaintive words had comforted Blake. He had never really felt the need before. But for some reason, he found the solace strangely reassuring on that occasion. But little did he appreciate the prophetic irony of what she had said.

He cherished the photograph and the sentiment; it reminded him of how uncomplicated things had been before the manuscript of Prospect Road had arrived at his office. It also marked one other significant moment in his life. The year he had officially taken over from Reggie Clanford as the owner of Clanford and Fox publishers and literary agents. A few months later, Catherine lost the unborn baby. Thinking back, Blake wondered if maybe that was when things had begun to change.

He gazed up at the ceiling, and his mind wandered back even further to 1968 when he had first joined Clanford and Fox as a new manuscript reader and copy editor. He was twenty-one and fresh out of university, gaining a double first in English Literature and History. He was unsure what he wanted to do with his life. He had considered going into television or the newspaper business. Then one day, while drinking in a Chelsea wine bar with Sean, an old friend from university, he mentioned this vacancy.

'Why don't you apply for this job?' Sean asked. He showed Blake the advert. 'It's a publishing company. I've already accepted another offer, so I'm not even going to the interview. There's no reason you shouldn't apply. You are better qualified than I am, so it could be right up your street.'

Blake thought it sounded interesting; he was broke, so he telephoned the company and arranged an interview. He was offered the job on the spot and accepted it, little realising just how much that decision would affect the rest of his life.

Blake got on well with Reggie Clanford right from the start. Reggie took him under his wing, and within a couple of years, he was treating him like the son he never had.

One day, Blake was in Reggie's office. They were discussing something completely innocuous when, quite unexpectedly, Reggie came out and said it. 'Blake, I want you to take over the business when I'm gone.'

'Me? But I've only been here for a couple of years. In all honesty, I don't know really know anything about it. Everybody else understands the business far better than I do.'

Blake was insistent about his lack of professional experience, but it brooked no sympathy from Reggie. His continued self-disqualification on the grounds of inexperience only further cemented Reggie's decision. He was the perfect man for the job.

'Yes, you do,' replied Reggie, smiling phlegmatically at Blake's modesty. 'It's not just about what you know. You… you have a natural flair for the business. You get on well with the authors, and you understand their silly little quirks, idiosyncrasies, eccentricities, whims, fancies, and occasional strange ways. That is what's important. This is a people business; we don't make anything here. We find dreams, fantasies, and illusions and put them on paper for people to read. Reggie gestured to a chair.

'Sit down for a moment, Blake, and let me give you some fatherly advice. Authors – and I use that word sparingly.' He made a wry expression – 'will happily inhabit their own existence with the ease of a tortoise permanently ensconced in its shell. Their most highly valued asset is the independence and freedom they have won by creating stories. Stories which other people want to read. Stories that allow their readers to temporarily escape their own humdrum existence. That freedom is most important to them. They work to be free of the world. And you must defend this status quo – to the death if necessary.' He added the last few words in a Churchillian tone - more for the dramatic effect than any literal sense. Blake smiled.

Reggie took another sip of coffee, leaned back in his old captain's chair, and gazed up at the ceiling.

'Over the years, I have come to the conclusion that writers live in their own microcosmic world. They are totally detached from the reality of a normal existence. This is essential if they are to continue creating interesting characters and engaging stories. They must be protected from the real world; reality and creativity are never good bedfellows. You must nurture their ideas and ambitions and listen to their problems, but never ingratiate yourself or give in to

16

obsequiousness. That would demean and eventually destroy the delicate balance and dynamic of your relationship. Do you understand what I am saying?'

Blake nodded, but Reggie was still staring at the ceiling.

Reggie looked back at Blake, and, in a hushed, conspiratorial tone, he continued.

'Hopefully, they will repay this empathetic indulgence by remaining loyal to our company once they become successful. Some of our current authors could have sold more books by switching to larger publishers. But writers generally write for something more incorporeal than mere financial gain. This much I know you understand.' He took another sip of coffee, 'this is the most important thing to remember above everything else.' He paused for a moment gathering his thoughts. He chose not to mention one more critical detail; he would talk about that another time.

'Did you know that Clanford and Fox have been agents and book publishers for over seventy years?'

'No, I didn't,' replied Blake, listening carefully. Visions of greater things were beginning to form in his mind.

'It was started by Joshua Clanford and Obadiah Fox in the early 1900s. They majored in writers of the ilk of Dickens and Conan Doyle, storytellers with a hint of darkness about them. Unfortunately, none of our authors has achieved quite the same recognition and popularity as Dickens or Doyle. But we have still had commercial success with the ones we have published, so we cannot complain. We have stayed in business to the present day, which is no mean accomplishment in these challenging times for the publishing industry. I am sure it will continue for another seventy years.' He smiled at Blake.

They had been salient words from the heart, and they made a deep impression on Blake. Now the business was his. Reginald Clanford had retired, and one year later, just before he died, he handed over the last remnants of control and all his shares in the company.

There was one other thing that Reggie had mentioned at the time, which suddenly came back to mind. It was about Freddy Fox,

Obadiah's son and Reggie's junior partner until he died in 1966 - a couple of years before Blake started working for the firm.

Freddie killed himself, leaving a puzzling note that nobody could understand. It merely said, 'For the sins that must be atoned.' It was all very enigmatic and made no sense to Reggie or Freddie's wife, Amelia. The other oddity was that Freddy had left his entire shareholding in Clanford and Fox to Reggie. And non to his wife, for some inexplicable reason.

So, Reggie Clanford owned all the shares in the company. Oddly, the legacy had been added as a codicil only weeks before Freddie died. Neither Reggie nor Amelia could understand why he had written this clause into his will, and neither would ever know.

'Not every suicide comes with an explanation,' said Reggie quietly, staring into the distance, 'but there is usually some rationale. In Freddy's case, however, there was nothing apart from the cryptic note. He was happy at work and home, and the business was doing well.'

Reggie had never gone into further detail except to say they had been best friends for many years, never having a cross word. Suddenly one day, Freddy's demeanour changed, and three months later, he committed suicide.

Blake's mind shot forward to 1982, just over two years ago. He had been sitting in the same office talking to his assistant Jamie about the schedule of manuscripts they had to read over the long May bank holiday weekend. Fortunately, or maybe not, he could work at home whenever it pleased him, doing what he enjoyed most: reading stories.

Manuscripts that had successfully passed through the first reading process in the outer office were then passed to Blake. This happened with Prospect Road, an autobiographical novel by Anthony Theodore Clackle when it arrived at the office that March. Jamie had read the whole manuscript, which he thought was promising. He then passed it to Blake with his editorial comments, ready for a final decision on whether they should publish it.

Prospect Road: Chapter One

Written by
Anthony Theodore Clackle
Thomas Drayton's Story

My name is Thomas Edward Drayton, and I was born in July 1947. It was a sweltering summer following one of the coldest winters on record. I do not remember being born; neither do I have any recollection of that long hot summer. I was only informed of these details after I had reached an age when I could understand their relevance.

My first full-colour memory of my existence on Earth was Coronation Day, 2nd June 1953, a national holiday. I was nearly six years old. Undoubtedly, all the preceding days had been blessed with colour as well, but for me, this one was the most memorable. It was so utterly different from all the other days of my life up to that point. It was a little overcast to start – it had rained overnight and left things a little damp. But the temperature warmed up as the hours slowly passed. It eventually became an unforgettable day, and I had a wonderful time.

Looking back, I remember it as a day full of promise - many promises, in fact, during a period of great excitement and overflowing enthusiasm. The lust for life had vanquished the cloud of despair that had hovered over us for so long.

There was a smile and encouraging words from everyone I met. 'Alright, lad' or 'Are you having a lovely day, my boy?'

We had been delivered from the carnage of a world war eight years previously. I was not actually around then, merely a by-product of the continuing celebrations after six years of bitter conflict.

Food rationing was still in place, but we had enough to keep our bellies happy. In the air, a hint of exhilaration and a sense of expectancy. The feeling that things would change was inescapable. No one seemed to know how things would change, just that they would, and it would "all be for the better," as everybody kept saying…

It was as if we were at the beginning of something beautiful, a journey into the unknown. It felt like those last few days of eager anticipation and excitement just before starting out on holiday. We had not arrived yet, but we knew that when we did, it would be fun, and we would enjoy every minute of it. The country had suffered from all kinds of shortages for years. But now things were going to be different - better. Fortunately, I did not suffer from these shortages, as I had never been aware of them in the first place. My mother used to say what you never had, you never missed.

Apparently, me and everybody else had a ubiquitous relative whom we all referred to as "Uncle Jim." No matter what the familial relationship was. I called him Uncle Jim, my mother called him Uncle Jim, and all the people in the shops, even the "old bill," called him Uncle Jim. It was all a little odd and very confusing at times. I found out later that being called Uncle was a local tradition. This was an epithet decorously granted to anybody who could always be relied upon to find whatever anybody wanted (within reason). Be it sugar, butter, nylons, coffee, bananas or even petrol, and of course, chocolate. He had been successfully plying his trade throughout the war and some years after.

He appeared to be utterly unaffected by the vagaries of Mr Hitler's attempts to prevent us from enjoying such luxuries and utterly oblivious to the government's rationing legislation (whatever that was). Parsimony and frugality were alien concepts to Uncle Jim. A complete contradiction to his liberal theories on free trade, which he would articulately defend on any night of the week in the Sailor's Return Public House on the corner of Prospect Road. Once again, as with so many of my earlier recollections, they almost entirely depend on third-hand information passed on to me much later in my life. But so vividly were they retold that I now feel confident that I must have heard them first-hand after all, however inconceivable that may sound.

Uncle Jim was a fascinating character. The like of which, undoubtedly turned up all over the country during this period, tinker traders who kept everybody adequately supplied with the essentials and a few simple luxuries. He carried on his lucrative business right up until 1954, when rationing eventually came to an end. After that, food, clothes, and luxury items became more generally available in the shops, if you had the money to buy them.

Just after that, like a wisp of smoke in a gentle breeze, he was suddenly gone, and I never saw him again. I often wondered what became of Uncle Jim.

I later learnt that he was of Romany extraction, a fact that was, a little oddly, always greeted with a hushed mysticism and mild disdain whenever mentioned in general conversation. I never did manage to work out precisely why this should make any difference to his innate ability to procure these little luxuries. Or why he was apparently exempt from conscription.

'Where do you come from, Uncle Jim?' I dared to ask him on one of his visits to our house.

He looked down at me and scratched his belly. 'You're a cheeky little sod, aren't you?' I smiled, and he gave me a piece of chocolate but did not answer my question. I later learnt that this was because he was *enigmatic,* whatever that meant.

Uncle Jim had been living with my grandmother during the war, apparently as a lodger. My grandfather (Grandad Bob) had been away in North Africa at the time. He was a bit unlucky, forty-three years old at the outbreak of hostilities and therefore still subject to the call-up.

During the war and for some time after it had ended, Uncle Jim brazenly drove around Portsmouth in his enormous pink Cadillac motor car selling black-market goods from its vast boot. I can vaguely remember the Cadillac making flying visits to various houses in Prospect Road around the time of the Coronation. The only reason I remember this is because the lurid colour stood out so vividly in a predominantly dour landscape. The warships moored at the end of the road, and the pavements were grey. Rusty corrugated iron, which was everywhere, was brown. Everything else that could be painted seemed to be painted black, and everything else not painted black was painted dark green. Bright colours were a rarity in those days.

Many years later, I pondered how Uncle Jim managed to avoid the long arm of the law for so long when he drove around conducting his business in Portsmouth's most outrageously ostentatious car. I concluded that they, too, must also have been grateful recipients of his generosity and trading activities. All this was, of course, apocryphal. Undoubtedly colourfully embellished over time. I was unaware of what Uncle Jim did until I was about five or six - by then, his luxury goods empire had begun to crumble.

Now was the time to rebuild our damaged country and mend our broken lives. We were encouraged to plan for the future, and most of us did, one way or another. My mother, Mary Florence Drayton, known by everybody as Flo, was always making plans for something or other. On Coronation Day, she dressed me up in some Satin supplied by the infamous Uncle Jim to look like Sabu the Elephant Boy. I believe he was a Kipling character immortalised in a popular film of the same name from the late 1930s.

My mother covered my body with a peculiar-smelling brown liquid, which she had concocted from potassium permanganate and mud as far as I could make out. She only told me this when I was much older and could process the information philosophically. As I later learned, my life would be peppered with many strange experiences relating to potions, mixtures, concoctions, and customs. Macbeth's weird sisters had nothing on my mother.

I remember trying to remove the stain between my toes weeks after the party had finished. Eventually, I had to resort to having a bath… ahhh.

Twenty years later, I distinctly remember using this exact same concoction to soak my feet (without the mud this time.) Apparently, it prevented them from smelling so cheesy, a severe problem when trying to attract members of the opposite sex (this was another suggestion from my mother).

Like most mothers, Flo played a large part in forming my views on life and what I could expect. "The world was my oyster," she would say. I did not know what an oyster was. "You just have to pick out the shiny little pearls." I didn't know what they were, either. But I smiled and made a mental note.

Fortunately, I also inherited her innate ability to think for herself. This would stand me in good stead for the rest of my life. It would not make me wealthy, but it would make me happy – very happy for a while. Fortunately, I did not inherit my mother's idiosyncratic tendencies, one of which was a peculiar ritual she enacted every Halloween. For some reason I could never fathom, she always used the occasion to play questionable games with the devil and the occult. This concerned me much, and I have often wondered whether she was sowing bad seed for the future.

On the night in question, several of my precious lead soldiers, Christmas presents, I hasten to add, would mysteriously disappear, never to return. Coincidentally, during the latter part of the evening, my mother would start to heat up a saucepan, which, unbeknown to me, had my lead soldiers in it. Once they had melted, she would have my sister Lizzie and me stand around a large basin of cold water. Then she would put her hand on one of our heads, utter a strange incantation, then drop some boiling lead into the water. This would instantly form a very odd shape, which she would retrieve from the water and carefully view before telling us what our futures held. As you can imagine, we were both in awe of this quasi-demonic ceremony, which she regularly conducted on the same night every year. That was until my army of lead soldiers was all gone. Little of what she predicted came true.

Flo made a turban out of green satin, which she carefully wrapped around my head. She completed the ensemble with a sort of Indian shirt and baggy trousers, which she had made from red satin material. She was a dab hand on the Singer sewing machine; most mothers were just after the war. I must have looked a picture wandering up and down Prospect Road, giving the impression of a refugee with serious sartorial issues. Or possibly a miniature trainee pimp from a Bombay harem (I did not know what a pimp was then).

My sister Elizabeth was dressed up as Nell Gwynne. Surprisingly, as Uncle Jim could not source real oranges, Lizzie had to make do with green apples painted orange. They may have been dipped in the same concoction I had been coated with. And so, we spent that fantastic day wandering up and down Prospect Road, in and out of everybody's house, eating and drinking whatever treats we were given.

The centre of the road was taken up with tables covered in Union Jack paper, and bunting was strung between the houses. Where there were houses still standing, that is. Directly opposite Number four, where we lived, the houses numbered one through to seven had been hit by a bomb and were no more. My Uncle Keith and Auntie Jenny lived at Number Nine. Families lived together in little communes in those days, much like today in some more deprived areas. But the family ties and community commitment were beginning to be eroded by radical social engineering. Back then, the terraced houses were small and basic, but the people were friendly. It was adequate for our needs. The new tower block developments were entirely different, deconstructing social interaction and divisively alienating communities.

I have never again experienced that same feeling of family togetherness, unity, and community as I did during those early years. Something was satisfying and comforting about living within walking distance of your relations. A sensation that I believe is primitive in its concept. Although tempered by the absence of privacy, I still found it profoundly friendly, welcoming, and heartening. There was a sense of well-being and wholesomeness. I suppose even a nod to puritanism in its most secular form. Utilitarian religion was also significantly important in those days.

We looked forward to baptisms, confirmations, and weddings, the affirmations of life and commitment. These were extraordinary days; Lizzie and I always went to church on Sundays. I did not know what it was all about, but I suppose it served as a moral compass giving us direction. That simple life lifted my spirits and roused my soul every single day. Something, sadly, that I do not believe happens quite so much these days. Now there is intensity, tension, and anxiety in almost everything we do. I am not that naïve to think that rape, murder, or robbery are any more prevalent today than they were back then. I just didn't notice it when I was a child.

On this unforgettable day, the tables were covered in plates of sausage rolls, lemonade, Cherryade, Tizer, crumpets, sandwiches, cakes, blancmange, sweets and even some chocolate. In the latter part of the afternoon, I remember hearing the distant sound of a plaintive trumpet, sounding like the United States cavalry announcing its arrival just in time to save the day. I regularly saw this heart-wrenching yet exhilarating spectacle on Saturday mornings when I visited the local fleapit, the Forum cinema. Then I began to feel the distinctive thud of the bass drum, relentlessly pounding out the infectious rhythm of life, becoming louder with every heartbeat.

Then suddenly, we were confronted with the awe-inspiring sight of the Salvation Army brass band swinging around the corner, marching majestically down Prospect Road. They were playing their hearts out as they made their way towards us with all the pomp and circumstance befitting this magisterial occasion. The buttons on their uniforms sparkled like diamonds in the afternoon sun. Their brass instruments, highly polished and gleaming, deflected streaks of sunlight in every direction.

All the older men – they were probably not that old, they just seemed that way to me – who had been drinking in the Sailor's Return on the corner came out of the pub with pints of beer raised in the air and cheered the band as it passed. It was an enormously rousing and uplifting occasion, and I felt oddly euphoric about the whole thing. It was something I had not experienced before and seldom since…

They continued down to the dockside at the end of the road, and for one terrible moment, I thought they were going to march straight down the slipway and into Portsmouth Harbour. My immediate concern was the appalling effect the mud would have on their shiny boots, but they did not. Slowly, with sweeping majestical elongation and precision, they turned through ninety degrees into the road. Then they carefully turned again and began marching back up the other side. Once again, they passed all the bedecked tables, and once again, they received a roaring ovation. Eventually, having made their way to the top of the road, they turned the corner. Then slowly disappeared into the sunset, continuing their journey to unknown destinations and destinies.

The celebrations went on into the night. I remember Lizzie and me looking out of the bedroom window down at the street below, completely mesmerised by the evening spectacle slowly unfolding before us. We watched as the tables were moved to one side, and the adults began dancing the night away to the sounds of Mantovani and the Joe Loss band on a record player. The street lights cast an ethereal glow on the proceedings. The sounds of laughter carried on long after we had eventually fallen asleep. I will remember that day for the rest of my life.

Prospect Road: Chapter Two
Written by
Anthony Theodore Clackle

The following day was also a holiday, so we, Barry, Carol, and I –
went down to the slipway at the end of Prospect Road to play in the
mud for a while.

The sailors on the destroyers and cruisers moored to the quayside
would throw pennies over the side for us to find in the sludge. They
always threw more money if Carol was there. She had already
mastered the art of smiling coquettishly, and her beguiling
expression of heartfelt appreciation for the small gifts raining down
seemed to work wonders. I was still relatively naïve in such matters
and didn't completely understand the hidden agenda. But
precocious Carol had already fully realised how best to exploit her
femininity.

Barry lived at number fifteen, and Carol lived on the next road
but always came to play with us. When I was about six or seven, I
thought I would like to marry Carol because she made such
splendid mud castles. When I went to her house for tea, her mum
always gave me a packet of Smith's crisps. Mind you, the Smith's
factory was not that far away, and everybody seemed to have a big
square tin of Smith's crisps hidden under the stairs.

I remember how the big blue lorries used to park overnight at the
end of the road on another bomb site. Some days we would walk
around the other bombsite and try to guess how many packets of
crisps were inside the lorries. Some days, you could smell the
boiling fat from the factory where they were made. In summer, you
could taste the cooked potato in the air. They only had one flavour,
potato, with or without salt, which came wrapped up in a little blue
twirl of waxed paper.

I remember one very terrifying experience with Carol. Well, not
exactly with Carol; it was more to do with her mum and my mum. It
was when we were about seven and pretending to be married. One
day, we went back to my house to play a game of mummies and
daddies in my bedroom and decided to get into bed as husbands and
wives do. We were cuddled up and happily chatting away,

completely oblivious to the sexual connotations of the situation. We had shared a bed many times before when we were much younger. Typically when my mum was going out for the evening, I stayed at Carol's mum's house overnight. It all seemed perfectly innocent to us.

Suddenly, my mum burst in, looking horrified. She began shouting, screaming, and leaping up and down, which frightened us both. I thought she had gone mad. We jumped out of bed, and then, for no reason that I was aware of, my mother started to beat me on my legs with a cane while continuing to shout at me. I did not have the slightest idea of what was going on. Then Carol started crying profusely, totally confused by what was happening. My mother did not let up on the raging and ranting and beating. Then, out of nowhere, Carol's mum suddenly appeared at the bedroom door.

There was more shouting, screaming, jumping up and down, and then whacking with another cane. It was absolute bedlam. Carol's mum started beating Carol's legs until they were covered in wheals and welts. We collapsed on the floor, crying our eyes out, without a clue as to why we were being punished. Eventually, it all stopped, and her mother marched Carol home. I stayed in my room for days, except when it was time for food, or I wanted to go to the toilet.

Ten years later, I began understanding what had gone through our mothers' minds. A classic example of childhood innocence being cruelly destroyed in an instant. Lost forever because of a simple misunderstanding and our parents' seriously flawed and hypocritical morality. They had judged us by their corrupt standards – a valuable lesson I would remember for the rest of my life.

Anyway, the tide was coming in, so we started to make our way back up the slipway to the road and went to play on to the bombsite where numbers 1, 3, 5 and 7 Prospect Road once stood. All the bricks had now been taken away, leaving lots of pieces of wood, complete doors, corrugated iron sheets, odd bits of metal (probably bits of a bomb with my luck) and deep trenches everywhere. Some had been used for dumping a variety of unspeakable things over the years. This, in turn, created a mysterious, musty pong, which I will never completely forget. The smell was always much worse in winter when the earth was wet. Years later, I would think back to those trenches and wonder how they compared to the First World

War trenches in France. As I grew older, I occasionally caught a whiff of something similar, invariably in an entirely unrelated environment. I would instantly be transported back to my childhood - the bomb site and our underground kingdom. It is so strange how an aroma, pleasant or nasty, can do that. Those moments happened less and less as I grew older.

We would cover the top of the trench with sheets of corrugated iron or old wooden doors. And as we were roughly the same height as the trenches, we could wander around our malodorous subterranean village, undisturbed by the rest of the world. I do not remember much about what we did there, but we would spend hours running around pretending to do something. We were possibly preparing our defence of Prospect Road against an invasion from outer space or even red Indians.

Whenever it was lunchtime or teatime, my mum stood outside Number 4 and bellowed out my name. I would pop up from our subterranean world with my head just visible above ground level and wave to her so she knew I had heard her. She always smiled when she saw me. I still remember that. Everybody in the road (possibly the next road, too) probably heard her. She had a loud voice – just how loud it could be, I found out during the bedroom incident with Carol. I thought then that my ears were going to bleed. Still, I think she loved me quite a lot.

During the daytime, my mum always wore one of those flowered housecoats and a scarf. I remember she would go through a routine of polishing the front doorstep with Cardinal red polish at least once a week. I think it was on a Friday because we used to have fish and chips for tea. I have no idea why she did this on Friday other than everybody else did it on the same day. Some Fridays, we would be *on duty* in our trench gazing across the road - watching the curious sight of our mothers polishing. It would entertain us for ages. All on their knees - head covered in cotton scarves, happily polishing their steps in perfect synchronisation while simultaneously conducting various unconnected conversations. This made no sense at all to me. I could only describe it as an incredibly surreal setting for a West End-stage musical song routine. Once again, this memory has been partially enhanced by the passing of time. Something which has undoubtedly lent it some enchantment. I would not have known what a musical was at that time.

Some house windows were still boarded up eight years after the war. Occasionally washing lines would be hung out across the road, with carpets hanging on them, making it look like a Moroccan marketplace. I did not know what to make of it then, and I still do not nearly thirty years later. The road had been blown to bits in places; a quarter of the houses were gone. And yet, amid all this carnage and destruction, my mum was polishing some bricks. It seemed an ironic juxtaposition. Maybe a bright, shining front doorstep was a beacon of defiance. Perhaps it was a bylaw that you had to keep your doorstep polished at all times?

I also remember a character known as Bertie Coggins, the local rag, bone, and scrap-metal merchant. All the stuff he collected was stacked inside and outside his junkyard at the end of the road. He stood out in my memory because everybody thought he was no more than a beggar. Then one day, he turned up in a brand new, dark-blue Humber Super Snipe motor car, the best car I had ever seen. This proves the old Northern saying, 'Where there's muck, there's brass.' Everybody spoke highly of Bert, or Bertram, as he preferred to be known after buying the Humber (though we all continued to call him Bert, much to his displeasure).

When I had no money, I would walk around the houses, gather newspapers, and take them to Bert. He would give me a penny a pound in weight. I also collected empty beer bottles and returned them to the pub for the deposit refund. I think it was about a halfpenny a bottle. All the money I made invariably went over the counter in 'Auntie' Maureen's sweet shop, just around the corner on Commercial Road. It also sold Woodbine cigarettes and matches. Next door to Auntie Maureen's was, and I am not making this up, 'Auntie' Doreen's.

Doreen Cover and her husband, Jack, sold fruit and vegetables. Both Maureen and Doreen (which always made me giggle for some inexplicably puerile reason) were good friends with Mum. They would come to all her parties - my mum loved to have a party - and they were always kind to me. Auntie Maureen – she was not a real Auntie – would bring me sweets when she came to babysit, so I was always pleased when Mum told me she was coming around.

Next door to Auntie Doreen was Eric Dimblebee, Barber and Hairdresser. What had always fascinated me about Mr Dimblebee was that as well as cutting hair, he also sold Durex 'Johnnies'. They were invariably stored tantalisingly high up in a glass cabinet right in front of you as you sat in the chair.

I knew what they were, more or less, or to be more accurate, I knew there was a tenuous link with sex, but I had no idea what that specific purpose was until much later in life. But the mysterious connection between barber and condom stuck in my mind for many years. Up to the age of thirteen, I genuinely believed you could not have sex until you had your hair cut. I eagerly looked forward to having my monthly snip. Half-expecting that something miraculous would happen to me one day, as it appeared to happen to the other men who entered Eric's shop.

'Something for the weekend, sir?' That immutable phrase was muttered surreptitiously into the customer's ear. I waited patiently for the day when it would be uttered clandestinely into mine, but it never was. Oh, those wistful days spent in expectation of wondrous things that would happen to me in the future. But they never did, not for a long time, not until I was nearly nineteen, despite having regular haircuts.

The following two shops were not there, just a large hole, then it was Wilson's the butcher and finally, The Royal Oak Public House on the corner. As I remember, there seemed to be a Brickwood's pub on the corner of every street in Portsmouth. All Brickwood's pubs were ornately tiled inside and out, usually in shiny dark reds, greens, and browns. Very depressing, really. Looking back, they were not dissimilar in design to public toilets and didn't smell any better either.

Further along, the road was a cemetery with tall iron railings running parallel to the main road. In the middle was a large ornate arched cast-iron entrance with two imposing gates. I half expected St Peter to be hanging around somewhere. The gates would open when the procession arrived with its latest arrival... I suppose departed might have been more technically accurate. Barry and I would often lean on the railings watching the proceedings - discussing the merits of being dead - in some depth. The list was endless: no school, no requirement to tidy our bedrooms, not having to be in bed early, not having to eat our greens, and not having to wash. On balance, though, we unanimously decided to stay as we were for now, as being dead looked a little bit boring.

I only sort of half-understood what was really happening. A few years later, I passed the cemetery and noticed all the headstones had been lifted and stacked against the back wall. I did wonder if there was a time limit on how long you could stay in the ground and whether that limit had now expired. But then, that did not make any sense. Some of the plots had only been filled a year or two earlier.

It turned out the church had sold the graveyard to a petrol company, and they were going to build a filling station on it. The next we knew, all the stones had gone, and a new petrol station with four pumps, a large canopy, and a shop had been built on the site. I often wondered what happened to the souls of the departed bodies that had not had enough time to make the final transition. One day in the future, I might find out.

Anyway, back to Prospect Road. Quite often, there were piles of horseshit left in the road from the tradesman's carthorses. Initially, canny Bert never bothered to pick up his horse's dung. He very kindly left it for budding entrepreneurs like me to handle that end of the market. I suppose if I had made a success of it, he might have considered taking me on as an apprentice shit shoveller. But I didn't fancy it as a career.

During the summer, especially during the holidays, Lizzie and I would collect the horseshit and then knock on doors to see if anybody wanted to buy it to put on their vegetables. Mum used to shout at me if I called it horseshit. She told me to call it garden manure or dung. I would wait patiently for the coalman or the milkman to pay the street a visit, and then I would be off.

'We're just going out to collect some horse shit, Mum,' I would shout endearingly up the stairs as we hurriedly left with bucket and coal shovel in hand. I especially used the shit word. I could be very irritating when I was young, having become aware of my mother's and her friends' delicate sensibilities. I loved hearing her shout despairingly, 'It's dung, darling, manure, or pooh, but not that word.' She always sounded so disdainful, which only made it worse as we found her oddly pretentious inflection even more amusing.

'Yes, Mummy,' we would reply and then wander off up the road saying to each other, 'It's not horseshit, darling, it's pooh.' To which Lizzie would reply, 'We are off to collect some poo... not shit... poo.'

'Manure sounds nicer,' I would say, and Elizabeth would reply, 'What! Nicer than poo or nicer than horseshit?' 'Oh yes, definitely nicer than horseshit.' This would be the general tone of the conversation as we wandered door to door. Until we got bored or found a new customer.

But of course, Mum knew best, as we would eventually come to learn. I did not realise then that she had plans for much better things for all of us.

'Would you like to buy some horse manure, penny a bucket,' we would politely ask when knocking on doors.

'Yes, please, they would say. Could you take it around the back alley?'

Lizzie and I would fall about in fits of laughter when a customer told us he was going to put it on his rhubarb... you know the rest.

A year or two later - the milkman, the coalman and the dustman stopped using horses and switched to electric floats and lorries with petrol engines. Hence, our supply of merchandise began to literally dry up. Bert, the rag and bone man, was the only trader left who still used a horse. I am sure he only did this to prop up the image of humble impecuniosity he had created. However, his new car had done to death any such illusion he may have thought we were labouring under.

As our last local produce supplier - stock was becoming increasingly harder to find. On top of that, Bert had become more astute and even sharper, which I did not believe was possible. He had obviously taken careful note of my profitable side-line. Bert was now collecting his horse's dung and selling it on his travels through the highways and byways of Portsmouth as "freshly made quality fertiliser." So that enterprise was coming to an end, as we couldn't afford a production facility. We still collected newspapers and sold them to Bert right up to the day we moved away.

The French onion man, who came on a bike, was always a slightly questionable character. I knew France was far away and could not figure out why he would come from France to England to sell a few rings of onions he'd hung around his neck. It just didn't seem financially viable even to my naïve business brain. I could understand the horseshit trade. On this, I was virtually an expert, knowing it inside out - back to front in a manner of speaking, and that made perfect financial sense, but his did not.

I stayed awake for hours at night, worrying about how he made a living with all the costs of going backwards and forwards to France daily. A few years later, I discovered that Onion Johnny had been living with Auntie Doreen's sister Doris all along. Her husband was permanently stationed in Hong Kong. Onion Johnny had done a deal with Jack (Doreen's husband) to store his onions in Jack's warehouse and store himself in Doris's bed.

So, he went to the warehouse daily and picked up more onions to sling around his neck. He would put on his silly beret and striped jumper, and then off, he would peddle for the day. Apparently, he had not been back to France since the end of the war. I later learnt that the onions came from a farm in Petersfield. I was learning something new every day. For some reason, everybody thought that Onion Johnny's onions tasted better than English onions. How little did they know?

The crumpet man came on a bicycle pushing a tiny trailer in front. That was not much use to me or my horticultural growth enhancement business.

I do not have many recollections of my dad from those days. He was nearly always away during the week in Andover, Bournemouth, Guildford or one of the many other faraway places where he worked. But I would see him on most weekends. He worked as a window dresser for Hepworth's. Many years later, in my early twenties, I reflected on this strange quasi-nomadic occupation he had chosen, forever travelling from town to town. Only then, after lengthy interrogative conversations with my mother, did I come to understand something significant. He had been rampantly homosexual for most of his life. His occupation facilitated his predilection towards younger trainee window dressers of similar persuasion. They were available in every town.

Occasionally he would bring one of the trainees home to stay with us for a few days. Heaven knows what the sleeping arrangements were, but fortunately, all this was unknown to me then. The promiscuity ushered in with the sexual revolution of the 1960s - along with the decriminalisation of homosexuality in 1967, was still to come. So I remained ignorant of such things.

Many years later, after learning the ways of the world, I would eventually understand the true nature of my father's inclinations and my mother's tacit acceptance of this peculiar ménage à trois. Despite this strange arrangement, my parents appeared devoted to each other and remained so until my father's death.

Much as before, my weekdays were taken up with school. But it had now become a little more serious, as we had to learn many subjects in preparation for an important exam that we would take when we reached eleven years of age. The outcome would determine whether we would continue our education at a grammar school and wear a nice uniform or at a secondary modern, where we could wear whatever we liked if we were not so bright – so I was told.

Evenings were still spent playing marbles and games in the street or messing around in the mud (usually only at weekends). I visited the underground kingdom less and less now. I had grown too tall and had to bend over to walk underneath the corrugated iron. If I behaved, I had been promised a bicycle for Christmas, so I was doing my best.

In 1955, somebody new arrived in our life: Uncle Bruce, my mum's brother. He was in the Navy and had been in Singapore since the war. But now, he had been posted home and started to live with us for a while. As Dad was still away most weekdays, I tended to treat Uncle Bruce more as a father than an uncle. We made battleships out of Player's cigarette packets with guns made from silver paper and matchsticks. Bruce was not married (at least I had never seen his wife), though as far as I know, he was not homosexual like Dad. Of course, I am writing this with the benefit of hindsight, which makes me sound far more aware of my surroundings than I was at the time.

Uncle Bruce smoked (RN naval issue cigarettes) and drank Old Navy Rum. Strangely, he never fell over, which could not be said for some of the men who frequented the Sailor's Return public house on the corner. I remember Bruce brought us some presents from Singapore when he came home. One was a 3D viewer scope, which looked like a pair of binoculars into which you placed photographic 3D slides. This allowed you to see the fantastic sights of the world in unique three-dimensional colours. It almost felt as if you were there. Bruce died suddenly in November 1956 after falling down a hatchway on his ship while still in the harbour.

The coroner's report said he was heavily intoxicated at the time. It was an ignominious end for someone who had courageously battled through six years of war and had been sunk twice without a scratch. My mother harboured severe misgivings about the verdict until her dying day, based on the simple premise that she had never seen him incapably drunk. She swore blind he was pushed, but it did not seem likely, as he was such a likeable person. There is a lesson to be learnt in there, somewhere, but I have no idea what it is.

Somewhat ironically, only a few months earlier, Bruce had a win on the pools, a sort of weekly lottery based on which football teams scored a draw each Saturday. If you managed to pick eight score drawers, that gave you 24 points - the jackpot! Bruce did not score 24 points, just 23, but that was enough to win him a prize of over £2,000. This was a lot of money in 1956. He gave half to my Mum, who said she would now buy a house in the posher part of Portsmouth. The house on Prospect Road was rented, but we did not move immediately for some reason and stayed for another six months. Something to do with the lease, I think.

My mum later inherited the balance of the pool's prize from Bruce. He had not spent a penny of it, so the future looked very rosy for all of us – except, of course, for Bruce…

Dad apparently did not earn much money, so Mum started taking in a lodger. She had the money from Uncle Bruce's Littlewoods Pools win, but that was 'sacrosanct', whatever that meant. She would say this whenever anybody mentioned using it if we were a bit broke. That did not happen very often, as Uncle Bruce used to bring us home many things when he was not away at sea, but of course, that had all come to a sudden end.

We usually only had one lodger who would stay Monday to Friday, so Lizzie and I would move into Mum's bedroom, and our room would be rented out. I remember we met some lovely people during that period. One, in particular, was Christine, who we called Auntie Christine. We called all the women Auntie, but oddly, all the men were misters until we knew them better.

Auntie Christine would remain a family friend for many years. What I learnt many years later changed my understanding of many events during this period. Christine was a beautiful woman. She was about twenty and worked on the next road in the corset and brassiere factory. I remember Christine came home very tearful one day, something I do not remember adults doing very often. She had a long talk with Mum in the front room (we were not allowed in). Christine was ill and stayed in bed for a few days, but she was as right as rain afterwards. Anyway, it turned out she had been pregnant and, with some help from my mum, she became un-pregnant.

She eventually married a footballer who played for Ipswich Town. My mum had many other friends, so life was always hectic but mostly enjoyable. When she gave us our pocket money on Saturday morning (if we had behaved all week), we would trot off to Woollies and spend it. So, come Sunday, I was broke again. Lizzie somehow used to save some of hers every week. I never understood how she managed that.

Sadly, in 1958, my adorable sister Lizzie was killed in a freak car accident. That left a big hole in my world. I missed her terribly, not least because she had been an integral part of the crop fertiliser business. She was the senior partner in charge of stock control. (I looked after sales and marketing).

I grew closer to my father after Lizzie died. But I always knew that he and my mother never really overcame her early death. I don't suppose any parent would. Sometimes I would come in to find them sitting together in the lounge, holding each other tightly and gently weeping over a photograph they'd had specially made. It was a sort of monochrome with some parts of it hand coloured. They kept it on the sideboard. These were the precious moments I always remembered long after I had forgotten many other things about them. Most fathers tend to be closer to their daughters, which was true of mine. I felt that something left him that fateful day and never came back. We still got on okay, although I tended to be closer to my mother as she was always around.

Until her death just a few years after his, she would staunchly defend him and vehemently condemn anybody who dared say anything untoward about his 'funny way' (as she put it.) I often wondered whether she really knew what they got up to, such was her trusting and empathetic understanding of his inclination.

Whatever memories they had together, only they shared, and they were something I would never fully understand. Every relationship that lasts a lifetime does so for reasons far beyond rational comprehension. My one regret is that I never really got to know my father until the very end, and I think he also had regrets about the time he had not spent with me when I was younger… It was a father-son relationship that never quite blossomed due to circumstances beyond his and my control.

This probably happens more often than it should in the busy, complicated lives that we all now lead. I feel sad when I think back to what might have been. Occasionally, I grieve for the lost opportunity to get to know the man my father was and the chance to understand what makes somebody what they become. We all start out as one kind of person. Slowly, through circumstances, destiny, and serendipitous luck, sometimes good - sometimes not so good, we change into a different type of person. I sometimes wonder what really controls this strange chronological metamorphosis.

Chapter 2
May 1982

Blake thought the narrative appeared relatively pedestrian to begin but still engaging in that nostalgic, retrospective way that selective memories can be. There were some oddities concerning how past and present tenses were interwoven, which was slightly unorthodox. But this did not seem to affect the flow of the story.

The characterisation worked well; it was convincing, the people seemed real, and the imagery slowly drew him deeper into the story. The dramatic momentum, so crucial at the beginning of any novel, appeared to be lacking. But one unnerving aspect kept Blake engrossed: the uncanny way the story seemed to diarise and document almost precisely his boyhood memories.

Most, but not all, the characters' names had been altered slightly. Everything else, somewhat uncomfortably, was almost precisely as Blake remembered it. At times, he felt he could almost reach out and touch the people he had once known thirty years ago but with whom, for one reason or another, he had lost touch. It was the tiny details that really spooked him. The Bert Coggins rag-and-bone character in Prospect Road he knew as Bernie Collins in real life. He had one eye that always looked in a different direction from the other. This used to worry Blake. He never knew for sure which eye was looking at him when he was negotiating the sale of newspapers or scrap iron. Bernie also had a very pronounced Glaswegian accent, which at times was utterly incomprehensible.

That detail was not in the book, but he knew it was the same person; there could never be two people described in quite the same way. The same could be said for the Uncle Jim character, except that the Uncle John he grew up knowing had only one leg, which explained why he had not been called up. He had bought an American Pink Cadillac car because it was automatic and could be driven by somebody with only one leg. Uncle John was also a bit of a boxer in his day (when he had two legs) and still taught boxing some nights in a gym at the end of the road. There was never a more bizarre sight than to see a man with a metal leg dancing around a boxing ring knocking over younger boxers, who were too afraid to hit him because they thought he might fall over. I never did see him fall over or be knocked down, for that matter.

These were all relatively minor differences, but they all made a kind of sense. Everything and everybody seemed to make some sense, which to Blake did not make any sense at all unless...

In the first chapter, the story recalled events and details that he clearly remembered, or as best as his memory would allow. In the second, however, something changed. The story began to recall specific details of events and people he had no recollection of. Blake found this oddly reassuring. The book no longer appeared to be telling his own life story. He could happily consign the previously unexplained similarities to serendipitous coincidence and the vagaries of universal generalisation. It was, therefore, of no personal relevance.

However, after rereading the second chapter, some of the characters began to rise from the pages, swirling around in oscillating circles, confusing his eyes and jolting his memory. Some of the details he remembered about Bert Coggins and Uncle Jim that were not in the book the first time he read it suddenly appeared the second time he read it. It was as if his remembrance of things past that had been initiated by reading the book released further tiny details that were lost somewhere deep within his brain. Somehow, reading the book had activated a trigger mechanism for the story to rewrite itself with the added details now recalled - neatly inserted into their appropriate positions in the revised manuscript.

The faint, flickering light of long-forgotten events began to form clear visions in his mind as the memory grew brighter. It was like an old magic lantern show of trembling images cascading across his optical vortex. Slowly the images became real people, and then they began to speak to him. It was then that he realised that these events must have happened to him after all; he had simply forgotten them – or had he? It was all very confusing.

He flicked back the pages and started rereading the book from the beginning to ensure he had not fallen asleep and dreamt the whole thing. For a moment, he even considered whether he could have written the story himself. Such was the attention to detail, which seemed to become more apparent every time he reread a line. And then maybe sent the manuscript to himself under an assumed name. Many famous writers did this to engender objectivity, but he had not. That was madness, and anyway, he was not a writer. He once harboured an ambition in that direction but found he couldn't do it – so he stopped and never tried again. He was now perfectly content reading and publishing other people's stories.

Anthony Theodore Clackle had written this story; it said so on the front page. He would never have come up with a pseudonym like that. It was so unreal it had to be genuine.

He finished re-reading the first two chapters and turned over the page to start Chapter Three, but it was blank. Blake flicked further forward, but there were no more words, just empty pages with a number at the bottom and the title at the top. This did not make any sense at all. He wondered if it could have been a printing error. He would speak to Jamie tomorrow and see if he had any explanation.

The next day Blake was a little late into the office and did not have the opportunity to mention the missing chapters of Prospect Road to Jamie. A typical Monday morning was underway with all the incumbent chaos it brought. After lunch, the pandemonium had more or less settled down. Jamie took the opportunity to pop his head around the door of Blake's office.

'So how did your weekend go?' asked Jamie jovially, but with a wry expression alluding to the chaotic few hours they had just endured.

Blake did not answer straight away but just smiled. 'okay… But that book you gave me to read… Prospect Road. I have a question.'

'Yes,' replied Jamie.

'Where's the rest of it?'

'I gave it all to you – the whole book,' replied Jamie, sounding mystified. 'Have you lost it?'

'No, no, I haven't lost it. I have the manuscript and all the pages. It's just the words that are missing,' replied Blake, a little indignant at Jamie's accusation. He suddenly realised how stupid that sounded.

'Missing? Repeated Jamie, squinting his eyebrows in a puzzled expression. 'What do you mean, missing?'

'Missing as in not there, invisible, non-existent. All I have is the first two chapters. The rest of the pages were all blank, apart from the page numbers and…'

'Well, I don't know what's happened to it,' interrupted Jamie. 'Page numbers?' He mused as an afterthought. A bewildered expression flashed across his face.

'Yes, page numbers at the bottom and the book title at the top, but nothing else in between – just fresh air.' He threw a moronic smile at Jamie. But Jamie held his bewildered expression for a few seconds, wondering if he had accidentally walked into an old Monty Python sketch.

'Well, it was all there when I read it... Oh well, never mind. I'm sure it will turn up. So anyway... apart from the missing words mystery, did you have a nice weekend?' It was the same question as before, but this time with a slightly different inflection, apparently changing the subject.

'Yes,' replied Blake, 'thank you. How was yours?'

'Good, good,' replied Jamie, not sounding overly enthused. He paused for a few moments to get the timing exactly right. 'Couple of nice bottles of the old Château du Plonk?' he suggested quizzically.

'Oh no, I know what you are thinking,' replied Blake curtly with a grin, suddenly realising where this was going. 'Totally pissed the whole weekend and spent it reading the blank paper. Well, that was not the case. In fact, I hardly touched a drop. I was working very diligently, I'll have you know, reading... or not, as appears to be the case.' He stopped for a moment, thinking about what he had just said.

'Well, I'll check my office,' said Jamie, smiling, 'but I'm sure there was only one copy, and I gave it to you. I'm certain I checked it before I put it with the other manuscripts you took, and I wrote my name and the date I read it on the first and the last page as always.' This was an old in-house ritual they had inherited and used for many years to ensure nobody accidentally read the same book twice.

'Fair enough,' replied Blake. 'I'll have a look in my study again when I get home tonight, just to be sure, but... if I don't have a complete copy, you will have to ask Mr...' He gazed skywards for a few moments, searching for the author's name.

'Clackle, Anthony Clackle,' said Jamie.

'Yes. An interesting name is it not?' queried Blake. 'Almost Dickensian. Do you think that's his real name?'

'Could be a nom de plume, I suppose,' suggested Jamie with a questioning expression.

'What did you make of the book?' asked Blake.

'Let me think,' said Jamie pausing for a moment. Now he was the one gazing thoughtfully skywards. 'That was the story about the young boy in Portsmouth set just after the last war... Grows up to run a small publishing business in London, ironically. A bit like you, in fact.' He initially said the words slowly, as if plucking them randomly out of the air. 'That's why I thought you would find it appealing. A few things happened along the way that kept me interested. It was more a series of reminiscences than pure fiction to start with; well, that's what I thought. But it was beautifully written, and it chugged along. The characters felt real – they drew me in, and there was an unusual plot development format, as I remember. Not something that I have encountered before, not in this format anyway. I thought it could do well. Retro reads are always popular. It could even be the basis for a decent television series – TV companies are continually looking out for stories centred around the fifties era.

'What actually happens?' asked Blake.

'I just told you,' replied Jamie.

'No, no, the specifics. Can you remember anything after the second or third chapter?'

Jamie was a little intrigued by this odd question. 'After the second chapter,' he repeated? Looking down at the floor, he pondered for a few moments, trying to disentangle the unique characteristics of this one particular book from the many others he had read the previous week. But, with a curiously blank expression, he looked back up at Blake and, peering over the top of his glasses through his bushy eyebrows, replied, 'I am sorry, but do you know what? I don't remember much about it, apart from the beginning, which is a little odd... I can usually remember the central storyline of most books I've read in the last six months, but...' Jamie was obviously struggling to remember what he could about the book, but try as he might, he could not bring any part of the story to mind.

It had slipped entirely from his memory, which was unusual for him.

'That is all we have, then. You can't have read the whole book,' replied Blake, half teasingly, 'that would explain it.'

'But I have. And I also made a list of editorial notes and comments,' confirmed Jamie, sounding very certain but slightly frustrated. 'I gave them to you with the book, but they were only about readability, composition, sector interest, sales potential, marketing angles, all the usual things. For some reason, my mind has gone completely blank on the central narrative. He sounded genuinely concerned about his sudden inability to recall anything relevant about the storyline. Especially as he had only just that moment declared it to be immersive and engaging. Not a particularly glowing endorsement if he could not recall anything substantive about the story. Maybe his short-term memory was failing… could it be a sign of early-onset dementia, he wondered… as he drifted off for a few moments.

'Look, I'll contact this Clackle guy and get him to send another copy, and this time I'll make a copy after I've read it.'

'Fair enough,' replied Blake. 'Let me know when…'

'I will, don't you worry,' interrupted Jamie pensively - evidently embarrassed by his shortcoming. He left Blake's office, closing the door quietly behind him. Blake continued reading some other documents on his desk and thought no more about the incident.

The following day Jamie popped into Blake's office again.

'That author, Anthony Clackle – Prospect Road – we spoke about yesterday…'

'Yes,' replied Blake, leaning back in his chair, drinking a coffee. His mind appeared to be elsewhere.

'There's a bit of a problem. Clackle's file is empty, and the letter that came with the manuscript and the copy of our letter to him is also missing, so we don't have a telephone number or address.'

'So, no way of finding him?' asked Blake.

'I can ask Susie to see if she can find a number for him in the phone book,' replied Jamie. 'He's bound to turn up somewhere with a name like that. Can't be too many Clackle's listed.'

Blake nodded, and Jamie left his office.

Chapter 3
July 1982

A few months later, Blake was at home for the weekend rummaging in his study, looking for a newspaper cutting about a new author he had read about, when he came across the manuscript of Prospect Road buried under some other rejected manuscripts which he had not yet taken back to the office. He remembered the problem he had encountered with the missing chapters and how Jamie could not find the writer with the unusual name — a name he could not immediately recall.

He and Jamie had all but forgotten about the manuscript. This was a shameful oversight. Blake knew that as long as he indolently held on to an author's story, the author would be clinging on to a slender thread of hope. He was shamefully blocking the channel of civilised protocol between author and publisher, the communication stream on which the flotsam of expectation travelled. The illusion of possible acceptance, publication, success, and critical acclaim was being unnecessarily prolonged by his irresponsible tardiness. The emotional and psychological trauma of anticipated recognition desperately clung to until the moment the rejection letter dropped through the letterbox. In an instant, extinguishing another dream. Two years' work written off with just a half dozen cursory lines.

This was the process all writers were conditioned to and prepared for; better than nothing at all. At least a rejection note meant somebody had read it... possibly.

But this time, rejection was delayed, intensifying the anguish being unintentionally meted out to the author.

He must do the honourable thing and do it fast, and he would - on Monday. He scooped up the scripts and placed them in a pile on his desk, in a prominent place, to remind him to take them back to the office, from where he could arrange for them to be reunited with their creators. He would probably pay dearly for this oversight. There was always a final redemption for lethargy from Thoth, the God of all writers, but hopefully not until the afterlife. But then he remembered they could not send Prospect Road back because they did not have an address for the author. In fact, they had never intended to send it back. They just wanted another complete copy of the book to read before making a final decision on publication. It all came back on him now. This oversight was only adding insult to the injury of neglectfulness already sustained.

But at least if he took it back to the office, it would become Jamie's responsibility, not his anymore. Thoth might be more merciful with him on the day of reckoning - when all publishers are brought to account for their shortcomings, tardiness, and oversights. Jamie would have to suffer the mythological consequences, not he – maybe his thoughts were all a little whimsical, but then publishers are, traditionally, a very superstitious bunch.

He stared down at the front cover of Prospect Road, innocuous, inauspicious, and unassuming. Just a simple typed title in Courier font at nine or maybe ten points, if he was not mistaken. An unusual font – most fledgeling writers typed out their first creations using modern typewriters or even one of the new word processors. They tended to be manufactured with one font – Times New Roman. But this one had the strike-on appearance of an older, conventional typewriter. Underneath the title was the writer's name: Anthony Theodore Clackle. There was something intimately esoteric about a hand-typed manuscript; it had the writer's feel, touch, and smell embedded in every page. You could almost sense the writer's anguish, punching out every letter and word to get each line down on the page exactly how he wanted it.

Blake could sense how the writer had painstakingly chosen a specific word. And how he had changed it many times to ensure he conveyed a particular message, mood, or atmosphere to the reader. Sometimes you could see the stains where tears or drops of sweat had fallen. It was all so intimate, a visceral relationship between writer, paper, and reader; it was like no other. The writer renders up his soul onto the altar of the empty page - the vehicle that will eventually convey his message to the reader through the magical interaction of black ink and white paper.

Once, on a visit to the United States, Blake had been offered the opportunity to see Ernest Hemingway's manuscript for The Old Man and the Sea. The original typed, presumably white pages were now a smoky buff brown, and some were curled at the corners.

There were various stains where whiskey or beer, possibly even blood, had been spilt on it, presumably Hemingway's. Many words had been crossed out and replaced, and whole sentences had been cut or moved to a different position. The story was only just readable, with all the alterations, stains, and scribbled notes in the margins. Several pages had obviously been screwed up and flattened out again for inclusion in the final draft. The document was a testimony of the writer's struggle to create the perfect story as he saw it. Only by looking at that sullied manuscript did Blake really begin to understand just what a writer went through to produce a finished work.

He had found it to be an incredibly moving artefact - from its pages emanated the soul of Hemingway and the agony he had confronted while writing the story. The memory of that manuscript always stayed with him, and he briefly returned to it every time he read a book he was considering for publication.

He felt an odd tingling sensation in his fingers and found himself irresistibly drawn back to Prospect Road. He sat down in his captain's chair, leaned across the desk, picked up the script, looked at the front page for a few moments, turned the page over, and began to reread the story.

After a while, he reached the part in the second chapter where Thomas Drayton recalled his feelings after his father had died. Thomas had become overly attached to him, even though they were seldom together.

Blake stopped reading for a few seconds and looked up. His father, Robert, had died prematurely a few years ago from a heart attack. He could feel a tear form in the corner of his eye and begin to roll down his cheek. Like Thomas Drayton, he, too, missed his father terribly. He had missed him being away so much while he was growing up, and by the time his father had realised just how much Blake missed his presence, it was too late to do anything about it.

Blake had never experienced quite so much uncertainty and confusion in his life. However, to a small degree, he could empathise with how Thomas Drayton must have felt. The book seemed to answer some of the questions that had never been satisfactorily explained to Blake about his father. Questions that he had never had the opportunity to ask or even thought about until now.

When Blake's daughter Claudia was born in 1978, His father's first words to Blake were that he could not wait for the day when he would watch her walk down the aisle on Blake's arm. Blake had one younger sister, but tragically, she died aged nine in a car accident. So, his father had never made that short walk with his daughter to the altar. With his death in 1979, neither would he see his granddaughter make that journey with Blake. Blake continued reading until reaching the end of Chapter Two. He placed the manuscript back on his desk, still open on the last page he had just read and looked at his signature under the last word, dated the 26th of March. That was when he had first read the manuscript.

Blake thought carefully about what he had now read several times and how the more he read it, the more it seemed to open a window. A portal to a parallel universe, one that allowed him to look back at himself as he was. Each time he reread the first two chapters, they appeared a little longer than before, with what seemed to be more detail. It was as if the chapters were self-populating with more information from his past with each reading. This only served to increase his bewilderment and confusion over what was happening.

He lifted the read pages, precariously attached to the blank pages with a green treasury tag, back onto the main stack and stared at the neat pile of paper. For no specific reason, he flicked the corner of the pages and returned to the end of Chapter Two to clarify how the story had stopped. He turned over to the next page. It was blank. Then, for some reason, he turned over one more page…

He was half expecting something but did not know what exactly - not until he saw the heading: Chapter Three!

'Chapter Three,' he mumbled in disbelief. There had never been a Chapter Three, of that much he was sure, but there it was, as plain as day. He could not understand where it had come from. Could this be a joke that Catherine was playing? Blake asked himself but quickly discounted the possibility. She knew nothing of the mystery of the missing chapters, seldom venturing into his study except to run the hoover around occasionally or bring him a cup of coffee. He turned over the page, and the words were there waiting… Waiting to be read.

Chapter 4
August 1982

With some trepidation, Blake began to read Chapter Three. It spoke of Thomas Drayton and his family moving to a more affluent part of town. It mentioned some people, some of whom he had some distant memories. The story moved on to when Thomas started working in a publishing company in London in 1968, *the same year Blake joined Clanford and Fox*. It recalled with unerring and increasingly detailed accuracy events as they had happened to Blake.

In July 1970, Thomas Drayton, now a book publisher, meets Kate at a new book release party. He married her in 1974, which was how Blake had met Catherine and, coincidently, the same year they were married. No longer were the characters in the book masquerading behind different names. Whatever bizarre plot he had become unwittingly embroiled in, or more accurately entangled with, was now morphing into reality. All the demarcation lines that separated fact from fantasy were increasingly blurred. The details of the two relationships were slowly seeping, bleeding into each other. Like black ink on blotting paper, the story slowly edged towards territories it had only casually visited before, leaving just a few smears. But now, it was obliterating everything that had once been visible. Before long, a dark mendacity would overpower everything. Their parallel worlds were heading for a collision.

Anthony Theodore Clackle named characters in his fictional story after people Blake knew in real life. For one split second, Blake considered whether he was going mad, suffering from some kind of paranoia or split personality disorder perhaps. In his mind, that would make perfect sense. But he also knew that a genuinely psychotic person would never countenance the remotest possibility that they were mad, so he quickly discounted that option.

Of course, he could be bipolar, that wonderfully erudite euphemism for manic depressives. Masquerading under the cover of political correctness, this word had surreptitiously crept into everyday language. A hobble-stick for suburbia. Like a drunk leaning against a lamppost, more for support than illumination. No, he was not depressed, either. This was merely the undramatic consequence of a strange synchro meshing of fiction and fact. It was as unassumingly trite and predictably ordinary as that. As soon as he accepted this, everything else would fall into place – but could he?

As he read further, the story told of the birth of two children, Michael and Carol. Blake and Catherine had named their children Max and Claudia. It also mentioned his uncle's tragic death and Reggie Clanford, the publishing company owner for whom Thomas worked. Blake stopped reading, took a bottle from his desk drawer, and poured a large glass of bourbon. He felt more confused now than when he first read the book's opening chapters a few months earlier. But now Blake was beginning to feel uncomfortable - ill at ease. A peculiar sense of foreboding was beginning to overwhelm him, something he could not control.

Repeatedly reading the story did not alleviate his concerns as he thought it might. He had reasoned that an element of familiarity with the text would weaken the visceral chill of truth and invoke contempt by assimilating the imagery into normality, but it had not. He became frustrated and infuriated with himself for not understanding or determining precisely what was happening. He came to the end of Chapter Three, where Kate gave Thomas a silver-framed photograph of her and their two children. That was a very poignant moment for him, and hard as he tried, he could not stop the tears from welling up behind his eyes. That had always been a very private moment for him and Catherine. Nobody else on the planet knew the exact circumstances or the precise words that Catherine had used. And yet, here it was, written down word for word by somebody he had never met or was ever likely to encounter, going by his experience so far.

Blake reread the section…

My school years were uneventful, filled with all the mundanity of education. After leaving school, I went to university and then, by chance, secured a job at a publishing company.

My life had now started to mean something, and in 1970 I met Kate, the woman who would become my wife, the woman with whom I would spend the rest of my life. We were married in 1974.

I remember one day, it was my birthday; Kate bought me a silver-framed photograph of herself and our two children, which I would always treasure. As she gave me the present, she whispered, 'Something for me to look at every day, to remind me that no matter what happens, we will always love you.' That was one of the most important days of my life; I felt I now had a purpose, a reason for being...

Blake's hand began to tremble, and the remains of the whiskey in the glass he was holding began to quiver as if an earthquake were about to follow, but it didn't, and the trembling stopped. He came to the end of the chapter and turned over the page, but there were no more words.

He flicked through the following empty pages two or three times to make sure he had not missed anything. After assuring himself, there was no more narrative, he scribbled his signature and the date underneath the last typed line and closed the manuscript.

Blake sat down for dinner with Catherine and the children at six o'clock. They discussed various things, including their eighth wedding anniversary in three weeks. They had decided to invite a few friends for dinner instead of going out, preferring the intimacy of a quiet dinner party at home rather than going to a restaurant.

After dinner, Catherine put Max and Claudia to bed while Blake cleared the table. Blake then went upstairs and kissed them goodnight. When he returned, Catherine had poured him a bourbon with ice and placed it on the table next to his chair. He smiled at her.

'Is there a problem?' she asked with a curious expression.

'No. Why do you ask,' Blake replied, sounding a little surprised?

'You just seem... distant, preoccupied, that's all. Something seems to be troubling you. I know that much.'

'It's nothing really,' replied Blake, not altogether convincingly.

'What is it? You might as well tell me now,' continued Catherine smiling, gently probing his inner thoughts. She knew he had never kept any secrets from her for very long. 'I'll get it out of you in the end, Thornton.' Blake smiled at her astuteness.

'I could resort to torture if necessary,' mused Catherine. 'I could sing.' Catherine sang appallingly with no sense of key, timing, or melody. 'You couldn't hold a tune unless you kept it in a bucket,' Blake had told her many times.

'All right, all right, anything but that,' conceded Blake.

Catherine playfully poked him in his stomach.

'It's just a book I've been reading. It's…' He paused, not knowing how to explain the curious events surrounding the manuscript.

'I read part of it a few months ago and then forgot all about it until today when I came across it again. It was buried in my study under some other manuscripts. So I thought I had better take it back to the office. I didn't think it was that good when I first read it. There were some unusual problems, but for some reason, I thought I would reread it before taking it back… It's just that…' He seemed a little distracted.

'It's what?' said Catherine, now a little intrigued.

'Well, it's a story about a publisher, like me, and the circumstances are a little like mine – ours, but it is a little odd; there is something about it that's…' He paused. 'Not right. It's a little spooky.' He twitched his nose.

'Well, what's it about? Is it professionally written, how does it end, and most importantly, would it sell?' Asked Catherine in the pragmatically prosaic manner she always adopted when dealing with any problem to do with a book.

'I don't know what it's about. That's half the problem. Apart from documenting somebody's life story, someone who sounds remarkably like me - us, in fact. It doesn't seem to have a central storyline. It's written in a naïvely yet engaging way that keeps you interested, but as for how it ends, well, that's the oddest thing of all.' He paused to take a sip of bourbon.

'Why?' asked Catherine.

'Well, it doesn't end. In fact, it stopped at Chapter Two when I first read it. That was the unusual problem I mentioned, but when I reread it today, I know you will think I'm going mad, but when I read it today, there was another complete chapter, which, somehow, I appear to have missed the first time I read it.'

Catherine did not say anything immediately but thought over what he had said. She waggled her drinks glass at him nonchalantly. He smiled and shook his head, indicating he had not been drunk and fallen asleep while reading the book, or whatever it was she was subtly alluding to. He did, however, begin to wonder about the issue of drinking. This was the second occasion in only a few days that somebody had made a passing reference to his bibulousness and how it might be affecting his work. But oddly, only in the context of Prospect Road.

Anyway, he did not think he drank to excess. Probably no more than a half bottle of wine for dinner, maybe one or two brandies during the evening, but not every night. Of course, there were the traditional G & T's on Sunday, but not before midday. Oh, and a bottle of wine on Saturday night if they went out for a meal. Occasionally he had a pint or two at lunchtime at the office if he was going out with a client or discussing a book with Jamie over lunch. Apart from that, he did not drink! Then he thought about what he had just thought about.

'Have they read it in the office?' asked Catherine.

'Yes, one of the junior readers read the first two chapters, liked it, and passed it to Jamie, who read them and requested a full manuscript which he also read. Then he passed it to me.'

'So, you have just been given the wrong copy,' said Catherine. 'It's as simple as that.'

'Well, no,' replied Blake. 'You see, we have a system for marking scripts, so we know who has read what. Whoever reads it signs it at the beginning and end or wherever they get to if they don't manage to read it all. Also, we all make notes, which go into a file on each book under review. The copy I have is signed by Jamie, who read the whole story and made detailed notes. He signed it at the beginning and on the last page. We only have one complete copy of the book, but all the pages are now blank after Chapter Three.'

'So how did Jamie read it?' asked Catherine.

'I don't know. He swears he read it cover to cover and liked it a lot, which is why he passed it to me.'

Catherine said nothing; she was as baffled by the conundrum as Blake was.

'Well, it sounds like someone has simply removed all the chapters after the third,' suggested Catherine.

'That could make sense, but why do I still have all the pages numbered and titled and Jamie's signature on the last blank page. And, of course, that doesn't explain how the third chapter suddenly appeared from nowhere while the manuscript was in my study.'

Catherine could not answer that one.

'What happened to the first copy you received?'

'I checked that,' replied Blake. 'It's still in the office, but only the first two chapters.'

'Let's have an early night, and tomorrow I will look at the book for you, and we will sort this out,' said Catherine confidently. Blake smiled. He knew there had to be a simple explanation. Hopefully, Catherine would come up with it by the time he returned home the following evening. She had a remarkable ability to solve complex problems with her uncomplicated woman's logic, and in some small way, this seemed to assuage some of Blake's concerns. He went to bed that night, still troubled but tried not to let it show. He even got a decent night's sleep after they had made love.

The following day, they were up early. Once breakfast was over, Blake went into his study and brought out the manuscript and ceremoniously, but still with some token resistance, handed it to Catherine. He was now having minor reservations about the manuscript. But nothing specific that he could put his finger on, apart from the apparent peculiarity of the missing narrative and the core similarity with his life.

'Prospect Road. See what you think.' He kissed her lips gently, then kissed Max and Claudia before leaving. The journey took just over an hour from Godalming to his office in central London. He usually spent the commute reading, but today he just gazed out the window wondering…

When Blake arrived home that evening, Max and Claudia greeted him at the front gate and took hold of his hands as they made their way back toward the front door. It was the archetypal cottage, with the traditional, white-painted picket fence adjacent to the pavement, a neat front lawn, and roses around the front door. This was something that Catherine had always wanted since she was a girl. It had been a lovely home for them over the last seven years, but with Max and Claudia growing up, it was now too small, and soon they would have to move.

He had not looked at the cottage in a while and suddenly realised how transitory everything in life was; nothing lasts forever, and everything changes eventually. It was an odd thought to come into his mind at that moment, tinted with paranoia and fragility, not something he was familiar with. But today, he had an inkling that what was happening with Prospect Road was somehow influencing him and possibly his family. His and their existence and the everyday things he took for granted could suddenly be overturned by events beyond his control. He began feeling vulnerable and exposed to forces beyond his normal comprehension. Yet, he had no reason to do so. He said a small prayer, hoping that Catherine may have discovered a simple explanation to the riddle and that everything would suddenly be okay. He also wondered if, maybe, he was becoming a little obsessed. There was no reason for him to feel that way, but then that was the nature of the beast.

'Mummy's in the back garden,' said Max as he and Claudia guided Blake around the corner of the cottage to where Catherine was swinging gently back and forth on the hammock. The script lay by her side on the cushion. She got up to kiss Blake and hugged him tightly in a way he found instantly reassuring, yet he could still sense a tiny element of inconclusiveness.

Blake looked over her shoulder, and just for a moment, he thought he could see an enormous grey elephant standing quietly in the corner of the garden nibbling on the grass. The Mahout sitting on its back in full evening dress, with a bowler hat and drinking a martini, did not help much by waving his glass at him.

And then it was gone. Catherine took Blake's hand, and they walked slowly over to the borders to see the flowers more closely – Blake casually snapped the head off a dead rose.

'So how was your day,' asked Catherine?

'Same as yesterday, still hectic.' But today, he sounded slightly less enthusiastic and more preoccupied than usual. Naturally, he wondered what Catherine would say about the book. He peered briefly over her shoulder to see if the elephant had returned - it had not.

'Martin rang,' said Catherine, wondering what Blake was looking for. 'Asked if we wanted to go for dinner this Friday. I said I would get back to him after we had spoken.'

'That would be good. How is he?' asked Blake, turning back to give Catherine his full attention.

'Fine. He has a new lady friend he wants us to meet. She's a writer and painter - a bit of an extrovert from what I can make out.'

'Writer?' he queried. 'Oh well, yes, that should be fun; he deserves a little excitement in his life again after all that's happened. It's been a long time.' He was alluding to the premature passing of Martin's wife, Ruth, some years earlier. They had been a gregarious and popular couple in the village, heavily involved in an eclectic array of local activities. Things began to change after Ruth suddenly and quite unexpectedly died in 1980. Martin slipped back into a less adventurous frame of mind, slowly withdrawing from social intercourse as many people do after a bereavement.

'Yes, yes it has,' replied Catherine.

'I do hope this isn't a pitch for a publishing deal,' remarked Blake with a cynically weary tone.

'No, it's not. I did ask Martin, but he said she writes stageplays, and a local am-dram society puts them on. She even does a bit of acting, but definitely no novels.'

'Oh, I see,' replied Blake breathing a sigh of relief. 'I apologise for jumping the gun - I was...' but he didn't finish.

Catherine smiled. They had gently tiptoed around the preliminaries of the yet unmentioned subject. But Blake had reached the point from which he could no longer continue without asking the question. The one that had been quietly hovering in the air above their heads. A giant balloon filled with water patiently waiting for the exigencies of thin rubber or nature to suddenly take control and drench them in a deluge of ice-cold reality.

'So, how did you find it?' There was a hint of precautionary restraint in Blake's voice.

Catherine pointed to the hammock, and they walked back and sat down.

'It was interesting... but as you said, it stops at Chapter Three. I can definitely confirm that much.'

'What do you make of the story and the similarities to our lives?' Blake sounded constrained as if he did not want to hear the answer. Or, at best, he wanted her to dismiss his suspicions as nothing more than speculation. The product of a publisher's overactive imagination.

'There were some,' replied Catherine, 'but probably no more than you would expect from many other people of our age.' She did not sound entirely convinced, nor did she seem overly concerned by the similarities.

'Some of it could be down to generalities,' she continued. 'Many people who grew up during the post-war period, I mean the second world war, of course…' She smirked at Blake to see how he would react to her tongue-in-cheek remark.'

'Very amusing,' replied Blake with a benign grin,' but he knew she was trying to make light of the awkward situation to assuage his fears.

'Well…' continued Catherine, 'they probably had remarkably similar experiences too.' But even as she said the words, she knew it sounded improbable. There were too many specific references that were obviously quite unique to Blake, to her and to their children. It would have been bordering on disingenuity not to acknowledge that those details were germane to Blake's uneasiness.

'Anyway,' said Catherine, 'with only three chapters, it's not going anywhere, is it? So, unless the rest of the book miraculously appears, you should just forget about it and put it down to a "strange experience".' She air-quoted the words and smiled, easing Blake's concerns. He nodded in agreement and kissed her.

Max and Claudia came over to the hammock and pulled at Blake's hands to get him to walk into the garden where they were playing in the paddling pool. He obediently went with them and sat down next to the pool as they both jumped in and started splashing water about. Blake watched them both enjoying themselves, utterly oblivious to the ominous ruminations running around his head. He knew he could not let his thoughts and concerns detract from enjoying these blissfully innocent times. He should take these fleeting moments spent with his children, treasure each of them as they came, and hold them in his heart forever. They would soon be gone, never to return, and only the memories would remain to comfort him in the years ahead. He thought no more of Prospect Road that day, but not before checking over his shoulder one more time.

Chapter 5

Blake returned the manuscript to his study and did not look at it again for a couple of weeks; he almost completely forgot about it. For some reason, he did not return it to the office as he had initially intended but left it on his desk among several newer scripts he had brought home to read. Life continued to move on much as before.

One Sunday morning towards the end of August, Catherine visited her mother's house with Max and Claudia. Blake opted to stay behind and have a leisurely day in the sunshine. Prospect Road had somehow risen to the top of the pile of scripts on his desk, and once again, he found himself drawn inexorably toward it. A little warily, he picked it up – not without some trepidation - and just for a few seconds, his mind flashed back to the last conversation he had with Catherine about the book.

He poured himself a large Jack Daniels from the bottle he kept in his study desk, went through to the kitchen where he took some ice cubes from the freezer and plopped them into his glass, and clutching the manuscript, walked back through to the lounge. The French windows were open, and a gentle summer breeze blew into the room, rustling the curtains for a few seconds. It was as if it were heralding a character's entrance in some amateur dramatic stage production, but no one entered, and the curtains became still again.

He sat on the sofa, turned over the cover page, and once again began reading this simple yet elegantly strange story. Not for one moment did he consider flipping to the end. There did not seem to be any point, so he just sat back and read the words, each appearing ever more poignant, personal, and pertinent than the last time he read it.

Once again, he became engrossed in the tale, and as he did so, his left hand slowly edged its way towards the small table next to his chair to pick up his glass of bourbon. He took a sip and gently swilled the ice cubes around in the glass. Momentarily distracted, he glanced at the smeary threads of water and liquor interweaving like the golden strands of a Möbius circle, with no beginning, no end – just an existence. Not dissimilar in some ways, he thought, to the story he was reading. Not at all the clearly documented but humdrum tale about his life from age five. That was just a cosmetic outer shell, the protective covering, the wrapping paper that would eventually be ripped away to reveal something more profound. The haze of obscurity would slowly lift, and what would be left would be the real reason for the story. It was leading somewhere; he was sure of that much. He just did not know where or to what.

It appeared to have been further enhanced since he had last read it. It was as if it was now being re-edited by someone who knew his past life as well, if not better than he did, or had at least recalled it better than he had. Instead of removing the weaker parts of the story, the inconsequential sections that ruined the rhythm of the writing and irrelevant phrases that did not fit, more detail had been added. This brought further into focus the stark realism, clarity and definition of the story, which already seemed alive. In the trivia – the minutiae – lay the credibility and integrity. But more than that, there was something else on which so much in life depended... truth.

The story began to recall little anecdotes and accounts of things that had happened long ago, things that he had completely forgotten about. Memories that had lain dormant for so many years were suddenly brought back into his consciousness. Once, when Thomas was about seven or eight years old, he had been invited to a friend's birthday party. But he did not have enough money to buy a present. His mother had no money as it was nearing the end of the week. So he had wrapped up a book that someone had given him a few months earlier to give to his friend. His friend unwrapped it and abruptly exclaimed, much to Thomas's embarrassment and the amusement of everybody else at the party, that this was the very same book he had given Thomas only two months earlier. The identical experience had haunted Blake since the day it had happened, and he had never forgotten it.

These were unimportant details that he would rather not remember, but the carefully chosen words now added a poignancy, relevance, and sentient authority to the tale.

He arrived at the end of the story, or so he thought, but turning over the last page, the one he had signed only a few weeks earlier, he saw more. The blank pages of Chapter Four had now been populated with more words. The empty space that had confused and confounded him on previous readings had now been neatly filled with sentences. Between the head title and the page number at the bottom, the story was approaching its inevitable climax.

He gingerly placed the manuscript on the sofa, stood up, walked over to the French window, and looked out into the garden. Somehow, he needed to affirm he was awake, not just dreaming, and that this was really happening right now, but how could he check? How could he know with any certainty that this was not a deception of the mind? He suddenly realised there was no way of confirming this beyond any reasonable doubt. Does anybody ever really know, he wondered?

Reginald Clanford had always playfully held on to the mantra that; 'Life, my boy, is all an illusion, made up of millions of stories, some true, some not, and there is no way of knowing which is which and in that respect, does it really matter. The only true reality is death…'

In a more prosaic and less dramatic tone, he would typically finish this insightful moral precept with something like…. 'Now all we have to do is print a few of the really memorable stories, and we will all make a jolly good living. And if, by chance, we can find just one story that has not yet happened but could…. Then that would be all the better for us, for the most intriguing, captivating, and enthralling of all stories would be the one, as yet, untold. That one would make us rich beyond our wildest dreams.'

It all sounded very whimsical and capricious. Just take a small selection of the stories that, one way or another, made up the flotsam and jetsam of somebody's life. Carefully distil them into a few hundred pages - publish them with an enticing cover, and we will all be set for life. The words just told the reader something that had already happened, and the same story could be retold a thousand diverse ways and probably would be over time; somebody had once said to him that there were only seven completely different stories, and every written word was fundamentally based on one of them.

Now those ordinary words took on a unique perspective. Until now, there had never been an underlying storyline that rested almost entirely on the narrative predicting a future that had already been lived but, by its very nature, one that could be changed.

If you didn't read the future, would it still happen? Blake wondered to himself.

He sat back in his chair and tentatively looked at the manuscript... to wonder if... The first three chapters had just been inconsequential narrative of no relevance, but was that about to change? He began to read.

Prospect Road: Chapter Four
written by
Anthony Theodore Clackle

I had been promoted to senior editor at the publishers. I was now in charge of deciding which books the company would select for publication. With this elevation came considerable responsibility. The company was now depending on my judgment regarding whether it should speculate substantial amounts of money promoting an unknown writer. One who might, with reasonable expectation, repay this investment many times over with worldwide sales of a stream of books.

It was a demanding responsibility, but I felt confident I could handle it. As with any publisher, the ultimate goal was to find the writer with the story that would change the world. The pot of gold at the end of a rainbow, the panacea for all ills. This was my quest.

We conscientiously read everything that came into the office, and if one of my assistants thought there was just a glimmer of hope, I would read it as well.

But still, I could not find anything that inspired me, something with the potential interest needed to warrant the investment of vast sums of the company's money. This went on for years, many books were shortlisted, and quite a few were even published, but there was never any realistic expectation of stratospheric sales. Some books are like that. They sell maybe a hundred thousand copies, which is reasonable; in fact, it is a considerable achievement for the writer. But for a publisher, it would only return him around two pounds on a hardback and far less on the paperback version. With all the marketing costs, albeit on a considerably smaller budget, and all the other office and production overheads, this did little more than keep the company ticking over.

What we desperately needed to ensure our continued survival was a major blockbuster. One that would sell in the millions and be reprinted in every country of the world. Hopefully, it would be turned into a film. A book that would continue to sell regularly, finding new generations of readers every few years. New readers who could contemporarily reimagine the same story.

I was looking for this, and this is what I eventually found one day when I was passed a hand-written manuscript. A story of unrequited love between a gardener/handyman and a novice nun set in Aix-en-Provence in the 1960s. It was beautifully written and brought me to tears; such was the passion embedded within its pages. Love stories were always good sellers, but with the subtle twist at the end, this book could not fail. I had found my Holy Grail. I read it repeatedly to be sure of how I felt – to convince myself that I had not just settled on it out of sheer desperation. But it was good, extremely good. In fact, it was the best story I had read in years... Each time I read it, I became more convinced of the potential success it could achieve. I passed the book to the company's senior partners, who agreed after reading it. They would publish The Chapter Room, a love story by Gideon Drew, a book that hopefully would embrace the world and change my life.

Chapter 6

Once again, Blake found himself engrossed by the story, drawn in by the perplexing parallels it seemed to be mirroring from his life. But now, there was a tiny glimpse of the future, which only heightened his curiosity. He flipped over another page to see what would happen next, but there were no more words. Just as before, the story ended abruptly. He slowly placed the manuscript back down on the sofa. For some inexplicable reason, he found himself treating it with some reverence as if it were a treasured antiquity. It had been a simple diary of events until now, some strangely similar to those that had happened in his life so far. Now it mentioned things that had yet to occur. Could the "The Chapter Room," novel mentioned in the story, exist, he asked himself? He had no recollection of seeing a manuscript with this title in the office and could only assume that this part of the story had yet to happen.

While pondering this puzzle, his mind drifted off to thoughts of how, sadly, most of Earth's inhabitants wandered through life hanging on in quiet desperation, never really knowing why they were here. For him, though, suddenly, there was a raison d'etre, a purpose, slowly unravelling before his eyes. No more existential confusion, just a mindful desire for illumination and clarification. He heard Catherine's car pull up in the drive and went outside to welcome them all back home. He felt relieved he was no longer alone with…

'Hello, Daddy,' exclaimed Claudia joyfully. 'We've been to see Grandma, and I made a cake.'

'Did you,' Blake replied quietly? 'You're a very clever girl.'

'I helped as well,' added Max, not wishing to be left out of the free-flowing adoration.

'No, you didn't,' interrupted Claudia haughtily, glaring at Max. 'All you did was eat some of it before grandma even put it in the oven.' Blake looked at Max, and Max smiled back with a nonchalant shrug of indifference.

'I was testing it for quality,' said Max in a faux managerial tone, wrinkling up his eyebrows as he spoke. 'I have to keep an eye on her; the kitchen can be a dangerous place.' He sounded protective and unusually mature for his age. Blake realised they were already little people with views, opinions and attitudes, little people just waiting to become big people.

'Good day?' asked Blake, kissing Catherine and hugging her gently while squeezing her bottom.

'It was lovely. How was yours?' replied Catherine, smiling and slightly surprised at his uncharacteristic assault on her bum.

'Obviously not too shabby… I sedili attaccano in pubblico, I am surprised.' It was a liberal interpretation; Catherine's Italian was a little rusty, but Blake understood her meaning.

'I'll tell you in a minute. Nothing alarming, just a little unusual,' replied Blake.

Catherine smiled with a hint of curiosity. Her eyes scrunched quizzically as she unloaded several bags from the car. His comment had naturally intrigued her. She thought she knew Blake better than he knew himself.

Blake grabbed the bags, and they walked back to the house. Max and Claudia went straight out to play in the garden, and Blake went into the kitchen to put the kettle on to make a pot of tea.

'Do you two want a cold drink?' he shouted out the back door.

'Yes, please, Daddy,' came the chorused reply. He poured two orange drinks, took them into the garden for Max and Claudia, and then returned to the kitchen.

'So, what do you have to tell me,' asked Catherine, settling herself at the kitchen table?

'Well, you remember that book I was reviewing, the one about…'

'Prospect Road,' interrupted Catherine. Instinctively, she knew what he was going to talk about. 'Yes, you gave it to me to read a few weeks ago. Well, the first few chapters, anyway. The one about the publisher's life story, some of which coincidentally just happened to be not unlike your dark and distant past,' she added with a hint of flippancy.

'It was more than a little similar,' he replied tersely. 'It was precise and exact in almost every detail except for the names.' Blake had assumed a stern, almost pompous expression. He may have thought it commanded respect and attention in the office, but it did not work at home, and trying it on with Catherine was doomed to failure as it always made her laugh aloud.

'Was it?' asked Catherine whimsically, pursing her lips into a tiny rosebud.

'Yes, it was, you know that,' replied Blake indignantly.

Catherine acknowledged her slight disingenuousness. 'And?' she added, tilting her head slightly.

'Well, I started to reread it today and…' He paused momentarily. Not for dramatic effect but to give himself time to allow his brain to revisit the content of the four chapters, in particular, the last one. 'There's now a fourth chapter.' There, he had said it.

'A what,' asked Catherine?

'I just told you, there is now a fourth chapter.'

'Where,' asked Catherine, with enquiring caution?

'After the third,' replied Blake glibly. He was still having a problem believing it himself.

'After the third.' echoed Catherine. 'After the third chapter, where there wasn't anything the last time I read it?'

'Correct,' replied Blake.

'And when did it app… materialise?' she asked, sounding more than a little curious.

'I came across the manuscript when tidying up and decided to give it another read while you were at your mother's, and there it was.'

'And there it was,' she repeated, with a hint of scepticism. But she refused to immediately surrender to the obvious. She looked Blake squarely in the eyes and realised he was not messing around with her. He was troubled and uneasy in a way she had not seen before.

'Have you had a drink today,' she asked?

'Not a drop,' replied Blake firmly. But he had, and he wondered why he had lied about it. This was not like him at all.

'Can I read it,' she asked quietly?

'Of course,' replied Blake. 'I want you to read it. I think you need to. If only to bring some sanity to this madness. If you can't, I don't know who can.'

'Right,' said Catherine, marshalling all her faculties into a plan of action. 'First thing – I'll make that tea.'

'Ah!' said Blake. 'Sorry, I did boil the kettle.'

'Then we can sit down and read it together.' She made the tea, and then they walked back into the lounge and sat on the sofa. She passed a teacup to Blake and glanced at the empty whiskey glass on the small table. She said nothing, but Blake noticed.

'Lemonade. It was just a lemonade, honestly. I wouldn't lie to you.'

'I believe you,' said Catherine.

'Thank you,' he timidly replied as if he had been scolded for being naughty. Catherine was not cross, but the manuscript and Blake's preoccupation with its contents were clearly beginning to try her patience.

'I'm ready now,' said Catherine, sitting at the other end of the sofa so she could face Blake. He took a sip of tea. She smiled at him.

Catherine picked up the manuscript and briefly flicked through to the beginning of Chapter Four. She looked up at Blake and, carefully choosing her words, cautiously asked, 'Not for one moment am I saying you have…' she paused, realising she was now treading on dangerous ground. Catherine would probably not have even asked the question if their marriage were not based on absolute, unimpeachable trust. She realised that just saying the words could damage their relationship irreparably.

Their marriage was stable, but every bond had a breaking point. A point from which there was never any going back. When the invisible golden thread was stretched to its limit and then beyond. After that, you could only move forward as if starting again. There could be no reliance on what had passed before. All the trust built over the years would have been destroyed. But that was sometimes the risk you had to take. Despite all her misgivings, she had to take the gamble and ask the question.

'You could have written this today while we were away…' The words seemed to hang in the air, suspended on a slender thread of faith, fidelity, and love. Catherine felt the air leave her body like an inverted body is exsanguinated when the throat has been cut. She took another deep breath in preparation for what might come next. Blake said nothing at first, and Catherine knew she may have made a terrible mistake, possibly the worst mistake of their lives together. It was a betrayal of trust, something that could never be reinstated.

His poker face was utterly unreadable. His brain was working overtime, more intensely than it had done in a long time. It was stumbling through the possible permutations that could be construed from those few words, but he was not conveying one speck of emotion or response to the extremities of his body. It was as if he had been suspended in a moment of freeze-frame animation that was being excruciatingly extended.

'Yes,' replied Blake after a few more painful seconds, possibly the longest she could remember, seconds in which their lives could have changed beyond all recognition, even moved beyond a point of no return. It was the time it took a happy smiling man, waiving from the back of a limousine, a man who once carried the world's destiny in his hands, to change his expression to utter astonishment and disbelief. His life was instantly blown away, and the world was changed forever in those few seconds. These few seconds could change Catherine and Blake's lives forever.

'You are right,' continued Blake, turning to smile at her with quizzical admiration. It was her integrity without concession that had first attracted him to Catherine. Only later, lying in bed, did he realise how stunningly attractive she was with her large deep brown Mediterranean eyes. Eyes of molten lava that could burn right through him if he did her wrong.

'I could have written it,' continued Blake. 'In fact, at one point, I was certain I had, such was my disbelief when I read it. I am going mad, I thought, but then… No, something else is happening.'

Catherine slowly let the air out of her body and breathed normally again. No damage appeared to have been done, and she quietly said a little prayer to herself.

'I don't know what is happening, but I didn't write it. Unbelievable as that sounds, and believe me, I know how ridiculous that is. I didn't write it because the book…' Blake paused momentarily; he had to ensure he was not losing his grip on reality. But he was certain he was still sane. He slowly glanced around the kitchen and then looked at Catherine, having absorbed all the things he recognised, all the everyday things he had always taken for granted, all the things that were now so precariously balanced on a knife edge, and then he said the words:

'The book is writing itself....'

There, he had said it. Either he was entirely around the bend, having suddenly developed some inexplicable schizophrenic condition, or he was dealing with something beyond his normal comprehension of literary fantasy.

Catherine stared at him but said nothing.

'The book is writing itself, I swear,' he repeated, more slowly this time, with heightened intonation. 'I thought somebody else was somehow writing the words and slipping them into the manuscript, but that isn't what's happening.'

Catherine did not know what to say. She had been temporarily struck dumb by his explanation of some supernatural intervention. This wasn't quite what she was expecting on her return home, having only been away for a few hours.

She glanced downwards momentarily, trying to get her head around what Blake had just said. She lifted her eyes and looked at the man sitting at the end of the sofa. This man she loved and adored had just figuratively opened his veins and let the blood pour onto the floor. Such was his incredulity at the circumstances that now seemed to be overwhelming and consuming him, taking control of his life and, to a lesser degree, hers.

'I believe you,' she muttered quietly. Blake looked at her for some sign as to which part she believed.

'That I am some sort of sociopathic nutter who has managed to develop a multiple personality disorder while on his own for a few hours, or that I've magically stumbled across an incredible self-writing book?'

'I don't believe you are mad or that you are writing the book. There must be another simple explanation. We have to try and work out what that is.'

'How?' said Blake, having spent the last few minutes sliding with terpsichorean agility from reality to abject desperation and then back to reality.

'Let's reread all of it,' said Catherine, 'to see if we've missed something. And if we don't find anything, I suggest we lock it away in a safe place where neither of us can get to it, and then we'll come back to it in a month or two and see if anything has changed.'

Concise, practical, and logical. All the qualities Blake seemed incapable of mustering right now but, fortunately for him, the very attributes he so admired in Catherine and which she had managed to marshal together at this crucial moment. Catherine had remained undaunted, unfazed by the strange conundrum now facing them, and had come up with a solution... No, not a solution, but more a navigable route out of this maze of confusion and misdirection.

'That sounds good, brilliant... Yes!' said Blake. He stumbled around for more suitable adjectives, but none were forthcoming; his brain seemed to have partially shut down. He moved down the sofa next to Catherine, and slowly with some trepidation, they opened the manuscript on page one.

'I'll make another cup of tea,' said Catherine. 'I think we need it.'

'Good idea,' replied Blake, endeavouring to regain his composure and sanity.

'We could have brandy,' suggested Blake, but Catherine's scornful expression quickly put paid to that proposal. She made two cups of strong tea and placed them on the table in front of the sofa before walking out into the garden to check on Max and Claudia. They had both fallen asleep on the hammock. Catherine came back into the kitchen.

'They're both asleep, so we should be uninterrupted for at least an hour.' They began to reread it through to the end of Chapter Four when the words ran out. They did not speak a single word to each other while they were reading.

'So, you started young,' mused Catherine, 'and you now have another wife, Kate, who you forgot to mention.' She smiled. 'That definitely wasn't there the last time I read it. I would have remembered that.' But the similarity in Christian names one a derivation of the other - began to unnerve her slightly.

'I agree, somehow that has been added, which means you would have had to retype large sections of the manuscript to squeeze in the extra details.'

Her expression said everything. She knew Blake was appallingly slow at typing and "hated it with a passion." A phrase Blake had carefully tried to explain to her on one of their first dates when he was trying to impress her. The expression, he had told her, originated from South America, where the indigenous Indians threw Passionfruit at foreign explorers, not without some justification. But Catherine harboured doubts about the credibility of that explanation finding it blatantly ridiculous. But it made her laugh, and that was why she remembered it.

Blake did not answer.

'The bit about the book sounds interesting.'

'The book?' queried Blake.

'The Chapter Room,' replied Catherine,

'What about it,' asked Blake?

'It has a nice ring to it. It could be just what you need. A blockbuster. Isn't that what you said a few weeks ago? If the book is writing your life, then maybe that's about to happen; you should look for it in the office.' Catherine said this more as a diversion from what they were trying to do. A welcome interlude after the uneasy period they had just experienced, one that gave Blake something more to think about.

Also, adopting Catherine's suggestion about a safe could prove beyond any doubt that he was neither an accomplice in some dark Machiavellian plot nor the instigator of this bizarre situation.

'Martin has a safe,' said Catherine, interrupting Blake's thoughts. Martin was a retired banker who lived next door and had been a good friend for many years. He and his wife Ruth had been regular Friday night dinner guests since before Max and Claudia were born, but not so much since Ruth had died.

'Perfect,' replied Blake. 'You take it round. Just tell him…' he stopped for a second to think, 'tell him whatever you think is best, but the one condition is he only gives it back to us if we are both together, or to you, but not me.'

'That sounds good,' agreed Catherine. She smiled at Blake. The tide of anxiety and apprehension threatening to engulf them over the previous hour slowly receded, their problem partially resolved. She took the manuscript to Martin. After explaining some, but not all, of its unusual characteristics, he happily agreed to place the book in his safe.

The Prospect Road manuscript was now safely locked away, being treated as a literal Edmund Dantès. Incarcerated for merely knowing the truth and prevented from being able to convey it.

Chapter 7

A couple of weeks later, there was a knock on Blake's office door, and Jamie stuck his head around the corner.

'Sorry to interrupt, but I have this one which you might want to look at.' He was holding a manuscript.

Blake stopped what he was doing and looked up at Jamie as an expression of indulgent enthusiasm flashed across his face. He beckoned Jamie to come in and sit down in the chair opposite his desk.

'We've all read it,' continued Jamie excitedly. 'It's that good. So, I thought it was time I brought it to you to read.'

'What's it about?' Blake asked casually but still with the air of eager anticipation that came with every new book passed to him.

It had, after all, been through the office screening system, and he trusted their judgement. He had no option. So by the time a book passed to him for review, he knew, with reasonable certainty, that it would, at the very least, be articulate and engaging.

It was no longer physically possible for him to read every manuscript sent to the company, such were the numbers now being received. Coincidentally, that was precisely what he was employed to do when he first came to work at Clanford and Fox in 1968, but the number of manuscripts sent in those days was far fewer. Nobody could have foreseen the development of the word processor in the 1980s inadvertently opening the floodgates to millions of novels being written by what could only be ingenuously termed as under-gifted amateurs. So, a filtering system became essential - to filter out the less-than-inspiring submissions.

His decision about a book's ultimate destiny depended primarily on whether he believed it could sell in sufficient numbers to make publication commercially viable. He reviewed many books that ticked all the boxes. But for one reason or another, he had decided they probably wouldn't sell enough copies to cover costs. So much was now being written that the writing quality, ironically, was no longer the most critical factor. Sometimes, something as base as notoriety was enough to sell a book in large numbers, irrespective of its literary worth, even after being severely edited.

Conversely, many classic pieces of modern literature languished in dusty drawers or on memory sticks. Many of which were destined to be formatted, ready for another life. They were all but forgotten, having been rejected by every publisher. Such was the paradoxical injustice of the writing profession.

He often wondered what would happen if the inexplicable electrical excitement coursing through his whole body when he read something outstanding suddenly deserted him. He would need to find something entirely different to do. Maybe he would become a gardener or a bricklayer, something perfectly defined by what it produced - something tangible. Something that no longer needed imagination - for imagination was essential to enable him to continue doing what he did. Real success was based on capturing the writer's intelligence having riotous fun with words - and the publisher's unquestioning, unwavering belief in the finished product without the benefit of any logical explanation or quantifiable rationale. It was a religion above all other religions, the communicator above all other forms of communication.

He knew the only way to define any story's real worth was to measure the degree to which it affected a reader. Did it make you want to change your life and become a different person? – A better person? Did it make you want to reassess how your presence affected other people? Did its very existence bring joy and pleasure to others, or did it simply leave you unmoved and unchanged?

Could you identify yourself with one of the characters, and was that good or bad? All these things come as part of the experience of reading a well-written book. As Reggie Clanford had told him many years before, 'A good story starts at the beginning and finishes at the end, but an exceptional story starts long before it begins and finishes long after the end.' That way, the reader becomes utterly immersed in the narrative. Furthermore, they are graced with the opportunity to re-imagine their own beginning and end. That transforms one story into millions of slightly different stories, one interpretation for every reader. This was the golden elixir of literary success. The reader is wholly enveloped in the tale and thereby becomes a part of it.

'It's a love story – unusual ending,' replied Jamie, 'but it's slightly different from the normal dross. Nicely written, well-drawn characters. As you can imagine, I found it hard to put down, which is normally quite easy for me. So, definitely not that bad for a first attempt.' He almost sounded patronisingly blasé about it but held back just enough to remain on the upside of cautious optimism. But then publishers become like that. In one respect, they were not dissimilar to literary critics; it was in their nature to be politely cynical, respectfully critical, and courteously negative. But never entirely going the distance and committing themselves, just in case...

They seldom found anything perfect at the first reading. These were the sort of people who would have described the Bible as painfully loquacious – thin on plot – with vague, unrealistic characterisation and obtuse, oddly derivative dialogue. An incessantly rambling dialectic narrative coupled with an unfamiliar development format. Sort of thing Tolkien, Nietzsche or Gandhi might have cobbled up after a heavy session on the vino.

'I think it could be great for the Christmas market,' continued Jamie. He knew more books were sold during Christmas than at any other time of the year except for the summer holidays.

'Yes, good. Can you leave it with me?' asked Blake, still not quite hearing every word. He was struggling to digest the company's latest half-yearly sales report. Going by the look on his face, it did not make for comfortable reading. 'I'll have a look at it when I get back from my meeting.' He glanced up at Jamie again and half-smiled.

He was going out for a 'media marketing conference' (a publisher's euphemism for a long-drawn-out boozy lunch) with Barrington Kane, one of Clanford and Fox's regular writers. He had just completed his ninth Inspector Chang Chinese detective story, and they needed to discuss how they would market this latest addition to the series. Invariably there would be many bookshops to visit for short readings, book signings, television interviews and various other media events. All this was even more significant now as a possible television drama series was mentioned, which would inevitably boost sales considerably.

The Chang stories were always good sellers, although a little banal even for Blake's catholic taste. Blake often experienced great anguish at Barrington's misappropriation of the definite article and his excruciating split infinitives. Nevertheless, his readers loved him, the prose worked and 'as that was all he had,' as his favourite writer Raymond Chandler once said, 'that was all that really mattered.'

Nevertheless, he was professionally and contractually obliged to read them and commit to memory every gory detail. In this respect, he had religiously and diligently fulfilled his obligation.

There was something compelling and strangely charismatic about this incompetent yet inscrutable detective with the glottal stop issue. It seemed to intrigue readers. He was forever leaving out the two t's in butter or pronouncing 'that is' as 'dat is', as in 'dat is very interwesting, but doesn't make logical sense because…' This was one of Chang's favourite catchlines before delivering a startling revelation.

He fumbled and bumbled his way around each investigation, making catastrophic errors. Either totally ignoring the blatantly obvious clues or discarding them altogether with a nonchalant hand wave. He would claim they were nothing more than 'red herons', a recurring phrase that his readers always found highly amusing.

He was ably assisted by a beautiful Chinese lady who did all the running around and research needed to help solve every case. Of course, she also brought the essential elements of sexual chemistry and tension necessary to complete each story.

With one staggering stroke of genius and panache in the closing chapter, Chang would invariably deliver a highly relevant (but usually teeth-grindingly abstruse) ancient Chinese maxim. After Chang's painfully drawn-out explication, the readers would inevitably be guided towards the exposure of the guilty party - a person you would have least expected. Samples of Chang's final Chinese aphorisms for consideration were:

'Cat with seven lives should never eat snow in June on a Tuesday.'

'Man, who falls into fast-flowing river, must quickly learn to sing in Italian.'

However, Barrington did have a large following of steadfastly loyal 'Changies.' They were the sort of bread-and-butter readers that kept the company ticking over and Barrington in receipt of an almost endless supply of beer tokens.

The secret of becoming a financially independent writer (and Barrington had comprehensively exploited this truism to the nth degree) was to catch and keep dedicated readers. They would religiously buy every book he wrote, no matter what. This guaranteed continuous and ever-increasing sales and a steady income for the writer and publisher. All the writer had to do was keep turning them out regularly. Readers invariably remained loyal to their favourite authors, and it would take some concerted and determined application by the author to alienate their faithful acolytes.

Barrington was the company's most famous writer apart from Desmond (Dezzi) Chandler, a lecherously rapacious middle-aged chef with his own long-running television series and a massive following of male and female fans. Many of whom he had, irrespective of sex or age, bedded over the many years the programme had been running. Dezzi ardently supported the aphorism that "every shag bought every book he ever wrote," and he had authored many books. It was a unique, if somewhat exhausting, way of building a loyal and faithful following. But he would endeavour to persevere on his quest because he was totally dedicated to increasing his book sales.

Dezzi would spend most of their lunchtime meetings regaling Blake, in detail, about his latest conquests. Blake found this insufferable and appallingly bad taste (no pun intended). Unfortunately, this was an essential element of being a publisher. It was necessary, in fact, essential, that Blake endured this monosyllabic, innuendo-riddled diatribe at least twice a year if he were to retain Dezzi as a client.

It was much the same with Barrington Kane but without the ghastly details of his personal indiscretions ladled over the linguine. Blake seldom ate much when out for lunch with Dezzi.

After lunch, Blake slowly made his way back to the office alone, musing over the many topics they had lightly brushed over while eating. He had left Barrington talking to a woman.

Barrington Kane was, in fact, a pen name; his real name was Walter Measal. In their infinite wisdom, the publicity department had decided early on that his name did not sound rugged enough for a writer of detective stories. So they had suggested a newer, punchier, macho-sounding pen name, which Walter quickly embraced.

Blake found Barrington mind-numbingly dull. But, out of common courtesy, he would put up with him bleating on about his latest Inspector Chang escapade for nearly two hours. Until - just as he was beginning to nod off, a Changie fan fortuitously interrupted their lunch. She gushingly introduced herself at their table, and Barrington, *out of common courtesy,* invited her to join them. This was the opportunity Blake needed to leave, and he quickly grasped the moment, made his excuses, and departed. As far as Blake was concerned, the interloper deserved all she would receive from Barrington for her bad manners.

As he meandered along the pavement, Blake thought about the enormous sacrifice of time he had to make in the line of fire. Either suffering the rambling machinations of a sexually rapacious reprobate or the inane mumblings of an inveterate bore. But such was his life, the one he had chosen. Oh, how he craved the conversation of an intelligent, articulate writer...

A little worse for wear and slightly shell-shocked, he made his way up the staircase to his office, arriving just after four to pick up some reports he wanted to take home and read that night. He noticed a manuscript that Jamie had left on his desk. It was the one they had spoken about earlier in the day. A scribbled note had been left on top – "Read this one. We all have, and it is good. The best we've read in ages." He picked it up, put it into his case with the other documents and wandered back out of the office, saying goodbye to the remaining staff as he went. He arrived home just over two hours later.

'Hi darling, how was your day?' asked Catherine as she walked up to kiss him hello, wrapping her arms around him and pulling him close for a cuddle.

'Same as always,' he replied, squeezing her bum. Several black coffees on the train had sobered him up from his lunchtime meeting - restoring him to some semblance of normality. 'There were delays with the trains due to the unusual heat. That's what the station announcer said, anyway. Apparently, the trains had been designed to run on lines with a different kind of heat.' He giggled to himself at his lame witticism. Fortunately, writing one-line jokes was not his livelihood; had it been the case, he would have starved to death very quickly.

'I waded through the sales reports today; they were a bit depressing for the first six months. Things have slowed down quite a bit. All we have in the pipeline is another one of Barrington Kane's Inspector Chang mysteries for the autumn. Hopefully, this will boost things along for Christmas.'

'Oh, I like those,' replied Catherine. 'They're hilarious... and quite naughty in places,' she added after a slight pause. It was a slightly stilted qualification. Blake made a mental note about her comment; it was, after all, singly objective, as he had not explicitly canvassed her for an opinion.

'How many is it now? Must be five or six,' she asked.

'Number bloody nine, would you believe,' replied Blake, astonished at his pronouncement.

He could not believe anybody liked the books, but they did, and they bought them in large numbers. No accounting for taste, he thought, but that was moving perilously close to popular fiction heresy. They were, in the main, poorly written, and the plots were weak, ill-conceived, half-baked, and unrealistic. There were no tangible police procedures. Something so precisely and accurately documented in most other detective novels doing the rounds. Procedures, which most crime fiction readers know backwards these days. But despite all these flaws, the books sold in their millions (after some severe in-house editing). Put simply, his readers loved his stories irrespective of and despite their literary value.

Blake compared the longevity of the Inspector Chang series to the Hayflick phenomenon. This determined that human cells will only subdivide a specific number of times before they cease to divide further because the DNA structure would have been so comprehensively degenerated by that point. Blake thought the original cracking storyline of the first book, a story he had enjoyed very much, had now been replicated so often that it was now in danger of running out of all and any originality. In fact, he was sure it had all but run out of steam by about number five. However, he had been proved wrong. The readers did not concur with his opinion. They continued coming back to buy – in ever-increasing numbers – poorly rehashed variations of the first book. Apparently, Mr Chang was on the road to literary perpetuity, and Barrington Kane was on his way to becoming a multi-millionaire.

Reggie Clanford had once told him that nobody ever went broke, underestimating the buying public's bad taste. Here was the definitive example to prove the point.

'Daddy!' exclaimed Max, with rising intonation - scolding his father for swearing. Until that moment, Max had been sitting quietly on the sofa reading - Blake had forgotten he was there.

'I'm sorry,' said Blake contritely, hunting around his trouser pocket for a one-pound coin. He dropped it, somewhat reluctantly, into the pink pig money box that Max had suddenly produced from nowhere and was waving under his nose. That was the financial arrangement they had come to, which worked both ways, but more so in Max's favour. Max, not surprisingly, had become incredibly careful with his language. He was making serious plans for the substantial number of pound coins that had now accumulated in the pig. He had no intention of giving any of them back under the reciprocal agreement.

'I thought you liked them?' asked Catherine curiously.

'I liked the first one. That was very entertaining, but it went downhill for me after that, but uphill for sales, so I stuck with it.'

'It pays the bills,' said Catherine philosophically.

'It does indeed, and it's very ungracious of me to be so disparaging and pious about them. It's a tad hypocritical, I admit, but they are bloody boring.' The pig reappeared on cue. Max knew there were always good pickings to be had when Dad came home, especially if he had had an unpleasant day.

'Aaaaahh,' said Blake, ruffling about in his pocket for another coin. 'But's there's hope yet.'

'Oh!' replied Catherine.

'I have this.' He produced the manuscript from his case that he had picked up as he left the office.

'The new Inspector Chang?' asked Catherine with a wry smile.

'No, no, it isn't. Actually, it's…' But Blake stopped, noticing that virtually all of the front cover was missing apart from a small area around the two punched holes. It looked as if the front page had been ripped off, possibly when he had put the manuscript into his case, but when he checked inside his case, it wasn't there either. The rest of the document appeared intact, but he checked the last page to ensure it wasn't missing. It was not.

'It's a new writer. Jamie says it is the best thing he has read in ages, and apparently, everybody in the office feels the same. So that has to say something.'

'So, maybe there is some salvation,' said Catherine wryly. 'We might be able to afford a sausage and two feathers for Christmas dinner after all?'

'Yes, maybe. We'll see,' replied Blake.

'Does it have a name?' asked Catherine.

'Yes, it does, but I don't know what it is. Nor do I know the writer's name. I've lost the front page.'

'Oh! So, do you know what it is about,' asked Catherine?

'A little. I read the synopsis on the train – it's a love story, that much I know.'

'That's good,' replied Catherine, but then she always liked love stories.

'It's set in a convent in a small village in France. It is about a conman hiding from the police and working as a gardener in a convent. He falls in love with one of the novice nuns, and then something unexpected happens. That changes everything.'

'Oh,' said Catherine. 'Well, that's a bit different.

Blake wandered into the lounge, sat down, and started to read the manuscript without a front cover.

It was intriguing from the first page, and he found himself swept up in the story almost to the exclusion of everything else happening around him.

Chapter 8
The Sisters of Mercy by Gideon Drew
Chapter Six...(The manuscript with no front cover.)

Charlie sat in his cell, reminiscing about all the good things that had happened in his life and how uncomplicated everything had once been before it all started to go terribly wrong. His recollection had been triggered by the exquisite fragrance of summer that surreptitiously wafted through the prison bars into his nasal passage to settle somewhere in his brain - in whatever part of the somatosensory cortex processed these feelings. His thoughts drifted back to a period just over a year before. To when it had all begun...

It was like any other day in Misericord, a tiny French village in the middle of nowhere. The air was warm, still, and heavy. The spicy fragrance of dianthus and lavender, which always seemed to overpower the other flowers, lingered lazily in the air. The pungent, erotic tang of jasmine, the nocturnal accomplice and third member of the aromatic triumvirate that scented the country tended to be stronger in the evening, a time of passionate endeavour. As they did every summer, the heady-scented co-conspirators had taken control of the countryside. A remorseless invasion of the senses by stealth and cunning intervention.

But it was the dianthus that Charlie would always associate with long, languid lunches with his dear friend and confidante Henri Pascal, owner of Café de Paris. Their intense lunchtime discussions would invariably be about the same four topics: politics, life, women, or religion, but mainly women. The lavender reminded him of the febrile afternoons of inconsequential passion he had shared with so many women who had passed his way, ladies who were now nothing more than distant memories. Or maybe it was the other way around. He was not sure; perhaps he was becoming confused. Maybe he didn't want to remember anything or anyone anymore – except one person – one woman.

The woman who stole his heart when he did not think he had one; his money, which Charlie never had until he met her; and his life, when he thought he was in complete control of it. He was not – she just made him feel he was. So much had changed, and yet nothing had changed.

Charlie wandered casually down the dry, dusty road to the village from the Convent of Le Sang de la Vie, where he had been working that morning. Dangling in his right hand was a half-smoked Gitane, the wisps of white smoke slowly curling behind him like a recalcitrant halo...

His other hand was in his trouser pocket, mindfully turning over some loose change. His beret was pulled down low and outwards to shade his eyes from the harsh midday sun. He looked at the ground as he walked, but his thoughts were miles away; they were always somewhere else, never where he was.

This was a journey he made most days between the hours of 12.00 midday and 3.00 pm when not otherwise engaged.

Today, the village was perfectly still. Still as if frozen in time, it was virtually deserted. Except, that is, for the sound of two unmistakably English women sitting at a table outside the café. Under the shade of a Heineken umbrella, they drank wine and chatted animatedly. A man sat alone at another table reading a newspaper while sipping a café noir. He did not look up. Charlie began to...

'Dinner,' whispered Catherine, not wishing to disturb Blake more than necessary while he was reading. This was an understanding they had whenever he started reading a manuscript during his regular working hours.

It was arguably a little regimented, even mildly dictatorial, but essential if he were to work productively at home. Usually, he would read in his study, but occasionally, he would sit in the lounge as today.

'Oh great,' replied Blake, sounding a little surprised. He laid the manuscript down on the sofa. 'I'm starving.' As he got up, he glanced at the old grandmother's clock; it was ten past nine.

'Ten past nine? That cannot be right,' he exclaimed disbelievingly. Maybe he had forgotten to wind it. He looked at his watch to double-check.

'Oh, it is darling,' replied Catherine. 'You've been reading non-stop since you came home. You even missed the children going to bed… you were so engrossed I thought it was best not to interrupt you.'

'Oh,' said Blake. He looked stunned for a moment, his eyebrows dropping in bewilderment. Seldom, if ever, had he become so engaged with a story that it had prevented him from sitting down with his family to eat dinner. More importantly, from saying goodnight to Max and Claudia.

'I am sorry. I just started on this, and…' Blake picked up the manuscript and showed it to Catherine, 'I have just become so absorbed by it, completely sucked in. It is a wonderful story. I know our marketing people use the same old clichéd phrases "can't put down" and "must read in one session" on half of the books we put out, but it's true in this case. It really is.'

'So, there is a chance I might be able to replace my old jalopy soon?' asked Catherine with a pleadingly, mournful expression. 'The old girl was on her last legs.' Catherine wasn't overly concerned about the car, but the old Volvo estate was beginning to show its age and regularly breaking down. Increasingly, she had to rely on Blake's car, which he, fortunately, left at home two or three days a week when he travelled to London by train. However, if hers did fail, it would invariably be on a day when Blake had driven to work. Another niggling concern was she would soon be taking Max to school every day, a round trip of eight miles. The journey was mainly down quiet country lanes, where an early morning breakdown could be a real problem, as she would also have Claudia in the car.

'If there is any justice, this will fly, and you can have a…' He hesitated for a moment. '…brand new Volvo estate and I can have the Bentley convertible I have always wanted. And we can have a decent holiday.'

'That would be wonderful,' replied Catherine, surprised at his bubbling jubilation. She did, however, ponder momentarily over the inequality over his choice of vehicles. But she would let that pass for now.

'I haven't seen you this elated since… since Chelsea beat West Ham, and that was years ago. Blake had always been a Chelsea fan through the good and the troubled times, and Catherine still remembered the good times because they had been so rare over the past three or four years.

'I am,' he replied. 'I really am. This could be it. The Holy Grail! This could be the one to put us firmly back on the publishing map at last.'

The business had not been immensely profitable, almost since Reggie Clanford died. His timing was immaculate. He died just as their bestselling novelist died, leaving nothing unpublished. That was an excellent opportunity that had just slipped through their hands through the lack of forward planning. Blake would not make that mistake.

They had Barrington Kane, Desmond Chandler and several other authors under contract who were consistent bottom-league sellers. But they had no prominent writer in the top twenty, where they had to be to make serious money. So, the company had been desperately looking for someone to fill that top seller void ever since.

Blake sat at the dining table and ate dinner together despite being a little past its best. It had been in the oven for a couple of hours longer than was strictly necessary. Blake poured a second glass of Niersteiner for Catherine and himself – they preferred the German Rieslings to the Austrian. He raised a toast to the unnamed book and its unidentified author. It was a bit odd toasting a book and an author without knowing the name of either.

'To the unknown writer… and his masterpiece.' They clinked their glasses together and drank the wine. Catherine smiled. She was glad to see some sparkle coming back to Blake's eyes. Just lately, she had become a little concerned about his preoccupation with work – and of course, the manuscript of Prospect Road, which she knew was still troubling him, although he hadn't mentioned it recently.

'You can't be certain it's that good. You haven't finished it yet,' said Catherine.

'Oh, I am.' he replied firmly. 'It's that good.' He smiled the smile of somebody who knew precisely what he had and what it could do for him, his family, the business, and his life. 'This book will change our lives; I am certain of that much.' Little did he realise just how much.

The next day was Friday. He caught the train into London and took the Underground as usual to Tottenham Court Road to get to his office in Denmark Street. On entering the office, he was immediately confronted by Jamie and two other assistant copyreaders, Julie and Rachel. They said nothing, but both just looked at him with vacant expressions. He sensed something was not right.

'What?' he exclaimed. 'What's happened?' He naturally assumed the worst. The first thing that sprang to mind was the possibility that maybe Barrington Kane had been murdered in a horrendous ritual killing. Not dissimilar to one of his own far-fetched storylines. This one having the significant added advantage of being for real, and as such, would obviously mean a considerable increase in sales of his complete back catalogue. That thought heartened him, and then just for a moment, he paused and reflected on how egotistical and self-serving that was. Nevertheless, he continued to speculate on the various positives this disaster might bring about.

An aficionado of literature and the English language had chopped him up in little pieces and fed him to his pet pig. Perhaps as recompense for the degenerative influence, he had inflicted on the general standard of grammatical literacy. An assassin after his own heart. He drifted off, daydreaming for a few more seconds, hypothesising on the various other gruesome ends that could have befallen Barrington. He had plenty of scope, nine books (including the latest magnum opus). They would undoubtedly go on to sell in incredible numbers thanks to the kudos of the unexpected marketing tactic of the author getting himself murdered. He was spoilt for choice, with at least three grisly murder scenarios in each book covering the full spectrum of surprise demise. Without a doubt, this was a truly generous, noble, and selfless act of bonhomie, even he pondered quietly to himself.

'Is he dead?' Blake blurted out eventually, having returned from a state of wistful distraction, now managing to string a few simple words together with mixed emotions. He realised that he was speaking the words he was thinking, and those words should not have left his mouth. He had let his imagination run away with itself, which was unforgivable in the circumstances.

'Who?' said Rachel, looking at him oddly and sounding confused.

'Barrington! Is he dead? Was he murdered?' asked Blake quietly, with a strained impression of empathetic concern.

'No!' said Jamie. 'Has someone told you something we don't know?'

'No, no,' replied Blake. 'It's just that... you – all standing there – to greet me. I thought...' Blake realised that he had completely misread the situation. Barrington was, in fact, untouched by man-eating pigs and probably halfway through his next book.

'Did you read the book?' asked Jamie.

Blake took a deep breath. 'Book? Which book?'

'The Sisters of Mercy, the one about a nun in a convent falling in love with the handyman.'

'Oh, yes, I have. Didn't know what the title was to start with. Somehow, I mislaid the first page, but I recognise the name now.'

'I found that on your desk,' said Julie.

'Ah, that's where it was,' muttered Blake.

He suddenly had an odd Deja vu moment; for no reason, Prospect Road popped into his head. He had temporarily forgotten about the book and then remembered where it was, quietly resting in Martin's safe. But there was something in there that he had heard before, possibly a name. But what was it, he wondered. The thought tempered his initial enthusiasm.

'What did you think,' asked Jamie?

'What did I think,' replied Blake, with measured indifference? He didn't want to appear overly eager, or they might start talking about a bonus, which would be slightly premature at this stage anyway. So best to appear a little non-committal about it and gently deflate their overly-exuberant enthusiasm. Of course, if the book did take off big time, it was customary to hand out bonuses, but all in good time, he thought. It was early days yet, very early days.

'Yes, it was quite good. We should have a chat with Mr...' The author's name had, either by deliberate intention or absent-mindedness, temporarily escaped Blake. The staff were slightly surprised and flattened by his less-than-enthusiastic reaction; they had half expected him to be as ecstatic about the book as they had been. Usually, he would be bubbling with excitement after reading something he really liked which had great potential. But strangely, he was not displaying any outwardly encouraging reactions at all.

Although he didn't mention it, he had, in fact, stayed up all night and finished the book. Many works are touted as one-sitting books but seldom live up to expectations - this one indeed was. He was utterly exhausted by the end, such was the intensity conveyed in the writing. The dialogue filled his brain with an ineffable passion. The experience had almost disturbed him to the point of paranoia, the fear of never again achieving this visceral interaction with a written work. It was a revelation, a sensation that he realised could be replicated by anyone who ever read the book.

The characterisation was so cleverly defined that Blake could swear he knew some of these people intimately. He knew everything about them. Every fault, every lie they had ever told, every indiscretion, every secret... every love they had ever known. By 5am, when he struggled to bed, they had become close personal friends, some of whom he had once loved and some he would have sacrificed his life for.

By the time he made it to bed, he had been reading non-stop for eleven hours, except for the short break for dinner. He was beginning to hallucinate on the opiate of aching emotion so cleverly embedded and enshrined within the narrative.

'It's Gideon Drew,' said Jamie, interrupting Blake's cerebral meanderings. 'I think he may be American.'

'Oh,' said Blake, with a noticeable downturn in the tone of his voice, as if he was slightly disappointed for some reason. 'Gideon Drew. Hmm... it has a nice ring to it.' He still couldn't quite place the name.

Yes, give him a ring and set something up. No! Wait. He stopped for a few moments to gather his thoughts. 'Don't ring him. Send a standard letter and ask him to arrange to come and see me. We don't want to appear too keen.'

Jamie looked at Blake a little oddly. He was not used to employing subtle psychological tactics when dealing with a potential new client. Especially one with a terrific book already under his belt and potentially many more to come. And, of course, there was every possibility that Gideon had already sent copies of the book to other publishers. Maybe they wouldn't be so tardy in responding if they felt the same as he did after reading it.

He could see a slight change in Blake's personality. It may have been infinitesimal, but it was there, all the same, something he had not seen before. Ruthless manipulation hiding behind the façade of subtle misdirection. It was an uncharacteristic trait, and it surprised him. He thought he knew every dimension of Blake's character, having worked with him for over five years, but he had not seen this aspect before. He took no further notice of his observation and put it down to the transient elation of the moment. Maybe Blake's brain had removed a few passive brain cells that had died and replaced them with new, slightly more aggressive ones. Who knows, he thought to himself.

'No problem,' replied Jamie as he wandered off to organise the letter.

Some weeks later, Gideon Drew rang the office, and a meeting was arranged for the third Thursday in September. Blake was quietly excited and overjoyed but kept his feelings in check. He'd had lengthy discussions with the marketing, publicity, and sales departments on how best to put together a promotional campaign with maximum impact for an unknown writer. He hardly bothered with the editorial department, as he passionately believed there was nothing they could add or remove to enhance the book one iota. In fact, their interference at any level could reduce the flawless integrity of the piece. It would be a bit like asking a monkey to edit Macbeth. It was possible, but it could take quite a long time.

Considering his editorial team's mental agility and literary experience, he thought that was probably a little disparaging. But it made the point in his mind.

This was unique in his publishing experience, a perfect manuscript without anything superfluous or irrelevant and devoid of any authorial padding. The story's rhythm was as perfect as Ravel's Bolero, building to a stunning crescendo that took your breath away before bringing tears to your eyes. It was just like having sex for the first time with a beautiful prostitute. You know it's wrong, but you can't resist.

Not that he ever had, but he had read about the experience in many books. He knew deep down that, just like illicit sex, the book must have a flaw, a tiny imperfection. No matter how small or indiscernible, it had to be there somewhere, but he couldn't see it yet, which made it so perfect. The book was wrong... but he couldn't resist.

Chapter 9

Gideon Drew was a quiet, well-mannered, unassuming man in his mid-twenties. When Jamie showed him into Blake's office, he did not sit down until Blake asked him. Blake looked at him and wondered why so much talent should be bestowed on one so young. He had once tried to write a novel but failed miserably, lacking the fire and genius to create anything original. Fortunately, he could see the creative talent in others, which was his salvation, but deep down, he felt bitter and frustrated that he had not been so blessed.

'Mr Drew, or can I call you Gideon,' asked Blake? He had an odd feeling that he had heard Gideon's name before, somewhere, but could not remember where or when.

'Gideon is fine, thank you, sir,' replied Gideon.

'I'm not a sir, Gideon,' replied Blake. 'Please call me Blake. We're a big family here; it's all very informal.'

'Oh, I see,' said Gideon. 'Right.' He seemed a little uneasy with the informality, which Blake quickly noted.

'Would you like some tea or coffee, Gideon?'

'Yes, please. Tea, thanks,' replied Gideon. Blake tapped on the intercom and asked Julie to organise tea and biscuits.

'Right,' said Blake. 'Let's make a start.' He smiled benignly at Gideon. 'Firstly, I have to say I think it's a very well-written book. Everybody in the office has read it and loved it.' *Not everybody had read it, only the editorial staff responsible for evaluation,* but it sounded impressive and inspiring if a little obsequious. A singular unequivocal testament and commitment by the company to one person's creation.

Blake nodded slowly as he spoke, a sort of brotherly gesture of comradeship. They were all in this together to make this book an enormous success. That was the message he was endeavouring to convey.

'The central storyline is original. The dialogue is honest… believable, which I can tell you is a real problem with many new writers. Not to mention a few established ones.' He was thinking of one in particular. 'They tend to write as they think people talk, not how people actually talk. It's surprising how many words people don't actually say – they convey the message in other ways. That is what you have done. "Less is more" – and you have admirably grasped that concept.'

The Sisters of Mercy was not that long; it was technically a novella rather than a novel, but that wasn't an issue worth worrying about. Blake remembered that Catcher in the Rye, Breakfast at Tiffany's, The Old Man and The Sea, and The Great Gatsby were of similar length, but it had not affected their success.

'As for the characterisation, I thought I knew Charlie and Anna intimately by the end. Their passion leaps from the page. They inspired me, made me want to be a better person, and believe me, for a hard-bitten publisher like me, that is some trick… No, I take that back. Not a trick, pure genius.'

Gideon remembered some virtually identical praise he had received many years ago…

Blake let that thought hang in the air for a few moments. He wondered whether he was overdoing it a bit, but what the hell, in for a penny… and to be perfectly honest, that was precisely how Blake had felt the first time he read it. 'The real impact lies in its unnerving ability to access areas of my brain that I was unaware I had. Existential sensations that for most authors would be as alien as something from another planet.' Blake smiled at that last comment.

'I didn't realise,' replied Gideon, not a hundred per cent certain what Blake was alluding to.

'I think with the right marketing campaign, this too could be a major success, even, dare I say, a possible classic.'

There, he had said it. The magical words guaranteed to make the most hardened, cynical writer cry with happiness, not that Gideon appeared to be either.

Even in measured quantities, sycophancy was a ploy Blake seldom resorted to. But on this occasion, he thought it appropriate for reasons he could not fully understand.

'We, the team, and I think it would appeal to a particular sector who are historically regular buyers and generally loyal to particular writers. This is where we see the continuity coming from. Once we have a successful book, we must follow it up with another of the same quality. It keeps the reader focused and intrigued and builds a relationship between you and them. Once you have proven your credentials, they trust you as a writer. They learn how your characters work and will buy your stories on trust. There is a bond between a writer and the reader. An invisible, intangible connection, a slender thread of commonality that links them together forever. It is like a love affair, a burning fire of desire; it just waits to be satiated, a thirst that must be quenched.' Blake had lifted large sections of that diatribe from various other books he had read recently and thought it suitable for recycling on this occasion.

'I understand,' said Gideon. Though exhilarated by the approbation being heaped upon him, he was beginning to find its intensity a little suffocating. He understood the importance of vivid, impassioned narrative in a story but was less prepared for such oratorical adulation.

'And to keep this love affair alive, we must feed the flame, this raging fire.' Blake was laying it on a bit thick, but he did this occasionally when the mood took him, and today it had. Deep down, he was still that frustrated novelist who couldn't finish his story. While Gideon Drew had most definitely finished his.

'There is much more to publishing a book than just the printing element.' Blake paused for a moment to allow Gideon to absorb that thought. 'There is a lot of psychology involved. Are you with me so far?'

'Oh yes,' replied Gideon. 'I understand that. So how can I help?'

'Well, you've done all you need to do regarding the manuscript. Our people will brush it up as necessary after the contracts have been signed, and then we will send it to you for final approval before we publish it. Right now, all we need to discuss is the publishing contract and the financial arrangements. If you wish, we can do that today or leave it for a week or two. It's entirely up to you. I can tell you the basic terms now if you want.' Blake was purposely not being too pushy. He knew that new writers generally grabbed whatever was offered when an offer was made. Having probably been rejected tens if not hundreds of times before by other publishing houses.

It was very much a mercenary dog-eat-dog business these days. Very few publishers took on new writers without some established commercial or media celebrity value. Politicians, pop stars, film stars, footballers, soap stars, all these people were guaranteed to generate sales, regardless of the quality of writing. But the content invariably lacked depth and lustre, even when heavily ghosted and edited. As Reggie Clanford so often said, 'Son, no matter what you do or how much you spend, you can't polish a turd.' Originally from Yorkshire, Reggie was a man of few words, but they were all wise, succinct and to the point. Despite this piece of erudite northern wisdom, many attempts were made, but all failed.

But this book did not need polishing; it already sparkled like an enormous, perfect diamond. Blake could see it, he could almost touch it, he could smell it, and he could feel it in his bones.

Blake spent the next hour going over the contract's specific details. Setting the royalty rates for the first and following six books and all the precursors and conditions, most of which seemed perfectly acceptable to Gideon. He did not try to renegotiate the royalty rates, appearing perfectly happy with Blake's terms. In fact, a little oddly, Gideon was more concerned with Blake being happy with everything in the contract before he signed it.

Blake tapped the intercom and asked Jamie to witness the contract signing. Jamie arrived a few moments later. As he entered the room, Gideon stood up and held out his hand. Jamie grabbed it and shook it firmly.

'Terrific book really enjoyed it. Charlie and Anna feel so real. I was fascinated by how the intimate depth of emotional perception was so cleverly portrayed. Are they based on people you know?' Blake had not thought to ask that question.

'Yes, they are, or were…. They are both dead now,' replied Gideon quietly, drawing a small breath. His head dropped slightly, eyes to the floor as if he were saying a prayer. Maybe he was. He was obviously saddened by their passing. 'They were good friends,' he added, almost in a whisper.

That revelation left an odd gloomy feeling lingering in the air. For a moment or two, Jamie and Blake were unsure how to proceed without causing further distress or offence. Gideon had clearly drawn heavily from that loss when writing the book.

'That's incredibly sad,' replied Jamie, breaking cautiously into the stillness. 'They were such inspiring people. It makes me realise how lucky I am to be here today.'

The compassion in Jamie's voice was evident, and it seemed to reach out to Gideon. He smiled at Jamie. 'Thank you so much. Nobody else has ever said that, except for Blake.' He turned and smiled at Blake, who smiled back.

'No, thank you,' said Jamie, shaking Gideon's hand once more before leaving the office. 'You've written a wonderful book.' He closed the door behind him, and Gideon sat back down again.

'Do you have any more completed books,' asked Blake casually, not expecting a positive reply? He was saddened that there was unlikely to be a sequel as the two protagonists had died so tragically at the end.

'Oh yes,' he replied. 'I have two other books I am finishing. They both still need work, but I could complete them within two to three months.'

'That's good,' replied Blake, 'but there's no rush. It will take three months before we can get this into the shops. So, plenty of time.' He smiled at Gideon again and leaned back in his chair. He could relax a bit now his work was done. The contracts were signed.

'It could be a hectic year for you promoting the book, so it's good that you have some writing already completed.' Gideon smiled again but said nothing more.

Blake looked at Gideon. Only now, after nearly two hours of conversation, did he really begin to see the person sitting before him. Blake had ceased to focus on the writer of captivating prose and could now look at the man. Gideon had dark features, short dark hair, a little goatee beard and large blue-grey eyes set back under bushy eyebrows. He was tall, about six foot two, and there was a definite hint of the Mediterranean about him. Possibly Greek, maybe Italian, but not American as Jamie had first suggested. He obviously kept himself fit. Gideon was a good-looking man; there was no doubt about that. This would help immeasurably with television interviews. He wore a gold wedding ring, but Blake thought it best not to say anything as he had never mentioned a wife. If he had, then surely he would have spoken about her at some point, was Blakes's reasoning.

'You must come to my house and meet the family some time. We live in the country, so maybe you could make a weekend of it, possibly over Christmas.'

'That's exceedingly kind of you,' replied Gideon. 'I would love very much to meet your family.' Blake briefly felt a cold shiver run down his back, tingling the hairs. He looked around to see if the window was open, but it wasn't. He thought no more about it.

They both got up and shook hands.

'Oh, there is one small thing I need to ask,' said Gideon.

'Anything,' replied Blake, who was already thinking about going home and not paying complete attention.

'The book title…'

'Yes,' said Blake,

'Well, that was only a working title. I have come to think of it as a little ineffectual, so I have changed the title to something more appropriate and relevant - in keeping with the story. It relates to where Charlie and Anna used to meet.' Blake was confused for a moment. He had read the book twice but remembered nothing about a particular meeting place. Just a room in the convent where the two central characters had met only once, to make love.

'Oh,' said Blake curiously. He was perfectly happy with the title as it was but didn't want to upset things over what could only be a minor detail. 'I can't see that being a problem. What is the new name?'

Gideon did not answer immediately but slowly turned around as if he were pivoting on the spot. For a few moments, he gazed at the bookshelves and the oak panelling as if searching for inspiration. But he did not need any incentive or stimulation, for he already knew exactly what he was going to say. Turning back to face Blake again, with no discernible expression on his face, he whispered:

'I'm going to call it… The Chapter Room.'

Blake collapsed awkwardly into his chair. His legs had turned to jelly, and his body began to shake gently. The name, he knew that name… The Chapter Room – Prospect Road. For months, the self-writing manuscript had been filed away in Martin's safe and the dustier reaches of Blake's memory; now it was back.

Blake looked up at Gideon and noticed his face had begun to change. Gideon gazed back at Blake with a disdainful, almost contemptuous glare that pierced right through him as if searching for his soul. His eyes burned with a fire of retribution and an intensity that he could only compare with the flames of hell… For a split second, Blake feared for his life.

'Are you okay?' asked Gideon innocently, concerned at seeing Blake fall unexpectedly back into his chair. 'Is that a problem?'

'I, I…' Blake could not speak. He could only manage to mutter something almost inaudible.

Gideon rushed into the outer office, looking for Jamie, seated at a desk.

'Jamie, come quickly. Something has happened to Mr Thornton.' Jamie ran across the room and into Blake's office. Blake had by now recovered and was almost as he was before he collapsed.

'What happened?' asked Jamie, sounding genuinely concerned.

'Mr Thornton fell back in his chair,' replied Gideon. 'I thought it was a heart attack or something.'

'Oh, it's nothing,' interrupted Blake, waving Jamie away as he was fussing a bit. 'I just had a dizzy moment. Lack of food, I think. Working the brain too hard without nourishment. Must be getting old,' he laughed self-deprecatingly.

'Do you want me to get you something?' asked Jamie.

'No, no, it's okay,' replied Blake, still slightly confused. 'I'll pick something up in a minute. I was showing Gideon out anyway.'

'I am sorry, Gideon,' Blake apologised. He cautiously looked up at Gideon, half expecting to see the bizarre manifestation again, but Gideon appeared perfectly normal. He must have imagined the whole episode; that was the only explanation he could think of. This really was a bit odd. 'Must be my sugar levels are down or something,' he mumbled as he got up. The words 'The Chapter Room' kept turning over in his head, echoing in the distance, but he tried to block them out of his mind.

'Anyway, Gideon, I won't detain you any longer, but I will walk down with you. I need to pop next door for a sandwich.' He smiled at Gideon again, a sort of reassuring glance. He hoped the episode hadn't frightened Gideon too much.

Blake politely ushered Gideon out of the office door. They wandered down the stairs to the ground floor, chatting amiably about the weather as relative strangers do, despite neither of them being remotely concerned one way or the other. They stepped out of the lobby into the sunshine.

'This is what I miss,' pronounced Blake, 'being stuck in an office all day.' He lifted his arms up to the sky in praise. 'Sunshine - wonderful, isn't it.' It sounded oddly trite for some reason, but Gideon took no notice.

Blake took hold of Gideon's hand and shook it firmly.

'Are you sure you don't want to go for lunch? It's a company expense now.' He smiled briefly, but Gideon didn't understand the in-house quip. Maybe he shouldn't have bothered. Blake did not want Gideon to think they were about to push the corporate entertainment ship of plenty out into the harbour. Having just signed a brilliant new writer who would make them a lot of money. Maybe he had overthought that one a bit; it was just an offer of lunch. He was still a little on edge, making him appear nervous, even a little irrational.

'No, not for me, but thank you anyway,' replied Gideon calmly.

'It's been a real pleasure to meet you,' said Blake. 'We are going to have a wonderful relationship. I can feel it in my ....' They smiled at each other again. It was a bit stilted, but that would fade with time as they grew to know each other better.

'Yes, we are,' replied Gideon with a smile.

'I'll let you know about that weekend thing,' said Blake.

'Yes, I'll look forward to that,' replied Gideon. 'Thank you. Oh, and the name change. That is okay, isn't it? You didn't say, what with the funny turn...' He smiled at Blake again.

'No, no, that is fine. No problem.' replied Blake. 'And you're right – it is a better title.'

As Blake wandered off to the sandwich shop, Gideon turned and slowly walked away in the opposite direction. Blake suddenly remembered some words he had read recently, and they made him shiver.

Chapter 10

Blake picked up a chicken sandwich and ordered a large, decaffeinated Americano with no milk to be on the safe side. He paid the girl who had served him, picked up his tray and sat down in the corner, where he could see the rest of the room. So, what was happening, he wondered. Was something unusual going on, or was this just his over-active mind suffering from plot overload from the relentless intake of so many different stories. Could they all be morphing into one fantastically outrageous story... No, that was ridiculous. He promptly discarded that preposterous idea. He took a sip of his coffee – a bite of the sandwich, then sat back and carefully reviewed the moments leading up to the incident in his office. Maybe it was all one huge coincidence. He had encountered stranger things than this before, but he could not remember exactly when. Probably because they were irrelevant and had faded harmlessly into obscurity.

But he did have the script from Anthony Clackle in Martin's safe where he, or more accurately Catherine, had locked it away back in August. That had predicted a part of what had occurred today. As much as he tried to rationalise the details swirling around his head, it didn't seem to come out any other way. He could put it down to coincidence and chance, but the statistical probability was heavily stacked against that possibility. It could have been an elaborately staged illusion or a trick of the light. Misdirection of the most intricate variety.

Prospect Road had clearly and unambiguously recalled much of what had already happened in his life. That was beyond dispute and could be easily explained away. But now, the book was predicting what would happen in the future and controlling the events. Was that possible? This was what he had to contend with and what could not be so easily explained.

Was this a good or terrible thing, he wondered? Blake took another bite out of the chicken sandwich. Glancing around the room, he noticed all the women staff were dressed up as clichéd French waitresses. Black tights, striped clinging tops, berets, little red scarves, black high heels, and rouge lipstick. The men all had large fanciful false moustaches and wore black aprons with a white towel flung jauntily over the shoulder.

For some reason, they had made a special effort to create a pseudo-French atmosphere in the coffee shop. Possibly because it was late summer and still warm, or perhaps they were celebrating a belated Bastille day. But then, nothing seemed to make sense anymore. The glass-panelled doors at the front of the café had been slid back. There were a half dozen tables outside with little umbrellas, all busy with customers taking in the late afternoon sunshine. He had completely missed all of this when he first arrived. Still preoccupied as he was with the events of the past hour.

One of the waitresses was Susan – and they had become good friends over the years he had been frequenting the café. But today, he had not recognised her when he entered. Out of the corporate utilitarian uniform he was accustomed to, she had blossomed into something breathtakingly beautiful. He watched as she slowly made her way around the floor. Picking up trays and cups, provocatively bending over from time to time (for his benefit, he felt sure) to pick up odd items that had fallen on the floor. Eventually, she arrived at Blake's table.

'Et comment allez-vous aujourd hui, Monsieur,' she whispered, in a deliberately affected sultry French tone so cleverly immortalised in a Seventies television series.

'Beaucoup mieux pour vous voir, j'aime te regarder travailler. Vous semblez avoir du plaisir' replied Blake. She smiled, and he saw something in her eyes, something he had not seen before – but then maybe he hadn't been looking. He was beginning to see everything in a different light.

'Peut-être que nous devrions nous amuser un peu plus,' said Susan.

'Maintenant vous jouez avec mon coeur,' replied Blake, moving his head slightly to one side and pretending to be mildly embarrassed by her suggestion.

Susan smiled and picked up his tray, and Blake watched her as she sashayed slowly back to the counter, swaying her body slightly from side to side as she did. She knew he was watching. He finished his sandwich and the coffee and bid farewell to Susan.

'Au revoir, petit derrière,' Blake whispered as he left. She smiled seductively and blew him a kiss. Once outside, he suddenly realised how out of character it was for him to even look at another woman, let alone flirt with one. Why had he done so today when he had been visiting the café for years? The thought had never crossed his mind before. He was probably no more than a few words, a drink, and a furtive assignation away from committing adultery with Susan. What was happening to him, he wondered. Was the vague possibility of impending financial success suddenly distorting his moral compass?

He was aware some people, even the Pope, would willingly switch the focus of his morality dichotomy to suit a theological argument. Catholics were under papal instruction not to use contraception even in a fleeting moment of illicit passion, yet abortion was considered a sin. Bizarrely, the twisted morality partially condoned using condoms for health reasons. I.e. to prevent the spread of disease, thereby paradoxically creating a sanctimoniously pious escape route for sinners and lovers. Religious hypocrisy had always confused him; this was just one example that had sprung to mind.

He looked into the tall, thin mirror, which was part of the shop front of the café and stared at the reflection he saw. He could see flashes of the man he once was and what he used to be, but more disconcertingly, he also caught glimpses of the man he was becoming, and he did not like what he saw. With all these troubling thoughts running around in his head, he slowly made his way back up the stairs to his office to get things started on The Chapter Room. His earlier concern over the name change was now dismissed as of little significance….

That night he arrived home a little later than usual because of the lengthy discussions that had taken place in the office that afternoon relating to the sales campaign for Gideon Drew's book. He kissed Catherine and asked if the children were still awake.

'Claudia is asleep, but Max is waiting for you.'

'I'll go up and say goodnight before we eat if that's okay,' Catherine nodded.

Max and Claudia were still awake and began jumping up and down when Blake entered their bedroom; they were overjoyed to see him. He kissed and cuddled them both before reading a short story, then kissed them once more, having tucked them into their beds. He was back downstairs just after seven-thirty.

'Look, before we sit down for dinner, could you pop next door and ask Martin if we could have a quick look at the manuscript? I want to reread the last chapter again. It has been nearly a month, and I've forgotten precisely what it said. I'd go, but we did say that he wasn't to give me the book if I was on my own.'

He smiled self-deprecatingly at the absurdity of the peculiar arrangement they had made. It now seemed so juvenile and immature to conceive of a situation where he could not trust himself. Catherine looked at him oddly at first; she had temporarily forgotten the arrangement. In hindsight, it really didn't seem to make any sense. Reading the book last time had been disturbing, but more so for Blake than her. He seemed to have taken it quite badly at the time. Catherine had even become slightly concerned over his sanity at one point, although she had not mentioned this to him. The thought of revisiting all that emotional trauma was not something she relished. Blake seemed to be in a positive frame of mind now, so possibly he had come to terms with it and wanted to move forward.

'You definitely want me to fetch the manuscript?' asked Catherine.

'Yes, if you don't mind.' He seemed very insistent but not in a belligerent way. He smiled at her reassuringly.

'Why now?' asked Catherine sounding a little intrigued.

'I'll explain over dinner. It's nothing important – just something odd that happened today.'

Mollified by his reply. Catherine dutifully popped into Martin's and returned ten minutes later, clasping the manuscript to her breast as if it were something precious.

'Martin's going away on holiday on Friday for two weeks, so if we want to put it back into his safe, we will have to take it back tomorrow at the latest. Is that okay?'

Blake nodded. 'No problem, we only need to have a quick read. We'll have dinner and a big G and T, and then we can have a look to see if there have been any changes or additions. You can take it back to Martin first thing in the morning. Agreed?'

'Agreed,' replied Catherine. 'You make the drinks; I'll serve dinner.

'Excellent,' said Blake.

Over dinner, Blake spoke to Catherine about the day's events but not the office incident. It didn't seem relevant. It was, but he had convinced himself that his sugar levels were too low, which was the reason for his collapse.

'I met a new writer today. You might remember I spoke about his book a few weeks ago.'

'Was that the one you stayed up all night to read?' she asked idly, sipping her gin and tonic.

'Yes, it was, actually. Shows you how good it must have been to have kept me reading it all night.'

'So, you've met him?' she asked casually.

'Yes, I have. He came to the office today to sign a contract.'

'Oh, so it's serious then?'

'Very much so. As I said a few weeks ago, I think we have a major blockbuster on our hands. If we promote it properly, it will make us a lot of money,'

'So, what's the author's name?

'It's Gideon, Gideon Drew.

Catherine paused for a moment deliberating over the name. She thought she recognised it from somewhere.

'Unusual name.'

'Yes, I suppose it is, but it suits him and sounds good.'

'Yes,' muttered Catherine, 'I suppose it does.' For no reason, she ran the name over in her head several times.

'He's a genuinely nice guy, very unaffected by it all. He really doesn't know how good it is. It's quite refreshing to meet a writer who is much better than he thinks he is. It's normally the other way around. I have asked him to come down to stay sometime, for a weekend, possibly in November or maybe nearer Christmas, whenever it is convenient when things start to move a bit. Just so you can meet him and can get to know him better. I've signed him up for a seven-book deal, so it could be a few years that we're together, in a manner of speaking. I hope that's okay.'

'No problem,' replied Catherine. 'Just give me time to get the room ready. It's full of junk at the minute. I will have to move it all around. Will he be bringing his wife?'

'Do you know what? I never asked. Don't even know if he is married.'

Catherine looked at him, slightly stunned, 'you never asked?'

'No, no, I didn't; it never cropped up. I was too wrapped up in the book. It just completely slipped my mind.

'I'll sort the bedroom out next week.'

'No rush. He won't be coming till around Christmas time.'

'Oh, right. Okay. You do realise we are starting to run out of room here. The house seemed big when we first moved here, but now....'

'When this takes off, we can buy a much bigger house with lots of spare bedrooms,' said Blake smiling. He sounded confident, and that reassured her. Their finances had been a little strained recently.

'So, what was the book's name?' she asked. 'I don't remember.'

'Ah, that's the interesting bit. Gideon originally called it The Sisters of Mercy but thought that maybe that sounded a little pious, so he came up with a better title... It relates to the place where the two central characters have their encounter.'

'Where they have a bit of the old, how's your father, you mean?' replied Catherine with her prosaic head on and a passing nod to a working-class accent.

'Well, yes, but Drew puts it more romantically, thankfully.'

'Sex, love, violence and a bit of mystery, that's what sells. That's what you told me. Has it got all four?'

'Absolutely.'

'Then I'm ordering a new Merc estate next week,' replied Catherine, giggling.

'Ah, got me there.' Blake smiled, and they clinked glasses.

'So, what's it called?' asked Catherine again, still smiling, 'You still haven't told me.' Blake put his glass down. He did not want a repeat of anything like the incident earlier in the day.

'It's called...' He took a deep breath. 'The Chapter Room.'

'The Chapter Room?' repeated Catherine, a little surprised. 'That's a strange coincidence.' She paused for a moment. She recognised the book title as the one mentioned in Prospect Road.

Catherine instinctively knew why Blake had asked her to fetch the manuscript from Martin.

'That's the book and the author mentioned in Prospect Road, right?'

The light-hearted tone of their conversation suddenly changed, taking on an air of hesitancy.

'Maybe. I'm not certain. That's why I wanted to reread the manuscript,' replied Blake with some hesitation.

'I see,' said Catherine. 'I'm certain that's the title mentioned,' she repeated, no longer sounding quite so buoyant. Catherine thought for a few moments more before continuing. 'Now, I don't want you to read anything untoward into this, but...' She paused, realising she had made an excruciatingly bad, ill-timed pun purely by accident. Fortunately, Blake hadn't noticed. She knew what she was about to ask would tread heavily and clumsily on his sensibilities, but she had to know the answer. The question had to be asked...

'So, whose idea was it to change the name?'

'Gideon's,' replied Blake firmly, without even stopping for breath. He carried on eating as if it were a detail of no consequence.

'Oh,' he suddenly added, putting his knife and fork down on the table. 'I see - you thought maybe I had suggested it.'

He took another sip of wine and put his glass down. He gave Catherine a reassuring smile, which said so much more.

'No, Gideon came up with that. In fact, I was happy with the original title. I rather liked the Seminarian overtone. I think that's the right word.'

'Seminarian?' queried Catherine; she had never heard the word before.

He gazed upwards and slightly to the left, invoking the medial temporal lobe to check the word he had just used.

'Do you know what? I'm not sure that is the right word, but you know what I mean anyway. It's about the theology of Christianity. The novice nun about to be married to Christ when her religious and moral convictions are unexpectedly subjected to the ultimate challenge. God or man? So, for me, The Sisters of Mercy worked well. But he is the writer, so...'

'Oh,' replied Catherine. 'I am sorry for doubting you, but with all that went on the last time we spoke about this, I didn't want to see you in that state again.'

'I understand,' said Blake. 'But now we know for certain I couldn't have written anymore, so if there is something, it's nothing to do with me.' His mind flashed back to the incident in his office.

Catherine nodded in agreement even though she was still unsure of what was really happening.

They finished dinner, put the plates and cutlery into the dishwasher, cleaned the kitchen, and then settled down in the lounge with their G and T's to reread Chapter Four.

'You read it first,' said Blake. Catherine looked at him, a little surprised at his sudden loss of curiosity.

'No,' she replied. 'We can read it together. We only have to cuddle up close.'

Blake smiled. 'You're not going to take advantage of me, are you?' There was a naughty glint in his eye, something she hadn't seen for a while. This was more like the Blake she knew, self-assured, confident, even slightly arrogant at times. But then, weren't all men, she mused as an afterthought.

'I might do – later,' replied Catherine. Blake sniggered like a schoolboy.

His manner was light as if he had temporarily disengaged from the more pressing matter at hand. This was more like how he used to be, back before the dark, ominous cloud of Prospect Road had reared its head and cast a shadow over their lives. It seemed to be loitering, ever-present, somewhere in the background, reminding them of its existence from time to time, like a tiny, cancerous cough.

Their married life had always been enjoyable, exciting, and amusing; at times, it was also a struggle, but they had endured it together. It had been like that for nearly ten years, right up to the beginning of 1982, just before the Prospect Road manuscript had arrived. The stress that would be caused by The Chapter Room was anticipated; it came with every new publication. But once Blake's job was done and the book was released, he would return to his usual easy-going manner. But the situation with Prospect Road had never been resolved by publication. It just lingered in the air like a nasty odour, and slowly this toxic mist began seeping into their lives, into every tiny corner. It seemed to be waiting for something, waiting to do something, but she had no idea what.

Catherine longed for the good days to return, the happy days – days of carefree abandonment when their love for each other was all that mattered. The births of Max and Claudia only further enriched that euphoria. Catherine could not believe how happy she felt. It was as if she were a princess who had found her Prince Charming, and they would live together in blissful harmony for the rest of their lives. The dream of every couple, she thought, but how few achieve it, she wondered.

And then, one day, through no fault of their own, everything began to change. Catherine tried desperately to hang on to her dream, but for reasons she could not explain, it seemed to be slowly slipping through her fingers like the sands of time running out. Something was taking over her life; something to do with Prospect Road was taking control.

Before they began to read, Catherine said a small prayer under her breath. A plea to whichever gods determined the outcome of such moments. The same God who decides who wins a lottery and who dies tomorrow. Or when a stone that has sat on the top of a building for a hundred years plummets to earth, killing an innocent passerby. Someone whose life until that moment had been relatively uneventful, but now and for eternity, an honourable member of a very exclusive club. "The touched by a statistical improbability Club."

In quiet desperation, she was clinging to the tiniest possibility that nothing would have changed in the manuscript. That every word would be the same as when they last read it. They could then happily agree to arrange for it to be sent back to its author with the customary rejection note.

They skipped the first three chapters and began reading halfway through Chapter Four…

Prospect Road – Chapter 4

… this was what Thomas had been looking for, and he found it when he was passed a hand-written manuscript one day. A story of unrequited love between a gardener/handyman and a novice nun set in Aix-en-Provence in the 1960s. It was beautifully written and brought him to tears; such was the passion embedded within its pages. Love stories were always good sellers, but this one couldn't fail with the subtle twist at the end. Thomas had found his Holy Grail. He read it repeatedly to be sure of how he felt about it. He needed to convince himself that he had not just settled on it out of sheer frustration at not finding anything better. But it was the best book he had read in years. Each time he read it, he became more convinced of the success it could achieve. He passed it to the company's senior partners, who agreed with him after reading it. They would publish the book. The Chapter Room. A love story that would embrace the world and change Thomas and Kate's life forever.

After that last line, the manuscript was signed:
Blake & Catherine Thornton
13th August 1982

They reached this point the last time they read it in August. But now, after their signatures, more words had appeared that had not been there before. Catherine's heart sank. Her prayer had not been answered, or maybe it had been – but not how she had expected. Blake looked at Catherine as if to say, "Should we read on?" But of course, there was never really any option. They couldn't stop now, even if they wanted to.

Prospect Road: Chapter Five
written by
Anthony Theodore Clackle

Over the next few months, Thomas immersed himself in the marketing and sales promotions for the forthcoming publication and the editorial elements that needed some fine-tuning. The pressure at work meant he spent less time at home, and Kate began to sense the first signs that he was drifting away from her.

He would leave at six in the morning and not return until nine, maybe even ten in the evening. By then, he was absolutely shattered with little interest in eating his evening meal.

He seldom wanted to engage in an intimate conversation when he eventually arrived home. It tended to lean towards practical matters such as household repairs, bills, or something to do with the children. Under normal circumstances, Kate would not usually mention these routine matters to Thomas; she would deal with them herself. But in an attempt to open a meaningful dialogue, she would now discuss everything that happened during the day, expecting it to move the conversation onto a more personal level. But it never did, and she was now beginning to feel as if her attempts at re-establishing communications with Thomas were doing more harm than good.

It was all to no avail. Kate and Thomas's relationship had lost direction and momentum and was almost entirely devoid of emotional dimension. It was as if they were acting out the final scenes from a domestic television tragedy where the inevitable end was clearly in sight.

They might exchange brief words during the evening, and then they would go to bed. Kate would lie awake gazing out of the window, looking up at the moon. Wondering how their once blissful existence had so suddenly, without warning, slipped away and left her in this desolate, lonely place. Only their children, a few friends, and neighbours helped ward off the feelings of absolute hopelessness and futility now slowly overwhelming her. With all their best intentions, friends and neighbours were still a poor substitute for the sense of joy and fulfilment she once derived from her close relationship with Thomas. The thought of his laughter, their conversations during the evenings and weekends, and their interaction with their children - all those things that would once have been sufficient to sustain her during the lonely days and nights when he wasn't there - were nothing more than a distant memory now.

She could remember a time when they would be lying in bed together, and he could be a million miles away, thinking about something or another. She would reach out and touch him gently and whisper, 'Come back to me,' and he would be there in an instant, back with her, and then he would ask:

'How did you know I was gone?'

And she would smile and say, 'I just knew.'

Now she would lie beside him in the dark just before they fell asleep and wonder what he was thinking. She knew he was somewhere else again, a million miles away, but she daren't reach out and take that chance anymore; the fear of rejection was too much to bear. There were no words that could heal his pain.

She still craved the warmth and tenderness of his love and affection and held onto the faith that he would return to her one day. She still believed in miracles, and even if there were no words spoken, deep down, she knew there had to be a tiny thread of hope, something for her to grab hold of and pull him back. But she didn't know how to find it any longer, so she patiently waited day after day.

She could recall things he had said the night before or even the weekend before, things they should do, plans they were making for the future, or arrangements to go out with friends. All this would keep her mind occupied and comfort her soul. The joke he would have made a few days ago would come to mind and make her smile again, possibly many times. Now there were no humorous asides to recall, and her days were spent without amusing reflections or memories. She would glance at Thomas, but he would have fallen asleep almost immediately. Kate was now utterly alone with her thoughts....

'Hi, sorry I'm late, darling. It's just so busy right now getting this book ready for publication. We have had so much interest from other countries from the proof copies we sent out that we never seem to get on top of it. I will be glad when it is published. At least we won't be under so much pressure in the office. It will be the printers with the problems then.'

But the conversation was lame, pedestrian, soulless and laboured. Just words - hollow words with no heart or meaning, just noise to fill an empty space where once there had been happiness and contentment. This was the avenue down which their relationship journeyed night after night, with futile gestures and meaningless acknowledgements. As the months slowly passed, it began to deteriorate even further into the trough of despair, the solace of fools, if that were even possible.

When they spoke now, it conveyed nothing of Thomas's real feelings for Kate… nothing about how they used to be, nothing about anything really…. It was just a monochromatic snapshot of their existence at one moment in time, without the benefit of any clear-cut definition between black and white. All shading and tonal variation – a mishmash of inconsequential greys fading to darkness.

For some reason, he could no longer convey how he once felt. It was as if the invisible conduit of communication that had always flowed between them had been irretrievably severed…

There were forces in play that neither of them could clearly understand. There seemed to be nothing left of what had once existed between them when they were once so much in love. This was the course and the nature of their existence night after night. After four months, it had already inflicted irreparable damage on their relationship.

Kate was once a serene and understanding wife, fully aware of the pressures her husband was constantly under. But she was losing traction, unable to hang on to what little was left, and it was beginning to show. She desperately needed some small sign of his love or, at the very least, an acknowledgement of her existence as a person and not just the keeper of the house. But even this, she was denied. So many nights, she sat alone, waiting for Thomas to return, and when he did, there was nothing. They continued in this manner for many months, their life on hold, in a state of suspended animation. The flame of their love was fading fast, like the final moments of a candle before it splutters and dies.

At times she began to imagine she could step back a few feet and see what was happening to her and Thomas as if she were another person looking in on them. She had become an Edward Hopper voyeur, peering into her life through a distant window.

This peculiar disorder continued for another three months, and she began to consider the possibility that she was losing control of her mind. Such was her detachment from the life she had been accustomed to. Kate started to drink secretly and even considered suicide at one point. But thoughts of the children and the devastation it would cause to their lives pulled her back from the edge. She tried to push the dark thoughts from her mind. But how long, she wondered, before they returned, seeking retribution for being denied that which they desired....

It was as if her thoughts were dark assassins of the night, seeking vengeance for unspecified sins, but they weren't. It was just her mind playing callous games....

Catherine and Blake stopped reading at the same moment and turned to face each other. Maybe it was another coincidence, but why now, at this juncture, when Blake and Catherine – Kate, as he occasionally called her in moments of anger – were also navigating their lives through a labyrinth of turmoil, chaos, and confusion?

Would they, too, fall into the well of emptiness and despair, this atrophied existence, just as Thomas and Kate had done? This troubled Catherine deeply, but she said nothing.

Blake looked at Catherine. 'This will not happen to us,' he swiftly reassured her, instinctively knowing what she was thinking. This was what being together, soulmates, kindred spirits meant, this indescribable, unfathomable sixth sense of communication, the untouchable, unseen, intangible force that deep relationships thrive and depend upon.

Blake responded firmly, 'We won't let it happen!' His eyes opened wider; she could see the tiny crinkles on his forehead. His eyelashes moved upwards, coming to attention as if responding to a command - his cute little ears twitched. He was firm and assertive, instantaneously responsive, for he had a good idea of what was going through Catherine's mind. He chose to confront the issue head-on, not sidetrack it or try to deflect it down some dark alleyway where it would fester and grow into something far worse.

This was Blake, her husband, speaking. Blake, the man she loved, the man she had always loved.

'What?' said Catherine. Her heart leapt at his magnanimous announcement. She was a little surprised at his directness and candour. He was saying there might be a slight problem, but he would not let it take over their lives. We are stronger than that, much stronger. Catherine was so relieved. Blake had said the words she so desperately wanted to hear. He had reached out and touched her and answered the questions Catherine wanted to ask but did not dare speak for fear of what the answers might be. Now, she didn't need to.

He was making a statement, a reassuring affirmation of their relationship. Something that was worlds away from the debilitating, soul-destroying nature of Kate's thoughts in the chapter of Prospect Road they had just read together.

'What this is saying...' He threw the manuscript on the floor, and it fell apart, 'we won't let it happen.' But conversely, in that same statement, he had acknowledged that Prospect Road was taking control of their lives.

'We will take the shrivelled little gonads of this nasty little monster and fry them in boiling goose fat.'

It was a ridiculous declaration to make, one that didn't make any sense. But it made Catherine laugh aloud and comforted her soul.

'None for me, thank you,' said Catherine politely, with an expression of jovial revulsion. 'Not overly keen on deep-fried testicles.' They both laughed out aloud again, together.

This was the Rabelaisian ingenuity she was more accustomed to. And which she much preferred to any wimpish concession to the apparent mystical premonitory power of a few thousand words in the manuscript now scattered on the floor.

'This is all bollocks,' said Blake. 'Pun intended.'

'I agree,' said Catherine. 'But let's not give up now. Let's read it to the end, and then we can decide what to do with it.'

'Right,' said Blake firmly. He knelt down, gathered the manuscript's scattered pages, and put them back in order.

'We need a drink,' said Blake.

Catherine went to get up, but Blake touched her arm. 'Not tea. I think maybe we deserve something a little stronger?'

Catherine nodded, and Blake went over to where they kept the spirits and poured another G and T for Catherine and a large bourbon for himself.

They clinked glasses, smiled, and both took a large swig before putting their drinks down and starting to read the next chapter.

Prospect Road: Chapter Six
written by
Anthony Theodore Clackle

And then, one day, quite unexpectedly, Thomas came home early, just after five o'clock. Kate went to the front door and opened it. It was a routine now, an automatic response to hearing his car pull up on the gravel drive. However much their relationship had deteriorated over the past nine months, she refused to change her custom of welcoming him home with a smile. Today, their two children, Michael and Carol, rushed to the front door to greet him as well, as they had not yet gone to bed.

'Hello, Daddy...' they chorused as soon as he entered the hallway. 'We love you very much and miss you when you are away working.'

This unexpected display of affection had not been preplanned or rehearsed, and Kate was as taken aback as Thomas. She glanced at Thomas with a mixed expression of wonder, concern, and astonishment, fully believing that he might have been maddened by this sudden outpouring of emotion. But he was not. Without hesitation, he acknowledged that his wife had not overtly orchestrated it. Thomas was overwhelmed, disorientated, and humbled by this ingenuous greeting. Try as he might, he could not hold back the tiny tears of joy that welled up in his eyes. At that moment, he realised he had completely lost contact with his life, wife and children, the only things that mattered. Could he maybe recapture those halcyon days, he wondered...

'Please, can we play together, Daddy?' chorused Michael and Carol plaintively.

Thomas dropped his briefcase by the door and gazed at Kate with a hollowed expression of lachrymose contrition. Consumed by shame, he realised the damage he had inflicted on their relationship. He knelt in the doorway and threw open his arms to embrace his children, holding them tightly, desperately hugging them to his body as he stood up. The tears were now rolling down his face. He looked at Kate and saw the woman he loved, the only woman he had ever loved, and she was lost and confused, and he knew this was his doing. Something had taken hold of his life and had nearly consumed his soul. It had threatened to drag him down into a sea of oblivion, and he had not seen it - he could not see it, for he was blinded by misdirection. He gazed at Kate, his eyes begging for forgiveness and redemption for the pain he had exacted upon her. She answered without reservation and without a single moment of hesitation.

In an instant, he was absolved, and he beckoned her over to join them. She cautiously stepped forward into his outstretched arms. The children were still clinging to his neck, and he kissed her passionately in a way he had not kissed her for many months... They all embraced, the children not really understanding what had happened, although they now felt much happier than before. The embrace never seemed to end, the tears rolled down Kate and Thomas's faces, and they kissed repeatedly. The carapace of dark confusion had been breached. The suffering was over; they were happy once again... for now.

Thomas's company published The Chapter Room two weeks later, and a few weeks later, it rose to the top position for weekly sales. It stayed there for nine months, selling over five million copies before it was released worldwide. It went on to sell another twenty-two million copies in the first year. The biggest-selling book the company had ever published and the most prolific book from any publisher for the last five years. Thomas was asked to become an equal partner in the company; his life would never be the same again.

Just six months later, Thomas and his family moved to a much larger house on the outskirts of Oxford. Some significant changes were being made in the office, and more people joined the company in anticipation of a continuing flow of successful new authors. Kate and Thomas were much happier than they had been for a long time and settled down to enjoy their new house and increased income. All was well for nearly a year until one day, while he was at the office, a call came through to the switchboard from Kate. It was redirected to his extension. She seldom rang him during the day, so Thomas knew it must be important. He picked up the phone with trepidation and listened intently as Kate explained what had happened. He slowly replaced the receiver in its cradle, picked up his case and walked out of the office without saying a word. One of his colleagues tried to speak to him to ascertain whether there was a problem or if there was anything they could do to help, but he did not hear them. He paused for a moment at the office door and turned to look back into the room, started to say something, but stopped and then, with a despairing expression of incomprehension and disbelief, he left.

Chapter 11

And there, once again, the story came to an abrupt end. Blake looked at Catherine, a little confused. Although the manuscript had clearly documented what was possibly going to happen, there was nothing particularly revelational in it apart from the mention of Gideon Drew and The Chapter Room. That could still have been a coincidence, however unlikely that was. The story was still little more than generalisation and supposition. However, they were confronted again with the *puzzle* of how the book *appeared to* be writing itself. This obviously concerned them both and had yet to be explained. There had to be a rational answer, but what could it be?

'What should we do?' asked Catherine after a few moments.

'What can we do?' replied Blake. 'What do we actually have? Nothing but words. We will have to wait and see how accurate it is. The only problem is, we don't know how long.'

'It has to be the same book,' said Catherine. 'It's the same name and the same author. That is too much of a coincidence, and surely the book will be coming out very soon anyway.'

'Hopefully,' replied Blake. 'We have some last-minute issues to sort out first, which could mean a few late nights for me at the office, but...'

'Oh,' said Catherine. A tiny cold shiver ran down her back.

'Like Thomas?' she asked gingerly.

'Well, yes, I suppose you could say that. But it won't be four or five months. It'll be a few nights at most.'

'Good!' said Catherine. 'We don't need to play into its hands...' She stopped suddenly. 'Oh, my God!' Catherine whispered under her breath. She seemed to be glaring into space.

'What?' exclaimed Blake, looking anxiously around, expecting to see something, but there was nothing.

'I just acknowledged the existence of...'

'What?' interrupted Blake.

'Someone or something... It no longer feels inanimate. It...'

'There is nothing,' said Blake reassuringly. 'You're just getting spooked by a few clever words, that's all.' Catherine smiled. Blake was right; the manuscript had put her into a nervous frame of mind for no rational reason. Her concerns were based almost entirely on nothing more tangible than some cleverly contrived passages in the book.

'That's what good writers do,' said Blake after a few moments. 'They make you challenge your beliefs, everything you hold sacred. They... make you re-evaluate what is important in life. Every story has to be a morality play, a metaphor for life. It must have a reason to exist to show us something we may have lost or forgotten along the way. Humanity, compassion, and kindness – the characteristics that make us human. It could be anything. It becomes a collection of meaningless words if it does not. Maybe that is what Prospect Road is all about. I don't know.' He smiled at Catherine and kissed her on the forehead.

'We can take it back to Martin's for safekeeping,' suggested Blake.

'Good idea,' said Catherine. She put the manuscript back into its envelope.

'Wait,' said Blake. 'Can you take it back out?' Catherine wondered what Blake was going to do. Nevertheless, she did as he asked. Blake produced his fountain pen.

'We still need to sign it... for what it's worth.' Catherine nodded and took the pen.

Having both signed and dated it on the last page with text on it, they replaced the manuscript in its envelope.

'Come on, you two,' shouted Blake to Max and Claudia, who were playing in the garden. 'We're just popping over to Uncle Martin's for a few minutes.

When they arrived at Martin's house, Max and Claudia went to play in his garden. Once they were out of earshot, Catherine and Blake confirmed the ongoing condition. The manuscript should only be released to Catherine. It should not be handed over to Blake under any circumstances if he was alone. Blake nodded his agreement.

Martin gazed at the two of them, slightly confused but said nothing. He wondered what might happen if Blake asked for it, and he had to refuse, but he put the thought to the back of his mind for the moment.

He continued to be quietly bemused and a little perplexed by the mysterious nature of the request but did not query the instruction. He was, after all, an ex-naval officer and had been conditioned to take orders and instructions without question during the war, many of which he never fully understood. His not to reason why, blah-di-blah, he mumbled quietly to himself as he placed the manuscript back into the safe and spun the dial.

Catherine and Blake had unresolved concerns about how the book was continuing to write itself. Hence, the rules of release were still relevant.

'Drink, you two nutters?' asked Martin, quizzically pursing his lips.

'Yes, why not,' said Catherine, relieved that Prospect Road was securely tucked away.

Knowing their regular tipples, Martin poured a gin and tonic for Catherine and a bourbon for Blake. He handed them the glasses before pouring himself a whiskey and soda.

'Cheers,' said Martin.

'Happy days,' replied Blake. Catherine smiled.

'I must apologise for our strange behaviour,' said Blake. 'I think maybe you deserve some sort of explanation.'

'Don't' worry about me, old boy,' replied Martin, 'I have never been the overly curious type. It's the Navy, you know. Teaches you not to ask too many questions. I remember what happened to the moggy.'

Catherine and Blake were a little confused for a moment.

'Moggy?' enquired Blake, sounding intrigued but moderated with caution.

'Tiddles,' replied Martin quietly, adopting an unusually sombre expression. He glanced at the ground philosophically as if remembering happier days.

'I didn't know you had a cat,' remarked Blake, slightly puzzled.

'I don't... not anymore. It was all a little unfortunate.'

'Oh,' said Blake empathetically. 'So, what happened?'

'It drowned.'

'Oh, I am sorry,' said Blake. 'Drowned?' he muttered quietly.

'Fell down the bloody well, didn't she.' Martin held his mournful expression for a little longer. His sorrowful eyes extracting every drop of emotion he could squeeze out of the moment while continuing to sip his whiskey.

Catherine and Blake did not know what to make of it. Not sure whether they should make some token gesture of sympathy for a beloved feline pet that had come to a watery end. A cat they never knew existed and had apparently been remarkably close to Martin's heart. Suddenly the penny dropped.

'You haven't got a bloody well,' said Blake.

'You never had a cat either,' said Catherine, laughing. 'You're just play-acting again.'

Max popped his head around the door. 'That's a quid you owe me, Dad.'

Martin just smiled and carried on drinking his whiskey. Blake rustled about in his pocket for a pound and dropped it in Max's box.

Martin gently hummed Ding Dong Dell….

The next day Blake went to work as usual. The advertising and marketing schedule for the official launch of The Chapter Room had now been set. Various television and radio chat programs had been booked to interview Gideon and discuss the book alongside a countrywide billboard and bus campaign. Blake was confident that with Gideon's rugged good looks and enigmatic personality, his media appearances could only further encourage book lovers to purchase the opus. The vagaries of success or failure in publishing often turned on such nebulous and pedestrian elements.

This was it. Everything the company had and considerably more was being staked on the biggest gamble of Blake's life. The turn of one card would dictate how the rest of his life would play out.

If the book did not make the sales he had predicted, the company would be in debt for years. Probably forever, and Catherine would never get her new Mercedes. Failure was now inconceivable. If this crashed, Catherine might even leave him, unable to face the ignominy of near poverty. Maybe that was a slightly over-egged assessment of the situation, but such were the niggling doubts running through his mind. He suddenly realised what a risk he was taking, not only with his personal life but also with his business career. One thing was certain: if it became a monumental disaster, he would never work in publishing again. The company would collapse, nobody would employ him, and he would become the iconic Jonah figure, the one to avoid at all costs. The one who sank the ship by dropping the golden anchor straight through the bottom of the hull.

Could he have lost his usually astute business acumen? He wondered if maybe he had lost track of all reason and objectivity for some ludicrously egotistical motive. Had he just blundered ahead, committing the company to a massive marketing budget beyond what they would typically spend on what was, after all, a debut novel by an unknown writer? But he couldn't mention these fears to anybody now; it was far too late for that. And anyway, everybody he had spoken to agreed with his decision. Indecision and prevarication at this stage of the game would be the kiss of death. It was 'Stand by your guns and prepare for action,' as Nelson had said at Trafalgar – or was that Davy Crockett at the Alamo? He wasn't sure.

Despite his reservations, he displayed no outward concerns about The Chapter Room receiving anything less than rapturous praise and adulation from the critics. He refused to even consider the possibility of a mediocre reception. Blake's unwavering belief in the absolute brilliance of the book was sometimes a little intimidating. It was as if contemplating anything other than a magnanimous literary triumph was a sin worse than blasphemy.

He had lifted the mindset of everyone in the office to a level where they now honestly believed this was one of the greatest novels written in the past ten years. They were the privileged few who were bringing it to the world's attention. A masterful piece of subliminal psychological promotion… Now all he had to do was convince everybody else in the world.

As the day drew closer, the atmosphere in the office became electric with anticipation. You could feel magic in the air. Rumours began percolating to the media that a rumbling giant was about to be unleashed on an unsuspecting public. A story that would move people to tears for years (as the advertising went). And then, on one Tuesday morning in early November, it started.

Chapter 12
Catherine and Gideon

The book was released late on Monday. Reviewers had stayed up all night to read it. They appeared on the breakfast television shows at 7.30am on Tuesday morning to give judgement. Their plaudits and praise were beyond Blake's wildest expectations. It was as if a new Bible had been written and released that day; such was the tsunami of emotion with which it was greeted. Blake had predicted possible sales of a half-million books in the first year. By 9.10am – ten minutes after most bookshops opened – 20,000 copies had been sold, and advance orders were taken for nearly 400,000. Blake's office was taken entirely unawares. The floodgates had opened, and shoals of frenzied customers had begun to feed.

A guardian angel had been watching over Blake that day, ensuring everything was perfect. It would return one day for settlement, but not just yet.

Sales crashed through the one million mark in the first month, bolstered by further glowing reviews from critics who usually gave established writers a tough time for decent books. But without exception, they all applauded this book's creation as one of the seminal moments in 20th-century literature. Gideon Drew is the new messiah of heart-rending prose equal to Dickens -Twain – Hemingway, or Lawrence. A popular, somewhat clichéd sobriquet.

In the beginning, the printers were unable to maintain supplies, such was the demand. Fights broke out in many bookstores when copies became available. Sales continued to rise as they approached Christmas, the year's busiest period. The bandwagon was galloping ahead at full speed, and Blake had to run extremely fast, metaphorically, to keep up with it.

In the weeks before publication, Catherine had suffered a few sleepless nights with Blake arriving home exceptionally late, sometimes not till the early hours. But any concerns she may have had quickly faded when the book was published. It was all Blake and his staff could do to fend off the torrent of approaches from established writers. Each amazed by the company's support for

Gideon Drew and its audacious marketing strategy. It was an enormous gamble, but it had paid off.

Catherine had a surprise for Christmas that year: a brand-new top-of-the-range Mercedes estate car appeared on the drive on Christmas morning with a giant pink bow wrapped around it. They had a fabulous Christmas, especially as the receipts from sales were already starting to trickle into the company's bank account. The bank manager even rang Blake on Christmas day to update him on the company's bank balance. He was old school and liked to keep his clients personally advised of any significant changes in their accounts. On this occasion, it was to inform him that the cleared balance had passed the million-pound mark in only seven weeks since the release date of The Chapter Room.

Gideon Drew had arranged to stay for a few days from Boxing Day. Catherine and Blake were looking forward to spending some time with the creator of the phenomenon that promised to change their lives beyond recognition. Blake secretly hoped Gideon would turn up with the manuscript for his next book, but he couldn't be too pushy. The company could only just cope with what was happening now with The Chapter Room. Publication of another book would have to be delayed by at least a year. If not even longer, to maximise the company's outlay on the current sales campaign. So there was no real urgency.

Gideon arrived at midday as arranged. Blake had half expected him to bring his wife or girlfriend. Possibly even his partner – these were enlightened times. Blake was prepared for all eventualities – but Gideon arrived alone. He wore a long black leather coat that brushed the floor. Black leather boots with shiny brass buckles, a pale green silk scarf wrapped around his neck and a large fedora hat with a tiny fawn-coloured feather sticking rakishly out of the rim on the right-hand side. Gideon now carried himself with the air of an ungodly character from an obscure eighteenth-century Transylvanian horror story, hell-bent on vengeance for an unspoken act of evil debauchery against an innocent virgin. Blake was drawing that from something he had read recently, something he still did when the opportunity arose, but not that often at the moment. These were the times when new manuscripts arriving at the office were instantly rejected without even being read, with the customary apologetic rejection letter.

Blake could not help but stare awkwardly at Gideon for a moment; he was stunned, bedazzled, and pleasantly surprised by the sartorial manifestation before him. His expression of astonishment and puzzlement coalesced into one of admiration at the transformation. He found himself at once starting to apologise. 'I am so sorry, but…'

'Please don't,' interrupted Gideon. 'I realise it's a little over the top, but you mentioned having minor reservations about my unexciting and introverted appearance at book signings. So, I thought I had better try to liven things up and go for something slightly different… the outrageous rock-and-roll superstar look.' He smiled at Blake, looking for approval. 'Is it okay?'

'It's wonderful, absolutely perfect. You'll sell thousands with that even if you don't utter a word…'

Blake felt relieved at what was potentially an uncomfortable moment. He ushered Gideon into the house, took hold of his suitcase and placed it in the hallway. Gideon took off his coat and hat and gave them to Blake, who dropped them on the hall table.

He was a remarkably handsome man, but he was different now; his whole appearance had changed dramatically, so much so that Blake hardly recognised him. His tousled, shoulder-length, dark hair (it had been much shorter when he had last met him) and tanned skin now gave him the vague appearance of a swashbuckling pirate. This would undoubtedly endear him to most women and probably some men at interviews. His eyes were a piercing blue, which was odd because Blake thought they were much greyer the last time he saw him, but he must have got that wrong, or maybe it was the light.

Blake's mind seldom drifted far from the mechanics of the business. Inwardly Gideon slightly bemused him, but he was nevertheless gladdened by the reformation. He had been harbouring some minor reservations about the marketing drawbacks of Gideon's shy and retiring nature. He knew that gregarious writers like Barrington Kane and Dezzi Chandler had mastered the art of public appearances. For this reason, they sold far more copies at signings and on promotional tours than shy writers ever did. This was an unfortunate fact but had to be borne in mind. Sales were already extremely high, but natural declension could set in unless a high public profile could be maintained. But any concerns he may have had were quickly dispelled. He knew beyond doubt that Gideon would electrify an audience with his reimagined characterisation of a romantic tragedian. Any minor concerns Blake may have had about Gideon's visual saleability were now firmly consigned to the waste bin.

Gideon's carriage and persona had also changed beyond recognition. He had acquired the aura of someone daring, flamboyant and risqué with measured charm. In only a few short months, he had miraculously developed a mantle of cultural eloquence. Under different circumstances, this would have taken a lifetime to achieve. It suited him perfectly and befitted his newly elevated position in the literary world, however transient and capricious that might be. Everybody he met would be swept up and carried away by his natural authority and charisma. It was perfect.

As they made their way to the lounge, Blake noticed an aroma similar to bay rum and lilies about Gideon. A strange, old-fashioned malodorous yet captivating pungency which seemed to radiate the delicate pall of age and death. It was as if it were protecting him from unforeseen adversaries,

This was a man who functioned best alone. He didn't need anybody else; such was the aura of self-possession he carried so adroitly. He was a man entirely in control of his destiny and mortality.

As always, Gideon was polite, quiet, and unassumingly enigmatic. On meeting Catherine, he gently took her hand and kissed it softly, his lips never quite touching her skin. Bowing his head almost imperceptibly, he never lost eye contact with her. His piercing cornflower-blue eyes seemed to be searching for something deep inside, and possibly, he may have found it.

It was an elegant propriety, something Catherine seldom encountered except in the Brontë sisters' novels. Gideon's smile was disarming, quickly putting her at ease. Yet she found it strangely engaging, as if they shared a dark, intimate secret. Burning a pathway straight into her soul, his eyes conveyed a reassuring message. *Even under the threat of death, I will not reveal our secret to a living soul.* But, of course, there was no secret, but that didn't matter, for she had already begun to falter and yield to the polarising magnetism of his charm.

Although the manner of Gideon's greeting surprised Blake a little, he took it to be no more than an academic eccentricity. He had assumed (incorrectly) that Gideon had attended one of the redbrick universities where he had probably witnessed similar foppish mannerisms first-hand. He neither approved nor disapproved but simply found the gesture entertaining and amusing. He did not, however, notice Gideon's effect on Catherine.

She felt confused, unsteady, and suddenly embarrassed by the unexpected attention she was receiving from Gideon – feelings to which she was not accustomed. Blake generally tended towards the more prosaic elements of love and amity. He was caring, considerate and attentive. When they made love, she felt a warmth and satisfaction that only came from years of knowing all the intimate secrets of someone else's body and them knowing all of yours.

She no longer swirled with Terpsichorean ecstasy whenever they fucked. Neither was she lost in that euphoric chemical high of the neuropeptide hormonal opiate induced by the release of endorphins - neither of them did anymore, but that didn't really matter…

That was the opening gambit of the courting ritual and soon passed. The first months of any relationship were always a whirlwind of confusion when the body's neanderthal cravings obsessively drove the mind. But despite the cooling of that uncontrollable physical lust, Catherine still loved Blake passionately. Sex was now primarily amusing, entertaining, gratifying and occasionally procreational. The corrosive elements had not yet taken hold.

Nothing as transient as a few days in the company of Gideon Drew would deflect her from this persuasion, and she strenuously endeavoured to retain her composure, giving nothing away. But then she found herself slowly weakening as she became enthralled by the idea of becoming embroiled in a passionate love affair. Such was the light-headedness he had managed to induce. It was a schoolgirl flight of fancy, an evanescent adolescent crush, nothing more. But why now? Why today, after nearly ten years of a happy marriage, was she suddenly being sapped of the strength she so desperately needed to resist. To defend herself from this intruder who had so easily charmed his way into her affection? She breathed deeply and opened her eyes wider, struggling to eradicate the fantasies in her mind.

On holiday in Samoa a few years ago, Catherine learned the word Tusitala. It meant a spinner of tales, a weaver of dreams and spells, and was used to describe the best storytellers. That, undoubtedly, was what Gideon was – and he had cast his spell on her. She began to wonder whether her close proximity to Gideon Drew was having some profound metaphysical effect on her.

Every time she read the Chapter Room, and she had read it many times, she saw various aspects of the narrative that seemed to relate directly to her and nobody else. This was part of the book's enigmatic riddle: its inherent ability to connect directly with every woman and man who read it, but to each, in a slightly unique way. Readers would slowly dissolve into the immersive narrative.

Maybe she had been unknowingly intoxicated by the pure romanticism embedded within every page, and she was confusing idealistic prose with the reality of life. This, after all, was the intention of every author. To engage the reader so intensely, they would be carried away from the mundane certainties of their ordinary lives just for a few hours.

This sort of thing had not happened before, but then she had not read a book like that for some time, if ever, and she had never met anybody like Gideon Drew. He was having an inveigling effect on her for reasons she did not understand.

Having recovered from her moment of disorientation, she introduced Gideon to Max and Claudia. They both smiled a little warily at first. They, too, were also clearly mesmerized by his presence. Never had they met someone with such an overt mystical charm. To them, he was more than just a storyteller. Blake had previously told them that a friend who wrote stories was coming to stay for a few days. He had embellished his portrayal of Gideon to engender a sense of mystery and intrigue. This, however, had proved unnecessary and clearly unwarranted - as he was now beginning to realise.

Max and Claudia had previously discussed the imminent arrival of the visitor. They had surmised from Blake's description that he was from another age, somebody who would regale them with mysterious tales of dragons, demons, monsters... and white knights.

After they had all been introduced, Catherine took Gideon upstairs to show him his bedroom, closely followed by two seriously entranced children.

 Blake remained in the lounge, gathering his thoughts, when something odd occurred to him. Gideon had attributed his extraordinary change of image to Blake's comment of - '*minor reservations about his unexciting and introverted appearance at interviews.*' But Blake, as he now recalled, had said nothing of the kind in front of Gideon. He would never have been so tactless. However, Blake had discussed the issue with Jamie and some marketing department staff. They had considered diverse options to rehash Gideon's image, but nothing had been settled. He wondered how Gideon had become aware of a conversation he was unaware of. As far as Blake could recall, Gideon wasn't even in London at the time of the discussion.

The whole family grew to know Gideon closely over the next three days. They each found him to be an extremely friendly, gregarious, and generous man. Someone happy to spend many hours entertaining them with a constant flow of hauntingly evocative tales. The spellbinding way he told them tended to enthral Catherine and the children more than Blake. It was as if the cynicism of age, the day-to-day pragmatism of life and the harsh realities of business had sucked some of the joy from Blake's life.

The worldly-wise perspective he had developed over the last few years had somehow cauterised his ability to enjoy whimsical diversions.

Gideon could create fascinating and intricate tales from miniscule incidents and the tiniest fragments of life, which he elaborately expanded into sweepingly cloudless legends. These would engross Catherine, Max, and Claudia for hours. This made the stories almost believable. Sometimes it was hard to distinguish precisely where fact ended, and fiction began.

He could entice you into his world of purposeless splendour and make you believe you never wanted to leave. He made you realise that what really mattered was not how many times you took a breath in a lifetime but how many times your breath was taken away. Gideon was a true Tusitala, and Max and Claudia were reluctant to leave the quixotic utopia he so quickly conjured up. He spoke little of his next book, only to say, somewhat strangely, that it would be even more captivating than The Chapter Room. All he would reveal was that it was another love story, but this time set in England, in and around Oxford.

It was intriguing to hear him talk objectively about himself and something he had created in the third person. It was as if half of him authored the books, and the other half critically reviewed them. A unique and enviable characteristic if it could be accomplished. One which he had succeeded in with admirable impartiality in his first novel. But then, in Blake's experience, this is what most successful writers had to do.

On the first night, as Catherine had requested, Gideon came down for dinner at precisely seven-thirty. He had previously mentioned a preference for writing between three in the afternoon till seven o'clock in the evening. This was the time when he was most creative and productive. For this reason, he did not wish to deviate from his regular work pattern. So, the timing for dinner was perfect, as far as he and Catherine were concerned.

'Take a seat, Gideon,' suggested Catherine, 'I am just about to serve dinner - the others will be here in a moment.' Gideon did not sit down straight away, preferring to watch Catherine while waiting until everybody else had arrived.

Blake, Max, and Claudia came through from the lounge.

'Evening, Gideon,' said Blake.

'Good evening, Blake,' replied Gideon, with the hint of a restrained smile. It conveyed something more than a casual pleasantry, but Blake did not notice. 'And good evening to you two,' continued Gideon, addressing Max and Claudia, who quickly seated themselves at the table. They both smiled at him coyly.

'It's a lovely room, beautiful view of the woods. In fact, it's a very charming house. You are truly fortunate, Blake.'

Blake was going to say, "Well, we hope to move somewhere bigger quite soon," but thought better of it.

'The woods have some historical importance. Something to do with a battle during the English Civil War, I believe,' he muttered instead.

'Interesting period,' murmured Gideon.

'We have lamb for dinner. I hope you like it,' said Catherine interrupting.

'That sounds lovely, thank you,' said Gideon. 'Do you have any mint sauce?'

'Yes, we do,' replied Catherine smiling. 'I like mint sauce too. Blake doesn't, though… hates the vinegary taste.' Gideon nodded, and they sat down and began to eat. This was how the evenings would play out over Friday and Saturday night. Casual, unobtrusive, non-invasive ordinary conversation. Questions, answers, views, and opinions, but nothing revealed of any consequence. But on Sunday night, something changed.

'If you would like to sit down,' asked Catherine, smiling at Gideon as he entered the dining room at precisely seven-thirty as he had the previous nights. 'I'll bring dinner through.'

'Wine,' said Blake, who was already sitting at the table, offering to fill Gideon's glass.

'Thank you,' said Gideon. Blake filled his glass, and Catherine and Gideon sat down and began to eat dinner. After they had finished dessert, Blake offered to take Max and Claudia to bed, which was a little unusual. Catherine smiled, happy to stay seated and relax after dinner and finish her glass of wine.

'Will you tell us another story before we go to bed?' asked Max.

'I think you have had enough stories from Gideon today,' interrupted Catherine. Gideon had been regaling them with stories from just after lunchtime until he went to his room at three.

'Maybe Gideon will tell us some more tomorrow.' She glanced at Gideon to ensure she hadn't inadvertently committed him to an arrangement he might not be willing to partake in, but he appeared perfectly amenable to the proposal. 'But you must go to bed now.' She then realised, somewhat embarrassingly, that she had rescued him from one obligation only to bind him to another.

Max and Claudia kissed Catherine goodnight, and both politely shook Gideon's hand, which amused him. They then both smiled and flounced up the stairs to bed.

'I will read them a story tonight to keep them happy,' said Blake, walking up behind them.

'It won't be as good as one of yours, Gideon,' said Blake smiling, 'you've probably spoilt them forever.'

Gideon smiled,

'Can you keep Gideon amused while I read to them?'

'No problem,' answered Catherine.

It was a throwaway line with no hidden agenda. But Catherine suddenly felt warm and could sense a strange sensation in her stomach.

Gideon and Catherine watched them all as they walked up the long staircase to the landing before disappearing. Gideon turned back to Catherine.

'I will have to leave about midday tomorrow to get back home at a reasonable hour if that's okay,' said Gideon, sipping his wine.

'Of course, it is. It's a shame you have to go. I know the children would love you to stay and talk about your life, but I know you must have lots of work to do,' she paused for a moment. There was the hint of something else in what she had said, and she was a little surprised that she had phrased it that way, but she had.

'What about you?' asked Gideon.

'Me?' replied Catherine.

'Would you like me to stay?'

'I'm sure Blake wouldn't mind,' said Catherine evasively while smiling at Gideon.

'And you?' repeated Gideon, 'what about you?'

Catherine did not answer straight away. 'Tell me, Gideon, pouring more wine into his glass and deftly changing the subject, 'where did you get the idea for the book? How do you write something like that? It's so personal, so intimate. Do you make it up as you go?'

'No, it's not all fiction... a lot of it comes from people I know... people I knew, and some from people I don't know.'

'But how do you do that?' asked Catherine, sounding intrigued.

His beguiling enchantment was beginning to entice her into his world. 'I watch them, people in love, and see the things they never see.'

'What sort of things?' asked Catherine probing curiously into what was now dangerously uncharted territory.

'Sometimes, things they want me to see,' replied Gideon. 'Things they want everybody to see. Signs of affection - touching hair as you pass or just a transient stroke of your body. If you analysed it closely enough, it would have to be something to do with possession - ownership - control... This is mine! – I can touch it! - But not you. That sort of thing. It's all about body language.' Catherine smiled but said nothing.

'Sometimes, I see tiny, infinitesimal things they don't want anybody else to see. The cold glance of remonstration, disapproval, hesitation... Minute hand movements and mannerisms - the turning away and reluctance to answer a question... and sometimes I see things they cannot see. Things that could mean all is not as it seems, little idiosyncrasies that could mean they may not even realise what is already happening. And sometimes, I see the same identical things, but they mean something entirely different – a desire – a yearning. I see all these things even though people may try to keep them hidden, and they do manage to hide them from most people, but it's always there if you look close enough and know what you are looking for.'

It was a surprisingly candid self-appraisal of his remarkable abilities. Catherine found it unnervingly uncomfortable listening to someone capable of delving deep into the psyche of a relationship. Someone who could accurately extract, deconstruct and analyse each tiny element simply by observing somebody.

She felt exposed and vulnerable, almost naked before the gaze of a man who seemed to know more about her and Blake's relationship than they did.

'Oh,' said Catherine, sounding a little surprised. He had not alluded directly to Blake and Catherine; nevertheless, the inference was there.

'You could be a dangerous person to know,' whispered Catherine.

'Could I... I didn't think so?'

'Maybe you just don't realise it.'

Gideon smiled. 'It's all to do with the things that go into making a relationship work, that delicate fusion, that… balance of emotion, feelings, passion… and need between two people.'

Catherine hesitated before continuing the conversation. Aware that if she wasn't careful, she might paint herself into a very tight corner from which there would be no escape, only submission. But curiosity and his charismatic manner drove her forward - like a fiery chariot hurtling towards the edge of a cliff. On the surface, she wanted to save the occupants, to scream out… and tell them to jump to safety. But deep down, in a desolate corner of her soul, the part she seldom ventured into, she had already surrendered to something else. Something much darker, something she cared not to think about. The image of the raging flames and cries of anguish from the trapped passengers was too enthralling, too beguiling to resist. So she stood quietly by and said nothing and watched and enjoyed the deliciously devastating spectacle as it slowly unfolded.

'I can understand emotion and feelings, even passion and desire,' she murmured, looking away for a split second as she uttered the last words. 'But need – isn't that a little like a dependency, a weakness?'

'Why did you look away when you mentioned desire?' asked Gideon.

'Did I?' asked Catherine, sounding surprised. 'I wasn't aware…' she stopped, realising what she had just done. She was doing everything that Gideon had just mentioned people subconsciously, unknowingly do, and now he was watching her.

Gideon smiled.

'I don't know why,' said Catherine. 'But isn't need just a weakness?' she asked again.

'No, it's something entirely different. A need exists in the absence of weakness. I see pure need as something that is added to the relationship equation, not taken away, like oxygen. We all need it, and yes, we depend on it. Without it, we would simply stop breathing. But that doesn't mean we are lesser mortals because we have that need. It's essential to continue living. We can't function without it. Does that make sense?'

'Yes, it does,' replied Catherine. She went quiet momentarily, looking at Gideon while preparing what she would say next. 'So, you are really a voyeur,' she continued, grinning mischievously, 'secretly peeking through invisible keyholes into other people's lives?'

Gideon smiled. 'No, not a voyeur, I'm.... You could call me an observer... of life, a witness... and when I see something interesting, I make notes... in my head.'

'To use in your next novel?'

'Possibly,' replied Gideon.

'Were they very much in love?'

Gideon looked at Catherine intently, then dropped his gaze to the table, thinking about what she had said. The sudden change in the narrative had caught him a little unawares.

'Who?'

'The people you talk about.'

'Yes, they were.'

The question seemed to trouble him slightly, and Catherine could sense this and began to feel a little uneasy. She decided to try to switch the conversation to something safer, neutral, and less immersive.

'Do you watch everybody,' whispered Catherine? Gideon lifted his eyes to engage hers again, their blueness radiating an almost ethereal luminescence.

'It depends...'

'On what?' asked Catherine.

'On whether they interest me.'

'Do we interest you?' Catherine asked tentatively. Her expression changed slightly. It was a perilously loaded question; she knew that. Any answer would take her to a place she had not expected to visit when they first sat down for dinner that evening. Until now, their conversation had been light, generalised, and non-specific. Typical dinner talk coupled with the inevitable curiosity about how a writer does what he does. But now Catherine had ventured into viscerally dangerous territory. Gideon moved his hand a few inches across the table and gently scribed the area just in front of her hand with tiny circles. For some strange reason, this simple gesture aroused an overwhelming sense of erotism in her, the like of which she had never experienced before.

He did not touch her, but she could feel another peculiar sensation on her neck and elsewhere. A phenomenon she could not recall ever experiencing. She instinctively glanced towards the staircase to see if Blake was coming back down…

'Yes, you both interest me very much, but you interest me more.' He looked directly at Catherine as he spoke. 'I am falling in love with you, Catherine. You have no idea how long I have been searching for you. It feels longer than a lifetime, but now I have found you… I want to be with you. When can we be together?'

In a few brief words, he had summarised precisely how he felt and what he wanted to do, leaving Catherine with only one decision to make. It was like the intuitive car salesman who always asked: "When would you like to pick up your new car?" Not whether you wanted to buy it… Gideon had already made that decision for her.

Catherine had to think about his words for a few moments. She wasn't sure whether he said what she thought he said or whether she had imagined it. She had drunk her fair share of wine that night and occasionally wandered off, lost in her dreams and fantasies. Maybe she had misheard him, but no, it was so blunt, honest, and without ambiguity that the only conclusion she could come to - was he had said the words. She just hadn't been prepared for what they were saying.

'I don't think I have ever read a story with so much intensity,' she uttered in confusion, her head spinning with his words. Changing the subject, yet again, was the only available tactic open to her; she needed something to give her time… time to think.

'Being in love is intense,' replied Gideon, 'and must always be so. When that has gone, all you have left are two lonely people, Two empty souls who appear to know each other. They may appear to love each other, but they are not in love. They simply inhabit the same space.'

He seemed to have done it again, succinctly summarising her actual state of mind into a few carefully chosen words. How does he know how I feel? She asked herself. Was he still talking about the characters in his book, or was he now talking about them? She wasn't sure. She wasn't sure of anything anymore. She wondered whether this was all part of an elaborate illusion, something he had somehow created, like one of his stories. He was dangerous and would drag her down, but she could not walk away.

'Are you in love?' asked Gideon.

'Yes, I am,' replied Catherine quickly, grasping for simple, explicit words.

'Are you, really?' asked Gideon again.

'You can't ask me that,' replied Catherine.

'But I have. I am looking for the passion and the desire, but I can't see it, not between you and Blake... So how can you be in love?'

'How are you two getting on?' asked Blake, re-entering the room.

'Fine, just fine,' replied Catherine, breathing a small sigh of relief at the momentary respite from Gideon's tender yet intense inquisition. 'Gideon was just making a few suggestions...' she hesitated momentarily, looking playfully at Gideon, 'about running away to sea, to get away from everything.'

'Damn good idea if you ask me,' replied Blake. 'We could escape all this chaos and the mayhem in the office. It's all your fault, you know.' he smiled at Gideon.

Gideon and Catherine smiled at the idea. But what they were thinking was not what Blake was thinking.

'Are the children asleep?' asked Catherine.

'Yes, they are just, at last. I had to explain all of your stories to them again,' said Blake looking at Gideon. 'You have so completely entranced their minds you will have to come over again to retell your stories - sometime soon if you can manage it. If you don't, I'll never be forgiven.'

Yes. You have also entranced my mind, so you will have to come again, thought Catherine.

'No problem,' replied Gideon. 'It will be a pleasure.' He smiled at Catherine. They continued to talk and drink long into the night before eventually going to bed around midnight.

The following day, after they had finished breakfast, Blake, Max, and Claudia said their goodbyes before walking off to the village, leaving Catherine to clean the breakfast things and see Gideon off.

Standing at the front door, he referred to the previous night's unfinished conversation.

'Remember what I said last night. I meant it.'

Catherine smiled, slightly embarrassed. She had sobered up now, and it was clear in her mind that the previous night's flirtatious conversation was nothing more than the wine talking. The tranquil surroundings and the poetic licence of a romantic novelist had been working overtime. And it was of no consequence. But his words left little uncertainty as to his intentions.

After Gideon left, Blake, Catherine and the children spent the last few days of the holiday visiting estate agents, collecting details of larger houses for sale in the area. Catherine put all thoughts of Gideon out of her mind. He had returned to his boat on the Thames, and it was unlikely they would meet again any time soon.

Chapter 13
1983

Catherine found their new home, a beautiful seven-bedroom Victorian manor house set in three acres of land with a swimming pool and tennis court. It was still within walking distance of the local village. Catherine and Blake had decided they liked the area they lived in very much and did not want to move too far away. Fortunately, *anything was now possible with the change in fortune at Clanford and Fox.*

They arranged to view the house a few days later, and before they had even entered, they knew it was the one for them. The interior was everything that Catherine had dreamt of. Apart from the usual requirement for a new kitchen, a couple of modern bathrooms and redecoration, it was perfect.

There would obviously be many other cosmetic things to change. But the layout was precisely how Catherine had always imagined it. Curiously, it was almost identical to a house that Gideon had visualised in one of his many stories.

They moved in just over three months later, at the end of April when the air was beginning to warm up after a hard winter. The work started almost immediately to make all the changes Catherine had planned.

Meanwhile, Blake was back in the London office orchestrating the European, Japanese, Chinese, and American publication of The Chapter Room. UK hardback sales had reached an astonishing one million copies, and now the paperback edition had pushed sales past six million. They received two pounds on every hardback copy as publishers, meaning Blake's company would receive over two million pounds from hardback sales alone. This was unheard of in the industry.

While at the office one day in early May, he received a telephone call from Martin, his old neighbour. Martin informed him there had been a severe fire at his house, and everything had been destroyed. Fortunately, by some curious twist of fate, the safe where the manuscript of Prospect Road was held had withstood the fire, and the document was undamaged. Martin wanted to know if Blake would like to pick it up sometime, and of course, Blake, somewhat reluctantly, agreed. They arranged to meet that weekend at The Lodge Hotel near where they used to live. Martin was living there until the builders had completed his house's reconstruction.

After Blake replaced the receiver, he remembered the last time he and Catherine had read the manuscript and the details in the final pages. It had accurately predicted The Chapter Room's critical acclaim, the high sales volume, and even their move to a village just outside of Oxford. It also mentioned a very tense period between Thomas and Kate. Blake and Catherine had not experienced anything as traumatic as the events mentioned in the book. So it appeared to be less than accurate in some details. It also never mentioned a fire. Maybe it was all just a coincidence, he thought. He tried to put it out of his mind, but it would not go away. There was still the nagging riddle of how the manuscript was being written. That was a mystery he had yet to solve. He tried not to think about it anymore that day and pushed the matter to the back of his mind. It would possibly make more sense if they reread the manuscript. Each time they had read it previously, parts of it became much clearer.

On Saturday, they drove over to the hotel where Martin was staying. As they pulled up, they saw Martin sitting on a bench in the courtyard in front of the hotel, having a drink and taking in the spring sunshine. His appearance was that of someone who seemed entirely at ease, without a care in the world. But then, that had always been Martin's general predisposition in life. He never really took anything too seriously anymore after, not after the loss of his wife some years earlier. He did not socialise as much as he used to when Ruth was alive, but he kept in touch with close friends.

As they exited the car, Martin stood up and walked toward them.

'Catherine, Blake, wonderful to see you. And you two,' he said, looking at Max and Claudia. He kissed Catherine on both cheeks and shook Blake's hand. He produced two lollipops from nowhere and gave them to the children, but not before glancing cursorily at Catherine to ensure that was okay. She smiled her approval.

'Hello, Uncle Martin,' chorused Max and Claudia. He wasn't their uncle, but Catherine and Blake had encouraged them to call him that, as he had been in their lives since they were born. Martin now lived alone, and what family he did have lived many miles away and seldom visited him. He was now in his mid-seventies but remained sprightly and animated, which amused Max and Claudia. They all sat down.

'Let me get you a drink,' said Blake.

'No, I'll get these,' chipped in Martin. 'There is a sexy little barmaid here, and I could be in with a chance. She thinks I'm loaded!' He laughed at the self-deprecatory delusion, making a sad clown expression, which amused Max and Claudia. They obviously didn't understand the hidden agenda (or so he thought).

'I don't want to disappoint her, not yet anyway.' He laughed again, and Blake and Catherine smiled back. 'It's not my money,' added Martin. 'I have a subsistence allowance from the insurance company, so it's on them. Mind you, I don't know how long that will last. The food's awfully expensive here but very nice, so I'm getting my three meals a day now, with wine,' he laughed. 'Normally only eat at dinnertime.' He pulled a funny expression as if he were a naughty child who had stolen some sweets from the tuck shop. 'Stopped eating breakfast and lunch after the "governor" died.' He was talking affectionately about his wife, who Max and Claudia had liked very much. Martin entered the hotel returning a few minutes later with a tray of drinks.

'Right, there you go, lemonade for you two.' He passed the drinks to Max and Claudia, then handed a beer to Blake and a gin and tonic to Catherine. 'Happy days,' said Martin, picking up his beer. Considering the disaster that had befallen his house, he seemed in remarkably good humour.

'So, how did the fire start? Have they told you yet?' asked Blake, wiping away a bit of froth from his mouth.

'Well, that's the strangest thing,' replied Martin. 'Well, the second strangest thing, actually. I was out for the day, and… do you remember Derek, the postman?'

'Very vaguely,' said Blake, nodding his head.

'Well, he was cycling up the drive just after eleven o'clock, and suddenly there was an enormous explosion from what Derek told me. He was blown off his bike and landed on the hydrangea bush, which broke his fall, but there was no other damage, fortunately, but had he come a few minutes later...'

'Lucky man,' said Blake.

'Yes indeed, not so lucky for the Hydrangea though, could be years before that recovers.' Martin smirked, and Blake laughed.

'So, do you know what happened,' asked Catherine?

'According to the fire brigade, it was a gas leak. That was their first conclusion.'

'Nasty,' said Blake.

'Then, after the explosion, what was left of the house burst into flames.'

'You must have upset the village mafia by the sound of things,' said Blake wryly, taking another sip of beer. 'The local W.I. was always a touch on the militant side. You probably forgot to pay for the last consignment of jam.' Martin and Blake both laughed.

'It's no laughing matter,' said Catherine, gently scolding Blake. 'Martin's lost everything he owns, all his memories, photos.' Blake briefly dropped his slightly jovial expression and apologised to Martin. But Martin didn't seem overly concerned, but then he never was. He obviously thought Blake's little joke was very humorous.

'Place needed redecorating anyway,' added Martin drollery. Even Catherine laughed this time.

'No, it's not as bad as all that.' I kept most of that stuff in the garage in one of those four-drawer metal filing cabinets. As you probably remember, that's quite a few yards from the house – or where the house used to be, anyway.' He laughed at his quip. 'I did lose a few photos, but there are plenty left. We took thousands of each other over the years but seldom looked at them afterwards. I don't think anybody looks at old photographs that often, to be honest. We put them in a box in a cupboard and don't take them out again for years and years until… I think most of us remember people in our heads, not in photos. I know I do. That's until our memories start to fail then…'

It was a telling and insightful statement, but sadly, inherently true.

Martin lifted his pint and took a sip. 'Now, one of the really odd things was the safe.'

'The safe,' echoed Blake?

'Yes, the safe where I kept my real valuables – and, of course, your document.'

'The manuscript,' replied Catherine and Blake in unison.

'Correct,' replied Martin.

'Can we play in the garden?' interrupted Max, pointing to a small area to the right of where they were sitting. There were some swings, climbing frames and various other amusements for children.

'Yes, of course, you can,' said Catherine. They both finished their drinks and ran off to the play area. Martin leant over to a briefcase by his side, took out the manuscript, passed it to Blake first, and then slid it to Catherine before removing his hand.

'Is that right,' he queried? Unsure if he had inadvertently embarrassed Blake.

'Yes, yes, it is,' replied Blake. 'Look, I think you deserve an explanation for our...'

'All in good time,' interrupted Martin. 'I haven't told you everything yet, not quite...'

'Oh,' said Catherine, wondering what else there could be to tell.

'Well... after the fire brigade had put the fire out and the structural people had checked out what was left, they found something very odd.' Martin stopped momentarily, introducing a spurious hint of theatricality to build the tension. This was typical of Martin, who was never one to miss an opportunity to dramatise an experience or add an element of intrigue. He had appeared in a few local amateur dramatic productions when Ruth was still alive, usually as an imperious ex-major or overbearing judge. So he tended to rely on a few hackneyed theatrical affectations occasionally to emphasise something or make it appear a little more interesting than it actually was. He had picked up these mannerisms from various theatre directors over the years.

He knew Blake published crime fiction, so he endeavoured to introduce an element of mystery and suspense into his story to make it a little more interesting. Blake did not immediately realise that Martin was making light of his experience. He had obviously dined out or at least had a couple of pints on the back of his recollection of events.

He continued: 'When the firemen got to my study, where the safe was, they found the room was virtually untouched. The rooms on the other three sides had been demolished or burnt out, but the study was… as it was. Even the ceiling was still there. And what is more, a burst water pipe sent a fountain of water directly over the safe as if to protect it from the fire. It was all very odd.'

Blake looked at Catherine but said nothing.

'It was as if your documents were being saved by some sort of divine intervention.' He emphasised the last two words by delivering them slightly slower and a couple of semitones deeper. He looked upwards and then furtively to his left and right as if he were acting out a second-rate espionage agent character in a Graham Greene novel. He had always been a fan of Orson Wells in Citizen Kane.

Blake and Catherine were no longer as cheery as when they first arrived. In fact, for a few moments, they became very subdued, lost in the realm of introspection, contemplating the unusual circumstances surrounding the manuscript's survival and the matter they had not bothered to mention to Martin.

'So,' said Martin, 'what were you going to tell me?'

In light of what Martin had just told them, Blake thought it wiser not to mention the unusual feature the manuscript appeared to possess. Martin had suffered enough traumas for the moment. He didn't need to have something else to worry about. Martin finished his drink.

'It was unimportant,' replied Blake, 'Would you like another drink, Martin?'

Martin looked at his glass. 'No, I'm okay at the moment, thanks. Oh, there was one other peculiar thing about the explosion.'

'Yes?' said Blake cautiously.

'No gas!' replied Martin abruptly.

'No gas,' replied Blake, momentarily mystified? Then he remembered. 'Of course, we didn't have any gas either, did we?' He looked at Catherine, who nodded in agreement.

'The gas company has never put the service into our area, so nobody has gas.' said Martin.

Blake thought about that for a second or two. 'So how did the…'

'…explosion happen?' finished Martin. 'That was the other strange thing. The fire brigade couldn't determine any reason for the explosion. They were certain it was gas to start with, but eventually, they had to rule that out when they found there wasn't any. All very odd.'

'Odd indeed,' repeated Blake, deep in thought. 'So, what caused it?' he asked quietly.

'They don't know. They think it might have been a build-up of methane or something from the farm, but that is some way away, so even that was a little improbable. As I said, a bit of a mystery.' Blake and Catherine both smiled but with an air of quizzical confusion.

'Anyway, we must be off,' said Blake, 'but you must come to see us sometime. Any weekend is good – just give us a ring.'

'I will,' replied Martin. 'That's exceedingly kind of you.'

'When you are all sorted out, we may ask you to retake safekeeping of our manuscript, if that's okay?' suggested Blake. 'You protected it very well so far.' Catherine gave Blake a reproachful glance but said nothing.

'Glad to be of service,' replied Martin.

'Have the builders said how long it's going to take?' asked Blake.

'Yes,' replied Martin a little despondently. 'About six months, so November time. Back for Christmas, I hope.' He paused for a moment, then smiled. 'Still, it gives me plenty of time to work on the barmaid.' He laughed, and Blake and Catherine smiled.

'Max! Claudia!' shouted Blake. 'We're going now. Come and say goodbye to Uncle Martin.' They both came over and said their goodbyes. Blake picked up the manuscript.

'Thanks again,' said Blake.

'Yes, thank you very much for everything,' said Catherine. She kissed him on the cheek and gave him a reassuring hug. It was probably a little more affectionate than necessary. But she was feeling extremely uncomfortable about the grief and destruction she believed they had brought to his door. They started walking back to the car, waving as they went.

'Anytime,' said Martin, 'anytime,' smiling amiably as they left.

Max and Claudia waved back as they skipped over to the car. Blake placed the manuscript in the back of the estate. Catherine and Blake were a little subdued during the ride home as they contemplated what Martin had told them.

After they arrived home, Max and Claudia went to play in the back garden, and Catherine went into the kitchen to make some tea.

'So,' said Catherine, 'this manuscript not only documents your past and predicts the future, it…

'Predicts the future?' interrupted Blake, a little surprised by Catherine's statement. 'I think that's overegging it a bit.'

'Well, I don't think so,' said Catherine firmly. 'It did foretell all of this.' She waved her arms around, indicating the house they were standing in. 'And the success of The Chapter Room.' Blake pretended he had forgotten, but he had been thinking about it since Martin's telephone call. So much had happened since then that he wasn't sure how much had been documented in the manuscript and how much was real, albeit that everything was real, one way or another.

'Are you sure?' replied Blake.

'Yes, I am, just read it; you will see how close it is.' There was an urgency in her voice that Blake had not noticed before. The mysterious explosion had obviously unnerved her. 'But of more concern now is that it appears to have a guardian angel protecting it.'

'Well, not quite,' replied Blake, quickly discounting that suggestion. 'Why would a "guardian angel",' he flicked his fingers in the air to put the words in inverted commas, 'try to blow it up, set fire to it… and then save it from destruction?'

'Maybe that was a message,' said Catherine after a few moments of thought, pursing her lips in an odd expression of intrigue and mystery. She rolled her eyes a bit to enhance the suggestion. She was desperately trying to make light of the incident, but deep down, there was a niggling concern that she could not ignore.

'What kind of message?' replied Blake, still in a whimsical state of mind but nevertheless taking careful note of Catherine's odd facial contortions.

'Don't ignore me, or this is what I will do,' replied Catherine, using more inverted commas and adopting a Dalek-type nasal voice.

'Don't ignore me,' said Blake thoughtfully. Any earlier hint of flippancy in his voice was fast ebbing away. He was carefully considering what Catherine had said. Even if it sounded a little melodramatic, she might have a point.

'What do you actually mean?' asked Blake.

'Well, maybe, it wants to be read, and you haven't read it for a while, so it got annoyed, and the only way it could attract our...' She thought about that for a few seconds, then changed the pronoun. 'Your attention was to... boom!' She threw her arms in the air, emulating an explosion. 'So maybe it's time you did have another look.'

Catherine had clearly accepted that something very unusual was happening. She also realised how ridiculous that last statement sounded, but what she was trying to say was, 'Run with it; let it be your guide.'

This was the real difference between men and women and why they had to have come from different planets, thought Blake. Men function in a practical world, impervious to anything that defies convention, accepting all the illogical rules as presented. But a woman can function without reason or accountability and will challenge anything if it has no real purpose. They will also quickly readjust their opinion and change direction if there is the remotest possibility that a different course of action could solve a problem. Women were seldom intransigent or concerned about losing face. Sometimes, Blake wished he could be more like Catherine, more like a woman when dealing with contentious issues. Despite its apparent lack of logic, there were times when her way indisputably worked.

'But I thought you thought I was writing it, sort of sleep writing or something?' asked Blake, still trying to get his bearings on exactly where they were with it.

'It did cross my mind just once, but not since, and definitely not since we put it in Martin's safe.'

'Right,' said Blake. 'Okay.' Case in question, he thought to himself. 'So, what do we do?'

'Reread it,' replied Catherine with disarming pragmatism.

Blake realised he had sounded a little obtuse, 'and weep?' he offered. Catherine ignored him.

'So! Just so I am perfectly clear on this - what you are suggesting is the manuscript indirectly arranged to blow up Martin's house because we…'

'Not we,' corrected Catherine hastily. 'Definitely not we. You. It was sent to you, not me.' For whatever reason, Catherine was now consciously endeavouring to place some metaphysical space between herself and whatever was causing the incidents. It was as if she had suddenly become unsure of something she previously had no issue with.

'Okay, sent to me, and all this is happening because I haven't read it for a few months?'

'Nearly six, I believe,' said Catherine.

'Six then,' agreed Blake reluctantly.

'So, we'll reread it tonight after the children have gone to bed,' said Catherine. Blake nodded his agreement.

'In fact, you don't need me to read it. You read it. If anything relevant happens, tell me, and then I'll read it.'

Blake looked at Catherine momentarily, unsure whether he was comfortable with that suggestion. Catherine flashed him an expression of reassurance, so he smiled back and began to read.

Prospect Road: Chapter Seven
written by
Anthony Theodore Clackle
Mary Drayton's Story

When Thomas arrived home, Kate met him at the door and kissed him.

'I'm sorry, darling,' said Kate. 'It was last night, all very unexpected, according to her neighbour. She had been to bingo and seemed perfectly okay, but when her neighbour popped in this morning, she was gone.'

'I haven't seen her for months... with all this going on,' replied Thomas. 'I should have gone to see her, shouldn't have left it so long.'

'We all leave it too long for somebody,' replied Kate philosophically, quietly trying to ease the remorse and regret that Thomas was obviously feeling. She had been badgering him regularly to ask his mother to come over to the new house and stay for a while, but he had never got around to it, and now she never would.

'I haven't told the children yet,' said Kate.

'I'll do that,' said Thomas.

'We can do it together,' said Kate. Thomas smiled. Kate had never gotten on that well with Thomas's mother, but she had never let that become an issue.

'We will have to go down tomorrow to sort things out for the funeral,' said Thomas. 'I'll ring the office in the morning and tell them I'll be away for a few days. I am sure they can cope without me for a little while. Could you ring your mother to see if she can have the children for a few days?' Kate nodded.

The following day, Kate and Thomas arrived at his mother's house just after seven o'clock in the evening. They were met by a tall, older woman who introduced herself as Adrianna. She was the lady who had spoken to Kate on the telephone the previous day and had arranged to meet them. She was elegantly dressed in a tweed skirt and jacket with chestnut brown stockings and sensible shoes. Not exactly obsessive, but precise nevertheless, in a practical way that suited her manner. She appeared a little austere, but that was to be expected under the circumstances. Not English, thought Thomas, who couldn't quite place Adrianna but thought he recognised her from somewhere. Adrianna promptly opened the front door for Thomas and turned the light on; the curtains had all been drawn.

'I am sorry for your loss,' she declared abruptly. 'I was your mother's friend, but I wasn't here when... She died alone; unfortunately, I'm sorry about that.'

Kate thought that was an odd thing to say. Adrianna had spoken the words more as a statement of fact than an affirmation of amity, but maybe that was just her way.

Maybe, thought Kate, as we grow older, we become crotchety, more impatient. Less inclined to waste what precious time we have left on the trivia of polite conversation. Maybe civility and courteousness are unintentionally sacrificed at the altar of honest intent, and bluntness becomes the order of the day. Then again, perhaps she was just making benevolent excuses for an old lady who was trying to be helpful but had forgotten or temporarily mislaid the essential niceties necessary to carry it off successfully. Kate suddenly thought how sad it was that Mary had died alone, with no one to talk to in her last few moments of lucidity. The last few minutes of light before she slowly slipped away into the darkness that lay beyond. And the last opportunity she may have had, other than God, to plead for forgiveness, expiation and atonement for sins unspoken before a witness on earth.

Thomas recalled something he had read recently. He couldn't remember where, but for some reason, it had stuck in his mind like an earworm, and it kept coming back. 'He walks quietly at your side or behind you in the shadows, and you don't even give him a second glance... and then one day he clears his throat, and you are startled by his presence...' Was she startled by his presence? Probably not. Did she have things she should have told him before she died? Possibly, but now he would never know, and probably it was best that way.

'We used to spend our days together talking. I will miss our conversations... I will miss Mary.' Kate and Thomas turned around to where Adrianna was standing; she appeared oddly reluctant to enter the house before they did.

Adrianna paused for a moment. 'I live just next door. If there is anything you need, please knock.' Thomas did not seem to hear her speaking. Adrianna turned as if to leave.

'Thank you,' said Kate, realising that Thomas appeared preoccupied and had unintentionally ignored Adrianna. He was gazing at the front door, and Kate presumed he was preparing himself for the moment he would step back into the house where he had spent his childhood years. However, his mother would not be there to greet him this time. For the first time in his life, he would enter the house and be met by a deafening silence. Mary had always loved classical music. The radio would be turned on first thing in the morning. And the music would resonate around the house all day, only to be turned off around seven in the evening when they would sit down to watch some television. His love of Debussy, Grieg and Brahms had been nurtured by this subliminal indoctrination. His appreciation of the great composers continued long after he moved away and had continued to this day. Something else he had to thank her for.

'I remember you,' blurted Thomas, suddenly returning from his momentary introspection. 'I must apologise. I was thinking back to when I lived here. You moved here just before I left, didn't you?'

Adrianna turned back to face Thomas. 'Yes, that's right,' she replied.

'I must have met you a few times over the past years?'

'You didn't come here very often,' replied Adrianna bluntly, with a hint of gentle remonstration. 'Mary eagerly looked forward to the times you did visit.' Thomas felt a pang of guilt, which was Adrianna's intention, but she was right; his visits were rare. Occasionally he would make a flying visit at Christmas. Twice in the last ten years, he had managed to get down for a few hours in the middle of summer. But Mary had not seen her grandchildren as much as she would have liked, and now she never would. Thomas pondered over the lack of consideration he had afforded his mother. He had denied her the opportunity to see her grandchildren, one of the few pleasures she had left in her declining years when all it would have cost him was a little time. He began to realise that not everything was conditional on a return on investment. Mary had never shown anything but love and care for him, and he had repaid her with abjuration. He began to experience the bitter taste of remorse and loss, a loss that could never be replaced.

'Oh, I forgot to give you these.' Adrianna passed Thomas the house keys she had been holding and a business card.

'That's the chapel of rest where Mary is. I told them you would pop in tomorrow. I hope that is okay. Oh, and I left some milk, bread, eggs, and a few things in the fridge. There wasn't much left, and what there was, I had to ditch… It was beginning to…'

'Yes, thank you,' said Kate. 'Thank you for sorting everything out.' Adrianna smiled and then made her way back to her own house.

Thomas stepped into the small hallway and continued through to the lounge. Kate followed him. For a moment, he stood in the middle of the room, gazing at all the reminders of his youth. It was almost as if he was half expecting his mother to appear.

'Let's get the bags,' said Kate. 'Then we can…' But she didn't finish, not sure what to say.

'Yes, of course,' replied Thomas, suddenly returning from wherever he was. He returned to the car, collected the two small suitcases they had brought, shut the front door behind him, and took the two bags upstairs to his old bedroom. The room was just how he had left it all those years ago, but it seemed smaller now, much smaller than he remembered. Mary had put in a new double bed some time back in anticipation of Thomas and Kate staying over for a few days. But it had never happened; the bed had never been used.

Chapter 14

Blake stopped reading and looked up at Catherine. 'Thomas's mother has just died… and they hadn't spoken for a long time. It was very unexpected. Apparently, he had stopped visiting her for some reason.'

Catherine was acutely aware of the similarity between Blake and his mother. They, too, had not spoken for some time, and she also had become quite frail the last time they had seen her.

'You should call her,' whispered Catherine, reading the unspoken thoughts hanging in the air. Blake had an obstinate look in his eyes.

'The last time we spoke, we had a row… about you.'

'I can't help it if we don't get on. She doesn't like me. I have tried.'

'It's not you; it's her. She always has to say something unpleasant. Why can't she accept you? We are married, after all.'

'It's what mothers do; they only want the best, especially for their only son. It happens to all mothers as they grow old. They can only see the child they carried, the son nurtured from birth, and now they see somebody else receiving all the benefits after they had done all the work. She only wants what's best for you.'

'You are,' replied Blake.

'I know that - you know that,' said Catherine, a little tongue in cheek. 'She just doesn't know it yet.'

'But when?' said Blake, still annoyed by his mother's stubborn belligerence.

'As long as it takes. Your mother doesn't worry me, so don't let her worry you. She will come around eventually. Just get her over for a few days, maybe this weekend. We can break her down slowly over time. We'll just have to be patient with her.' She smiled, and Blake leaned across and kissed her.

'I'll ring her tomorrow, I promise,' said Blake. Catherine smiled.

'I'm going to have a bath,' said Catherine. 'You carry on and tell me what happens when I come back down.' She got up, kissed Blake, and wandered up the stairs. Blake continued reading………

Prospect Road: Chapter Eight

written by
Anthony Theodore Clackle
Mary and Julian's Story

'Do you want anything to eat? I'm starving,' said Kate, calling up the stairs to Thomas.

'Whatever you can find. I'm not all that hungry right now.' He returned to the lounge, sat at his mother's desk, and casually pushed up the roll-top cover while Kate started preparing dinner.

There were ten compartments, each neatly marked with tiny handwritten labels: Household Bills, Insurance, Circulars, Letters, Legal, Motor Car, Will, Sundry Other Items, Repairs, etc. Florence must have become very methodical with her correspondence after her husband, Jonathan, died. She had not always been so, as far as Thomas could remember. That had always been his father's responsibility.

He took out the envelope marked 'Last Will and Testament of Mary Florence Drayton' and looked at the words. He wondered what the word 'testament' actually meant. It had biblical connotations that somehow did not seem that relevant anymore. He pulled the paper-knife from the compartment marked 'Letters', slit open the envelope and removed the document.

'Are scrambled eggs on toast, okay?' shouted Kate from the kitchen, unaware that Thomas had come downstairs.

'Yes, that's fine, thank you.' replied Thomas quietly.

'Oh,' said Kate, sounding surprised before turning around to see Thomas seated at his mother's desk in the lounge. 'I didn't realise you were back down. What have you found?'

'It's Mary's will. I thought I should read it.'

'Yes, you should.' replied Kate.

He began to read what was, in effect, her final 'to-do' list – the only one she would be unable to complete herself, the one she would entrust to her son. It included details of her funeral arrangements.

As people grow old, they become fixated on preparing for their death and do everything possible to tidy up their affairs as best they can. Some people meticulously prepare their funeral arrangements down to the last detail to ensure their final farewell is conducted precisely as intended. They make detailed instructions about which hymns they would like sung and which people should be contacted. It was as if they were afraid that their passing would go unnoticed. Unseen and unmarked if the final ceremony they would be attending was not appropriately planned. Mary would have wished for her entrance to eternity to be trumpeted with blaring horns and raging chariots of fire.

The will was much as he had expected. Apart from a few bequests to the two grandchildren, Adrianna, the local cats' home, and a donkey sanctuary, most of the estate came to him. Mary had always loved donkeys. He carefully refolded the will, replaced it in its envelope, and placed it back into its compartment. He noticed the small bundle of letters in the Private section. They were carefully tied together with a faded red ribbon, not unlike the ribbon used by solicitors for tying up defence barristers' briefs.

They were probably correspondence between Mary and his father, Jonathan, going by the way the ribbon had been neatly tied and the careful attention to detail in the way his mother's name and address had been written on the first envelope. He pulled the bundle of letters out, quickly flicking through them but not actually intending to read them. That was when he noticed that the alternate letters, presumably the replies she had written to his father, were in her handwriting but addressed to a Mr J. Clackle. To an address, he did not recognise. He wondered why his mother possessed the letters she had sent Mr Clackle.

Curiosity got the better of him, and reluctantly, he opened the first letter addressed to his mother. It was dated 12th July 1950, one year before he was born. On closer inspection, he noticed it was in handwriting he did not recognise. He flicked to the last page, which was signed 'Your ever-loving Julian.' Not a name he knew. The letter was well-thumbed and had clearly been read many times. As Thomas began to digest its contents, he wondered who this Julian Clackle was.

Kate came through from the kitchen with two plates of scrambled eggs on toast and placed them on the table.

'Dinner, darling. I'm sorry it's a little unadventurous. I'll pick a few more things up tomorrow.' She went back to the kitchen and brought back two cups of tea. Thomas placed the letter back down on the desk. The room was eerily quiet, so he walked over to the Roberts radio perched on the sideboard. It was in the same place it had stood for as many years as he could remember. He turned it on. A piece by Debussy was introduced, and Thomas and Kate sat down at the dining table to eat.

After a few moments, the sound of 'Clair de Lune' slowly filled the room, perfectly matching his contemplative mood. Thomas thought how fortuitous it was that this piece of music was being played at that particular moment. The melody perfectly matched how he felt. Its slow tempo and heartbeat rhythm gently caressed his tormented soul. Mary had dedicated much of her life to ensuring that Thomas had peace and tranquillity in his childhood. Protecting him from the world's harsh realities until he was ready to face them. Now he was beginning to realise just how much he had neglected his mother in her closing years. Hardly repaying her at all for all she had done for him.

A wave of guilt and remorse engulfed him. That was something he was now going to have to live with. Nothing could alleviate the guilty thoughts running around in his head; only time would ease the sadness and feelings of regret he now felt. They finished dinner, cleared away the dishes, and Kate washed them in the sink. Thomas sat back at the desk and resumed reading his mother's letters.

'I'm going to sort the bedroom out, then have a bath,' said Kate, making her way up the staircase. Thomas looked up from the desk and half-smiled.

'I'll come up and scrub your back,' he replied quietly. His voice had a solicitous tone, with just the tiniest innuendo. But he wasn't fully committed to the suggestion – his mind was elsewhere.

When Kate returned, she took out a book she had brought with her and began reading. Thomas was still at the desk but was now retying the faded red ribbon around the bundle of letters, just as he had found them. He carefully placed them back into the compartment in the desk. He wondered why Mary had not destroyed the correspondence and what she must have been thinking about during her last days.

His thoughts turned to Dylan Thomas's verse, something he and his mother had read a thousand times together. However, until now, he had never really appreciated its defining relevance.

'Do not go gentle into that good night. Old age should burn and rave at close of day; Rage, rage, rage against the dying of the light.' His mother always added another 'rage' when she recited the poem, passionately believing that Thomas had made an unforgivable miscalculation in the lilting cadence of one of his most significant verses. She was never averse to cutting comments about any of the great poems, books, or pieces of classical music if she felt they warranted criticism. Freely giving her advice or even partially rewriting a part of it if necessary.

Some people become obsessed with leaving anything behind that might show them in a less-than-perfect light after death. Best to destroy indiscreet photographs taken when the potential for embarrassment sixty years in the future, had not been considered. The paradox is that removing such evidence eliminates the portal through which future generations could clandestinely and respectfully observe past personality, character and temperament.

Oddly, if discovered a hundred years later, such objects would be feted as quaint artefacts. Highly collectable items of harmless or, at worst, mildly risqué ephemera from a bygone age. Something of little or no consequence to the memory of the original protagonists. Possibly even something to enhance a faded reminiscence. A moment of startling revelation and honesty never previously envisaged.

Thomas turned to Kate and quietly, without any intonation - apart from an underlying sense of confusion - said the words that had been running around in his head since he had placed the letters back into their compartment.

'I'm not sure I know who I am anymore.' Thomas's eyes appeared to focus on something far away in the distance, a long way from Mary Drayton's lounge.

'Sorry, darling,' replied Kate putting her book down. 'I don't understand.'

'My father may not have been my father, after all. My father could be somebody else altogether.'

'If your father wasn't your father, who was? I presume it's something in those letters you've been reading.'

'Well, yes, sort of... possibly,' Thomas replied hesitantly. 'I don't know.' He clasped his head in despair, gazing at the floor.

Kate looked even more confused. 'Nothing good ever came from reading other people's private letters.' Kate spoke in the homily tone she often adopted at moments like this, a tone Thomas hated with a passion bordering on psychotic. Her dispassionate responses, philosophical clichés, and innate resistance to overreaction to any situation sometimes drove him to a state of near apoplexy. Of course, he knew she was right, but that only worsened things. Sometimes he just wanted her to scream at him in a mad tantrum and throw things at him in frustration... but she never did.

With his head still in his hands, Thomas looked up at Kate and continued, 'What I don't understand is why she didn't burn the letters if she didn't want me to read them? That would have been an end to it, and I would have been none the wiser. But she didn't, which meant she did, and I have, and that means she must have had a reason.'

He had to run that over in his head several times after saying it to make sure it made sense. He could be just as obtuse and obfuscated as Kate with her bumper-sticker philosophy when it was called for.

'But does it really matter?' asked Kate, ablating Thomas's carefully considered rationale with a few simple words.

'Of course, it does,' replied Thomas. 'Where we come from defines what we are and what we will eventually become.' It was a sweeping statement delivered with intensity and simplistic clarity. 'We are what our parents were, but more so. It is the very nature of life that each generation becomes stronger and cleverer. Survival of the fittest – natural selection and all that. *Those with the ability to survive also have the propensity to flourish.* If it were not so, we would all be condemned to oblivion.'

'I didn't realise you thought so strongly about it,' replied Kate, slightly surprised by this unexpected and heartfelt philosophical outpouring.

Thomas half-smiled. 'It would have been nice if she had told me while still alive. I could have asked her some questions about him then.'

'Like what?' asked Kate curiously.

'Well, who he was, what he did, what became of him.'

'Wasn't that in the letters? She must have mentioned something about him.'

'Well, yes. There's a lot of information in the letters about him and his life,' replied Thomas. 'But that doesn't really tell me anything about him as a person.'

'But you had a father, a real father. Doesn't that count?'

'Yes, of course it does, but...'

'Well, what was his name?' asked Kate.'

'Clackle - Julian Clackle, and he was married to a lady called Rosemary.'

'Clackle,' said Kate, rolling it over her tongue. 'Strange name. And he was married?'

'Yes, so it appears,' replied Thomas.

'How odd,' thought Blake. 'I wonder why Anthony Clackle should introduce a character with his surname into the book.' He made a mental note to mention that to Catherine when she came back down, and they resumed reading...

'Katie Clackle,' pronounced Kate authoritatively, rolling the words around in her mouth and testing the sound they made. 'Kay-Te-Clack-Cool.' She pronounced each syllable as if deciding how to deliver the words best. 'Christ, what a mouthful! I would have sounded like some demented harridan.'

Thomas laughed.

'I've decided I'm perfectly happy with Drayton. That's just fine,' said Kate.

Thomas smiled. Maybe he was going a bit over the top about the whole thing, while Kate, as usual, was being sensible and taking it all in her stride.

'It's still odd she never mentioned it,' said Thomas.

'She must have had her reasons,' said Kate. 'Maybe she just didn't want to tell you while your father was still alive, and after he died... well, maybe she thought there would be no point.'

Thomas pondered over Kate's words, which in a way, seemed to make some sense.

'I wonder where he came from,' said Thomas thoughtfully, 'and I wonder what happened to him.'

'What else do the letters say?' asked Kate.

'Well, Julian Clackle, or Daddy as maybe I should now call him…' He looked up at Kate and grinned. 'Well, he mentions various things, personal stuff mainly, between him and Mary. But amongst all that, he starts to write about something else that happened in the past.'

'When exactly?' asked Kate, intrigued by Thomas's questionable attempt to introduce a mysterious dimension to the proceedings.

'It was around the turn of the century.'

'Oh right, well, that is definitely the past,' replied Kate.

Thomas nodded, acknowledging Kate's whimsical frame of mind.

Kate decided it might be better to listen with a little more solemnity. She pursed her lips for a moment, her face forming the most convincing expression of riveted interest she could muster. With a playful flick of her hand, she gestured to Thomas to continue.

Thomas responded accordingly. 'Oh, and by the way, I have a brother, I think.' He did not sound too sure.

'A brother?' exclaimed Kate with a quizzical expression.

'Yes, well, half-brother, a Mr Anthony Theodore Clackle no less.'

Blake stopped reading just as Catherine came down the staircase in her dressing gown, her head covered in a towel; in that way, only women can wrap a towel around wet hair.

'This is all very peculiar,' said Blake, laying down the manuscript. 'The letters Thomas found confirmed that his real father was Julian Clackle, not Jonathan Drayton. Mary had an affair with him, became pregnant, and Thomas was the result, but she carried on living with her husband as before.

'And never told him?' asked Catherine.

'No, never, from what I can make out. Julian Clackle also had another son a few years earlier with his wife, a half-brother to Thomas. They called him – and this is where it becomes more confusing – Anthony Theodore Clackle. The writer of Prospect Road.' Blake looked blankly at Catherine.

'So, the book is an autobiography?' said Catherine, a little bemused. 'But why is it foretelling events happening in our lives?'

'I don't know. It's all very confusing,' replied Blake.

He read on…

'Oh,' said Kate, musing over what, if any, ramifications this latest revelation might have. 'Well, that's something you didn't know. What else do they say about him? Do they mention where he is?'

'No, they don't – well, not so far. But this is the part of the letter I want to tell you about.' He sipped the whiskey he had been slowly pouring into his glass. 'Julian goes on to talk about this young author back in the early 1900s who sent his first novel, A Sacrifice of Souls, to the book publishers Clanford and Fox…'

Blake stopped reading and stared at the words: Clanford and Fox. His company… Why was this book now talking about his company?

'Now it's mentioned the business,' exclaimed Blake, completely mystified.

'What?' replied Catherine.

'It now mentions a publishing company called Clanford and Fox. My company.' Catherine said nothing. Increasingly intrigued by the coincidence, Blake read on…

'There were two partners in this company. It was newly formed and did not have much money. They read the novel and agreed it was so good it could become a huge seller. Then they began to have concerns about whether the writer would stay with them. Once he realised how small a company Clanford and Fox was and how new they were to the publishing business, he might take the book elsewhere. They had never published a major book, and the author would quickly find this out if he visited them, which he would have to do at some stage.'

'And?' said Kate, now becoming absorbed by what Thomas was telling her.

'They thought they might lose their first client before he had signed a contract. But they also knew that publishing this book would virtually guarantee them immediate success. So, they decided to do something about it, and Joshua Clanford proposed a plan. It was unscrupulous, dishonest, and highly unethical. But they were new to the publishing world and hungry for success, so they pushed any reservations they had to the back of their minds.'

'What did they do,' asked Kate? Thomas now had her full attention.

'They decided to steal the book and claim they had written it themselves, or more precisely, Joshua would claim to be the writer. Then they would publish it through their own company.'

'But surely that's illegal. It's theft – plagiarism. They couldn't possibly get away with it,' remarked Kate, seriously disturbed at the thought, especially as this was Thomas's profession. The fear of something like this loitered in the darkest corners of the minds of all aspiring writers. Many believed the novel they had sweated over for two or three years was a unique masterpiece.

In many cases, it was seldom more than a collection of disjointed sentences. These would be embellished with unrealistic dialogue centred around an implausible storyline. But that wasn't always the case, as was the situation with this book…

'Yes, it is,' replied Thomas. 'All those and more. But in those days, most writers only wrote one copy by hand. Seldom were duplicate copies made, so it was much easier for a book thief without moral integrity to commit theft with relative impunity. Even Shakespeare borrowed and plagiarised other writers and was already famous.'

'Then what happened?' asked Kate.

'Well, A Sacrifice of Souls was published in 1912 by Clanford and Fox, purportedly written by Joshua Clanford. They never expected it to be anything more than a moderately successful novel. They thought it would make them financially independent, but not enough money for them to worry about the original author making a big fuss.'

Blake stopped reading again and looked up at Catherine with a bewildered expression…

'Now the letters go on to mention another author and something that happened back around 1912. Apparently, this author crafted a story that his publishers stole from him. Then they published the story through their company but under their own names.'

'Can they do that?' asked Catherine.

'No! They most definitely can't, but apparently, they did.'

'Then what happened?' asked Catherine.

'That's as far as I have read,' replied Blake. He carried on reading.

'But it made a lot of money?' speculated Kate tentatively.

'Oh yes, an enormous amount of money for those days. It began to sell in vast numbers all over the world.'

'Then what happened?' asked Kate, sensing something ominous was looming on the horizon.

'Well, the author did turn up at their offices about a year later and was justifiably outraged at what they had done. There was a furious argument about authorship, but of course, he had no evidence to support his claim. Eventually, they had to have him forcibly ejected from their office after he became violent. They never saw him again.

'The last thing he did as he was being thrown out was to swear to take revenge on them for what they had done.'

'And did he?' asked Kate.

'Well, apparently not. The next thing anybody heard was about a year later. The author's wife had left him after their son died of something or other; the letters don't say what exactly. The author could not afford to pay for a doctor as he had no money, and without money, you died from almost everything back then.

'By now, he had stopped writing and worked as a casual labourer. He had started drinking heavily, and then one day, he just disappeared. One of Julian's letters mentions that his estranged wife heard a few months later that the author had joined the Army and he had gone to fight in Turkey in 1915.

'Nothing more was heard of him after a battle at Mesopotamia. His friends thought that he was dead or had simply disappeared again, but nobody was sure. That was until news filtered back to his wife that he had been transferred to France around 1916. He was killed not long after, at twenty-four, while carrying out an unbelievable act of heroism. He had single-handedly saved the life of his commanding officer, carrying him across the battlefield on his shoulders for over four hundred yards under constant enemy gunfire. Just as he arrived back at his lines, he was shot by a German sniper. But the details are all very vague, so the story could have been fiction for all anybody knew. A muddy mix of conjecture, speculation, assumption, and harmless fabrication. A year later, the estranged wife died in poverty. All very wretched for all concerned.'

'And was that the end?' asked Kate.

'Well, no, not quite. In fact, this is where the story becomes even more intriguing. You see, Julian, my "father", explains that around 1920, the writer, Gideon, turns up again. His full name was Gideon Drew, by the way. Did I mention that?'

'No,' replied Kate. It meant nothing to her.

'Anyway…'

Chapter 15

'Christ!' exclaimed Blake. With his mouth hanging half-open, he turned to look at Catherine, standing by the open fire in her dressing gown, gently rubbing her hair with a towel.

'What?' replied Catherine with casual indifference.

'Now it mentions Drew.' Blake scratched his head.

'What?' repeated Catherine, unsure what Blake had just said.

'Gideon Drew. The book says that Drew was the author of a book called A Sacrifice of Souls.'

'But I thought Prospect Road was about Thomas Drayton and his family and some letters he had found.' Catherine felt a cold shiver run down her back at the mention of Gideon. Her heart missed a beat. Suddenly, she found herself paying closer attention to what Blake was saying.

'It was,' replied Blake, 'but...'

Catherine interrupted. 'And I thought Prospect Road was written by an Anthony Clackle.'

'It is,' replied Blake, trying to explain. 'That's what I was about to say. Anthony must be Julian Clackle's son. The book is an expository denouement – a way of explaining something that happened long ago - something to do with The Sacrifice of Souls, Gideon Drew, and Joshua Clanford. Joshua, Julian's birth father, is acknowledged as the book's writer, although Gideon wrote it.

I think Anthony wrote Prospect Road to explain not only the events that brought about his existence but something else.'

Catherine was beginning to grasp what Blake was trying to say, but there still seemed no rhyme or reason to any of it. Nothing really made sense. And in the back of her mind, never far from the forefront, was the recurring mystery of how the book continued to write itself with gathering momentum and ever-increasing prescience.

Although she had previously had reservations about its authorship, she was now reasonably sure that Blake had nothing to do with writing it. She walked over to the half-open window and gazed out into the garden. Her head was full of questions, but which could she ask, and which should she leave unspoken? The sky had begun to cloud over, and a slight drizzle was starting to fall. She could hear a gusty summer wind blow up and just as quickly die away. As if endeavouring to drive an approaching armada away from its intended invasion of Crete or Iraklion.

Catherine had recently read about the Trojan Wars and how the gods' control of the winds had made such a difference to the outcome of the invasion. Whenever she heard the winds swirling, she thought of the gods controlling the elements. It was still warm, and the heavy air had an indefinable aura of peace and tranquillity. Something you only ever experience in summer. The faint sounds of rumbling thunder could be heard in the distance, sounds that heralded a change.

'But the book was predicting our future and recalling events that happened in your past... and now you say it's talking about Gideon Drew. So how does that connect to you, and when did all that happen? Didn't you say it was...'

'It was over seventy years ago,' interrupted Blake again. 'It's something to do with Clanford and Fox. They were the publishers mentioned in the letters and the people who stole the original book. That is the connection. My company is the link...'

'But why does it suddenly mention Gideon Drew now?' asked Catherine hesitantly. 'That just doesn't make any sense.'

'I don't know. I haven't a...' Blake lifted the manuscript and resumed reading. 'Maybe it's....' but he didn't finish. He was caught up, once more, in the story of the letters.

After a few minutes, Catherine interrupted him again. 'Does it say anything else about him?'

'Who?'

'Gideon. Gideon Drew.'

Blake looked up, intrigued by Catherine's question. 'No, not so far. Why?'

'It's just very odd that it should mention him, isn't it?' She paused for a moment as if looking for some affirmation. 'Don't you think?' This wholly unexpected development had clearly unnerved Catherine and was obviously playing on her mind. A mist of prescient guilt lingered in the air, but Blake didn't appear to notice it. She had also unintentionally referred to the manuscript as an animate object. No longer just an abstract collection of words and recollections that had been slowly forming a syllogistic assumption in her mind. But what that assumption was, she wasn't too sure, and now she was even less so. Putting two assumptions together did not always produce the answer you expected.

'I must admit that it's a slightly spooky coincidence that the manuscript mentions a Gideon Drew writing a novel called A Sacrifice of Souls. A book stolen by Joshua Clanford and published with him being acknowledged as the author,' replied Blake, deep in thought. 'And that I have a phenomenally successful client with the same name. But the book they are talking about was written around 1912, so Gideon would have to be well over ninety years old if he were the same Gideon, which is laughable. So obviously, it is a different Gideon, or he has aged extremely well.' A grin crossed Blake's face. 'I'll just pop up to the attic for a moment and check,' he added light-heartedly, but the Wildean reference was lost on Catherine. She was otherwise preoccupied.

'Yes, he would have to be, wouldn't he?' murmured Catherine. 'And that's ridiculous because Gideon can only be in his early twenties, twenty-five at most. I'm sure of that.' Her mind flashed back to Christmas and the proposal Gideon had made.

Blake glanced at her for a second, surprised at her precise and remarkably explicit assessment of Gideon's age. He had never mentioned it before; if anything, Gideon looked younger.

Blake read on…

Prospect Road: Chapter Nine
Written by
Anthony Theodore Clackle
The Letters: Thomas and Kate

'Do you want me to read the letters aloud, darling?' asked Thomas. 'It might be easier for you to understand what is going on rather than me giving you a summary of the contents. I'm probably missing some salient elements.'

'But should you be doing that at all?' asked Kate. 'They are private, after all. If your mother has left them for you, I think it is reasonable to assume that she only meant for you to read them. But I can't see how anything can be gained from poring over some old love letters anyway. I wouldn't like it if somebody looked at ours, not with the...'

She didn't go any further. Thomas thought over what Kate was saying.

'I understand, but I still think my mother must have left them for a reason. I think either you should read them, or I should at least read some of the important parts so that you know exactly what I know.'

Kate mumbled something incomprehensible, and Thomas started to read the letters out.

'I'll only read out the letters that make sense,' said Blake, reiterating what Thomas had just suggested to Kate in the manuscript while desperately trying not to sound patronising.

'I think that may make it easier for us to understand.' Catherine nodded and took another sip of her wine.

THE FIRST LETTER
12th July 1950
from Julian Clackle to Mary Drayton

My Dearest Mary,

I felt I must write to explain and apologise for my behaviour last week and beg your forgiveness. I realise you may not wish to see me again, but I hope that somehow you can find it in your heart to forgive me. You were so kind in allowing me to unburden a problem that has been troubling me for so long. Something I have not been able to discuss with another living soul.

Now at long last, just as I feel there is a chance that I can put all that has happened behind me and move on with my life, I have once again fallen back into a trough of despair, secrecy and half-truths. I am still hiding behind a cloak of anonymity that has engulfed me for so long and threatens to consume my very existence.

I know I can trust your discretion, and I hope you feel the same way about me as I do about you. I believe we have grown closer each time we have met over the last few months.

I know when I told you last week I was already married and had been since 1946, you were understandably more than a little surprised that I hadn't mentioned this to you before, but there was a reason. I did not intend to deceive or hide the truth these past months. The problem was, the closer we became, the more certain I was that if I tried to tell you the truth, you would consider this to be the first betrayal. You would end our relationship and never want to see me again.

The first lie does so little harm, a tiny slip of the tongue that remains uncorrected for the sake of expediency. But it grows exponentially with each further lie to support the first. Each one creates its own trail of deceit and deception and profoundly enhances the earlier untruth. Expanding the deception to levels never anticipated at inception. I feel this may be a failing of all men, never realising at the beginning how something so good might end so badly. If only I could have found the strength and courage to have been honest in the beginning, but I could not. I will never forgive myself for that inadequacy.

Possibly this is due to cowardice or a foreboding apprehension or, worse than that, the fear of losing you. I don't know – I will never know. But if it can be some small recompense for the pain I have caused you, I would like to try and explain the intricate details of my past. Hopefully, this will help you to understand what has happened and why I have acted the way I have.

If you do not wish to continue our friendship, and I will understand if that is how you feel, then so be it. But if you believe we can overcome this together, then to my dying day, I will be forever in your debt.

Please write and let me know how you feel and whether you could find it in your heart to forgive me for my weakness in not being more candid with you from the start.

THE SECOND LETTER
22nd July 1950
Mary to Julian

Dearest Julian,

Your letter arrived today, and for many hours I deliberated on whether I should open it at all. But after considerable soul-searching, I eventually plucked up enough courage to do so. Initially, I read and reread the contents with some bewilderment and concern. But my feelings have now segued into thoughts of hope, deliverance, and optimism for the future.

When you first told me you were married and had been so for four years and that you also had a son, my immediate thoughts were that our friendship should end. Before, it became more complicated than it already is.

You have Anthony to consider and your wife Rosemary, who, as far as I understand, you still feel affection for despite what you have said. This aspect confuses me. And it casts doubt on the possibility of our relationship continuing. I believe we are just passing through a phase in life's journey, and this part will end soon. We will both have moved on and gone our separate ways or possibly just continued on the path we originally chose.

But then I think back to the first time we met in the park. We spoke for hours about such simple things as the fantastic colours of the flowers and the beauty of the trees. How, each year, they return just as beautiful, if not more so than the year before, and how wonderful life would be if it were the same life cycle for people.

It seems ridiculous now, but in those first few hours of meeting you, I realised I could fall in love again. More importantly, I wanted to fall in love again. Within those first few hours of meeting you, I told you I was imprisoned in a loveless marriage. I thought I did love him when we married, but I was only eighteen, and I didn't know what love was and still didn't until I met you. As I told you when we first met, our relationship had changed to one of total indifference toward each other after six years of being together. I wanted to leave but had nowhere to go, so I stayed. Jonathan works hard, and we have everything that anybody could want. But we never enjoyed our own company, and for some reason, we could not have children, which may also have made a difference. I felt oddly trapped in a place with nothing to stop me from walking away but the fear of freedom and loneliness. Some days I feel I am merely enduring a brief, joyless life. In reality, it is nothing more than an intermission before the eternal infinity of death comes calling. But now I know there is a reason to live and enjoy every moment of our short existence on earth. You have done that to me; this is how you make me feel.

When we spent that first afternoon in that hotel, something glorious happened to me that I find hard to put into words. Suddenly, I felt alive again. I felt a passion and a longing inside my heart that I have never felt before, yet somehow, deep down, I know it is something I have always wanted. They were feelings I was sure would last a lifetime, and when I looked into your eyes, I saw the happiness you were feeling and knew that you, too, desired what I desired.

Please write and tell me if there is anything you want to say that might help me understand. I want to see you, but I think it would be best to know everything there is to know about each other before we can meet again. I hope you will understand my reluctance to allow this relationship to develop further before I can surrender my heart and soul to you unreservedly. Experience has taught me that everything comes at a cost, and I need to know the price for the happiness we both desire.

I will always love you, no matter what.

Mary
xxx

Catherine felt an odd feeling in her stomach as Blake read the words. It was like a forewarning, a premonition of something, but she didn't know what.

THE THIRD LETTER
7th August 1950
Julian to Mary

My Dearest Mary,

Thank you for your kind reply and thoughtful words, which mean so much to me.

You deserve an explanation, and the best way to do this is for me to start at the very beginning and try to explain what has happened to bring us to this wretched juncture in our lives.

Firstly, I should tell you that Hilda and Harold Clackle adopted me when I was one year old. My real father (or should I say the person I believed to be my real father) was a man called Joshua Clanford.

In early 1916 Joshua Clanford (I prefer not to refer to him as my father, and I will explain why later) began courting my Mother, Madeleine Allbright. My mother inherited a fortune from her father after he died in 1915, and it was this that first attracted Joshua to her. It was no coincidence that this relationship was cemented just as the income generated by the book had been entirely squandered by Joshua and Obadiah on their depraved and extravagant lifestyle.

Joshua and Madeleine were married in September 1916, and for a while, she found Joshua attentive, charming, and captivating. She felt happier than she had ever been and never envisaged for one moment that he could ever change, but about a year after they married, he did. Having replenished his wasted fortune with another, he resumed his former debauched lifestyle of heavy drinking, gambling, and womanising. There were times when he was still kind to her, but as time wore on, they became less and less frequent and slowly, Joshua began to despise her for her piety.

According to Hilda, my adopted mother, Madeleine, was faithful to her husband for over four years. Even though he continued to spend her money entertaining other women. Then one day in 1920, Madeleine met somebody who, by all accounts, really cared for her, and she fell in love with him. But because she would not leave her husband, Madeleine's lover broke off the affair, and she never saw him again.

But by this time, however, she was pregnant. I was born one of twins, the other being my sister. Temporarily engrossed with the joy of having children, Joshua became more caring and attentive toward Madeleine once more. But somehow, he found out about her affair. Realising he was not our father, he demanded that Madeleine put us both up for adoption. Joshua wanted nothing to do with the legal procedure and left it to Madeleine. He just wanted us out of his life as soon as possible, and it was my mother who had to arrange what must have been the most heart-wrenching and traumatic event in her life.

When I was nine months old, Hilda and Harry Clackle adopted me in 1921. Another couple adopted my sister. Joshua and Madeleine were never intimate again and began to live separate lives in the same house, seldom speaking and never socialising together. Madeleine's day-to-day existence became very subdued. Her only release from her interminable incarceration was the clandestine journey she took once every week, without fail, on a Thursday afternoon to the other side of the town.

You may wonder how I know all this, and I will explain. Madeleine used to visit my adopted parents, Hilda and Harry Clackle, on a Thursday. Joshua always went to his club on Thursdays and never returned until the early hours of the following morning. Madeleine would play with me and talk for hours to Hilda about the things that Joshua had done. I never realised that she was my birth mother. She always pretended she was just one of my adopted parents' friends. This was an arrangement they had agreed to so as not to confuse me over my parentage.

Somehow, Joshua found out that she had been secretly visiting me and instantly forbade her from making any further contact. I never saw my birth mother again and didn't find out who she was or that I had a sister until many years later. A little time after this, Madeleine, in what I can only presume was a severe state of depression, threw herself under a lorry dying instantly.

Hilda and Harry attended the funeral with a small number of other mourners, including a stranger who introduced himself to Hilda as Gideon Drew. He mentioned that he had known Madeleine some years before and, oddly, asked about my well-being, which is why Hilda remembered him. She thought it best they didn't mention that they were my adopted parents.

Joshua did not attend the funeral. He now had all her money, which was all he had ever wanted. A few months later, in 1927, Joshua married Olivia. Just over one year later, in 1928, Olivia gave birth to a son.

For the next twelve years, my life continued without incident until just before I left home to join the RAF in 1940. On my nineteenth birthday, fearing the worst, Hilda told me some details she thought I should know about my past. That was when I found out my birth mother was Madeleine Clanford. They explained why she had been forced to give me up for adoption.

On the 20th of May 1941, both my adopted parents were killed in a freak accident. I had been flying with the RAF for over a year by then and still alive, which I can tell you was some achievement. I was now based near Chichester. There, I met and fell in love with Rosemary, the girl I would eventually marry in 1946.

The one thing Hilda didn't know and obviously couldn't tell me was I had a sister, and that sister was Rosemary. Neither did Rosemary realise she had a brother. Her adoptive parents had never told her. They probably never even knew themselves.

I only filled in the blanks through a chance meeting on a train going to London in 1949. I started a conversation with somebody who told me he had been at my wedding three years previously, but I couldn't remember him. He told me his name was Gideon Drew, and he said he had come to the wedding out of respect for Madeleine. He had known her back in the 1920s and met her husband, Joshua Clanford, my supposed father, but that was before everything changed.

He also told me that Madeleine and Joshua Clanford had twins, and they had both been adopted. One was called Julian, but he couldn't remember the girl's name but thought it might have been Rosemary. As you can imagine, this came as a shock to me. He also mentioned that Joshua had another son as far as he could remember. This was by his second marriage to Olivia. They had named him Reginald.

It was an odd encounter, as the man only appeared to be in his mid-twenties. He must have had a good war or a comfortable life because he must have been at least forty-five to have known my mother. It was only afterwards that I began to consider something else. The remote possibility that he could, in fact, have been my father had it not been for the anomaly of his age; he seemed no older than I was.

That was when I started to put it all together. Working out all the names, dates, and places in my head, I realised that I had, in fact, married my own sister, Rosemary Brierly – previously Clanford. But by then, it was too late to do anything about it. Our son Anthony was born in 1947 and was nearly two years old. He had some minor mental retardation, hearing problems and severe physical problems, which gave him an unusual limp. We were told his disabilities were incurable and would worsen as he grew older. The doctors could not explain what could have caused the debilities other than to say that it appeared to be some form of inherited genetic disorder.

I obviously didn't know what had caused the infirmities, not until I had that conversation with the stranger on the train in 1949. This secret and the reason for his disabilities have tormented me ever since - realising that his problems and his tortured life were all my making.

I immediately ceased intimate relations with Rosemary, and after a few days, I explained everything. As you can imagine, she was devastated, not least because she was still deeply in love with me. In time though, she came to realise that everything would have to change. I was beginning to think the nightmare would never end, and then I met you.

I still felt incredibly close to Rosemary, and I still do. She had done nothing wrong, and neither had I, but I now feel only brotherly affection. All we have left is the tangle of absolution to unravel and our son Anthony to look after. Of course, we could not stay married - it would not be correct. So, we divorced over a year ago. I hope you can understand what has happened, and maybe after reading this, you will be able to see me again, and we can talk.

I look forward to your reply,
Your ever loving Julian.
xxx

Blake put the manuscript down and looked at Catherine.

'So, what do you think is happening?' Blake sounded very confused. 'The whole thing is just becoming curiouser and…' He abruptly stopped himself from playing out the hackneyed cliché. It would have doused the ember of credibility he was endeavouring to imbue into his reading of the document. Catherine did not answer; she was miles away, deep in thought.

'Catherine!' said Blake.

Catherine suddenly returned from wherever she had drifted off to and looked at Blake with a glazed expression. She gestured for him to continue.

'Are you sure you want me to read this aloud? Wouldn't you prefer to read it yourself?' he asked.

'No, no. I'm fine. I can think more clearly when I am listening to you. Please go on.' So, he did.

'That was the last of the letters. It just goes back to the story now,' said Blake.

Prospect Road: Chapter Ten
Written by
Anthony Theodore Clackle
Joshua's Story

After Gideon disappeared in 1915, nothing more was heard from him. His friends assumed he was dead, possibly killed in the war, but he was not. He turned up again in 1920, having made a considerable fortune from his interest in a gold mine in South Africa.

The first thing Gideon did on his return to England was to purchase an elegant townhouse in London's popular Mayfair district. From here, he would quickly develop a wide circle of influential friends. Friends who would assist in his aspirations to immerse himself into the society crowd - the places the Clanford's and the Fox's frequented. He was no longer the shy, withdrawn person he once was. His appearance and manner had changed considerably. Gideon now used a different name, so Joshua Clanford did not recognise him when he first met him at a gambling club one night.

It is often found that those who acquire vast sums of money from felonious deeds are less prudent with the proceeds. Less so than they would have been if they had earned them through legitimate endeavours. Joshua Clanford and Obadiah Fox had made a considerable fortune from the book they stole from Gideon Drew in 1912. But by 1916, the income from book sales of The Sacrifice of Souls was declining and no longer sufficient to support their extravagant lifestyle. Having had no luck finding another bestseller to boost their finances, Joshua and Obadiah decide on another course of action to prop up their ailing publishing business.

To this end, they drew straws to decide who should propose marriage to a Miss Madeleine Allbright. She was a wealthy but remarkably unattractive heiress, and they both wasted no time making her acquaintance. They knew that she was not only available but also eager to marry. Joshua drew the short straw, proposed, and they were married a few months later, in October 1916. The fortunes of Clanford and Fox were temporarily replenished.

By all accounts, Gideon Drew was a remarkably handsome, refined, articulate, wealthy, and well-read raconteur. With his charming natural manner and soft, mellifluous tone, it was no problem for him to strike up an innocent relationship with Madeleine. By 1920, she had suffered four years of being virtually ignored by Joshua. She was a woman whose affections could be easily manipulated. Given that Joshua was not paying her any attention and spending his – or, more accurately, her – money on other women. Before long, Gideon and Madeleine had embarked on a passionate but, for obvious reasons, clandestine affair. It lasted some months and resulted in Madeleine becoming pregnant. At this point, Gideon made a sudden and hasty withdrawal from the scene, sold his house and disappeared again. His work was done, and the first part of his plan was now complete.

Madeleine had twins, a son, and a daughter, whom Joshua and Madeleine named Julian and Rosemary. The birth came as a pleasant surprise to Joshua. He had no recollection of having intimate contact with his wife for several years. Preferring to satisfy his carnal desires with other more attractive women or even the occasional whore. However, as he often arrived home very drunk, Joshua assumed that he must have had intercourse, possibly while in a state of bibulous stupefaction. He thought no more about the matter for over a year, happy in the knowledge that at least his wife had managed to produce a son and heir and a spare daughter.

One afternoon, however, while napping in his club with a copy of The Times draped over his head, he was awoken by a raucous and ribald conversation between two other members. They were discussing the rumours that he, Joshua, had been cuckolded and was unknowingly bringing up the offspring of that liaison as his own.

'Did you hear about old Clanford?' exclaimed Major Erskine-Blythe.

'No, what about the chap?' replied Judge Matthews, sipping his sherry.

'Rumour is, memsahib was tubbed by her secret lover in her husband's bed while old Clanford was out playing a round of golf, would you believe.'

'How did he do?' asked Judge Matthews.

'Hole in one, I imagine,' replied Erskine-Blythe drolly.

The judge spat out his sherry in surprise. 'Wasn't she the plug-ugly one?'

'Face like a pig's arse,' replied Erskine-Blythe. 'Probably why old Clanford kept her at home under lock and key.'

'Thought she might frighten the dogs,' replied the judge, grinning. They both laughed aloud.

'I heard she had a few bob, and Clanford's business wasn't doing too well... He likes the gee-gees and the tables, and he's not averse to a bit of hokey-pokey either... and that's not cheap.'

'Ah, I see,' replied Judge Matthews, sipping his sherry. 'Still, he should have done the honourable thing and kept her pleasured at least. Could have popped a brown paper bag over her head if she was that doggy.' They both laughed aloud again, much to the chagrin of the other sleeping members.

'Quite right. Fair do's, I say, fair do's. If he wasn't doing the decent thing, then....'

'Do you, er... keep the old girl... you know?' muttered the judge a little indelicately.

'Me? God, no,' replied Erskine-Blythe. 'Dear little thing hasn't got a brass farthing to her name, so don't need to bother. Anyway, can't be doing with all that lark, not at my age. Upsets my indigestion.'

'Right. Right,' said the judge. 'Understandable... well, I think it is very decent of the chap to take them on. All that responsibility for the next twenty years without any reward or compensation.'

'Or nookie, for that matter,' added Erskine-Blythe with a grin.

'Well, not from the wife, anyway. She obviously gets all she wants elsewhere.' They both fell about laughing again, despite further disgruntled looks from the other members trying to sleep.

Joshua stood up and stormed out of the club, much to the embarrassment of the two members. They had been unaware of his presence and were left looking rather sheepishly at each other before bursting into laughter again.

He immediately returned home to confront his wife with the slanderous rumour he had heard. They had a raging argument, and she eventually conceded that Joshua was not the father of their children, blaming this on his inability to perform. Madeleine argued vehemently to keep the children, but Joshua refused. Eventually, she conceded to his demands that both children be adopted.

So, Julian Clanford became Julian Clackle. Despite Madeleine's affair, Joshua refused to divorce her. Acutely aware that she still had indirect control over the remains of her inheritance, the part he had not yet managed to spend. This tortured existence continued until Madeleine committed suicide in 1927.

'Oh, I see,' said Catherine. 'So, a run-of-the-mill tale of infidelity, betrayal, deceit and money. All very interesting, but hardly earth-shattering and not particularly original. All very much the same as today, really.'

She appeared a little deflated by the story, somehow expecting something more. Her harsh and oddly cynical generalisation of the immorality of men caught Blake by surprise. He had always considered her to have a balanced, non-judgemental perspective on life. But this uncharacteristic outburst displayed a dimension he had not encountered before.

'That's not the end,' he added guardedly, at which point Catherine's interest perked up again.

Blake read on:

Then, in 1928, in furtherance of his plan, Gideon Drew embarked on another affair, this time with Emily Fox, the wife of Joshua's partner Obadiah Fox.

One year later, Emily had a son, Freddie. Gideon was the father, but this time the husband, Obadiah, didn't find out about the infidelity. Six months later, Obadiah and Emily Fox were killed in mysterious circumstances while on safari in Kenya. Twenty-five per cent of the company's shares automatically reverted to Joshua Clanford. The other twenty-five per cent passed down to their son Freddie, whom Joshua Clanford, without a moment's hesitation, offered to bring up... as his own son.

Chapter 16

'This Gideon Drew sounds like a right evil bastard,' exclaimed Catherine.

Blake looked up at Catherine, a little surprised by her outburst of righteous indignation.

'He's not getting to you, is he?'

'No, not at all, it's just that he seems to be ruining everybody's life and...'

'It's only a story. It's not true,' said Blake reassuringly, still slightly surprised at her unexpected reaction. 'It's not like you to become so angry over a fictitious character. Sounds like he's getting to you,' he repeated. 'Praise indeed for Anthony Clackle.'

'You forget,' interrupted Catherine, 'this story also details our lives, and this Gideon character sounds very un-fictitious to me.'

'In places, it's similar to our lives, I agree,' replied Blake, 'but that is just a coincidence – serendipity – chance even. Different writers often create similar stories simultaneously without ever seeing each other's work. Anyway, he hasn't ruined our lives at all, just the opposite.'

Catherine did not answer. Blake was right on that detail, but she knew that more in the book had happened to them than Blake knew about, and more could happen in the future.

'I can only imagine that the Gideon in the book is possibly the grandfather of the Gideon we know,' said Blake. 'That's the only explanation.'

'Well, it's one explanation,' replied Catherine, unconvinced and, by implication proposing another far more fantastic possibility.

'No! That is ridiculous,' replied Blake, aware of what Catherine was alluding to. He picked up the manuscript and carried on reading. The book appeared to be self-writing much faster than before, and he could see many more newly written pages he had yet to read. 'Maybe there's an explanation in the pages I haven't read yet.'

'Maybe,' said Catherine, but she was no longer so concerned with what had been written as with what had yet to be. 'Maybe we should give the book to Gideon to read? Maybe he could give us an explanation about his namesake.'

Blake did not answer but stared at Catherine, thinking about her proposal. He finished reading the new pages of the manuscript and then passed it to her to read but kept her off-the-cuff suggestion in the back of his mind for further consideration.

Prospect Road: Chapter Eleven
written by
Anthony Theodore Clackle
Hilda and Harry's Story

On a warm summer's day in 1940, a few days before he was about to leave them to start his training for the RAF, Hilda and Harry Clackle sat Julian down in their kitchen, and Hilda began to tell him a story.

'Before you leave... there is something we think you should know, something that could be of some significance to you one day.' Harry nodded, but looked uncharacteristically solemn, which unnerved Julian a little; it was not an expression he had often seen his father wear. Just once, when he was fourteen, had he seen that same look, just before his father had sat him down and told him that his dog Perfidia had died during the night. It did not bode well. Julian loved his mother and father dearly; they were gentlefolk, simple farmers, and they loved him; he knew that. The saddest thing he had ever had to do was tell them he had signed up to join the RAF and would soon be leaving them. That broke their hearts, but they realised they should not stand in his way if Julian wanted to do that. As a farmer, Julian was exempt from conscription. But he would not allow an agricultural dispensation to stop him from serving his country.

'We are not your real parents,' said Hilda reluctantly, uncertain about how he would react. 'We adopted you when you were very young.'

'Adopted?' he exclaimed. 'But I don't understand. How? I have lived here for as far back as I can recall. I don't remember anything else, or anybody else come to that.'

'You were just one year old when we...' Hilda hastily added.

'Oh, I see,' replied Julian. He went quiet for a few moments while his brain laced together the various disparate elements of this confusing revelation into one cohesive thought. It caught him completely unaware, but he wondered if it was that important now.

'So, does it really matter?' he asked. 'You are my parents. You are all I know, the ones I love. Whoever my other parents were, they obviously did not want me, and you obviously did, so is there any more to be said?' It was all very matter-of-fact, more than Hilda and Harry could have hoped for. They were expecting some remonstration for the secret they had kept from him for so long, but none was forthcoming.

Julian cared passionately for many things, but he was a pragmatist, not someone to dwell on what had gone before. He was more concerned with what was happening now and what might happen in the future - not what had happened in the past. Hilda and Harry were heartened by the knowledge that he did not believe they had kept the secret from him for no reason other than his knowing would have served no purpose at the time.

'Do you want to know the details? Asked Hilda. 'It is only right that you should know if that is what you want, but it is up to you.'

Julian rose from the table, walked over to the window, and gazed out on the courtyard scene he had grown up with, all he had ever known. A few chickens and ducks were fluttering about, and he could see the cows in the meadow just the other side of the lane, happily chewing the cud. It all seemed so peaceful and idyllic. In the arable field just beyond, for as far as the eye could see, were the lilac-coloured flowers of the new potatoes just peeping through. Yet behind the bucolic tranquillity, a world war was played out, one in which thousands of people had already been killed. Many more were probably being killed at that very moment - somewhere. And yet here, right now, it was a warm, quiet summer's day, and now there was this revelation, the last thing he could have expected. The entire world seemed to be in chaos.

Julian turned around. 'Yes, maybe I should know. It will probably make no difference now, but....' He didn't finish the sentence, letting the words remain unspoken.

Hilda took a deep breath, and Julian turned back to continue gazing out the window.

'Your mother... Madeleine Clanford was her name, she was a lovely lady, and we got to know her really well over the years she visited us... you.' Julian listened intently as Hilda recounted the story. Harry sat quietly and said nothing; any pain he may have felt, he kept to himself; that was his way. Julian should have noticed the subtle reservation in the context of Hilda's account, words unspoken - just out of sight, but he didn't, not straight away. After Hilda finished telling the story, she said, 'Julian, we love you more than all the world.'

Julian turned to look at his parents, 'So she did visit me?'

'Yes, she came here almost every week for three years. Seeing you for just a few hours each week brought her so much joy. Even then, she had to hold back and not allow herself to become too attached because she knew it could never become anything more than just a friendship.'

'But why didn't I know who she was?'

'Madeleine insisted we didn't tell you. You thought she was just a friend of ours that came to visit us, but really she was coming to watch you grow up.'

'But weren't you afraid that maybe one day she would come and say she wanted me back?'

'Yes, we had thought of that, but as I said, she was a lovely lady and honourable, and we were your legally adopted parents, so we thought it would do no harm. We had what we had never had, a son, and she had what she needed, which was the opportunity to see you. This would have been denied her under any other circumstances. It seemed to work, and there was never a problem until...'

'Are they still alive?' interrupted Julian. Hilda went quiet momentarily, looking at Harry and then back at Julian.

'Joshua Clanford is still alive, but he is not your father... Suddenly for no apparent reason, Madeleine stopped visiting you. Then she sent us a note saying that Joshua had found out about the meetings and had forbidden her from making any further visits. So now, Madeleine had no contact with either of her children. Just over a year later, we heard she had committed suicide. Madeleine sent us a note on the day she died... It said she could not go on not seeing you anymore, so her life was over. She thanked us for all we had done and asked that we always look after you.

Julian said nothing for a few moments.

'And my real father? Did she say who he was?'

'No, she never did.'

Prospect Road: Chapter Twelve
written by
Anthony Theodore Clackle
Julian's and Joshua's story

Julian left the only home he had ever known and went off to war. Except for a few odd weekends and one other specific occasion, he did not return until after the hostilities ended in 1945. Julian fought a long, challenging, and ferocious Battle of Britain in 1940. Four months of non-stop attrition took the lives of nearly all his friends and many pilots he never even got to know properly. He felt old and weary at twenty-two, when boys aged eighteen had joined up, learned to fly, gone to the local pub for their first pint and a singsong and were dead within three months.

He often lay in bed and wondered why it was that he had managed to survive nearly five bitter years of conflict when so many others had perished. Had he been granted this reprieve for a reason? He didn't know – he thanked God daily for his deliverance. By the war's end, he had been promoted on three occasions. But he couldn't help but wonder if this was due almost entirely to him not suffering the misfortune of being killed in action. That constant thought took the edge off the achievement in his mind.

Tragically, neither Hilda nor Harry survived the war and would never see him proudly wearing his wing commander's uniform. They were killed in the last German air raid over London in 1941 when a lost bomber plane had fatefully dumped its payload on their farm in the countryside. So, all the people through which Julian might have been able to find his birth father had been severed, all bar one.

After the war ended, Julian tried to contact his father. He wrote to Joshua Clanford several times, but oddly, he never received a reply. Then one day, in December 1949, Joshua sent him a letter asking to see him. They arranged a meeting at Joshua's house in London.

When Julian was ushered into Joshua's drawing room, he was confronted by the sight of an old man now imprisoned in a wheelchair. He looked very much as if he were not long for this world. By Julian's calculations, he was still only about sixty years of age, but he appeared nearer to a hundred, such were his infirmities. It was hard to tell for sure because the curtains had been drawn tightly. The only light in the room came from the flames of the open fire and the shimmering glow from the candles carefully placed around the room.

There was an overpowering stench of putrid urine in the air. Somebody, presumably Joshua's nurse, had endeavoured to neutralise by placing large bowls of freshly crushed English lavender and Jasmin about the room. This, if anything, only made the problem worse. The stomach-wrenching sweet yet rancid aroma brought back bitter images of a horrific episode from Julian's past. Memories he wished he could erase from his brain but never would.

The incident happened while he had been based at RAF Tangmere in Sussex, just outside Chichester, in 1943. He had to watch one of his closest friends dying, trapped in his burning Spitfire, which had crashed in a field of rotting cabbages to one side of the runway. Try as he might, he could not get close to the plane and could not save his comrade from the blazing inferno. He had no choice but to stand, watch, and listen to his friend screaming in agony as he was slowly burnt to death. All the while, he was inhaling the smell of the decomposing vegetation intermingled with the acrid stench of burning flesh and oil and, bizarrely from somewhere else, the aroma of Lavender. It would remain in his memory forever.

Initially, Joshua's face appeared to be moving, but only when Julian drew closer did he realise why. His bloated features were heavily pockmarked and inflamed, covered in erupting pustules, many of which oozed a greenish pus. His nurse, who never left his side, carefully wiped away the discharge with a small towel and dabbed cream, some form of antiseptic, onto the sores. Joshua's hands were also bloated and riddled with arthritis, his fingers the shape of small bananas.

'I like to sit in the candlelight, and do you know why,' he asked, pausing? It was obviously a rhetorical question; he understood the value of timing.

Julian did not answer.

'It enhances my enigmatic charm... my charisma,' continued Joshua, 'complimentary lighting is so important, don't you think?'

Julian still said nothing. He thought if he remained quiet, Joshua would ramble on and maybe tell him something relevant.

Joshua laughed croakingly at his self-deprecating quip.

The nurse smiled, happy to see her patient laugh.

'I commend you for your gracious manners, sir, and your patience, fortitude and intellect...' He paused briefly to see if Julian would react, but he did not. 'I am jesting with you, dear fellow. Nothing could enhance my appearance. I am as ugly as a gargoyle sucking lemons and have all the charm of the plague.'

Julian smiled guardedly at Joshua's remark. It was not what he was expecting.

Joshua beckoned to Julian to take a chair, and Julian sat down.

'So why are you here, boy?' asked Joshua, trying to smile.

'Because you invited me and because I want to know about my real parents, and you are the only person who knows anything about them.'

'I will tell you what I know, but I doubt it will be of any comfort if that is what you seek.'

Julian said nothing.

Joshua explained what had happened over thirty years ago and how Madeleine had betrayed him with another man. But Julian had his own version of this account, one he had lived with for many years and preferred to believe was nearer to the truth. Julian could not believe the lies he was being fed. He thought that syphilis had probably distorted the facts in Joshua's brain, just as leprosy had disfigured his face. This was just more bile that he wanted to leave behind to fester and thrive after he had gone.

After he'd finished retelling the story, Joshua took a tiny sip of the water by his side and looked directly at Julian.

'Leave us, woman,' he croaked abruptly to his nurse. She obediently left the room. Possibly, she had become conditioned to his harsh mannerisms and was blessed with a forgiving nature. More likely, however - was she was content to endure them because of the remuneration she was receiving.

'You are a fine-looking man, Julian Clackle,' remarked Joshua. 'Looking at you now, I realise I may have been a little rash in allowing you to be adopted. I should have been more forthright and kept you and thrown your mother out, but she insisted.' He was lying, but that is the prerogative of the old and the dying. One of the last acts of contrary defiance they are still capable of. One they choose to exercise if they so desperately desire bitterness and uncertainty to live on after they have departed.

'But you weren't my father. I thought that was the problem all along,' said Julian.

'Maybe, maybe not. We'll never know now, will we?'

'My mother killed herself because of what you did.'

'I didn't do anything. Your mother killed herself because she could not be with him. She didn't care about you or me.'

'That's not how I heard it,' replied Julian defensively.

'Everybody tells the same story about the same event from a slightly unique perspective, and each version will differ slightly from all the others. Isn't that the way of the world?'

Joshua took a deep breath and continued. 'Put ten men in a circle, stick an ugly naked old hag in the middle, and ask them to describe not only what they can see but also what they cannot see. I wager you that each man will describe her slightly differently depending on where exactly they are standing. Those who see her hideousness will describe her exactly as they see her.

Those whose view is partially obscured – will describe what they can see. With a generosity of heart, they imagine what they cannot see, believing it to be the truth. But not with any intention to mislead. Reality is the natural declension of truth. Such are the vagaries of honesty. Isn't that what is happening here? Truth is nothing more than an illusion that changes when seen from a different viewpoint. You will see that for yourself one day.'

Joshua tried to look up at Julian, waiting for his reply.

'I only want to find my father, my real father, the man who loved my mother... your wife.'

'But maybe I am your father,' said Joshua. He was enjoying this moment, tormenting Julian. It was probably the only mental activity he had left in which he could indulge himself now he was housebound and confined to a wheelchair. His days of decadence and debauchery - all a hazy half-forgotten memory now. All that remained for Joshua - to pass the time of day was something to taunt Julian with - something he knew, but Julian did not.

'No, you are not my father. I would know if you were. All that you have told me is a lie. My father is…' He paused. 'I don't know. Only you know that.' He looked bewildered. 'And if you don't tell me…'

'Drew,' interrupted Joshua, 'Gideon Drew, that is your father's name. The mysterious Gideon Drew who ruined all our lives.'

Joshua sighed, taking a deep breath and wheezing a little. 'This man, the one you have been searching for, but for one reason or another have been unable to find…'

'Yes,' said Julian, half expecting a startling revelation.

'Well, maybe, just possibly, he no longer exists. Have you thought about that?'

'What do you mean?' asked Julian.

'Well, you've said you can't find any trace of him, so what does that mean? You tell me. I never knowingly met him, and when I did, he was masquerading as somebody else. I only wish your mother had never met him, and if she were alive today, I wager she would rue the day she did. That was the worst day of her life.'

'I would have thought that was the day she committed suicide,' replied Julian bitterly.

'That was caused by Drew,' retorted Joshua.

'The way I heard it, you forced Madeleine to give up my sister and me for adoption because you were not our father. When you found out she was visiting me at my adoptive parents, you stopped that as well… That sounds like a convincing reason to blame you for her death.'

'That's all lies.'

'Did you know I married Rosemary?' asked Julian.

'What!' exclaimed Joshua, sounding genuinely surprised.

'I married my sister, Rosemary, because I didn't know who she was when I met her, and we had a son.'

Joshua was too stunned to say anything.

'That was your fault as well,' said Julian, 'placing us with two different families and ensuring they never met. I don't know how you did that, but that was the result.'

'That was nothing to do with me. Madeleine dealt with the adoptions, not me,' pleased Joshua.

'Adoption that you forced her to arrange. You were in control. You were always in control.'

'Ahhhh!' Joshua screeched. 'Get my nurse. I need some ointment on my face.' Joshua appeared to be in some distress.

'In pain, are you?' asked Julian quietly without emotion.

'Yes, excruciating pain all the time.' Julian smiled very discreetly.

'He's crippled, you know, in constant pain and deformed, all because I didn't know who I had fallen in love with.'

'Who's fucking crippled?' mumbled Joshua, now distressed and confused.

'My son, Anthony Clackle, that's who.'

'That's not my fault either,' said Joshua. 'Get my nurse!' he demanded again, but Julian took no notice.

'I think it is – I believe everything is your fault. Somehow you have brought this all down on your own head. Now is the time of retribution for what you have done. Fortuitously, I am here to witness you suffer the agony you so rightfully deserve for your sins.'

'Believe what you like!' shouted Joshua, wincing in agony. 'You're no fucking angel… killed many innocent women and children during the war, I bet. I saw what your lot did to Dresden - that was evil personified in every form imaginable, a hundred thousand innocent people burnt to death. At least I never killed anybody.' Julian ignored the unwarranted taunt.

'Have you sorted out their kith and kin and asked for their forgiveness? No, I warrant you have not?' croaked Joshua, his voice now a low, pitiful rumble.

'Why have you caused so much pain and sorrow to so many people? That's what I would like to know?' asked Julian.

'Who do you speak off?'

'Well, you are dying horribly to start with - of something that smells utterly revolting and looks disgusting, but that is of no consequence. But my mother – your wife committed suicide, my son is physically deformed, your partner and his wife both died horribly in Africa, your second wife drowned at sea, Freddie committed suicide under strange circumstances, shall I go on?'

'I told you, none of this is my fault,' replied Joshua, that is all of Gideon's making.'

'But why would he do that?'

'Because he can.'

'Because he can!' repeated Julian, sounding confused, 'what does that mean?'

'One day, you will find out it wasn't me.'

'I don't believe you,' said Julian.

'That's up to you. I don't care anymore.'

'I don't think you ever cared for anybody except yourself.'

'Get me that fucking nurse,' shouted Joshua again. His face appeared to have erupted, with pus now oozing from every boil.

'Can you go now,' pleaded Joshua, 'and leave a dying man in peace?'

Julian smiled at Joshua's discomfort, taking pleasure in the moment; he knew this moment would never come again. He stood up, walked to the door, opened it, and beckoned the nurse to return. He turned around to Joshua. 'I will find him one day, and when I do, I will know the truth, and if you are responsible, I will wish you to hell.'

'Too late. I'm already there, old bean,' replied Joshua grinning with self-satisfaction at his curt reply.

'Not yet, you're not,' said Julian, 'not yet.'

'Will you find him,' asked Joshua? 'I doubt it, and let me give you one last piece of advice.' He slowly lifted his head once more with every ounce of strength he could muster to look at Julian. The glow of the candlelight threw a soft, creamy light over Joshua's face. It highlighted the grotesque, gargoylian features that Julian could now clearly see had taken over his whole body. Joshua coughed, and blood dripped into his handkerchief. 'Be careful what you wish for, boy, be very, very careful, for you may find things you wished you hadn't found, things you couldn't have dreamt of in your worst nightmare.'

His head slumped forward as he fell into a deep sleep. The nurse smiled at Julian as if to say, 'You'll get no more from him today,' so Julian left Joshua's house, never to return.

Joshua died a few days later in excruciating agony, possessed by a demon right up to the end. He repeatedly screamed the same phrase, 'You may never take my soul,' until his last breath. One more part of Gideon's plan had been concluded.

Julian continued his search for Gideon Drew.

Chapter 17
June 1983

And there the story ended, but Blake could not sleep that night and lay awake for many hours in the darkness, deep in thought.

The next day at the office was as busy as ever with the Chapter Room's planned release in the United States. The developments mentioned in the Prospect Road manuscript he had read the night before now pushed firmly to the back of his mind.

The day seemed to roar away from him, especially just after two o'clock when the New York publisher's office opened. Then just after three, he had a telephone call from Catherine, which was a little unusual. He half expected her to say his mother had rung and she was coming over for a few days, but she hadn't. She had died suddenly earlier that morning. At first, it didn't seem to have any effect; the commotion in the office was misdirecting his sensory awareness. His brain was running at full capacity and was simply incapable of processing any more information at that moment... And then, one tiny scrap of information came from an unexpected quarter. Just four little words found their way into the specific part of his brain that dealt with incoming grief, and suddenly it all made sense.

'I am so sorry, Blake, but your mother has died,' whispered Catherine as compassionately as she could. She was only too aware of how it would affect him after reading about Thomas's mother dying in Prospect Road the previous night.

'What!' he cried with disbelief. The first reaction – nearly everyone's first reaction at receiving a message like that was complete disbelief and incredulity. Amid all the din in the office and confusion in his head, he had received a message that refused to register in his brain. It just didn't make any sense at all. It was all gibberish.

'What did you say?'

'I'm sorry,' said Catherine, 'Your mother has died. The police have only just rung me. I thought you would want to know straight away.' Blake did not answer - letting the words sink in and find the place where they would lay for the rest of his life.

'I... I'll leave now. Should be with you in about an hour or so.' The past began to whirl around in his head. Suddenly he was thrust back to Coronation Day. He was dressed up as a little Indian prince, wandering up and down Prospect Road. He could see his mother polishing the Cardinal red front doorstep. Then she was beating him with a cane for some unfathomable reason. He could see the Salvation Army band moving down the road in slow motion, their feet not quite touching the ground but hovering just above it. The music was fading in and out, loud then soft, distant then close, distinct then blurred. He could not understand it; it just didn't seem real.

'Blake! Blake! Are you okay?' He couldn't see where the words were coming from; was it from somebody in the band, he wondered... He turned around to see Jamie standing in front of him. Years ago, back in the 1960s, he had once experimented with the drug LSD, dramatically changing his perception of reality; this was what was happening now... a distortion of everything that generally kept him firmly rooted on the ground.

He knew this was coming - that this moment would happen one day, but still, he could not process the words or make the words make sense. For some reason, he couldn't do anything about it... How did he know? He scrambled around in his brain looking for an explanation, and then he remembered last night, reading the manuscript... That was how he knew. Anthony Clackle had told him in the story. But he hadn't really been taking any notice until now.

Seven days later, Blake buried his mother in the tiny village cemetery. Next to St Mary's Church in Bindle-Dean, close to where his father had been buried four years ago. It was a warm summer's day, and a gentle southerly wind blew through the trees. An idyllic setting for a burial, if there can be such a thing. There must have been at least two dozen of Florence's friends there. Mostly people whom he did not know or didn't think he knew. Some of them must have been from when they lived at Prospect Road and Wadham Road. They all spoke of Florence as if she were a second mother, and they all remembered him.

'Haven't you grown up,' said one of the ladies?

'Yes, I've noticed that' - Blake thought to himself.

'I don't suppose you remember me, but I used to bounce you on my knee. Em...'

'You were a lovely little boy then,' another one of the ladies chipped in. Was that a backhanded way of saying, 'You look like a miserable bugger now,' thought Blake.

Blake wondered about their relationship with his mother, but it didn't matter much now. They were happy to have known her, so she must have brought some joy into their lives, and few of us can say that.

Standing by the graveside, he thought about the manuscript and how it was now effectively up to date for want of a better phrase. Yes, it had predicted a few things might happen, and they had, but was there much further it could go? Could today be a final valediction before the manuscript left his life forever, or at best, ceased to have any effect on it? He hoped so.

Nearly all those attending the service returned to Florence's house afterwards. They enjoyed the traditional fare of cucumber and salmon sandwiches, tea, and sherry, prepared by one of Florence's neighbours, who was also a good friend. Coincidentally, the lady's name was Adrianna, the same name as Mary Drayton's neighbour in the manuscript, but neither Blake nor Catherine felt inclined to mention the letters or the strange premonition to her.

During the afternoon, the ladies, whom Blake scarcely knew, approached him and warmly shook his hand. They thanked him for something unspecified and paid him a compliment about his mother. This was a little unnerving as he became increasingly uncertain about precisely what they were alluding to or thanking him for. Initially, he just acknowledged their comments and remarks. But then he began to feel a little guilty and awkward, such was the emotion and sincerity conveyed in their words. These people were speaking about his mother in a way that Blake had never seen her, but strangely, they had. He began to wonder if there was more to her than he realised. The evidence he was repeatedly confronted with today indicated that maybe there was. He should have made more effort to heal their rift, but he had not. Perhaps she had authored the book to attract his attention. She knew all the facts. Yes, that must be it. That was a possible explanation. She could have been masquerading as Anthony Theodore Clackle, sending him the manuscript, and then coming around adding chapters when he was out. She didn't have a key to his house, but that was of little consequence to a woman like Florence. She was never one to be thwarted by such mundane trivialities as keys or access to a safe.

That would so neatly answer so many of the questions he had. It all seemed so obvious to him now, and it all fitted so nicely into place, which was why he hadn't seen it before. All these so-called ladies were probably in on the plot as well, all part of a conspiracy. They would continue sending him chapters Florence had written before her untimely demise. The only question was why, and that had been answered comprehensively by them all being here today. All except his mother, in a manner of speaking; she apparently was there, but only in spirit. It was all a ploy to get them back together. How devious, how talented he thought, conspiratorial cunning worthy of the Borgias. She was so much more than just a mother, so very much more. But why the praise from her friends, he wondered. That didn't quite fit any pattern he could think of. In fact, the more he thought about it, the more unlikely it became. But he was merely scratching about on the surface when the answer was far more proprietorially profound.

'We must be going now,' said one of the ladies dressed in black. Most of the women present were not dressed so formally, but five were, and she was one of them.

'We've had a lovely day saying goodbye to Flo; she was such a lovely lady.' The four other ladies in black nodded uniformly in agreement, looking not dissimilar to a row of bobbing dogs in the back of an old Ford Cortina. They all smiled - it was perfectly synchronised. A vision of Macbeth's weird sisters, the goddesses of destiny, suddenly sprang into Blake's mind for no reason. He furtively looked around for a boiling cauldron, but there wasn't one. There was also something else odd about them. They were all approximately forty years old, whereas his mother was sixty-three, so they were little more than teenagers when she knew them... It seemed an unusual relationship.

'Thank you for coming and being so kind,' said Blake.

One of them stepped forward. It was clearly pre-arranged, as the other four stayed back, presumably to hear what she would say.

'Hello Blake, I'm Nancy, an old friend of Florence, and I would just like to say that she loved you very much. You do know that, don't you?' Blake did not answer but nodded his head nonchalantly.

'She was hoping to mend things before she…'

'She was a hard woman to understand,' interrupted Blake defensively.

'We all know she could be stubborn. She didn't mince her words or suffer fools, but she has helped nearly every woman in this room one way or another, so we tended to look past the bluff, crusty exterior and see her for who she really was. All that other stuff was just a façade, something to protect her. Sadly, you didn't see what we could see.'

'I tried. I was going to…' started Blake, but continuing was pointless. 'I was going to', 'if only's and 'what ifs' are all so incredibly sad because they all mean the same thing. It's too late to change something that has already happened, and there's never any going back. He followed them to the front door and bade them farewell as they left Flo's house and his life forever. As the evening wore on, the rest of the mourners slowly departed. By seven o'clock, just Blake and Catherine remained to clear things up.

'It's very odd how they spoke of her,' queried Blake, washing the cups as Catherine dried.

'They loved her. She was a good friend,' replied Catherine.

'Was she more, though?' asked Blake.

'More! What do you mean,' asked Catherine?

'I don't know. It's just that I don't remember my mother ever mentioning any of those people.'

'Well, you wouldn't. You hardly ever went to see her, and anyway, you were very young when those ladies knew her.'

'Hmm,' said Blake meditatively. 'Do you think she wrote Prospect Road?'

'I don't know,' replied Catherine. 'It would seem remarkably farsighted of her, especially the premonitory bits. I mean, how could she have predicted her own death when it was due to natural causes. That's still some trick?'

'Hmm,' replied Blake again, weighing up the odds. 'Some people have done it before.'

'Have they?' replied Catherine, unconvinced.

'Right, we'd better be going. The babysitter will be wondering where we are.'

They turned everything off, locked up the house and left his childhood home forever.

Chapter 18
September 1983

With some reluctance, Blake had put the manuscript of Prospect Road into their house safe after collecting it from Martin. There, it had lain undisturbed since the funeral.

A few months had passed, and it was now the beginning of September. The summer had been hot but much cooler now and no longer so humid. Catherine was, at long last, getting the new house into some order. Blake was incredibly busy in London with The Chapter Room's American publication and arrived home late most nights. Martin had rung and left a message saying the rebuilding of his house was progressing well. Hopefully, it would be finished by October, and would they like to come over for dinner and celebrate the completion of work sometime in November?

Max and Claudia had spent the summer exploring their new house and gardens. Finding lots of old sheds and outhouses scattered around the grounds that had not been mentioned when they first visited the property with their parents.

Nothing out of the ordinary had happened since the funeral. Catherine and Blake were both beginning to think that maybe it was more than a coincidence that everything had become less tumultuous since Florence's death. Neither of them had mentioned this stillness for fear of upsetting the karma or, more accurately, this peculiar state of tranquillity that now appeared to exist. Nor had they bothered to read the manuscript for some time. There had been no reason to. Then one day near the end of September, on the 24th, Catherine's birthday, she received a telephone call out of the blue. She picked up the receiver expecting it to be Blake apologising once again for being held up at the office, but it wasn't.

'Hello, Catherine, how are you?' asked the quiet, gentle voice on the other end of the phone.

It was one of those rare pivotal moments in her life. Some weeks earlier, she had been browsing in an old backstreet antique shop in Guildford. She had come across one of those heavily distressed, hand-painted signs with a cliched philosophical platitude burnt into it. The sign read, 'What really matters in this life is not how many times you breathe, but how many times your breath is taken away.' Today her breath was taken away, sucked out as if she were a balloon suddenly deflated. She thought back to that shop and the sign she had not purchased for some reason, although she was deeply moved by the sentiment. For one fleeting moment, air didn't seem to exist anymore. She felt like she was drowning in her own existence but then inhaled, and everything went back to normal – or as normal as she could expect in the circumstances.

She recognised his deep, intoxicating tone but did not answer immediately – she was physically incapable. Her throat was suddenly bone dry, and her brain was racing with confusion. This was not what she was expecting, and she was correspondingly unprepared.

'I'm fine,' she eventually answered in a faltering tone, hinting faintly at a mix of surprise, curiosity, and anticipation. She instinctively knew that even remembering Gideon's name could prove a psychological disadvantage. Nevertheless, she surrendered to his expectant tenor; responding any other way would have been churlish. 'It's Gideon, Gideon Drew, isn't it?' she affirmed in her best attempt at insouciance and vague detachment, but it didn't really work.

'Yes, it is. I'm surprised you remember me after all this time,' replied Gideon quietly. Touché thought Catherine. That will teach me to try to be smart.

He wasn't surprised, but he knew better than to appear over-confident. That would smack of arrogance or, worst still, manipulative contrivance.

She had thought about him almost every day since their last meeting. Maybe for only a minute or two, but he was never that far from her mind.

'It hasn't been that long. It was only Boxing Day when you came to stay,' replied Catherine a little too swiftly. She muttered something incoherent under her breath and nearly bit her lip. That was her second mistake, and she scolded herself in her mind. She could not afford to make a third mistake. It would irredeemably condemn her as nothing more than a moronic gauche schoolgirl out of her depth with the preliminary verbiage of an adolescent relationship. This was not her at all. Christ, what has he done to me, she thought. She should have dithered halfway… at least for a few moments. It would have created a fleeting element of inconsequential indifference, a hint of vague indecision. But now, she had clearly confirmed that she may have been counting the days, hours and possibly the minutes and seconds since the last time they had spoken.

'Yes, that's right,' replied Gideon slowly and quietly - happy to allow the conversation to progress in this strangely casual manner, 'but that was last year, over nine months ago.'

'Yes, it was, wasn't it,' said Catherine. She pretended to sound surprised. 'How time flies. So, tell me, how have you been,' she asked in a courteously innocent tone. 'Blake tells me the book is going really well in America… and Australia, I think… You must be delighted.' That was better, she thought—just a hint of uncertainty.

'I could be happier,' replied Gideon. In everyday conversations, there are always cleverly constructed questions with an opaque agenda. Some are quite deadly, often with no apparent means of escape, but the cleverly fashioned answers are more lethal. Answers that snare the unsuspecting victim into an inescapable trap. Especially when uttered from behind the cloak of invisibility that a telephone conversation affords the enquirer. No chance to gauge the real agenda from a fleeting expression or involuntary gesture.

'Oh,' said Catherine, 'are you unhappy?' Christ, she thought to herself, closing her eyes momentarily in disbelief at her own naivety. I have done it again - invited him to pour his heart out, and we have only spoken for a few moments. Gideon did not answer her question. Catherine was relieved.

'Would you like to go for a drink sometime?' he asked. Having just been excused from one potentially embarrassing moment, Catherine was less inclined to refuse his invitation.

'Blake rarely gets home before ten most nights, so that could be a bit…'

'I meant just you,' interrupted Gideon. It was oddly blunt as if to infer his invitation was obviously just to her anyway. And surely, she must have realised that.

'Oh, I see. I wasn't expecting that. I am a married woman, you know,' replied Catherine being playfully coy, but that was precisely what she expected. She twirled her fingers in her hair girlishly while carefully taking stock of the situation.

'What were you expecting?' enquired Gideon.

'Oh, I don't know. As I said, I wasn't expecting anything. And I definitely wasn't expecting to hear from you, so.' Maybe I just about recovered from the opening catastrophe, thought Catherine. Gently clenching her fist and mouthing a silent 'Yes'.

'It's only a cup of coffee, so will you come,' asked Gideon again?

'When?' said Catherine nonchalantly.

'Whenever suits you.'

'I usually go shopping on Thursdays. The childminder stays all day just in case I get held up, and she picks Max and Claudia up from school, so that would be good.'

'I could meet you in the Lodge Hotel restaurant in Lansbury. Say at one o'clock. Do you know it,' asked Gideon?

'Yes,' replied Catherine. A friend of ours is living there at the moment. His house is being rebuilt after a bizarre accident.'

'Oh, should we meet somewhere else then?'

'No,' replied Catherine. The Lodge Hotel is fine.

'Right,' said Gideon. 'Thursday it is. You must tell me all about this bizarre accident when we meet.'

'I will,' she replied. The conversation went quiet for a moment.

'Till next Thursday then,' said Catherine, filling the void.

'I look forward to it,' replied Gideon. 'Oh, and a happy birthday for today.'

'Thank you,' replied Catherine sounding a little surprised. 'How did you know?'

'You told me at Christmas.'

'Did I?' said Catherine, who had no recollection of mentioning it.

'During one of our conversations over dinner. I have one of those memories for dates and places and things.'

'Oh,' said Catherine, still a little stunned.

'Bye-bye,' said Gideon, once again a little abrupt, but that was his way, not his intention.

'Bye,' said Catherine. She hung up the phone and sat back on the sofa in silence, trying to remember when she had mentioned her birthday, but she couldn't remember any conversation they'd had when the date was mentioned. Then Catherine thought about the lunch date with Gideon… Should she tell Blake? She wondered. Of course, she should; why wouldn't she. And yet, for some reason, she felt the urge not to. But why? she thought, and why was she suddenly having mendacious thoughts she had never experienced before? It was all a little confusing.

Chapter 19

Isabella arrived as usual on Thursday just after ten. After updates on village life and a cup of tea, Isabella started the cleaning. Catherine went upstairs to pick out what *to* wear for her coffee date with Gideon. She tried various outfits, balancing elegance with the practicality of shopping, and eventually settled on something that she thought was attractive but not too obvious. Catherine then addressed the matter of underwear, considering the various options available. But having let her imagination briefly wander into the realm of fantasy, she eventually, after some considerable deliberation, settled on something discreetly appealing but practical. There was no requirement for a sexy but not particularly comfortable G-string today; she was only having coffee.

She left just after eleven and arrived at the Lodge a few minutes after one. She saw Gideon waving from his table as she walked across the car park to the front beer garden's seating area. What he had blurted out at Christmas suddenly flashed through her mind, but she carried on walking anyway, albeit with some slight trepidation. Having mentioned the meeting with Blake, there was no reason for her to feel anxious, but she still did. In fact, Blake was pleased that she had found the time to entertain Gideon. He usually took clients (especially his bestselling authors) to lunch regularly. But he had been overwhelmed with work recently and had neglected this particular publisher-writer responsibility.

Looking as majestic as ever, Gideon gently embraced Catherine and kissed her softly on both cheeks. She could smell the heavily scented cologne on his body. But beyond that, there was something else, something warm, sultry, and aromatic. It momentarily deceived her senses, distorting reality, transporting her to some exotic place, conjuring up the distant sounds of an Arabian marketplace as if by magic. Tingling bells and wisps of marijuana smoke entwined with the beautiful flashing colours of the night. Whirling dervishes danced faster and faster as if they were about to sacrifice their souls into a swirl of infinity to defend their very existence. And all this from just one inhalation of the air surrounding his body, but then maybe that was the intention.

'I am so glad you came,' he stuttered, a little uncharacteristically. There was an unexpected air of vulnerability and nervousness about him that Catherine could not help but find endearing. She forgot any concerns she might have had; his reassuring manner put her instantly at ease. Maybe her recollection of their last meeting, like so many remembrances of things past, was not how it had been; she had simply misread the signs, and her mind had been playing tricks.

Today she could plainly see the difference in their ages. Gideon must have been in his early thirties, according to the occasional comments that Blake had made in passing, but he looked no more than twenty-five. There had to be a portrait tucked away somewhere in an attic, she thought, before berating herself for being so petty. Anyway, Blake had already made the very same comment a few months ago, so it wasn't even original. How little did she know how close to the truth she really was.

She was thirty-nine, happily married, a mother of two children, but getting close to ringing the half-time bell. In the cold light of day, the naivety of her quasi-adolescent infatuation was clearly evident. Christ! She thought, with a tiny stretch of the imagination, and in a bad light, I could pass for his mother, for God's sake. She glanced around at the other diners to see if anyone was watching them, but none were.

Even though she had taken the Lord's name in vain twice in one sentence, for which she quickly admonished herself as a good Catholic, she realised the situation was untenable. The prospect of her and Gideon never being anything more than acquaintances riled her sensibilities; it was an affront to her comprehension of human equality. Nothing more than the tangential oscillation of two diaphanous circles colliding in space.

Why should she be denied the intimate affection of a man she desired just because she had been born at the wrong time? With some reluctance, she let the moment pass.

'Would you like a coffee?' asked Gideon.

Catherine smiled. 'Yes, please. I'll have a skinny latte, thank you.' Gideon went into the restaurant to order the coffee.

Catherine tried to relax and began to think about things to say when he returned.

'One skinny latte,' pronounced Gideon on his return as if there were some agenda to her request.

'I have to watch my figure after two children. I could go to seed very quickly if I'm not careful,' she half-smiled. She wasn't deliberately pitching for a compliment but instantly realised how crass that sounded.

Gideon smiled but did not answer with the hackneyed reply she was half expecting. They both took a sip of coffee in silence.

'Is that espresso?' Catherine asked, looking at Gideon's small black coffee, hastily attempting to fill the void, 'I've always thought espresso was too strong. Blake drinks it that way. I prefer it much weaker. I'm sure it keeps him up at night.' Gideon smiled at the accidental innuendo she had thrown in at the end but said nothing. Catherine realised she was talking in short, monosyllabic spurts, lacking fluidity, bordering precariously on the edge of inane superficiality.

This was harder than she thought it would be. This was not how she usually was. She would have to make a conscious effort to breathe deeper and talk slower.

'Blake likes to read to three or four o'clock in the morning sometimes,' continued Catherine, still a little too hurriedly, 'if he is reading an engaging story. Sometimes I wake up in the morning, and he's still reading – not even bothered to go to sleep. Do you...'

Gideon put his forefinger to his lips and made a gentle shushing sound. Catherine felt slightly embarrassed, realising she had been rambling on like a ditzy schoolgirl with a puerile crush on her teacher. She even thought she was going to blush for a moment. Then she found her brain telling her body, "You are thirty-nine, for Christ's sake. You don't do that kind of adolescent blushing nonsense anymore. Get real."

'Have you ever seen Rosencrantz and Guildenstern are Dead? It's a play by Tom Stoppard,' asked Gideon, interrupting her meandering thoughts. He knew she was somewhere else.

Catherine was a little surprised by the sudden change in the direction of the conversation.

'Yes, once or twice,' she replied guardedly. Unsure where this puzzling diversion was leading. She took another sip of coffee. 'I first saw it just after I left uni... and then again a few years ago, I think, with Blake.'

'What did you make of it,' asked Gideon? It was a rhetorical question – he knew the answer he was expecting. There was an absolute generosity of spirit in the question. It was as if he were trying to bridge the invisible divide between them that only she could see, but he could sense.

'What did I make of it?' she repeated, 'I don't really know, to be honest... Nobody has ever asked me before, so I...' She stopped and thought about this strange question, and her mind began to backtrack to the last performance she had seen three years previously.

'As I recall, I think it was about two off-stage characters from Hamlet, minor characters. They discuss and re-enact various scenes from the play to demonstrate the confusion and loss of morality in life in general and, more specifically, in their lives; a sort of analogy, I suppose. All this is happening while they wait for their scenes to arrive. I guess it was like an alternative view of the Hamlet story to the one the audience sees. The exact opposite, in fact. The view from the other side of the play, if that makes any sense. Two people who can see the play and the audience simultaneously - observing how each reacts to the other. A play within a play about a play, if that doesn't sound too abstruse or pretentious.'

Gideon smiled as a wave of serenity washed over him. He appeared enthralled by Catherine's explication. It was as if he had been searching all his life for a kindred spirit, someone who understood things the way he did, and now, at last, he had found that someone. Somebody who could fulfil that role, that vacancy that had remained unfilled for so long since...

'That makes perfect sense,' he replied. 'Exactly what I thought for so many years, until one day I reread it, and then I found something else, something even more important.' Catherine felt exhilarated. She so enjoyed this feeling of worth and enablement, the sense of intellectual empowerment he so easily conveyed - and instilled in her. Catherine was becoming part of something more, something substantial, something powerful. It engendered a sense of invincibility - immortality that she had never experienced before. She was tantalised by his words, unable to resist the tsunami of verity and actuality sweeping over her body - inhabiting her soul and bewitching her mind.

She had never felt undervalued by Blake, and her life fulfilled everything she had ever dreamed of, but this was entirely different. This involved exploring a region of her mind, an area into which she had never ventured before and probably never thought she would. This was the danger.

'I believe it's about the inevitability of coincidence – chance – fate. Serendipity if you like,' continued Gideon. Slowly ensnaring Catherine into his labyrinthine plan. 'How small decisions can affect the whole of our lives and sometimes beyond. Can you see how that could make a difference?' he asked.

Catherine did not reply, unsure exactly what he was now alluding to.

Gideon continued, 'They could have taken control of events, and the outcome would have been entirely different, instead of which, nearly everybody dies.' Gideon looked at Catherine and smiled for a moment. In an instant, the smile was gone, replaced by something else, and for the first time, she felt a cold shudder of uncertainty run down her spine.

'But then if they didn't die… it wouldn't be Hamlet anymore; it would be something entirely different,' said Catherine.

'Yes, it would, you're right, and that's my point…' Gideon was demonstrative and assertive; he wanted Catherine to understand his feelings. 'But Shakespeare wanted it that way, so that's how it is.'

'Erm,' replied Catherine lamely, still unsure where this was going but certain of one thing. She was now falling inextricably under his spell, intoxicated by the passion of his words.

''I am so sorry, I do blabble on sometimes,' remarked Gideon apologetically, in what was apparently an attempt to lighten the intensity of the conversation.

'Blabble?' said Catherine, smiling, and scrunching up her nose, never having heard the word before.

'Yes, blabble. It's a nonsensical fusion of gabble and blabber. It's a word I made up, but that's what I do... when I'm anxious - when I feel vulnerable.' It was a clever subterfuge, and it worked.

Catherine laughed at Gideon's creation. She muttered the word a couple of times to feel the sound of it ripple over her lips and smiled again.

'So, you are anxious?' said Catherine, sounding surprised, 'I thought I was the anxious one.' They both smiled and took another sip of coffee.

'He only wrote comedies and mediocre drama until his son died, you know. After that, he started writing dark tragedies. The first was Hamlet.'

'I didn't know he had a son,' queried Catherine.

'Hamnet... that was his name, oddly. Died of the plague when he was about eleven years old.' Gideon pronounced the words slowly in an oddly stark, matter-of-fact manner that lacked any depth, feeling or compassion, which surprised Catherine for a second or two. She would have expected such a fact to be conveyed with empathy. But there was nothing, just cold, lifeless, soulless pragmatism.

Gideon continued. 'You see, in a way, we may only have the best tragedies ever written because, by chance or fate, his son died, and then his mindset changed. It was a creative trade-off... To feel, to understand pain and grief, he needed to experience it first-hand. That was the deal he accepted, the deal he did with...'

Catherine thought that was an odd thing to say.

'Had his son lived... then we would probably only have ever known him for comedies, and what a tragedy that would have been.'

They both laughed at the lame witticism.

'Do you think everything in life is a trade-off?' said Catherine.

'Possibly. Maybe a compromise.'

'Between what,' asked Catherine?

'What you want, desire, need, and eventually settle for.'

'Have you settled for something?' asked Catherine.

'Oh yes, I definitely settled for something. Something I want, something I need.' Gideon leaned halfway across the table and kissed Catherine gently on the lips. She did not have the strength to resist. She could feel the warmth of his body bleed into her soul through the conduit of two tongues gently exploring unexplored territory. She could not resist; she did not know how to.

He leaned back slightly and smiled, then continued talking... Catherine could not take her eyes away from his. She needed to understand what was happening.

'In fact, we probably wouldn't have known Shakespeare at all except as an irrelevant footnote in the annals of literature. It would be as if he didn't exist, or existed in a very minor capacity, unlike us...'

'We can't do this,' blurted Catherine pulling back, sitting bolt upright in her chair.

'Do what?' said Gideon, with an expression of childlike innocence.

'This,' Catherine replied, waving her hands in small pope-like gestures. 'Making small talk... talk that always leads somewhere... somewhere I don't wish to go.'

'But we just have,' replied Gideon. 'We can't just go back and pretend it didn't happen. It did. The moment has passed, it is now enshrined in our memories and history forever, and it cannot be erased. Time has moved on, and so have we; that is destiny...'

'But it's wrong on so many levels,' pleaded Catherine. She sounded desperate to redact the moment, but it was no more than a token gesture.

'I must be ten, possibly fifteen years older than you. I'm married, have two children and a lovely house, and my husband is your publisher and...'

'You haven't mentioned love.'

'Love? I don't love you,' replied Catherine abruptly.

'Not me,' replied Gideon quietly. 'Blake... You didn't mention love.'

'Oh, I see,' replied Catherine, suddenly realising her implicit omission. Half her brain processed the comment for a fraction of a second while the other half tried to rationalise its implication. 'Of course, I love Blake. That's a given.'

'Is it?' replied Gideon. 'I would never consider love as a given. It must really be there, not just assumed or taken for granted. You have to see it every day, in a smile, a word, a kiss, or a touch, but it has to be there, or you have absolutely nothing.'

'You don't understand marriage. It's not all wine and roses. There are lots of things that make it work. Boring, mundane, everyday, ordinary things, as well as wonderful things like love. It's a melting pot of many different emotions and...'

'But I do understand it,' interrupted Gideon, 'more than you will ever know. You see, I watched one marriage die, and that tells you so much more about two people being in love.'

Gideon leaned across the table again, gently taking hold of her upper arms. Slowly he drew Catherine closer and kissed her. In a way, she had not been kissed for a long, long time. She could sense the desire in his mouth, feel the strength in his arms, and see the intensity in his eyes. She tried to resist, but her brain was not passing the message to her body.

At that precise moment, the world she knew began to crumble. The next thing she clearly remembered was lying naked in the hotel bedroom, having made love to Gideon for what seemed like days but was, in fact, just a few hours. All that had passed before that moment now seemed very hazy.

She vaguely remembered him kissing every inch of her body and tasting every opening. But perfect clarity was lost in the delirium of ecstasy she had experienced. No, not experienced, she thought, experiencing, for that is what she was doing. This wasn't over. This feeling was constant, insatiable, relentless, and unforgiving. By six o'clock, they had been making love for over four hours without a break, something she had never done before, not even as a teenager. Gideon made love to her in ways that made her feel like she had never actually made love before. She had only been a willing participant in the act of rudimentary sex. This was many things, but never just sex. His strength and stamina had quite astounded her. She never realised the levels of ecstasy she could achieve, the frenzied heights of passion to which she could be taken when wilfully encouraged.

They dressed and went back downstairs to the lobby just after seven, where they kissed and parted with few words. Everything they had to say to each other that day had already been said.

Catherine made her way to her car, still hazy with a miasma of sleepiness that had begun to overwhelm her, still unsure exactly what had happened that afternoon. Before driving off, she lowered the front windows to allow the rushing air to revitalise her senses as she drove home, eventually arriving just after eight. Walking back towards the house, she could feel the gentle aching in her lower back, thighs, and hips. This was because her legs had been apart and manoeuvred into so many unfamiliar positions during the afternoon. Most of the time, they were wrapped around Gideon's waist.

She thought back to Gideon's words about inevitability and chance. She wondered whether this day had been preordained, whether it would have happened no matter what she did. Maybe she had no choice. Perhaps now, this was how her life would be, irrespective of anything that had happened before. She did not have the good fortune of Rosencrantz and Guildenstern - unable to evaluate cause and effect and probable outcome if circumstances changed. But she knew she would have to continue down the path she had taken, no matter what. Nobody could know what could happen, and nobody would know what had happened. She was determined that nothing would change. Her life would continue as before, but now with one glorious additional dimension.

She arrived back home just after eight. Isabella was still there; Blake was evidently running late.

'The children are in bed. I have read them a story and made you lasagne for dinner.' She was very precise in all she did and said. Although Romanian by birth, she had spent several years in Germany and had absorbed some Teutonic mannerisms.

'Do you need me for anything else, Mrs Thornton?' asked Isabella. 'You look like you have had a very hectic day,' she added innocuously. 'I can make you a cup of tea if you wish.'

'No, no, thank you,' replied Catherine more sharply than was actually necessary. 'I'm sorry – I just need to sit down. Thank you very much for today. I will be fine.' Isabella smiled, and Catherine smiled back, a smile which turned into a grin when she thought about what Isabella had said when she first arrived. Yes, it had been a hectic day, one she would remember for an awfully long time. No doubt there would be moments in the following days and weeks ahead when the odd twinge in her thighs would make her smile discreetly to herself again.

Chapter 20

Two weeks later, Blake went to the office as usual. He had removed Prospect Road from the safe while Catherine was still asleep and slipped it into his case. Blake had not mentioned this to her as he wanted to reread the last few chapters unhindered by the constraints of their arrangement. The agreement had only been made to dispel any suspicion that Blake might be secretly writing the new chapters. But since he knew he was not writing the book, it didn't make any difference now. Chapter Ten had filled in a few more gaps. However, one of the central unanswered questions revolved around Gideon Drew, the character in Prospect Road, and his relationship to the novelist of the same name whom Blake now represented. That enigma still intrigued him.

There was also the question of why the mysterious Anthony Clackle had sent him the manuscript but made himself completely uncontactable.

Blake mulled over everything that had happened so far and what had been predicted in the manuscript. Then, while idly gazing out of the train window at the trees frantically rushing by, he suddenly realised something. If he concentrated hard enough, he could see the dense woods just beyond the trees and all that was happening thereabouts. It was as if the train wasn't moving at all. The trees closest to the carriage became a blur, and the harder he concentrated on the woods, the less he could see the trees close to the track. They almost seemed to disappear. That was it, he thought. A bigger picture had been wholly obscured because he was looking too closely at the details.

He made some quick notes in the margin of the script about what had just occurred to him. It made a lot of sense, admittedly in a very abstract manner, but it still made sense to him. He made a mental note to discuss his thoughts with Catherine when he returned home that evening.

It was just after lunchtime when the telephone rang. The house was strangely tranquil as the lull before a storm. Max and Claudia were at school, and Isabella had finished for the day. Catherine was contentedly daydreaming in the conservatory while drinking a glass of wine. Her thoughts were somewhere else entirely. She was utterly unaware of how much her life – all their lives – would change forever once she had taken this call.

She casually reached across to lift the receiver and put it to her ear. Before she could say anything, a voice came on the line. A resonantly evocative tone that she at once recognised.

'Catherine... it's Gideon.'

Catherine said nothing at first. It had been nearly two weeks since that afternoon. Since then, she had heard nothing from him. Even entertaining the nebulous possibility that their brief liaison was nothing more than an overly contrived one-night, no -afternoon stand. Although, a little whimsically, she noted that they had not remained standing for very long. A tiny smile flashed across her face.

For a few moments, her mind flashed back to those few breathtaking hours of passionate rapture. More specifically, to the memory of his naked, sexually aroused body prowling around the bedroom, never taking his eyes off hers. Stalking her like a lion before it pounces on its mesmerised prey – she, the victim, unable to defend herself against the onslaught that would follow. She could remember his long dark mane of hair restlessly flailing as they gyrated in a rhythm of ecstasy. He was possessed of an energy that she found increasingly impossible to match; he was beginning to engulf her body and inveigle her soul, and she was losing all control over what was happening. His constant incantation, a charm-like spell of words she did not recognise. They exsanguinated every other thought from her mind. Her body felt as if it had been flensed to the bones with enchantment as a sense of declension of her very being began to overwhelm her. It had all become very confusing as she became lost in the euphoria of the illicit assignation.

She could remember drifting in and out of semi-consciousness. A state of mind that had not been artificially induced by drink or drugs but by the remorseless demand on her body's energy reserves. She had never experienced anything as intense before, not even when giving birth to her children.

After what they had experienced that afternoon, she found it impossible to believe he would not want to see her again. She knew she should not see him, but the gravitational magnetism pulled her into the centre of something she could not understand. Something dark and evil, a centrifugal force swirling faster and faster and far too strong for her to resist. As the moth is inescapably drawn to the naked flame and is eventually burnt to death, she also felt the inexorable inevitability of the vortex she was being drawn into.

Her mind raced in circles, thinking about what had been said the last time they met. Christ, she thought, I'm already thinking about sex, and he's only spoken three words. All these thoughts passed in a fraction of a second...

'Gideon... It's nice to hear from you. How are you?' Unsure of the protocol under these circumstances, she thought it best to appear semi-formal until she could evaluate the reason for his call. For all she knew, he could be ringing to speak to Blake. But then again, he would also know Blake would be in the office at that time of day, so maybe not.

'I was wondering if we could...'

'What!' interjected Catherine in a half-hearted attempt to chastise him. 'You tell me you love me, take me to a hotel, fuck my brains out all afternoon and leave me so exhausted I can hardly walk, and then you ignore me for weeks and have the nerve to...' She realised she didn't know what he was going to say next.

'I am sorry I didn't call, but I love you, Catherine, and I need to see you again. I need to explain.'

Some words do take your breath away, and these did. They took the air from Catherine's body and the anger from her heart.

'Explain what?' asked Catherine, settling down a little after her initial outburst.

'I want to hold you in my arms and feel your naked body beneath me. I want to make love to you all day and all night, forever...'

The words hung in the air. Catherine knew what they would mean, and more than anything else, she wanted the same - to be with him again to the exclusion of all others. 'You haven't rung me for nearly two weeks, and I thought... I thought I was just one of your dilettante dalliances, and that was it.' She had vented her anger at being ignored, but it was a submissive retort. It lacked the necessary fiery venom essential to validate the intent.

'I understand how you feel completely, and it wasn't a casual fling; I...' He paused to compose himself before speaking, but now a little slower than before. It would give Catherine time to process the depth and honesty of his words.

'I took advantage of our relationship, and Blake's kindness and generosity, and I thrust myself onto you and your family, and I am sorry...' It sounded like a genuine act of contrition for the sin of desire. Inexcusably, the word thrust instantly excited Catherine. Inwardly, she tried to rebuke herself for her puerile reaction but failed miserably. Not since her schooldays had such an innocuous phrase had such an animalistic effect on her. It was childish, the misinterpretation of an entirely innocent remark that would have produced a giggle from an adolescent teenager - but not from a mature woman with two children. She was embarrassed but could also feel a strange tingling in her pelvic region. It was not something she had often experienced, but she could feel it now... and she liked it.

Gideon continued. 'I felt guilty for betraying Blake and taking advantage of you. I wanted to leave you alone for a while to let you decide whether we should stop this now or continue.'

'I want to see you and be with you,' replied Catherine without taking a breath. There was no hint of hesitation or indecision; this was what she wanted, and she wanted it now.

And so, the affair began...

After a few months, they had settled into a regular routine. They would meet at 'Clanford', Gideon's new house. In reality, it wasn't a house, more a palatial mansion set in thirty acres of land and ornamental gardens. It was just a twenty-minute drive from Blake and Catherine's house. The estate was once owned by Joshua Clanford, the original partner in her husband's firm Clanford and Fox when the company was formed in 1911. Joshua had died many years ago, and the house had stood empty for a long time. Gideon had bought the house just over nine months ago and restored it to its original Edwardian glory. He had moved one step closer to his goal; ironically, it was also one step closer to oblivion and nothingness. They would meet every Tuesday and Thursday afternoon at one o'clock and spend the rest of the day eating, drinking champagne, dancing, and making love.

Isabella stayed late both days to collect the children from school. Blake rarely arrived home much before eight in the evening.

Sometimes he would return even later if they had a marketing, media, and development meeting, which happened twice a month, generally on a Thursday. These usually ran on for a few hours after the office had closed.

Life was exciting again for Catherine, and she seemed to have completely forgotten how much in love with Blake she once was. It was as if Gideon had cast a spell over her. The relentless delirium of the affair continued for six months. Until one day, just moments before reaching orgasm while riding on top of Gideon, she shouted at the top of her voice, 'We're having a baby!' She was so overjoyed at making the announcement and simultaneously climaxing that she didn't notice the subtle change of expression on Gideon's face. The pleasure he was now experiencing was beyond Catherine's comprehension.

She gently uncoupled herself from Gideon. They embraced passionately for a few minutes before falling back on the bed to rest.

'That's wonderful news,' said Gideon. 'Just what we were waiting for. That completes everything.'

'Yes, it does,' replied Catherine, unaware of precisely what Gideon was referring to.

'What shall we call the baby,' asked Catherine, lighting a cigarette? She never used to smoke but had started to in his company; it was necessary.

Gideon thought for a moment, staring languidly at the ceiling, seeing only visions he could see. 'Mephisto. I want to call him Mephisto. It commands respect. I had a distant relationship with a man of the same name many years ago; he helped me greatly when times were hard.' He thought about his first meeting and their contract, now nearing completion. He could still extend it for another fifty years if he played his cards carefully. A smile touched his lips, but Catherine didn't see it. She was also staring at the ornately plastered ceiling and watching the painted cherubs playing innocently in a heavenly setting.

'You've never mentioned that before,' said Catherine wistfully.

'It was when I was a struggling writer.'

'Oh, I see… Mephisto,' said Catherine, trying the name out to see how it felt. 'I've never heard that name before.'

'It has a Greek origin.'

'I don't remember you ever mentioning any of your family before,' said Catherine.

'That's because they're all dead now.' Gideon's reply was oddly blunt, almost abrasive as if he were unconcerned by their existence.

'Oh,' said Catherine apologetically. 'I am sorry. I didn't realise.'

'Nothing to apologise for,' said Gideon, still gazing upwards with an odd expression, somewhere between immense satisfaction and bitter regret.

'And if it is a girl?' asked Catherine reluctantly, now a little wary about what name Gideon might propose.

'Not likely, but I will leave it to you if it is. I have always loved the name, Alicia...' He paused for a few moments as some old memories crossed his mind. 'That's another family name that's close to my heart.' A tear formed in the corner of his eye, but Catherine never saw it.

'That's a lovely name.'

'But it will be a boy, I am sure of that,' replied Gideon.

'Oh,' said Catherine, a little surprised. 'Right. I should break the news to Blake and start making arrangements.'

It was an explicit declaration of intent. Catherine paused momentarily to think about whether she should say what she was thinking, but before she knew what had happened, the words had passed her lips.

'Should we move in together?' It came out sounding a little sheepish, and she wished she had thought about it a little longer, possibly making it sound less passive. It had the unattractive ring of desperation about it, which was not her usual manner.

'Oh, I hadn't thought about that,' replied Gideon, slightly surprised.

Catherine was a little taken back at his reply. She had been labouring under the misapprehension that moving in together was an inevitability, a natural progression. In reality, it had never really been on the agenda. For a moment, she wondered whether she had completely misread the signals. Her mind began to race with uncertainty and confusion. This unexpected scenario had not been factored into the plan she had formulated.

'You could move in here, I suppose,' continued Gideon with a smile after what seemed an interminable pause. His qualified suggestion alleviated her immediate concerns, but she could still detect an almost infinitesimal hint of reservation in his tone.

'Yes,' replied Catherine, 'that would be wonderful; this is an amazing house. The children...' Then she stopped, suddenly realising that she had two other children who had slipped her mind... This was all becoming a little unreal. There were so many more things to consider in this complicated proposal that she had not foreseen. There was also Blake and how he would react to all of this.

'How far have you gone with this?' asked Gideon.

'How far?' she replied, unsure what he was referring to. It seemed an odd question.

'The baby. How far gone is he - are you?'

'You're absolutely sure it's a boy then,' replied Catherine, smiling with just the tiniest hint of surprise.

'Absolutely. I have knowledge of these things,' he replied enigmatically.

'Do you?' she replied curiously. 'Nearly three months.'

'Three months!' exclaimed Gideon. 'Why didn't you mention it earlier?'

'I needed to be sure.'

'And is it...?' He stopped.

'Yes, it is yours,' answered Catherine. 'We, Blake and I, haven't had sex since your bloody book went ballistic last year.' This wasn't strictly true, but near enough. 'Blake is too tired to do anything by the time he gets home except sleep.' She smiled at Gideon; she wasn't really blaming him for anything.

'I will have to send him another manuscript to keep him busy,' said Gideon, smirking.

'Yes, you do that,' whispered Catherine, rolling over to perch herself back on top of Gideon. 'And in the meantime...' Slowly, Catherine began to move up and down on Gideon's manhood. Smiling with all the enraptured passion of a woman wholly entranced by the joy and fulfilment of the moment. Oblivious to the malevolent clouds jostling for position on the horizon.

Chapter 21

Catherine arrived back home at just after seven-thirty. Isabella had already put the children to bed and prepared a simple spaghetti Bolognese for dinner.

'Hi Issy,' said Catherine. 'Is everything OK?'

'No problem, Mrs Thornton. Everything fine.'

'Good, good,' replied Catherine, smiling to herself for no apparent reason.

'Are the shopping bags in the car?' asked Isabella curiously, noticing that Catherine had not brought them in with her.

'Oh no,' replied Catherine, suddenly realising her oversight. 'I... I met an old friend I hadn't seen for ages, and we had some lunch and got chatting, you know, and I never got around to it. I'll get something tomorrow. It doesn't matter.' Such fleetness of mind was occasionally necessary to preserve the deception, but it became a little more complicated each time. She usually picked up some shopping on the way home to support her Thursday alibi, but today she forgot. Everything she and Gideon had said about the proposed change in living arrangements was still running around in her head.

'I understand, Mrs Thornton.'

'Catherine,' replied Catherine. 'Please call me Catherine. Mrs Thornton sounds so formal. It's as if... as if we weren't friends, but we are friends, aren't we?' asked Catherine plaintively. Catherine had asked her many times before to call her by her given name but to no avail. Isabella preferred the detachment of formality.

'Yes, of course, we are,' replied Isabella, smiling apprehensively. The old maxim about familiarity breeding contempt was never far from her mind.

Catherine had never explicitly mentioned friendship before; it had been taken for granted. Catherine smiled back.

'So, you will remember,' asked Catherine? She spoke with casual conviction, a temperament undoubtedly partly brought about by the earlier consumption of the best part of a bottle of Madame Clicquot's magical elixir of life. Champagne invariably deceived her brain into believing circumstances were far more convivial than they really were. Conventional social barriers would vanish until sobriety and reality eventually returned, which was the case today. But she wasn't so much as drunk on the alcohol as she was elated with her vision of the future—however much of a delusion that might have been.

It was an odd question, thought Isabella. Of course, they were friends. But there still had to be clearly visible demarcation lines when one person bought the time of another, no matter how close the relationship was. It was necessary - essential, in fact, for the borders to exist; it established distinct parameters for each of their responsibilities. No ambiguity, no inconsistencies, and therefore no misunderstandings. But today, for whatever reason, Catherine wanted something different. The introduction of distortion and blurred obscurity on the borders, a touch of undefinable greyness around the edges. Calling Mrs Thornton - Catherine seemed inappropriate, but nevertheless, if that was what she wanted…

'I will try to remember,' said Isabella.

'Good,' replied Catherine, 'good.' She appeared to be pleased that they had come to an understanding.

As Catherine disappeared into the walk-in-larder, Isabella started to put her coat on.

'Drink before you go?' Catherine asked, suddenly reappearing, brandishing a bottle of Pinot Grigio she had liberated from the wine cooler. She wanted to continue enjoying the ecstatic euphoria she was experiencing at that moment - for a little longer. 'It's icy cold…' Catherine added enticingly - gently waving the Pinot at Isabella.

'Yes, that would be nice,' replied Isabella after a few moment's deliberation. She was a little surprised at the gesture, as Catherine usually let her go the moment she arrived back home. She removed her coat, placed it on the chair, and sat at the table. Catherine poured her a large glass of wine and a small one for herself but remained standing, leaning against the sink unit.

'To… life,' toasted Catherine. 'To the love of life.'

Still feeling like she should be a little restrained, Isabella picked up her glass and leaned over to clink it against Catherine's. 'To the love of life.'

'You seem very cheerful today,' asked Isabella.

'I am. All my plans are slowly coming together.' She turned to look out of the window into the garden. 'There will be a few changes soon, but…' She thought for a moment and took another sip of wine. 'It will all be for the better.' She turned back again to face Isabella and smiled.

'I am glad, replied Isabella.' I am happy that everything is going well for you.' Catherine had never really listened to the Germanic inflection in Isabella's voice before. The intonation, emphasis and nuance were all wrong, but her dedication, reliability and honesty were beyond question. She had been their children's nanny, as well as their cleaner and an occasional cook since they had moved to the new house back in early 1983. Max and Claudia had taken to her at once, as had Blake and Catherine.

'If I tell you something, can we keep it between ourselves?' asked Catherine guardedly.

Isabella did not answer straight away but took another sip of the Pinot. 'A secret?' she asked inquisitively but tempered with a distinct hint of reservation.

'Yes,' replied Catherine.

'From whom,' enquired Isabella, whispering over the rim of her wine glass? There was a definite hint of restraint in her tone. The confidant had now become the cautious inquisitor.

'Everybody,' replied Catherine, 'for now,' she added as a qualification.

'Is it important?' asked Isabella with a further hint of caution.

'Very much so,' said Catherine.

Isabella took another sip of wine and put the glass on the table.

'Would it jeopardise my position,' asked Isabella evermore cautiously? Measured restraint, the sagacious Germanic influence now coming further into play. She was as curious as any woman would be in a similar position. Being entrusted with a confidence would strengthen the bond between employer and employee, but with any secret comes immense responsibility and an element of risk. Once you were partnered to a conspiracy, there was an implicit mutual declaration of intent to deceive. There would never be any going back to the way things were before. The dynamics of a relationship change from that point forward, and whatever die had been cast could not be uncast. All this weighed heavily on her mind. She wondered whether she may have overthought this simple request far beyond its material significance. Possibly she had, perhaps not, but she had been asked once before to keep a secret, and it had not ended well.

'No, not at all,' said Catherine leaning over and refilling Isabella's glass while waiting nervously for her reply. She also wondered whether she may have disturbed the delicately balanced symmetry between them and inadvertently compromised their relationship. But the balance was now tipped, and that point had been passed. The question was already answered. If Isabella declined to answer, she would still, forever, be in possession of knowledge about some unspecified information and, therefore, an accomplice by default to something - despite being unaware of what precisely she was an accomplice to. A paradoxical trap from which there was no escape.

'You can tell me if you wish,' replied Isabella reluctantly. She reasoned that on the balance of probability, it was more likely than not to be something innocuous and of no consequence.

Catherine did not answer straight away; she was carefully choreographing what she was about to say so that the salient facts were unveiled in the correct order of significance. How she revealed and conveyed what she would say was as important as what she was about to say. She took another sip of wine and carefully placed the glass back on the worktop.

'I'm having another baby.' She waited for Isabella's reaction.

'Oh!' exclaimed Isabella loudly,' her lips drifting apart in astonishment before her face lit up in relief and joy. 'That is absolutely marvellous. I am so happy for you, for you and for Mr Thornton, and for Max and Claudia. You are all so fortunate. This will be a lovely time for you all. I am so, so...'

Isabella could not get the words out, so she jumped up from her chair and hugged Catherine, completely overwhelmed with emotion. Catherine automatically responded, relieved she had told someone she could trust explicitly.

'So how far pregnant are you?' asked Isabella, briefly taking hold of Catherine's hands and squeezing them affectionately.

'Three months,' replied Catherine, smiling as she tried to figure out which day it had been and where they were. They both went back to sit down at the kitchen table.

'So, it will be here for...'

'There's a little more,' interrupted Catherine, looking slightly pensive but believing the time was right.

'More?' said Isabella, still looking overjoyed at the news. 'Don't tell me… It's twins, yes? If you worried about me, I could help you with them; babies not a problem. I will be here to help you whenever you need me, no matter what.'

'This could be a problem,' muttered Catherine.

Isabella's expression changed. 'A   problem? Oh, I am sorry…' Her hands shot across the table to grasp hold of Catherine's again, holding them both tightly. 'We can deal with this together if you want. Now I understand why a secret.'

'No, I don't think you do,' said Catherine hesitantly.

'So, what is problem,' asked Isabella? Catherine didn't answer immediately but just gazed at Isabella for a few moments. She was studying the genuine concern in how she spoke and looked while trying to figure out if that would change immeasurably, even irretrievably, once she had said what she was about to say.

'Blake is not the father.'

'I'm sorry,' said Isabella, unsure if she had just heard what she thought she heard.

'I said, Blake is not the father. I've been having an affair with… and well… he's the father.'

'Oh, I see,' said Isabella, subdued and confused by the confession. 'But how, why…? Or maybe I shouldn't ask.' But she continued, suddenly realising her revised position in the arrangement. 'Do you want to tell me more, or do you want to just leave it there?'

'Of course, I have to tell you more. I want to tell you everything. I don't know what is happening; that is why I wanted to talk to somebody, to you, the only person I can trust with this.'

'Don't you have close friends or family you can talk to as well?' asked Isabella, suddenly feeling vulnerable.

'No, not really. It would put all our friends in a very awkward position; we have known them for so long. That's why I needed to tell you.'

'I see,' said Isabella. She took hold of Catherine's hands and held them tightly one more time. 'Do you love him?'

'Yes,' replied Catherine. 'I love him more than anything in the world. I have never known a love like this. I... I would give up my children for him if I had to.'

Isabella was slightly taken aback by that revealingly stark declaration. In the past, she had many relationships, some with married men. She had many friends who had had relationships that had come and gone, but none, as far as she was aware, had ever come close to avowing such a sacrifice for a man.

'What do you mean,' asked Isabella?

'I have to be with him and our baby. I can't continue to live with Blake... hopefully, he will allow me to take the children with me, but if not...'

'I am sure it would never come to that,' replied Isabella reassuringly.

'Probably not. Blake is not an unreasonable man. He will see that that would be best for them.'

'Are you going to tell him tonight?' asked Isabella.

'No, I'll tell him tomorrow. Then we'll have the weekend to decide what will happen.'

'So, you don't need me to come over?'

'No, we'll be okay. I will call you on Sunday night if anything changes. I'll see you on Monday as usual if I don't call you.' Catherine picked up the bottle, but it was empty. 'Ah,' she said, turning to Isabella. 'Shall I open another one?'

'No, I had better go,' replied Isabella. 'I don't want to be arrested for being drunk in charge of a bicycle, and you will have to give up wine as well... for a while.'

'Yes, I know, I have been easing back slowly anyway,' she pointed at her smaller glass, 'but now,' she made a cut-throat gesture with her hand and frowned, 'I will have to give it up completely.'

'I can drink yours for you and tell you how it feels if that would help,' suggested Isabella. They laughed, and then Isabella got up and put on her coat. She turned to Catherine, who was now standing in floods of tears. Isabella took hold of her, and they held each other very tightly.

'I really don't know what is happening to me, Issy. This is not like me at all. I have never looked at another man since the day I first saw Blake, and then suddenly, a few months ago, we met, and now my head is all over the place. It's almost as if he has cast a spell on me.'

'We'll talk some more next week, but if you want to call me over the weekend, that's okay any time.'

Isabella picked up her bag and left. Catherine sat down in her chair and stared out the window, trying to figure out what had happened over the last seven months, almost without her realising it. In fact, it had really started before that, but she just hadn't been aware of it.

She went back into the larder, brought out another Pinot Grigio and slowly inserted the corkscrew, thinking about what she had said and had done. Then realising that she shouldn't drink any more, she pushed the cork back into the bottle and put it into the fridge.

Chapter 22
April 1984. Saturday

The following day Blake was sitting quietly at the desk in his study, idly reading the newspaper, when Catherine came in with two cups of coffee, one of which she placed on the desk. She took a sip from her cup before sitting down opposite him.

'Thank you, darling. Are the kids up yet, asked Blake, looking up at Catherine?

'No, not yet. I wanted to have a word with you first. There is something we need to talk about.'

'Oh,' said Blake light-heartedly, laying down his newspaper. 'That sounds a bit ominous.' He pulled a "have-I-been-a-naughty-boy?" expression to humour her but noticed she did not appear to respond as he had expected. In fact, she didn't seem to be responding at all.

'Is this important?' asked Blake, now a little concerned.

'I think it is,' replied Catherine quietly.

'Oh,' said Blake, the corners of his mouth dropping as he adroitly adopted a more sombre expression. 'Have you dinged the car?' he ventured in a cheerfully restrained tone, 'because if you have, that's really unimportant.'

'No, I haven't dented the car. It's nothing like that.'

'Oh,' repeated Blake. He could sense the conversation drifting into uncharted waters.

'I have a confession to make,' said Catherine curtly. She didn't mean to sound abrupt; it just came out that way. The anxiety and apprehension that had kept her awake the previous night had faded - now supplanted by an unexpected inner strength. For a moment, her mind flashed back to thoughts of Gideon and to making love, and this, too, seemed to stimulate and energise her spirits, quelling any doubts or concerns she might have had. Freshly invigorated, she continued with what she had decided she must say and do.

Blake didn't say anything, sensing that this was not the moment to speak. He opened the palms of his hands as if to say, 'The floor is yours.'

'I'm leaving you... I have met somebody else. We are in love, and I want to move in with him... And I'm having his child.' There, she had said it all, everything that mattered. Succinctly, no rambling, no hesitancy, no prevarication. She was proud of herself.

'Oh,' said Blake for the fourth time, but the threat of mortal danger had already flashed past and cut him down in its wake. 'You're leaving me, and you have met somebody? I don't understand.' His arms fell to the table. 'Is it something I've done? Because I am a little confused... I wasn't aware we had a problem.'

He looked stunned and could not have moved out of his chair even if he had wanted to. His body had turned to lead... It felt much the same as that moment in his office eighteen months ago when Gideon told him about the change of name for The Chapter Room. It was so unexpected and instantly brought to mind all manner of disconnected thoughts that had been dwelling harmlessly in the back of his brain. Suddenly they were coming together and starting to make sense.

'And you say you are having a baby? But how? I don't mean how; when; when did you even find the time? No, that's the wrong question. What I want to say is, are you really leaving me, and is it an irretrievable situation?'

In these situations, all the right questions are asked, but they always come out sounding wrong. Blake was being confronted by a full-frontal attack on his life and every aspect of it. And yet, he was already looking for ways to resolve the problem and rescue the situation. This was Blake, the man she had fallen in love with; these were the personality traits she had always admired in him. His honesty, integrity, and ability to make her laugh when everything was going wrong - and his stubborn refusal to accept anything detrimental to their relationship. A relationship that had so overwhelmed her when they first met. There was little chance of a snappy witticism rectifying this situation.

They, Catherine at first, then Max and Claudia, had always come first; everything else was a distant second. That had been his priority until two years ago when suddenly everything had begun to change, from the moment The Chapter Room first arrived in his office. But that was all in the past, and today all that would count for nothing. Catherine wanted something else now, something that only Gideon could give her.

'Yes, I am leaving, and it is an irretrievable situation. I am truly sorry, but I have met him, and we have fallen in love, and I am not in love with you any longer... and there is no going back to how things were. It is as simple as that. It's nothing to do with you. No, I'm sorry, that is not what I mean. What I meant to say was you have done absolutely nothing to cause this. You are the innocent party. This is all me, all my fault. I drifted into something I didn't understand and completely lost control. I can't live without him. I am so sorry.'

'As simple as that?' You've met someone else,' replied Blake, picking out the phrases that seemed so unreal. 'You make it sound so matter-of-fact. It's... it's almost clinical, the way you have conceived this... this plan... this devious plan, and then executed it with such utter brutal efficiency. You have comprehensively fulfilled your objective without a shred of compassion or consideration for the enormous, devastating consequences it will have on all of us. Do you know what? I am absolutely stunned beyond belief by this. For the first time in my life, I am at a complete and utter loss for the right words to convey exactly how I feel...' It is like you have carried out an autopsy and removed all my vital organs...and now I am empty.

Catherine thought he was managing remarkably well to find all the right words and express himself so eloquently under the circumstances. Oddly, she felt as if she was viewing his protestations as part of an audience and not an active participant; detachment was a strange feeling.

Blake also felt detached from reality. It was as if his cognitive powers had been temporarily withdrawn. He was left floundering around, flapping like a stranded fish on the mud. When the tide turned, it would leave him behind. He had to default to pedestrian aphorisms and clichés.

'How long have you planned this?' he exclaimed, his voice slightly raised, which was unusual for him. He never thought he would experience this moment, but here it was. The bitterness, the venom, the anger, and the hostility welling up inside him.

'I didn't plan anything. It just happened.'

'How long has it been going on?' asked Blake, now juggling days and times in his head. Of course, it was possible; he had been working late two or three nights a week on Gideon's book for over a year. Sales had passed the thirty million mark, and they were now deep into negotiations with three companies for the screen rights. That meant even more of his time, which he had deprived his family of, and now he was paying the price.

'Just over seven months as an affair, but it started before that.' Catherine was being brutally honest, which, if anything, made the pain even worse.

'What do you mean, it started before that? When did it start?' shouted Blake.

Catherine pulled back slightly, a little surprised at his raised voice. Undoubtedly it was entirely justified, but she couldn't recall him ever shouting at her, not once in all the years they had been married. Suddenly she became reluctant to be more specific, but she had no choice. The proverbial genie was now out of the bottle. All the nasty little grubby details would come out eventually, so she might as well get it over with and make a clean breast of things now. Hackneyed clichés were not the vernacular she would usually resort to. But those were the first things that came into her head. She racked her brain to ensure she was correct with the dates before continuing.

'Boxing Day 1982,' she declared with perfect precision.

'Boxing fucking Day? How the fuck did you meet somebody on…? Oh, fuck me… It's Gideon, isn't it, fucking Gideon?' He was usually more inventive with expletives when the need arose, but nothing much else would have served so adequately at this juncture. The Anglo Saxons had much to be thanked for in that department - suddenly flashed through his mind.

Catherine said nothing, but that was enough.

'So that little bastard I've been working my bollocks off to make rich repays me by shagging my wife.' There had to be a sort of metaphor in the irony, but for the life of him, he could not see what it was.

'It wasn't quite like that. It didn't start out that way, it…'

'It never does, does it,' interrupted Blake? 'But that doesn't matter now, does it?' 'It's how it finishes that matters.'

'Quite,' said Catherine, staring intently at Blake, trying not to second-guess what he would say next. Blake appeared to have settled down a little now.

'I can't believe what he has done to us. I can't believe what you have done to us.' Blake was quieter now; the wave of fiery condemnation had passed. He hadn't come to terms with it, but he knew that shouting and swearing wouldn't get him anywhere. 'So, what's the plan?' he asked brusquely.

'Well, I don't know, actually. This isn't a plan; we just agreed that I should tell you today and work it out from there.'

'What about the children?' asked Blake, realising they were as much a part of this as he was.

'I was hoping you wouldn't object to them coming with me. Of course, you will see the children whenever you want, and we won't be living that far away. Gideon has a…'

'I know where Gideon's fucking house is,' interrupted Blake.

'Yes, of course, you do. I forgot. I'm sorry.'

'I'll not fight you over the children…' Blake looked remarkably calm now, disturbingly so, and strangely in control of the raw emotions that were undoubtedly boiling inside.

'But I thought that…' started Catherine, sounding slightly surprised.

'No, I would love them to stay here, but if we went to court, I would lose, men always lose, and I would probably be even worse off. And Gideon now has far more money than I do to spend on lawyers.'

'I promise you will have all the contact you want with them.'

Blake smiled. The one thing he knew about Catherine above all else was that she always kept her word, and if he had the comfort of that, then that was all he needed. She had been entirely open with him about the affair, and she had bitten hard on the bullet of anguish and had chosen to break the news to him in person. She could so easily have slipped away during the day, any day, and sent him a letter, but she chose to face him and face the consequences.

'Okay, okay,' said Blake. 'I will leave it to you to let me know when…'

'Thank you,' said Catherine.

'What for?' said Blake.

'For being so civilised about it all.'

Blake smiled. 'I love you, Catherine, and this changes nothing. You may not be here anymore, but I will still love you. Remember that. There is always hope; where there is life, there is...'

It was an unusual thing to say, thought Catherine, but Blake was an extraordinary man in so many ways.

Catherine could feel tears welling up and turned to quickly leave Blake's office. She collapsed in the lounge, but this time, Blake did not come out to comfort her, unlike all the other occasions when she had begun to cry, for he was already crying his heart out. This time she would cry alone.

Chapter 23
Sunday

Blake sat alone in his study on Sunday morning, watching the sunrise and listening to the dawn chorus. He had tried to get some sleep in the spare bedroom, but that had not proved particularly successful. He had spent most of the night going over what had happened and how it was that the manuscript of Prospect Road had so methodically detailed the events of his earlier life. And then segued seamlessly into predicting the events that were happening right now.

The manuscript appeared to be the instrument through which those changes had been affected. Blake considered whether not reading the book could have any influence on the eventual outcome. Maybe the events only became real once he had read them. Perhaps he should stop reading it. No, he couldn't do that. Maybe he should destroy it. No, he couldn't do that either. There would be no going back then. At least now, there was a chance of doing something. He just didn't know what.

Blake began formulating a pattern, a paradigm for what was happening, but it still didn't make sense. Somehow, he knew everything that had happened over the past few years was part of a much larger plan. The book was trying to communicate with him... send him a message, but what was the message? That was what he could not figure out. It all seemed to go back to when Reggie died in December 1981, and Blake took over the company. That's when everything started to happen. The manuscript of Prospect Road arrived only a few months later, and then in August 1982, Gideon Drew's book turned up.

It wasn't just Catherine leaving him. That was only a tiny part of something much bigger, but what, why, and, more importantly, how could he find out? If he could answer those questions, then maybe he could change everything. Even put it back to the way it was. No matter how meticulously drawn up - every plan has a flaw, a minute, fundamental weakness that, if carefully exploited, could bring about the failure of the whole project. All plans were created by humans, and all humans were fallible.

The Germans, the Romans, the Greeks, Napoleon and the French, Attila and the Hunnic horde, Genghis Khan, Mongols, and even the English had plans to conquer the world. But each project had a tiny flaw, and each plan failed profoundly. It was a vague analogy out of all proportion to his situation, but it was the first to come to mind. There had to be a link, a thread of commonality between their demise and his position.

There was also the element of chance, the unknown factor, that too could affect the outcome.

It had all started with the manuscript of Prospect Road and its writer, Mr Anthony Theodore Clackle. Blake's office had never managed to contact Clackle despite many attempts, and there had to be a reason for that. That was where he would begin.

He opened the wall safe in the study, took the manuscript and laid it on the desk. He would need to reread the whole thing to figure out the hidden message. But before he started, he went to the kitchen to make a fresh cup of coffee and returned to his study to begin. He turned over the first page, and then, out of habit, a ritual he had only adopted whenever reading this book, he flipped the pages over to the end. He couldn't see his signature, so he flipped back a page, and there it was, at the bottom of the final page of Chapter Twelve. However, in the space of only a few weeks, one more page had been added to the story. It wasn't a whole page, just a heading and some notes...

Notes for 'Prospect Road' Chapters 13/14/15.

In these chapters, Kate decides to leave Thomas after starting an affair with the writer Gideon Drew.

She discusses the affair with her housekeeper?
Expand....
Thomas considers suicide?
Kate discovers she is pregnant with Gideon's baby?
Kate moves in with Gideon. Y/N
Gideon has cast a spell???
Who is the mysterious Gideon Drew?
Julian searches for Gideon. Does he find him?
Is anybody going to die? Who?

What would happen if Gideon…?

Some of the details corresponded with what had already happened. Some were a little enigmatic, but the message was clear to see. Blake had just not realised what Anthony had been trying to tell him.

And that was it: Just a few words on what the following chapters could bring. In fact, life had moved on well past this point. For the first time, the reality of events had overtaken the written word. Blake thought about that for a few moments – maybe, as the chapters had not yet been written, there was a possibility that the plotline and outcome could change. If so, how exactly could he make that happen? There was possibly a time element involved, but how would he find that out? Questions, questions.

Clackle had to be the key. Blake knew he had to find him; he was the only person who could provide an answer to the puzzle. Maybe there was even a chance he could save his marriage, sanity and probably his life if he could find him, but how.

Chapter 24
Monday

Blake spoke briefly to Catherine on Monday morning before leaving for the office. She confirmed that she would not be moving out until the beginning of the following week to allow them time to prepare the children and make all the necessary arrangements. It all sounded remarkably affable and civilised, but Blake refused to be baited by the strange calmness with which Catherine appeared to be handling the transitional stage. As on Friday night, it was all conducted with a frighteningly detached and dispassionate air. It was as if they were arranging to go away on holiday to Devon for a few days, not making what was, for him, the most dramatic change ever in his life.

When Blake arrived at the office just after ten, he pulled out their file on Anthony Clackle. It was still very thin.

Jamie popped his head around Blake's office door.

'Morning, Blake. Good weekend?' Blake mumbled something incoherent.

'Good, good,' replied Jamie, not taking too much notice. 'Look, I need to review some figures with you sometime today. It's the calculations the lawyers have come up with for the screen rights for The Room, so…'

The office staff invariably reduced a popular book's title to something slick and catchy given half a chance, typically the title's first letters or the last word. It sounded cliquey and buzzy and invoked an elite club-like aura for the people dealing with a specific book. It was undeniably spurious, even a little pompous, but it infused them with a sense of inflated self-importance that helped compensate for the paltry wages they received. In reality, it was all a little sad.

'…we need to finish everything before presenting it to Gideon.'

Blake looked up. 'No problem. Just give me a couple of hours to go through this.' He waved the Road file at Jamie.

'Prospect Road?' said Jamie, sounding surprised. I thought we'd dumped that one on the back burner. Isn't half of it still missing or something? Bit of a dead duck.'

'No, I've…' Blake hesitated for a moment. They had turned the office upside down, looking for the missing chapters, but without success. It would appear a little unusual if Blake suddenly produced a substantial proportion of the missing section out of thin air without a reasonable explanation. And, of course, he didn't have one, not one he was prepared to throw into an open arena for discussion anyway.

'I was just wondering if there had been any more communication from Mr Clackle. I thought we could follow it up if…' He was fumbling around and not sounding particularly convincing. Jamie gave him a curious glance.

'I would have thought you had enough on your plate right now with The Room.'

'I do, I do, but that won't last forever. I just thought…'

'We did receive a letter from him about a month ago. It's in there.' He pointed to the file. 'I didn't mention it because we were busy with…'

'Oh, right. I'll have a look then. Come back about twelvish, and we can go out for lunch and run over the figures, okay?'

'Right,' said Jamie, smiling as he shut the door behind him.

Blake opened the file and took out the letter from Clackle.

March 14th, 1984
Clanford & Fox
Denmark Street
London

Dear Sirs (or Madam),
Many apologies for troubling you, but I wondered whether you had had a chance to read my manuscript for 'Prospect Road'. I appreciate that some aspects of the story may appear a little far-fetched, even for fiction, but I can assure you that this story is based partly on first-hand information from a reliable source. I felt compelled to write the story, as I believe my time on this earth will not be for much longer, and I must finish it and hopefully find a publisher before I am done.

I have no idea who or what the story is about, but I know that it relates to somebody who must be aware of what is happening to them and that there is also a family connection. If the book is published, that person may just read it, saving that person's life. This is merely a message to that lost soul.

There are forces in play that militate against me. I feel their powers growing stronger day by day as they try to impede every word I write and destroy my faculties. Nevertheless, I must do my best to have the work published, even at the risk of death.

Please excuse the melodramatic tone of this letter. It was not intended that way, but that is how I feel about it. Hopefully, you will respond and let me know whether you would be interested in considering publication. But if not, I would be grateful if you could return the manuscript. I do not have the strength to write another copy, and I would like to send it to another publisher. I am still physically able to discuss this book with you if necessary, but not sure for how much longer.

Best regards,
Anthony T. Clackle
Farthingales
The Green
Chiddingfold

The address was in a little village outside of Haslemere, which wasn't too far from where Blake lived, only forty-five minutes by car. It appeared to be some sort of hospitalisation facility. Blake made a note of the address, put the letter back into the file, and dropped it back on his desk.

On Tuesday, he phoned the office and left a message saying he would be late as he was visiting a client.

He stood outside the towering main entrance of Farthingale's Dignity and Comfort Care Centre and looked up at what had once been somebody's ancestral home.

A once beautiful building set in glorious grounds now sadly reduced to a utilitarian facility for the care of the wealthy elderly and infirmed, he presumed. He made his way into the reception area, where he saw a large, smartly dressed woman in a business suit and sensible shoes remonstrating with a man who appeared to be a cleaner. On seeing Blake enter, she instantly ended her conversation. She made a small, unfamiliar gesture to the man she had been speaking to, and then he left. The women then marched towards Blake in a distinctly military fashion with an expression that could only be described as a business smile.

'Can I be of any assistance?' she politely enquired, leaning slightly to one side as she said it. 'My name is Brenda. I'm the senior day manager.' She said all this in an entirely different tone from the one she had used only moments earlier with the man Blake assumed was a humble serf in her kingdom.

'I must apologise for not making an appointment, but I wonder whether it would be possible to speak to one of your...' Blake paused for a moment, unsure of the correct term... 'patients?' he tendered tentatively.

'We prefer to call them house guests,' replied Brenda, still smiling, her tone now coloured with just a smidgen of inverted snobbery. It was obviously an expensive establishment if it had this sort of defence system in place, thought Blake.

'Yes,' replied Blake. 'A guest by the name of Clackle,'

'Clackle?' enquired Brenda, 'Ah, you mean Anthony, don't you?'

'Yes, that's right. Anthony Theodore Clackle.'

'A genuinely nice gentleman, if I may say so. I had the pleasure of meeting him when he first contacted us. That was before...' Her expression suddenly changed, and she hesitated before reaching for a register under the desk.

'Oh,' said Blake, unsure where the conversation was going.

There was silence for a few moments while Brenda flipped through some records. Blake glanced around the reception area, which must once have been the main entrance to the house. It was probably filled with beautiful antique furniture and family portraits before. But its grandeur had been severely diminished with the installation of temporary offices made of blue felted moveable panels, two reception desks, and half a dozen austere metal filing cabinets.

'Yes, he's in the Waterloo Wing, in...' said Brenda, interrupting Blake's historical musings. She flipped over another page, 'The Copenhagen Suite.' She glanced up at Blake with an air of superior intellect, pronouncing the name with a smirky self-satisfied expression. It was as if it were some rarely known fact she had probably picked up from a television quiz show. 'The suite was named after...'

'The horse, ridden by The Duke of Wellington at Waterloo 1815,' interrupted Blake.

'Ah, yes,' said Brenda, squinting with just a hint of disdain. 'Not too many people know that.' Her smile turned to a scowl. She had probably used this trinket of historical trivia many times to impress new visitors to the establishment. So, she was a little irritated that this relatively obscure detail was more widely known than she had realised. And even more perturbed by an absolute stranger stealing her thunder.

'He was stuffed,' said Blake blankly.

'Who, the Duke of...?' replied the woman indignantly before Blake interrupted again.

'The horse. The horse was stuffed... after it died, that is. Not the Duke.'

Brenda half smiled and murmured something quietly to herself.

'Are you a relative?'

'No, just a business acquaintance… and a friend,' he promptly added. He lied, believing it to be a necessary falsehood in the circumstance.

'Oh, I see. Well, Anthony is not particularly communicative, you know.'

'Oh,' said Blake. 'What do you mean?'

'He's virtually paralysed, head to toe.'

'That's strange. He only wrote to me about a month ago and didn't mention it then.'

'I'm afraid his condition has deteriorated dramatically since then,' replied Brenda.

'Can he speak?'

'Not really, as far as I am aware.'

'Oh well, we will have to get through as best we can with sign language, won't we,' replied Blake optimistically. He had come this far, and he was not giving up now.

'He can't move his hands,' said Brenda, reinforcing her earlier statement.

'We'll manage,' replied Blake, smiling.

'Follow me; it's quite a long walk.' Blake obliged as she briskly marched off down the main corridor.

'Interesting term, Dignity and Comfort Care Centre. Is it a hospital or a recuperation unit?' Blake asked innocently.

Brenda stopped and turned to face Blake with a vacant expression of curiosity.

'Neither. Do you not know what Anthony is here for,' she asked?

'I know he's ill,' replied Blake bluntly, instantly realising how obtuse that sounded.

'He's dying, and soon. That's what we do here; we help them through their last days.'

'I apologise. I didn't realise he was that ill.'

'He wasn't,' she replied sharply. 'He came to see us about a month ago and told us there was nothing wrong with him, as far as he knew. But he had experienced a premonition that he would suddenly deteriorate and probably die before the end of this month. It was all very precise. He paid for everything upfront, including collection from the hospital. Then, on the exact day he had predicted, he collapsed, was diagnosed with a terminal brain tumour, and was brought here.'

'But it's the twenty-eighth today,' said Blake.

'Yes,' said Brenda with a derisive smile that said, *"You're very quick, aren't you?"* 'So, we are not expecting him to last beyond Friday. He's been correct on everything else so far, so we see no reason to doubt that he will be correct with his final prediction.'

She exuded matriarchal arrogance. Her job was to ensure that guests died in comfort, with dignity, and hopefully on time. While under her care, they would be extended every possible courtesy, and visitors were of secondary importance as far as she was concerned.

After a few twists and turns, they arrived at 'Waterloo' and made their way to the Copenhagen Suite. She showed Blake into the suite and gave Blake one final instruction before leaving.

'Try not to tire him out; he's only got three days, so he deserves to spend them peacefully.' She obviously cared deeply about her "guests." He wondered if he should make a booking here for when his time came – but hopefully not just yet.

The nurse who had just finished feeding Anthony smiled charmingly at Blake before pushing the meal trolley towards the door. She closed it behind her, and they were alone. He walked over to the bed to see a man who looked roughly the same age as he was but was preparing to die. Blake suddenly realised just how fragile and short life really was.

Anthony just stared, his eyes glazed and fixed.

'My name is Blake Thornton. I work for Clanford and Fox, book publishers. You sent me a manuscript… Prospect Road.' There was no response.

'You've written the book about my life, but I don't understand how you know so much about me and why you have written it.' Still, there was no response. Blake thought for a moment.

'I have met Gideon Drew, and we are publishing his book The Chapter Room, the book you mention in Prospect Road…'

The moment Blake mentioned Gideon's name, Anthony's head began to turn very slowly toward him, and his eyes widened, suddenly becoming alert. He started to say something, but it was no more than a whisper. Blake drew closer to Anthony, who whispered the words again:

'You may never take my soul…'

'You may never take my soul,' repeated Blake.

Clackle smiled as best he could with his eyes - his facial muscles were no longer functioning.

'Who?' said Blake. 'Is it Gideon Drew?'

Clackle looked disturbed, visibly frustrated because he could not pronounce the words he was so desperately trying to say, but Blake was beginning to understand.

'It is Gideon,' suggested Blake. Anthony relaxed, and his eyes smiled again. So, it was something to do with Gideon.

'The manuscript you sent me appears to be writing itself… is that really happening?'

Anthony's eyes smiled again. At least they had a basic form of communication. Anthony couldn't speak… but if he smiled, it meant yes, or that he agreed.

'Why is it doing…?' Blake stopped. He could not ask a direct question, only propose an assumption. That made it far more challenging. He would have to think carefully about how he should phrase the questions if he wanted answers that meant something.

'If…' He paused for a second, unsure if he wanted to know the answer to his next question. If it wasn't the answer he hoped for, then all was lost anyway, so what had he to lose?

'If the manuscript that I have only pens a summary of what might happen in the next unwritten chapters… does that mean…?' He paused again. 'Does that mean that… the chapters could turn out differently from the initial summary?'

It sounded like a complicated question, but there was no easier way to put it. Anthony thought about it for a moment. He seemed to be running it through his mind to ensure he understood before answering. His face was still turned to face Blake, and slowly, a smile entered his eyes. Blake's heart almost skipped a beat; at last, there was a chance he could change everything. He just needed to know how to change it.

'How can I change it?' asked Blake before realising he could not ask that question.

'Is there a way I can change it?' Anthony's eyes smiled again.

'But how? I don't know what questions to ask.' Now Blake was becoming a little frustrated – as frustrated as Anthony must have felt.

'Please help me,' said Blake. 'Please help me save my family...' It was a desperate plea, and Blake cursed himself for having to beg a dying man for help, but he didn't know what else he could do. Anthony's lips began to open, and Blake drew closer.

It was almost inaudible, a ghostly whisper, just a few words slowly muttered. 'Pass Cath to Gideon...' he took a shallow breath and continued, '... and it will end.'

The last word seemed to linger on Anthony's lips like a final breath slowly fading away. But what could that mean? Pass his wife to Gideon, and it will end? That didn't make any sense. She had already decided to leave him and live with Gideon, so how could that make a difference? How could that change anything? Anthony could not know what had been happening over the last few days and knew nothing about the other things that had already happened... And what would end, he wondered? His life had almost ended anyway, having almost lost his wife and children to Gideon. He was more confused now than when he first arrived. Anthony may have given him some answers to the puzzle, but he had also inadvertently created more riddles and questions.

Anthony turned his head back to face forward, and his eyes closed. He was not going to utter another word that day.

There were so many other questions he wanted to ask. Would Prospect Road still carry on writing itself if Anthony died? Why had the complete book been sent to the publishers initially with an ending, but now only the first twelve chapters were visible? Why, in fact, had the book been sent at all? Who was Gideon Drew?

Blake got up and gently touched Anthony's face. There was nothing more he could do today.

'Thank you, thank you for everything,' he whispered. Anthony's eyes smiled, but Blake could not see them as they were shut. Blake said goodbye to Brenda, who was now back at her desk by the front door, gave her a card and asked her to contact him when...

Blake drove home knowing that he would have to discuss this with Gideon at some stage, but he would have to reread Prospect

Road first. There had to be a clue somewhere in the manuscript relating to Anthony's final words that day.

Chapter 25
Tuesday

Blake arrived home just after three o'clock, which was early for him. His desire to return to the office had declined dramatically over the past few days, especially after visiting Anthony. He had always been a highly motivated individual and an enthusiastic employer. His driving passion had always encouraged and inspired everyone to work as industriously as he did. This is what made the company so successful. No one complained about the occasional late night that had to be put in to finish a project or even coming in at weekends when necessary. That was the commitment you signed up for; it would never be a nine-to-five job.

Book publishing was not a profession for the faint-hearted. It wasn't a profession at all. It was a sadomasochistic art form, almost as much a self-inflicted vocation as writing was. You don't choose it; it chooses you. Nothing exacts so much intolerable pain and intense anguish as writing, editing and publishing a book, apart from reading a bad one.

It demands complete and absolute dedication; it is closer to religion than business. The publisher must have an unfailing belief in something when there is no tangible evidence available to indicate the work has any commercial value. He must rely on his own gut instinct and little else. That is what all publishers depended upon, this and their gut judgement on the literary value, an ability honed from experience alone.

Their business succeeds or fails, lives or dies, on this judgement alone. Nobody alive can honestly read a book and say with absolute conviction that it will succeed. But every day, publishers make that call because that is what they do; their existence depends on it.

For this reason, Blake decided it would be better if he did not go in, at least not until he had come to terms with the changes about to occur in his personal life. His frustration and bitter frame of mind would undoubtedly spill over into the office, creating tension that could affect the efficacy of what they had to do. He would return when matters had been resolved.

Max and Claudia greeted their loving father at the front door, hugging him and chatting about what they had done that day. But for the first time ever, Catherine held back in the hallway, not exactly cowering in the shadows but carefully monitoring the situation. Watching her family go through the routines they had gone through so many times before. Blake glanced up, caught her eye briefly, and gently smiled. Not the impostor's triumphant grin over the minor victory of being greeted so warmly by his children when she had chosen to desert him, but the simple expression of joy, happiness, and gratitude at being greeted at all. Something which they had created together over the last ten years. It was magnanimous and generous and honest and courageous – and it hurt. He wasn't sure how he would be greeted today.

Catherine could feel bitter tears welling up behind her eyes, so she quickly returned to the kitchen to carry on preparing dinner. Gideon had warned her that there would be distressing moments like this during the few remaining days she had agreed to stay at the house, so she was prepared for it. But nothing could adequately prepare her for the emotional trauma she had chosen to receive. He had also told her there would be moments when she would experience self-doubt and even thoughts of self-recrimination for what they were doing. But he assured her that that was a natural emotion in anybody as caring and considerate as she was. She should disregard such false feelings. Standing back and quietly watching this drama play out before her wasn't easy. Catherine wondered how it was that Gideon was so knowledgeable about such viscerally intimate feelings. Had he once experienced the same situation she was going through right now? If so, then when, she wondered. Maybe she should ask him… but then again, perhaps not. That could jeopardise the relationship that now existed between them. But then, surely, the essence of a long-term relationship was the ability to share all earlier experiences without becoming emotionally involved in what had happened in the past. Only by exposing them to daylight and open discussion could they be relegated to where they belong, ancient history. She would have to ask him one day, but not today; today was not the right time.

The greeting over, Max and Claudia returned to the lounge. Blake popped his head into the kitchen.

'How are you? Sorry about all that. I realise it was a bit…' That hurt.

'I'm fine, fine, thank you,' replied Catherine, 'you're early.' She seemed a little surprised but not overly so.

'Yes, I went to see somebody, but by the time I'd had lunch, it seemed pointless going back to the office, so I thought I would call it a day.'

'Right,' said Catherine. She took a deep breath and plunged in. 'I've spoken to Gideon, and he says I don't need to take any furniture. So I will take my clothes, some personal things, the children's clothes and some of their toys. But I will leave enough for the weekends if that's okay.' She waited with some trepidation for the expected fallout…

'Yes. Yes, that's fine,' replied Blake, sounding surprisingly sanguine about her pronouncement, as if he were not concerned about the pedestrian trivialities of separation. He knew she would hardly pillage the house; that was not her way of doing things.

'Look,' said Blake, oddly hesitant. 'If you don't object, and I will understand if you do, I would like to chat with Gideon on neutral ground just to discuss everything. You know, what with me being his publisher and his agent and us having contracts and things…'

'That's not a problem, Blake. I am sure we can work this whole thing out so that everything is just f…' She nearly said fine but realised that that would be pushing his sensibilities too far. 'We can talk; you can talk to him. I am sure you won't come to blows. I will call him if you want me to and…'

'That would be good,' replied Blake, 'thank you.'

'Dinner won't be till five,' said Catherine, not really knowing how to continue the conversation. Moments like this would always be a little awkward until she finally left. Tiptoeing around on eggshells very accurately described the situation, and it was something to which she was not accustomed.

'That's fine,' said Blake. 'I know I'm back a little early; I have something to do anyway. I wanted to start rereading a manuscript I have.'

'Oh,' said Catherine, trying to make conversation. 'Which one? Anything we've spoken about?'

'Prospect Road, actually,' replied Blake.

'Prospect Road. Oh,' repeated Catherine. 'The odd unfinished one about…' She stopped – she didn't need to finish. He knew what she was going to say.

'Yes, that's right. In parts, it was, wasn't it? All a little unusual, but then life has been a bit unusual lately.' He smiled and went to his study. He opened the manuscript, which was still on his desk and began to read it until Catherine called him in for dinner just after five. They all sat down and enjoyed the meal much as they always had on weekends when he wasn't working. It reminded him how much things would change, but he did not let it show.

'I've spoken to Gideon, and he has suggested that maybe you could meet him at the Green Dragon in the village,' said Catherine as she cleared the plates.

'Can we come to see Uncle Gideon?' chipped in Max.

Blake looked at Catherine, slightly surprised at Max's comment, 'Uncle?'

'That is what I have told them to call him for now, and they do know him…'

'But Uncle,' said Blake, with just a touch of indignation.

'It's all I could think of at the time,' apologised Catherine.

Blake shrugged his shoulders and let it go. 'When?'

'Can you do lunchtime tomorrow? I know you have the office, but maybe…'

'That's not a problem,' Blake interrupted. 'I've decided not to go into the office again until you move out next week. I won't be able to concentrate on what is happening, so it would be pointless. Don't worry, I won't cause you any…' He paused momentarily, searching for the right word. 'Difficulty' was the one he landed on, not very convincingly. 'You know what I mean.'

Catherine smiled. She knew Blake well enough to know he would keep his word. Blake smiled back at Catherine, then returned to his study to continue reading Prospect Road.

The next day Blake arrived at Green Dragon at the appointed time. Gideon was already sitting outside nursing a pint with another on the table.

'I got you one in. Bitter, isn't it?'

'Yes, that's fine, thank you,' replied Blake.

He spontaneously put his hand out to shake Gideon's but then withdrew it, realising that the gesture was inappropriate. Historically, the practise of shaking hands was to show someone you did not have a weapon in your hand; he didn't, but he had considered it. Gideon made a mental note and smiled at Blake.

'I understand,' said Gideon. 'Look… Blake,' he said firmly, delicately encapsulating the essence of condescension and patronage into one word. 'This wasn't what I had expected to happen. This whole thing came out of nowhere; it caught us both unaware. I hope you can understand that.'

Blake did not answer immediately but sipped his beer before continuing. 'I'm here because I don't want to upset my children by arguing with Catherine in front of them. It would serve no purpose. I know the way this works. I've seen it enough times in the books I've read to know all the likely scenarios and how they usually play out. So that's why I am taking it the way I am and why I am talking to you amiably today.' He smiled at Gideon. Gideon found it slightly disturbing.

'Right, I see,' said Gideon, sipping his beer but sounding slightly relieved.

However, I do have some things I don't quite understand, and I was wondering if you could help me with these… unresolved oddities? Blake had taken on an oddly curious yet benign expression. A friendly interrogator - if there could be such an oxymoron.

'It would help me see things better if I could clear up these anomalies.'

'Anything at all,' said Gideon. 'If it's about money or anything like that, I can assure you I will look after Catherine and the children. You need have no fears there.'

'No, it's not about money. I know you have no problems in that department. I am your agent and your publisher, after all. And as for my children, I will have them at weekends and some of the holidays. Obviously, I will continue to support them anyway.'

Gideon half-smiled his acknowledgement of Blake's intent. 'So, what is it?' Gideon asked.

'Well… I went to see a man yesterday, another writer. His name was Clackle, Anthony Theodore Clackle. Have you ever heard of him?'

'No, can't say I have. Why?' replied Gideon.

'That's odd because he seems to know you and in some detail, so it would appear.'

'Oh,' said Gideon, appearing unconvincingly surprised.

'Two years ago, he sent me a manuscript about the life story of a man called Thomas Drayton and his wife. Her name was Kate.'

'And?' said Gideon, still none the wiser.

'Well, it's odd. You see, this manuscript he sent me is unusual for several reasons.'

'Oh,' replied Gideon. 'Please explain.'

'Well, firstly, and this is quite bizarre, the book recalls all my past life up to the present day, but under the pseudonym of a character called Thomas Drayton.'

'That is very unusual, but…'

Blake interrupted. 'That's not all – you see, it also writes itself.'

'I don't understand,' said Gideon. 'If this Clackle guy sent you a complete story, then surely it's already written?'

'Well, you'd think that, wouldn't you?' said Blake. 'That would make sense, but as I said, this one is different.'

'How?' said Gideon. 'Please explain; I'm intrigued.'

'Well, when he sent the original manuscript to the office, somebody else read it. Jamie, in fact. You know Jamie, my assistant, don't you?'

'Yes, of course. We speak most weeks.'

'Quite,' said Blake. 'Well, when he read it, it was complete; it was finished. He liked it, so he gave it to me to read, which is when it went a bit odd. You see, when I first read it, there were only two chapters and nothing else, just blank pages. The next time I read it, a few weeks later, another chapter appeared. The first two chapters had also been filled out with more detail. You know how it works with writing, and that's how it went, right up to Chapter Twelve, which was quite recent, and that is where I am now.'

'Very mysterious,' said Gideon, 'and fascinating.' He scrunched his eyes up a little.

'Ah no, that's still not the mysterious part; that's yet to come. Getting back to Anthony Clackle, who, as I said, I went to have a chat with, well, he could not physically communicate with me very much as he was completely paralysed, you see. Struck down suddenly with a very nasty brain tumour, which, oddly, the doctors couldn't see when he first complained about severe headaches. But hey presto, a few days later it suddenly appeared, and it's goodnight Vienna for Mr Clackle.'

'Tragic,' remarked Gideon, continuing in his trite, laconic vein, which annoyed Blake a little.

'Is he dead yet?' asked Gideon.

'No, not yet, but soon, in a few days.'

'Dead by Friday then?' suggested Gideon as if the timing was as expected. Blake thought it was an odd question but didn't pursue it further.

'The bizarre thing was,' continued Blake. 'Mr Clackle had already booked his place in the care facility a few weeks earlier when he appeared to be in excellent health. He told them that he had had a premonition that something unpleasant would happen to him, and he wanted to be fully prepared. The care facility manager was reluctant to process Mr Clackle's request on such a nebulous and unsubstantiated self-diagnosis of imminent death. But Mr Clackle insisted and offered to pay them in advance, so the booking was accepted. This was strictly on the understanding that he would die within two months. If he didn't die, he would have to leave.

'Very proactive of Mr Clackle. It's a shame we don't all receive similar premonitions. It would make final exit planning a lot easier,' replied Gideon with a shadowy tone of introspection.

Blake thought this response was also slightly odd; it wasn't so much what he said but how he said it. As if he were aware of another option, but that wasn't possible.

'Anyway,' continued Blake, 'I happened to mention you and your book The Chapter Room in passing, and do you know what, just those few words seemed to rally him around for a few moments. It was very inspiring.' Blake smiled, then continued, 'His eyes lit up, and he even managed to move his head slightly. That must have taken some considerable effort. According to the nurse, he was totally paralysed up to that moment. Then Clackle said something strange, well he didn't actually say it - he just managed to mumble it, and do you know what he said?'

In mock surprise, Gideon threw his arms into the air and replied, 'I've absolutely no idea, but it must have been an inspiring moment for you.'

For the very first time, Blake could see a small chink in Gideon's armour. A tiny speck of darkness in a shining light. It was not alarm or even anxiety; it was unease. Gideon was undeniably looking a little uncomfortable over something that Blake had said...

'It was very enigmatic, almost cryptic. He said...' Blake paused briefly, looking directly into Gideon's eyes to gauge his reaction. 'Pass Cath to Gideon, and it will end.'

'Just that – nothing else,' asked Gideon? He looked bewildered.

'No, just that, but he appeared very anxious about it,' replied Blake.

'Probably delirious. The drugs can do that,' suggested Gideon.

'Possibly, but to me, it seemed that just the sound of your name was enough to stir him into making one last supreme effort. To utter the words with absolute clarity. But still, they didn't appear to mean anything, so why did he go through all that effort? I asked myself. He seemed so clear and precise, and they were virtually the last words of a dying man.'

'Was he possibly referring to Catherine?' queried Gideon innocently. 'Cath – Catherine?'

'Yes, I thought about that, but he never met her.'

'Well, maybe he read my book and was making a suggestion. That is the effect it has on some people, I am told. Or maybe it's one of those strange philosophical imponderables people mutter in their last lucid moments on planet earth. Salient advice to those still living on how to live a better life, maybe? As it is, you've already fulfilled his wishes anyway, haven't you, so he should at least die happy.'

Blake thought that was a stunningly arrogant thing to say, possibly no more than he should have expected, but he refused to be drawn.

'Yes, I have, haven't I? That could explain it,' said Blake in a conciliatory fashion, but in his heart, he didn't believe it. Gideon was still his biggest client, so he couldn't really tell him what he was thinking.

'Anyway, the manuscript mentions Julian Clackle, Anthony's father, who could have been immensely helpful with my queries. But unfortunately, he died about four years ago, so I can't speak to him.'

'So, it's a semi-biographical novel?' asked Gideon.

'Yes, you're right, that's what I thought. Anyway, Julian and Rosemary, his wife, had a son, Anthony. But Julian also had an affair with Mary Drayton, the wife of Jonathan Drayton. They have a son called Thomas, who marries Kate. They are the couple I mentioned earlier that appear to have a similar life to Catherine and myself. They also appear to be the main protagonists of the story.'

'It's becoming extremely complicated,' remarked Gideon. 'Far more so than the storyline in my book'.

'Yes, it is, but if you can bear with me a little longer, I'm nearly there now.' Gideon nodded. 'Now, here's the strangest thing. You see the character Gideon Drew, not you obviously because in the book, this Gideon Drew was born in 1890 and would be about ninety-four now at least, and you...' Blake smiled wryly. 'Obviously, you are not that old... are you?' He added the last few words after an oddly elongated pause.

'No, only just twenty-five,' replied Gideon promptly without expression.

'Yes. I realise that,' said Blake. 'Just twenty-five. So lucky to be that young... aren't you?'

Gideon did not answer immediately but smiled puzzlingly while mulling over Blake's curiously rhetorical question. 'That is a fabulous story, and I'll tell you what. If by any chance your Mr Clackle doesn't finish it, and that's beginning to sound highly likely...' he flashed Blake a strangely demented facial expression appearing to emulate someone in the final throes of death. Blake thought that to be deplorable and inexcusable - but didn't respond. He did, however, make a mental note.

'I would love the opportunity to contribute and tidy it up,' added Gideon, 'for a small acknowledgement, of course – if that would be helpful.'

'That is very generous of you, Gideon. I will bear that in mind. Anyway, I'm still not quite finished with the story. It turns out that Julian had a sister, but for some reason, they were split up at an early age and adopted by two different families. During the Second World War, Julian met Rosemary in a village near Chichester. Not realising they were related, they started a relationship, and in 1946 they were married. One year later, they had a son Anthony. Unfortunately, Anthony was born with serious genetic and physical deformities that the doctors could not treat. Sometime later - it must have been about three years - by a stroke of remarkable coincidence, luck, or unbelievable misfortune, Julian made the acquaintance of a stranger on a train to London. During their conversation, it became apparent that their families were closely related. Then the stranger told Julian something that Julian had never thought possible.'

'What?' said Gideon a little prematurely.

'Well, it was a complicated story, but to cut to the chase, he told Julian that he and his wife Rosemary must, in fact, be brother and sister. This, of course, instantly explained Anthony's medical problems. Not long after that, Julian and Rosemary were divorced.'

'Who was the stranger?' asked Gideon incuriously.

'Can't remember, but it's in the manuscript. Anyway, that's it, more or less it.'

'It's a wonderful story,' said Gideon.

'Well, in a way, yes, I suppose it could be. But I still haven't mentioned some other minor details in the letters from Julian Clackle to Mary Drayton. In one of the last letters, you see, it mentions a Joshua Clanford...'

'Clanford... My house is called Clanford. That's an odd coincidence,' remarked Gideon.

'Not really,' said Blake. 'You know him, in a manner of speaking.'

'Do I?' replied Gideon, 'Who is he?' asked Gideon innocently.

'Well, he's the Clanford in Clanford and Fox Publishers, but he's dead now.'

'Now that is an odd coincidence,' remarked Gideon.

'Yes, I thought so, to start with, but there's a little more. And this will help you quite a bit if you decide to finish off Prospect Road.

Apart from being a plagiarist, Joshua Clanford was a charlatan, drunk, gambler and a womaniser by all accounts. While he was out playing every night, his wife Madeleine embarked on a love affair, and do you know who she had an affair with? Believe me, this will surprise you.'

'I've no idea,' said Gideon, 'it all sounds absolutely fascinating.'

'Gideon Drew, no less.' replied Blake, with an expression of utter surprise blended with the absolute certainty that it was no surprise at all to Gideon.

'Amazing,' said Gideon. 'My namesake, no less. Now that really would make a delightful story. This Gideon sounds like a right bastard.'

'Yes, he does, doesn't he? But what I don't understand,' continued Blake, 'is why this Gideon character should start an affair with Madeleine. By all accounts, she was plum ugly, a bit of a gargoyle. That is the bit that confuses me. So if you could think of a decent reason for Gideon taking up with Madeleine in the first place, we could be on our way to another winner.'

'Yes, we could,' said Gideon. 'I see what you mean.'

'Anyway, I will undoubtedly see you soon, so I will leave you with that conundrum, and maybe you could think over the proposal re Prospect Road. Let me know if you want a copy, and I will send one to you.' Blake stood up to leave and then sat back down to face Gideon for a few moments longer.

'You will treat Catherine and the children well, won't you? She doesn't deserve anything less, despite all that has happened.'

Gideon was a little surprised by this declaration. 'That is very magnanimous of you, Blake. I really appreciate you taking such a civilised view on things.' Blake smiled, even though his heart was breaking deep down, but there was no way he would let Gideon see that. He still had a few things to do before everything was entirely settled. He finished his pint, stood up to shake Gideon's hand, and walked away, leaving Gideon, for once in his life, a little bewildered.

Gideon stayed at the pub for another half hour, wondering why Blake was being so reasonable and accommodating. It wasn't something he had factored into his plan.

Chapter 26
Wednesday

Blake arrived home just after four o'clock, having driven around the countryside for a while mulling over the events of the past five days, but more particularly the last few hours. He thought back to the previous Friday when he had arrived home with expectations of an enjoyable weekend, possibly visiting a country pub or maybe a country fair on Saturday and doing some essential shopping with his family on the way home.

On Sundays in summer, he and Catherine would do some work in the garden and spend time with Max and Claudia, catching up on what had happened in their lives and taking careful notice of the tiny physical changes that had invariably occurred over the course of the week. Changes that he seldom detected during the week - as he usually arrived home mid-evening. By which time, they would both already be in bed.

New vital words may have been learnt and were now permanently committed to memory, ready to be rolled out at any opportune moment. New abilities learned, new goals achieved, old problems conquered or overcome. To crawl, to sit up, and then for each of them, the momentous day they would take their first unassisted steps. Before he knew it, they would be wilfully running everywhere with gay abandonment, oblivious to life's vagaries and cruelties - fates and fortunes. He clearly remembered the first day they began to walk, a treasured memory hopefully only ever seen once in a child's lifetime.

But in just a few days, all that would change forever. The past was for Blake to keep and treasure. Memories nobody could take away. But the future would now be entirely different from how he thought it would be. He would no longer be a significant part of it.

Alternate weekends spent in their company would be the only opportunity for him to experience the tiny changes in their characters. Changes that may have occurred during the previous two weeks. The refinement and development of idiosyncrasies that would intractably and imperceptibly mark their individuality for life. Max was now seven and Claudia six, but Max was by far the quieter of the two and much preferred to curl up in a chair with a book rather than watch television. He had begun to show a remarkable ability to not only read and absorb books but to question their credibility, integrity, and validity in a world of words. But Blake would no longer be there to answer the questions he might ask; that would now be Gideon's role.

Max had already come to realise that it was essential to keep an open mind about anything he was reading. Invariably the writer, whoever he was, would always accentuate a biased perspective on the subject matter, which could be severely tainted by a lack of objectivity. Undoubtedly, there will always be other interpretations. Max didn't quite put it that way, but that was the message he unintentionally conveyed.

Blake found this characteristic profoundly exhilarating in somebody so young, particularly as it was his flesh and blood. He harboured a secret desire that Max might someday come to work in the family business. In readiness for when the moment came to hand over the reins and stand aside, as Reggie Clanford had done for him. From time to time, Blake would propose outlandish or ridiculous scenarios - to evaluate how Max would explore and interrogate the integrity of the suggestion and endeavour to detect the flaws and weaknesses. He found these moments immensely pleasurable and rewarding. They brought him and Catherine great happiness far beyond any they had previously experienced or had expected in their lifetime. Apart from the joy of being with each other... but that was now coming to an end.

These were the things he would miss, the growing-up part. One weekend in two would now be spent alone, with endless hours to reflect on how things used to be. Would this change in their circumstances alter Max's and Claudia's characters' outlook on life? Would it weaponise the betrayal, for this was, unquestionably, what it was, a betrayal of the contract - and would that do immeasurable and irreparable damage? Would they be better or worse people for their trials? All these questions troubled him deeply.

The house was eerily quiet. Before Blake left for his meeting, Catherine mentioned that she would do some shopping and take Max and Claudia with her, as Isabella would have finished by then.

He poured himself a large glass of bourbon without ice and sat down in his study to skim over Prospect Road again. After about thirty minutes, Blake wandered back into the lounge and poured himself another bourbon. He didn't usually drink so fast at this time of day, but the first glass did not appear to have induced the dulling effect he so desperately craved. He sat back at his desk, took a large sip, and leaned back in his chair.

The room slowly began to turn, and for a moment, it felt like he was on a carousel ride at a travelling fair. He made a mental note to slow down his whiskey intake; he had gulped down a glass and a half in no time, and that was never a good idea on an empty stomach. He closed his eyes briefly to stop himself from feeling giddy, but that didn't help. Then he noticed that some of the books had started to float out of the bookshelves and slowly spiral around in the middle of the room. One by one, different books came sharply into focus, hovering in front of him, then withdrawing to allow another to take its place. Most of the books eventually made their way back into the bookshelves from whence they came, leaving just three spiralling around in front of him: Prospect Road, which had not been published yet, but he could clearly see the title; then came The Chapter Room, he knew this one well, it had made him and Gideon extraordinarily rich - and then a third book came into view... The Sacrifice of Souls. He could faintly remember the title. He hadn't published the book himself, but it was the first title that Clanford and Fox had published back at the beginning of the twentieth century, over seventy years ago.

The three books began to morph into one larger volume, which started to glow red hot like a furnace - before a wraithlike image of Gideon appeared, hovering in the air, with the flaming book swirling faster and faster around his head. Gideon's raging eyes were on fire. Then the book burst into flames, and the image of Gideon grew much larger and moved closer to Blake as if it were about to engulf him, but Blake fought back with all his might... and then there was darkness.

The next moment Blake was back at his old university, wandering around outside, appearing confused, and he could see that everybody else was staring at him. He ran up to the top of the stone steps leading to the front entrance to the main building but then slipped and began to slide all the way back down the stairs on his heels, but somehow remained upright. When Blake reached the bottom, he stood up, still slightly dazed. In the distance, he could see a girl pedalling furiously towards him. When she arrived, he realised it was Catherine, but she was only about eighteen years old - but he never knew her at eighteen. And then she spoke…

'Blake… Blake, are you okay?'

Blake opened his eyes. 'What?'

'Are you okay? You were asleep in your chair, waving your arms about. I thought you were having a seizure or something.'

Still half-dazed, he looked around the room. 'I was fighting off monsters, killing the demons,' he exclaimed. His eyes look petrified.

'What?' replied Catherine, looking confused and concerned for his sanity.

'I was…' Then he realised what he was saying. Fighting off demons. Christ, that is for children. I am not a child anymore; I put the monsters away when I became a man. I am no longer a child… But now he knew what he had to do. Some of it had already been done. Now, he would have to finish it if he wanted to win Catherine back.

'I was having a nap. No, I must have fallen asleep and had a daydream.'

'Looked like a nightmare to me,' said Catherine.

'Yes. Yes, it was. But I think it's nearly over now.'

'You are okay then?' said Catherine, completely missing the real implications of his reply.

'Yes, yes, I'm fine,' said Blake. He had to focus his mind for a few more moments, as he still wasn't a hundred per cent certain where he was. Had the last few weeks all been a horrible nightmare from which he had just returned, or had he, in fact, just returned to the nightmare?

'Have you been drinking?' asked Catherine.

'Yes, I had one, possibly two,' replied Blake.

'I've told you before not to drink on an empty stomach. You know how it affects you.'

'I know, I know,' replied Blake apologetically, but he was reasonably sure he had not drunk that much.

'You will have to look after yourself when I'm…' she did not finish the sentence.

Gone, thought Blake, finishing her sentence for her. That is the word, gone. Can't you bloody say it? He felt a little belligerent. The bitterness of recrimination was beginning to well up inside, but he said nothing and gently bit his lip till it hurt.

He smiled. 'Yes, of course, I will. It is just like you said, I didn't eat. I was reading, and I forgot.'

Catherine glanced at him, and an expression of reproach and concern flashed across her face. She was madly in love with Gideon, but that had not extinguished all her feelings for Blake.

'I've arranged to stay over at Gideon's house tonight. I hope that is alright?' It sounded like a request, but it was not; it was an explicit declaration of intent. It was all so matter of fact for Catherine in this new relationship. It was as if she had been drugged or was in a trance and was not aware of what had happened or what effect it would have on other people. It was probably not the best timing to mention this now, but she thought the sooner said, the better. Now was not the time for hesitancy or indecision. The executioner who procrastinates inflicts infinitely more pain and suffering than the one whose aim is swift and true and kills with a single strike.

No confusion any longer, thought Blake; this was the reality. He had returned to the nightmare and would have to ease back on drinking in the afternoon, that much he knew for sure. But what was that dream all about? He could recall every detail, every moment. It was so vivid. It couldn't possibly have been generated solely by the alcohol, he reasoned… The Sacrifice of Souls? Why had that particular book featured in his dream? He had never given it a second thought before. Maybe he should read it. And then everything suddenly became clear, and he remembered what he had to do.

'Fine, no problem,' replied Blake. For some reason, Catherine's declaration that she was staying over at Gideon's that night did not register as being of any concern at that moment. In fact, it didn't seem to register at all. There was a time when he could not have conceived of hearing those words without being emotionally destroyed, but those feelings were now held in a kind of cryogenic suspension. Far more pressing matters that had to be quickly addressed were whirling around in his mind.

Chapter 27
Thursday

Catherine arrived back at the house just after eight in the morning. It was Isabella's day off, and everything seemed strangely tranquil. Fortunately, it was half term, and the children were not up. Blake had been up most of the night reading and drinking, despite the previous day's reprimand, and had fallen into a deep sleep before waking up and eventually getting to bed at just after three o'clock. Catherine had already showered at Gideon's, so she went straight to the kitchen and started preparing breakfast.

'Breakfast in fifteen minutes,' shouted Catherine up the staircase after a few minutes. She could hear movement upstairs, so she knew they were awake. Max and Claudia wandered down the stairs in their pyjamas ten minutes later.

'Aren't you dressed yet,' asked Catherine? It was a rhetorical question to which Max responded with a confused expression. Claudia did not answer. They smiled sweetly, then dropped into their chairs. Blake came bounding down the staircase a few minutes later, fully dressed and apparently unaffected by the previous night's drinking. Even if he had been, he would have been ill-advised to mention it.

'Morning, Catherine,' said Blake, smiling without a hint of reservation. It was as if he had forgotten everything that had happened the day before.

'What are you up to today?' asked Catherine casually. It was a suitably vague enquiry; she knew she no longer held the franchise on asking searching questions about his private life. The sacrificial lamb of innocence and truth had been well and truly slaughtered on the altar of betrayal. That baton of privilege had now been passed firmly to Gideon.

'Nothing at all, I just feel... I feel good.' He smiled at Max and Claudia, and they returned the gesture a little warily. He buttered some toast and ate it slowly before drinking his coffee.

Catherine was strangely unsettled by Blake's tacit acceptance of their revised living arrangements. She found it unnerving that he had only once raised his voice over the sudden and dramatic change to their lives, before suddenly accepting and embracing it with no further resistance. Blake's cheery disposition permeated through to Max and Claudia, who had become almost sanguine about the whole matter. Catherine and Blake sat down at the table for an oddly enjoyable breakfast. Blake enjoyed these rare moments; he always had.

'Any more coffee or orange, anybody?' asked Catherine.

'No, thank you,' replied Max and Claudia in unison. 'Can we see Uncle Gideon today,' continued Max? Blake pushed his cup and saucer over to Catherine, and as he did so, he looked up into her face. She could see his expression had changed, not dramatically, but sufficiently to register some hurt deep inside on hearing Max's plea. For a few brief moments, Catherine did not look away but continued to gaze at Blake, hoping that she might be able to gauge what he was thinking, but she could not. That tenuous bond, that fragile golden thread of commonality that once ran between them, had been irretrievably severed.

'I don't know; we will have to ask Daddy.' They all looked at Blake.

'I have a meeting later this morning that will take a few hours, so no problem. What time do you expect to get back?' It was a peculiar question, and the implications were not lost on Catherine.

'I'll just go for a few hours, so we could be back by one o'clock if that's okay.'

'Are you staying there tonight?' asked Blake blankly.

'No, not tonight,' replied Catherine.

'Okay, I'll see you this afternoon,' replied Blake, smiling.

They all helped clear the breakfast table, and Max and Claudia went out into the garden. Blake went into his study and opened the safe. He lifted the manuscript of Prospect Road but did not remove it; instead, he fumbled around for a large old brown envelope beneath it. The words Clanford and Fox were written on the front in neatly handwritten italics. Company Documents. Underneath, a small list of the contents had been typed onto a faded white label:

1) Articles of Association & memorandum.

2) Certificate of Incorporation.

3) Minutes of various AGMs.

4) Share certificates.

Blake put the envelope into his leather satchel and dropped the two self-closing tags. He glanced around his study to see if he needed anything else. Having satisfied himself, he did not; he walked back across the hall into the kitchen where Catherine was tidying up after breakfast.

'I'll be back about one, all being well. The traffic shouldn't be too bad today.'

Catherine was about to ask where he was going, but she changed her mind for some reason.

Chapter 28

Taylor Bedridge was one of the new split-discipline practices dealing with accountancy and law within the same office. Blake had found this to be of great benefit to him as it saved him considerable time when dealing with the increasing number of clients' intertwined legal and financial affairs. Most of whom he now acted for as an agent.

Many newly successful writers were unfamiliar with the business side of the publishing and writing world, so he would direct them straight to John Taylor of Taylor Bedridge. John had solved many niggling problems over the years.

John came into reception and shook Blake's hand.

'Good to see you, Blake. Please come on up.' John led him through the labyrinth of offices to the first floor, where his office was situated.

'Take a seat,' said John pointing to a chair. John's secretary came through and asked if he would like some tea.

'Yes, please,' replied Blake. 'White, two sugars, thank you.' The secretary smiled and left.

'So,' said John. 'You've intrigued me. You mentioned the disposal of assets on the telephone, but with an unfamiliar prerequisite.

'Well, briefly, I need to know whether it can be done without the recipient knowing,' said Blake.

'Before I can answer that with any certainty, I need to understand what precisely you want me to do. What you are asking… is highly irregular, to say the least. I need to be certain I have not misunderstood your instructions. Also, I must check whether it is even legal. But, based on what you have told me so far, I do not think that will be an issue. Of more importance are the financial implications, which, to put it mildly, are extremely onerous and need to be very carefully considered. They will have an inestimable effect on Catherine, the children, and everybody who works for you. You do realise that?'

Blake nodded but said nothing. He carefully listened to every sentence, word and syllable being painstakingly explained and his proposals' ramifications.

'The worst-case scenario could see you bankrupt and lose everything you have if your plan doesn't work. I have presumed that behind all of this, there is a plan, a reason?' He looked sternly at Blake to ensure he clearly understood what he was saying. Now was not the time for indecision, hesitancy or uncertainty. There was no room for manoeuvre or retreat after the transaction had been completed.

'I fully understand everything you have said,' replied Blake. 'If necessary, I will sign a declaration exonerating you from any responsibility whatsoever for my actions.'

'Can you tell me why?' asked John.

'I can't. If I did, first you would think I had taken leave of my senses…'

'I already think that,' said John interrupting. Blake smiled.

'…and secondly, you wouldn't believe it. But I promise you this much: after it is all over, one way all the other, I will explain… if I can… if I am able….' John was a little unnerved by the last few words. They smacked of Machiavellian melodrama, but this was not play-acting; this was real, of that much he was sure.

'When do you want this matter concluded?' asked John.

'The sooner, the better,' replied Blake. 'I can't break this enchantment until your part is done and I have finished mine.'

It was an odd, enigmatic phrase; John wondered if it was some sort of analogy, though he didn't know what. As far as he was aware, what he was being asked to do would change everything; there was nothing else.

'I will have a small document drawn up before you go. It will only take a few minutes. You must sign it and have it witnessed by an unconnected third party and then returned to me. I will then arrange the transfer.'

'My bank is just across the road. If I have the manager endorse it, will that be okay?' asked Blake.

'That would be fine,' replied John.

Blake got up from his chair to leave, but before taking the second step, John jumped out of his chair and quickly walked around the desk to grab Blake's hand. As he did so, he put his other arm around Blake's shoulders and pulled him close to hold him in a tight embrace. Blake returned the embrace. He needed an ally right now, and John was there when he needed him. He would not forget.

'Be careful, my friend,' said John, 'I have a very odd feeling about all this. Will I see you again afterwards?'

'Of course, you will. It may be a while, but you will.'

John smiled. 'If there is anything else, just let me know. We have been friends for a long time and...'

'Thank you,' said Blake, 'but you will have done enough.'

John said nothing but clasped Blake's hand with both hands and shook it one more time.

As Blake left the room, John whispered under his breath, good luck, old friend. May the Gods be with you.

Chapter 29
Thursday afternoon

Blake arrived home just after one, but Catherine had not yet returned. He went into his study, picked up the telephone and called the office.

'Hi Carol, could you put me through to Jamie?'

'No problem, Blake,' replied Carol. There was a short delay while the extension rang.

'Blake,' said Jamie, 'how are you?'

'Not too bad. Sorry I haven't been in this week, but something cropped up.'

'No problem, we're just about managing the empire without you, but we will need you next week. There's a few…'

Blake interrupted, 'Jamie, I must ask you to do something for me.'

'Anything,' replied Jamie. 'You're the boss.'

'I know this will sound ridiculous, and it won't make any sense to you at all, but it is crucially important to me.' Blake heavily stressed the word "crucially."

'No problem, whatever it is, I'll do it,' said Jamie enthusiastically.

'But you don't know what it is yet,' said Blake?

'You want me to murder somebody,' asked Jamie?

'No,' replied Blake, 'it's not that bad.'

'Right,' said Jamie. 'Then it's not a problem.'

Blake took a deep breath, 'The company published a book many years ago. It is still on our back catalogue for occasion reprints; it was a big seller around the early 1900s. It's called A Sacrifice of Souls.'

'You want me to get a copy from the archive?' asked Jamie.

'No… It's a little more than that. I want you to arrange for a small reprint run of, say, one copy.'

'One copy? The printers can't print one copy. I think the minimum is a hundred,' replied Jamie, 'but we probably have a few copies somewhere that haven't been pulped.'

'I will have to have a hundred, then. There will be some small amendments, so we need a new print run.'

'No problem,' said Jamie, sounding a little intrigued, 'Are there many changes, or can you tell me over the phone?'

'I'll fax over the details. How long will it take?' asked Blake.

'If it is still on their reprint list, as you say, then a few days, maybe a week.'

'Good,' said Blake. I will send over the details as soon as I have finished this call and leave it with you to arrange. Oh, and I won't be in till Wednesday or Thursday next week. Terribly busy here for a few days.'

'No problem,' said Jamie. 'Hopefully, we will have the reprints here by then.'

'That would be good,' said Blake. 'Thank you.'

'No problem,' said Jamie. 'Anything else?'

'No, no, thank you. I'll leave it with you.'

'And that's it?' Jamie asked, sounding surprised at the relatively trivial nature of the request - he had expected something more significant, even life-threatening, but maybe that was because he read too many crime thrillers.

'Yes, that's it,' replied Blake.

'Right. I'll see you next week then,' said Jamie, still intrigued.

'Yes, next week. Good-bye.' His mind seemed to be somewhere else.

Blake put the phone down, slipped a sheet of paper he had previously typed into the fax machine, and punched in the office fax number. The device made a funny churning noise, and the paper slowly disappeared. He sat back in his chair and wondered what next week would bring. Had he set something in motion that might have been better left alone? Maybe it would all come to nothing, and it was all a tremendous waste of time and effort, but then perhaps not. But it was too late now to go back.

The whole thing was based on a capricious notion that had come to him in a dream - the last words that Anthony Clackle said. "Pass Cath to Gideon, and it will end." He wondered if he had read too many stories over the years and was now confusing reality with fantasy and make-believe.

Whatever the outcome, he could not sit around and wait for the inevitable. He had to take a chance. Life is about taking chances occasionally; the important thing was the balance of probability: Was the gain worth the gamble? He didn't really have any choice, and anyway, it was now all in the lap of the gods; everything was - there was never really any chance of going back.

There was just one last thing he had to do.

Chapter 30
Friday

Blake awoke early on Friday; he hadn't slept much during the night. His family's imminent departure and the plan he had set in motion were playing on his mind. Over and over, Blake replayed the two possible scenarios in his head. He was as confident as he could be that the likeliest outcome was the most probable outcome, and that would be what he wanted to happen. But that still didn't alleviate the unmistakable sense of fear and foreboding. But fear of what, precisely? That was what he kept asking himself. The unknown, the conclusions he had not considered, the possible reactions from Gideon he had not factored into the equation. All these played on his mind, like a carousel going around and around, each taking its turn to face him before slipping out of view to be replaced by the next.

During dinner the night before, Catherine had mentioned that she wanted to start packing some of her clothing and personal things the next morning, along with some of Max and Claudia's clothes. She had arranged for some cardboard packing cases to be delivered the following day so that she could hopefully finish over the weekend. She had also arranged for a removal lorry to transfer the cases to Gideon's house on Monday morning.

'Is there anything you want me to do,' asked Blake? It was a situation he clearly did not know how to handle. He was floundering a little, endeavouring to figure out the correct etiquette under these circumstances.

Should he help his wife, who was about to leave him, and thereby effectively become an accomplice by default in the conspiracy to break up his marriage? Or should he stand back and let her do everything. That seemed the more natural yet belligerently unaccommodating option? He just didn't know.

'No, we can manage,' said Catherine. She felt as awkward as he did. 'Look, I know this is very distressing for you. Why don't you go out for a few hours while I make a start on this? It might be a little less traumatic for all of us if…'

Oh great, thought Blake, you want me to bugger off and sit in the pub and get drunk all day while you pillage and plunder the remnants of my life - our life. He knew she would not do anything unreasonable or remove anything that meant something to the two of them without consulting him. Nevertheless, he knew there would be tiny spaces and voids everywhere once she had completed packing the boxes. Where once sat a familiar photograph or a curio, a memory of different times, happier times, there would now be nothing. Something would become conspicuous by its very absence.

Fundamentally, each room would still look the same as it was. Only when subjected to closer examination would we notice the subtle idiosyncrasies that make every dwelling space unique. Only then would each room appear to have lost something that had once made it warm and welcoming. Each room would be a few shades closer to a hotel room's cold, clinical, unemotional colour. The aura and the atmosphere of a house occupied by a family of four would be demonstrably and immeasurably different from that of a house occupied by one lonely man. Nothing could conceal that.

'I have a few things to do as it is,' said Blake, 'so we can have breakfast, and then I'll leave you to it.'

'That would be good,' said Catherine. 'I'll put some coffee on.'

They sat at the table, ate toast, and drank coffee silently, for there was little more to say. Just as they finished, Max came downstairs.

'We are going on a long holiday to Uncle Gideon's,' said Max, innocently unaware of what was happening.

'And me,' said Claudia, suddenly appearing from nowhere.'

"We" means all of us,' retorted Max, 'except Daddy. He's not coming.'

'Yes,' said Catherine, 'Daddy is staying here to look after our house.'

Those few innocently spoken words reduced Blake to tears. He hurriedly left the room so as not to let his children see him crying.

'You will both be coming back to our house to see Daddy and stay over the weekend every couple of weeks,' said Catherine in a slightly louder voice to ensure Blake heard it. It was a vain heartfelt attempt to lessen the pain she had unintentionally inflicted.

"Our house," thought Blake. He wondered if it was a gentle hint that it was jointly owned. An overture before impending matrimonial proceedings. Divorce? He had not considered that aspect, but they would have to discuss it before long. Living in suspended animation was not an option. Even that inevitability was subject to the law of unintended consequences. No matter what arrangements were made, he still had no idea how this situation might eventually play out, despite everything he had done to manage the situation.

Blake went back into the kitchen.

'Right, I'm popping out for a few hours. Be back around two, okay?'

'Yes,' said Catherine. 'I can only do so much each day. I am feeling...' She did not finish, but Blake knew what she was trying to say. He kissed Max and Claudia and then left.

The weekend passed with little incident. Catherine packed her boxes, and as the sun was shining most of the time, Blake sat in the garden, half-reading a book while pondering the proceedings he had set in motion. Occasionally, he would look up at Max and Claudia, happily playing, and wonder how the outcome would affect Max and Claudia. He had no real idea how it all might end...

Chapter 31
Monday

On Monday morning, the removal people rang early to say their lorry had broken down and it would be convenient to make the collection on Wednesday instead. That was the day Catherine intended to move out anyway, so she agreed to the rescheduled arrangement. She called Gideon to tell him about the change of plan and confirmed she would pop over that night.

During the afternoon, there were a couple of telephone calls.

'Blake,' shouted Catherine from the house. 'It's Jamie at the office.' Blake made his way back to the house and picked up the receiver.

'Jamie,'

'Hi Blake, how are you?'

'Fine, taking in the sunshine at the moment.'

'Sounds good. It's horrible up here, the air con's broken, and it's as muggy as hell on a Friday.'

Hell, on a Friday, thought Blake... good name for a book... He never really switched off. 'How can I help you?'

'That book, A Sacrifice of Souls. The printers pulled all the stops out, and they will arrive later today. What do you want me to do with them?'

'Ah,' said Blake mulling over the options, 'I could come up tomorrow... yes, that would be best. I can't trust the post as I need them by Wednesday.'

'Are you sure?' said Jamie.

'Yes. I am. I need to pop in town to see John at Taylor Bedridge anyway, so I can kill two birds with one stone.'

'Fair enough. I will see you tomorrow. Enjoy the day.' Jamie hung up, and Blake stood momentarily with the receiver still in his hand, pondering how he would stage-manage the next part of the plan.

'Did I hear you say you were going to London tomorrow?'

'Yes, I'll be out for most of the day.'

'Would it be okay if I took Max and Claudia over to Clanford House for the day, as you won't be here,' asked Catherine cautiously? For some reason, she did not say 'Gideon's but referred to the house by name. Somehow, it seemed less offensive. Less of another shard of humiliation tearing into his flesh. 'If you don't want me to, I….' she began.

'No problem,' interrupted Blake. 'I won't be here, so… What time do you think you might return?' It was all very civilised and adult but somehow smacked of more Machiavellian treachery being subtly orchestrated by Gideon. Those thoughts were never far from his mind. He did not think of Catherine or the children that way; they were innocent parties, nothing more than pawns in Gideon's game. Gideon was the instigator, the controlling personality, the man he had to confront. The man he would eventually face when the last card was played.

Chapter 32
Tuesday

Catherine woke early and went downstairs to the kitchen to make some coffee. She had not slept particularly well during the night but still needed a shot of caffeine to get her brain working. She sat at the breakfast table, poured two cups of coffee, and pushed one cup across the table. Blake was already dressed and sitting at the table. He had been reading the newspaper but had put it down. It felt a little awkward.

'Can I speak to you for five minutes?' asked Blake, which seemed odd as they were facing each other and drinking coffee. But the inference was that he wanted to discuss something of significance.

'Of course,' replied Catherine, looking a little guarded.

'Look, this is a bit embarrassing, but I want to ask you to do something for me.'

'What,' said Catherine?

'When you next see Gideon, could you discuss whether he would be prepared to set up an arrangement to protect you and the children? Until such times as the divorce comes through, and I presume you get married? Just in case something happens in the...'

Catherine interrupted, 'He's already done so.'

'He has?' queried Blake.

'Yes. Gideon has changed his will so that we will be provided for should anything happen to him. I know you would not see us starve or be without a roof over our heads, but I did not want to take the house or half the business from you. That would not be fair, and Gideon has agreed.

'So, you have already discussed this,' said Blake, slightly surprised.

'Yes, yes, I have. I thought it was important to sort that out as quickly as possible to avoid any problems later.'

'Yes, I see,' said Blake.

'In the event of his death...' Catherine paused momentarily to allow the words to sink in, 'he has left everything to the children and me. He has no other family, so you have nothing to worry about.'

'Good, good,' said Blake. I'm relieved by that; it had been playing on my mind a bit.'

Catherine smiled at his continued concern for her, then, thinking about what he had said, realised just how hard that must have been. Blake briefly mulled over Gideon's provisions, noting how conveniently they fitted in with his plan. Maybe things were going to turn out okay after all. He even managed a smile.

'Looks like a lovely day to go to the office,' said Catherine glancing out of the window and changing the subject.

Blake smiled, finished his coffee and stood up. Then he leaned forward instinctively to kiss her before sharply withdrawing and apologising profusely. For a fraction of a second, his brain had temporarily disconnected itself from reality. He quickly put his jacket on, grabbed his bag and left without saying another word. Catherine went back to bed for an hour, pondering the incident she had just experienced in the kitchen.

Blake arrived at the office building just after ten o'clock and took the lift instead of the stairs. As he stepped out, he noticed the two large half-glazed oak doors in front of him, with the words Clanford and Fox Publishers – Est. 1911 painted in brown lettering on the glass. He had been through the doors thousands of times but had never looked at them. They were the original doors, the same ones that Gideon Drew had walked through in 1912 if Blake was correct in his assumption.

He greeted everybody with his usual smile as he passed through reception and the front office to his office at the back. He sat down in the old brown leather chair. The chair he stubbornly refused to replace and the one that Reggie Clanford had used. The one Reggie had always considered his lucky chair and the one he liked to sit in whenever making an important decision. It had also served Blake well so far. He looked at the silver-framed photograph of Catherine and the children, the present she had given him on his thirty-fourth birthday when everything had been perfect. He smiled momentarily at the memory, and then the smile disappeared, replaced by the look of a sullen, angry, tormented soul. Jamie popped in.

'Hi Blake, good to see you. Everything good?' asked Jamie.

'Getting there,' replied Blake, quickly changing his expression.

'The book, it's over there.' Jamie pointed to three boxes next to one of the bookshelves, 'I put one on your desk for you to check the changes. How come the…'

'It's a long story,' Blake interrupted. 'An awfully long story, but I will explain it to you soon, just not today if that's okay.'

Jamie looked intrigued but left it at that.

'I'll get you a coffee,' he said.

'That would be great; I want to read this just once more.' He took the tattered manuscript of Prospect Road from his bag and laid it on the desk alongside a copy of The Chapter Room by Gideon Drew. That had now sold over thirty million copies in hardback and paperback. Then he pulled across the brand-new edition of A Sacrifice of Souls, a novel by "Gideon Drew." Inside the book was a small addendum and corrigendum on the second page, something never before seen in Clanford and Fox's published works.

Addendum and Corrigendum

When this book was first published in 1912 by Clanford and Fox, the author was stated as Joshua Clanford, a business partner. At that time, the publishers had no reason to doubt the veracity or integrity of the authorship claim. No counterclaim or objection was ever received by the publishing company by any other party claiming authorship. Therefore, the publishers went ahead with the publication of the work in the full and honest belief that it should be attributed to the pen of Joshua Clanford.

However, Clanford and Fox Publishers' further investigations during 1983–1984 revealed serious doubts about the authorship's original claim, which has now been wholly substantiated. Beyond any reasonable doubt, we are currently satisfied that A Sacrifice of Souls was indisputably written by Mr Gideon Drew in 1911. We now acknowledge Gideon Drew as the factual author of this work. We humbly apologise to Mr Gideon Drew and his family for any material loss or personal anguish they may have suffered because of this error.

We are now pleased to acknowledge Mr Gideon Drew as the correct author of this book. To fully authenticate the reassigned copyright, prescribed copies for libraries and institutions will be replaced with the corrected edition.

Blake Thornton
Managing Director
Clanford and Fox
Publishers and Publishing Agents.

About three o'clock in the afternoon, Blake had a call put through to him from Taylor Bedridge. John confirmed that the transaction had been completed and the details lodged at Companies House.

Chapter 33

Tuesday

Blake arrived home just after six to be greeted by Max and Claudia at the front door. He kissed them both, took off his shoes, dropped his bag on the chair by the front door and walked hand in hand with them into the lounge.

'We have had a lovely day at Uncle Gideon's, and we are going to stay there for a holiday from tomorrow,' said Max. Claudia smiled in agreement. She seemed a little subdued, however, not as jubilant as Max.

'Will you be coming with us, Daddy?' asked Claudia.

'No, no, I won't. I have a lot to do here, and I'm terribly busy at work, but I am sure you will have a wonderful time.' Claudia seemed oddly reserved and a little disappointed by Blake's reply.

'I love you, Daddy,' said Claudia unexpectedly. It was simple, plaintive, honest and hurt like hell. Blake felt a lump come up in his throat, and he knew at once that despite her tender years, Claudia had detected something was amiss by the tone of his voice.

Like all women, she had an inbuilt, highly developed sixth sense, an instinct that told her when something was not quite right, but she still didn't know what it was. Max had missed the altered state altogether, but then men often do.

'Gideon has a swimming pool,' said Max.

'Has he?' replied Blake. 'Well, that will be great fun for the summer.' He was just going through the motions for their sake. He refused to put a dampener on Max and Claudia's expectations. They had done nothing wrong and had no comprehension of what was happening. He could not ruin their hopes and dreams just because his life had been destroyed.

They all sat down to their last meal, a quiet affair, with Catherine not saying much. After dinner, Blake went to his study to continue reading A Sacrifice of Souls, which he had started to read on the train home. Catherine, Max and Claudia watched television and Max and Claudia went to bed at around seven-thirty. Catherine carried on watching the TV more as a distraction than for its entertainment value before popping her head around the corner of Blake's room and saying goodnight at nine-thirty.

'Do you have a few minutes, Catherine?' asked Blake.

Catherine looked a little surprised. They'd had plenty of time to discuss anything he wanted to talk about over dinner, but he had remained relatively subdued.

'Yes, of course,' she replied. Reluctantly she entered Blake's study and sat down.

'I'm not going to lecture you or anything like that. You know how I feel about what is happening and how you feel, so there would be no point. But there are some things I think you should know.' Catherine looked a little uncomfortable but said nothing. She had half expected something like this at some stage, but due to the imminency of her departure, she had assumed it would not happen after all.

'There is something very unusual about Gideon, something I can't explain, something significant that you need to know.'

Once again, Catherine said nothing; she felt she owed him something, if only a courteous benevolence. She acknowledged what he said with a half-smile, anticipating some minor revelation. That would not affect what was happening, but she felt obliged to indulge him on this occasion. Once he had finished saying what he wanted to say, it would be over, and that would be an end to it. It was a small price to pay before her new future began.

'I don't know who Gideon actually is,' said Blake.

'I don't understand,' said Catherine. 'You're his agent, publisher and friend until… He is a good writer, as it turns out and a nice person. I love him, and he gets on well with the kids. He has a nice house; what else is there to know?' Catherine sounded a little confused by Blake's statement.

Each word of praise, another twist of the knife, thought Blake before replying.

'Gideon wrote another book.....'

'He hasn't mentioned that,' said Catherine.

'It was a remarkably successful book - sold millions of copies,'

'Are you sure?' asked Catherine, now sounding slightly intrigued. 'Why have you never mentioned it? I thought you said The Chapter Room was his first novel.'

'That's what I thought until I did some research – and this other book is also mentioned in Prospect Road.'

Catherine became slightly subdued momentarily as she recalled the self-writing manuscript they had repeatedly been reading for the last two years. The book which had unnerved both of them at times.

'I thought we had agreed that it was nothing more than coincidence, an example of literary synchronicity,' replied Catherine defensively.

'Possibly it is, but A Sacrifice of Souls isn't.

'A Sacrifice of Souls?' repeated Catherine. 'What's that?'

'That was the first book that Gideon wrote.'

'How come I have never heard of it?' replied Catherine, now beginning to have misgivings about what Blake was saying.

'He wrote it some time ago,' replied Blake. 'In fact, quite a long time ago, in 1912.'

'What do you mean in 1912? That is ridiculous… That's… seventy-two years ago. That would make Gideon over ninety. You must have him muddled up with someone else, someone with the same name. His grandfather, maybe? Well, no, it would have to be his…' She thought for a moment, working out the possibilities in her head, '…his great-grandfather. That's who must have written it; that would make sense.'

Blake said nothing at first; he let Catherine run her mind over what she had just said.

'We published the book,' said Blake.

'You? How? When?' replied Catherine, sounding surprised.

'Not me exactly, but Clanford and Fox. It was the first book they ever published. Originally the author was acknowledged as Joshua Clanford, one of the original partners in the business. He stole the book from a Gideon Drew and published it under his name.'

'But why?' said Catherine.

'Money,' replied Blake, 'just money. It's as simple as that.'

'How do you know all this? It doesn't make any sense at all.' Catherine was still having a problem taking in what Blake was saying. It all sounded unreal, like one of Gideon's weird fairy stories.

'It's all in the final chapters of Prospect Road, but more importantly... if you ask Gideon, I very much doubt he will deny it.'

'The book must be wrong. The age thing is ridiculous,' replied Catherine. 'Gideon is twenty-five, not ninety.'

'That's what I kept telling myself, but I've spoken to somebody who knew the truth, and that's what he told me, in a manner of speaking.'

'Who?' asked Catherine.

'Anthony Clackle.'

'The mysterious writer you could never get hold of?'

'I did, actually. I managed to track him down just before he died. His father knew Gideon in the 1940s. So, I believe the book is correct in almost every detail.'

'So, what happens now?' asked Catherine.

'Well, nothing much. I have redressed the matter of Gideon being acknowledged as the author of the book, and I have had an amended edition printed with an apology on behalf of the company.' With some trepidation, Blake leaned down to the floor, lifted a copy of A Sacrifice of Souls, and placed it on the desk in front of Catherine.

'It's not a bad book; I can see why Joshua stole it.'

Catherine picked up the book, handling it a little warily for some reason. She looked at the front cover and flicked through the pages. 'I should give this to Gideon.'

'You should. It rights many wrongs done to Gideon, and it belongs to him.'

'Or his grandfather,' suggested Catherine.

'Maybe, but I don't think so.'

Catherine smiled at Blake's odd presumption but was disinclined to disagree with him. It would have been churlish at this point in time.

'Will he be pleased, do you think,' asked Catherine?

'I think his tormented soul will, at last, be at peace,' replied Blake, 'he will receive the recognition he deserves at last.'

Catherine did not know what to make of that. 'I still don't understand the year thing. There must be a more obvious explanation.'

'I'm sure there is. Hopefully, Gideon will explain everything to you if you ask him. What reason would he have not to?' He smiled compassionately at Catherine, and she smiled back.

Blake had spoken as if he did not have an explanation either. He did have one, but not one he was inclined to discuss any further that day or any day for that matter.

'Thank you, Blake, for what you have done. I know you didn't have to do this, but it will make such a difference for Gideon.'

'I know that too,' said Blake. 'I know that too,' he repeated quietly. Catherine went to bed; Blake poured himself a large bourbon, sat back in his old green leather chair, and thought about what he had done and what might now happen. He did not know for sure; in fact, he had no idea at all. Once again, it was all in the lap of the gods.

Chapter 34
Wednesday

The removal lorry arrived at eight o'clock on the dot. Once the three men had drunk their obligatory cup of tea, they began removing the cardboard boxes that Catherine had so carefully packed. Blake sat in the garden while they worked, drinking coffee and reading the newspaper. He appeared unconcerned, almost sanguine, about what was happening. When the removal men had finished, the lorry drove off, and Catherine returned to the garden with Max and Claudia to say goodbye.

'We'll be going now,' said Catherine.

Blake jumped up, appearing a little surprised.

'Oh, right. Well, you all take it easy and don't work too hard unpacking and things. There is plenty of time to do all that in the weeks ahead. I hope it all goes well.' He leaned forward to pick up Claudia and Max and cuddle them.

'Now, you two must be strong little soldiers today and help Mummy, as she is going to be extremely busy in your new house. Can you do that for me?'

'Yes, Dad,' replied a perplexed Max. 'I still don't understand what is happening, Dad.' For some reason, Claudia chose to remain silent.

'Mummy will explain everything to you. There's nothing to worry about.' That seemed to reassure him and put his mind at rest. Blake smiled at Catherine. He kissed Max and Claudia and put them back on the floor.

'I love you both, don't forget that.' Looking up at Catherine, he added, 'I love you too, Catherine – always remember that. No matter what happens in the future, I will always love you.' It sounded a little ominous to Catherine, and she flashed him a curious look.

'You are going to be all right, aren't you?'

'Yes, I will be fine; you are the one setting out on the adventure into the unknown, not me.' That seemed to satisfy Catherine's concerns. She kissed him on the cheek and left with Max and Claudia, walking out of the garden for the last time as a family.

It must have been around eight o'clock that evening when Blake drove up to Clanford House. The imposing driveway was lined with copper beech trees on both sides. Blake had always favoured the copper beech because of its unique reddish-brown leaves in summer. They reminded him of something, but he could not remember what at that precise moment. He parked the car and grabbed the envelope lying on the passenger seat. He looked up at the magnificent Georgian-style mansion before him, wondering what must have happened there when Joshua had been in residence.

He rang the front doorbell and waited to see who would open the door. Would it be Max, he wondered, as he usually did at home, but it was not; it was Gideon.

'Blake, I wasn't expecting you,' said Gideon, looking surprised. 'Do come in. The children would love to see you. I'm not sure where they are right now, but…'

Blake interrupted. 'No, I'm not staying. I've just brought this around. It's rightfully yours, and you deserve it for everything you have suffered over the years.'

Gideon looked perplexed. 'What is it?' he asked.

'I am sure you will understand. Hopefully, it will bring you what you seek.'

'Sounds very enigmatic,' replied Gideon, reluctantly holding his hand out to take the envelope. 'It's not a writ, is it?'

'No, it's not; it's a gift,' said Blake, smiling. 'Just a gift for your new life together, that's all.'

'What do you mean by all I have suffered over the years?' asked Gideon curiously. 'I wasn't aware that I had suffered anything.'

'Haven't you?' asked Blake, feigning surprise. 'I think you have endured a great deal: the loss of your wife, the death of your son, the theft of your book, and probably a few other things along the way. And, of course, the loss of your soul. At some moment in your life, you reached a point when there was nothing more to live for, and somebody made you a proposition that was too good to be true. What did you have to lose? So, you took it, but now maybe I think you regret that decision and are looking for salvation. All this retribution has cost you far more than you anticipated.'

Gideon's expression changed.

'I think you've got the wrong end of the stick, old chap,' he replied in a mildly condescending manner. He possessed the infuriating ability to roll dismissal and disrespect into a gentle jibe, which you could easily miss if you weren't paying attention. Blake wondered whether he had ever tried that tone on Catherine... He would have received short shrift had he, despite her current besottedness.

'You think so?' said Blake.

'Yes, I do,' replied Gideon firmly.

'Well, that's your prerogative. Maybe I am wrong, and if I am, I humbly apologise but enjoy the gift anyway. Did Catherine give you the other item I gave her to give to you?' enquired Blake casually.

'No, she hasn't given me anything yet, but it has been a bit hectic today with the moving-in, as you can imagine, so maybe...'

'Yes, maybe later,' replied Blake.

Gideon cautiously took the envelope. 'Thank you, Blake.'

'No problem. Speak soon,' replied Blake. He turned and began to walk back down the steps towards his car.

'Blake!' said Gideon, shouting after him just as he reached his car.

Blake turned, 'Yes.'

'This other Gideon person you speak of, my namesake, the one mentioned in Prospect Road.'

'Yes,' said Blake quietly. He now knew for certain he was right. This was the moment Blake had waited for. He could feel the cold shivery sensation of vanquishment run down his back.

'Do you think he loved his wife?'

Blake stared at Gideon momentarily, deliberating over the question and the many other unasked questions buried deep within the words. Then, slowly he made his way back to the bottom of the steps and stared up at Gideon standing at the top.

'Of course, he loved her, he loved her more than anything in the world, and they had a son, and he loved him too. He loved them both more than life itself.'

'Then why was he so bitter?' asked Gideon wearily.

'Because he had lost them, and there was no going back, no matter what the deal was, he would never see his wife or son again.

That is why '*he is*' bitter. He paused momentarily on the words "he is" to emphasise their relevance. That's probably why he spent his life taking revenge on...'

'Can he be saved?' interrupted Gideon.

'I don't know. Only he knows that and the terms of the arrangement.'

'The arrangement?' asked Gideon. 'What was this arrangement?'

'A sacrifice. A sacrifice of Souls,' replied Blake. 'That's what I think it was.'

'Oh,' said Gideon, 'I see. Do you think he was a good person?'

'I don't know. I imagine he was, once. He didn't appear to be an inherently bad person. It was just some terrible things that happened to him. They changed him, made him different...'

Gideon smiled. 'Well, thank you, Blake. That will help tremendously when I finish that story off.'

'No problem,' Blake replied. 'Any time. Bye.'

Gideon shut the door, and Blake walked back to his car.

He looked at the house for a few minutes before driving back home. He had done all he could. He had read Prospect Road and The Sacrifice of Souls repeatedly, and he was sure he was right, but only time would tell now.

Chapter 35

'Who was at the door, darling?' asked Catherine as she stood in the kitchen making tea.

'Oddly, it was Blake,' replied Gideon as he read the documents he had been handed.

'What did he want? Not a problem, was it?'

'No, far from it. Actually, I'm a little confused.'

'Why?' asked Catherine.

'Well, you're not going to believe this, but he appears to have transferred all the shares in Clanford and Fox Publishing to me.' Gideon continued reading the documentation.

'What!' exclaimed Catherine, carrying a tea tray into the dining room.

'All of them, every share,' replied Gideon.

'To you!' said Catherine, looking puzzled. 'But that doesn't make any sense. I could understand if he had transferred them to us but to you?' She placed one cup of tea next to Gideon and the other on the small table beside her chair. 'That doesn't make any sense.'

'He has written you a letter explaining why,' said Gideon.

'Read it out. I'm intrigued,' said Catherine, 'or, more accurately, totally confused.' She sat down and sipped the tea as Gideon read the letter aloud.

Dear Catherine,

I apologise for what may appear to be my rather odd behaviour regarding the share transfer. I will endeavour to explain the reason for my actions. As I mentioned yesterday, a certain Gideon Drew wrote a book over seventy years ago. The book was stolen by Joshua Clanford of Clanford and Fox Publishers, the company I once owned.

It was a remarkably successful book, making considerable money for Joshua Clanford. However, shortly after the book was published, Gideon's son became ill with tuberculosis. He needed treatment in Switzerland, but Gideon could not afford to send him, and his son died. Gideon's wife left him not long after that, cursing him for being such a fool, for allowing the book to be stolen and for having no money to save their son. About a year later, she, too, died of a broken heart, still grieving for her son. Gideon disappeared for a while and was presumed killed in action during the First World War. He resurfaced in 1920 as a wealthy and successful businessman.

Gideon started an affair with Madeleine Clanford, Joshua Clanford's wife, as retribution for Joshua stealing his book. Madeleine had an illegitimate son, Julian, who was subsequently adopted by the Mr and Mrs Clackle. And Julian Clackle later married and had a son, Anthony. Anthony wrote all this in his book Prospect Road. I believe he sent this to warn me about Gideon's intentions to steal you from me. It was a final act of revenge against Clanford and Fox, even though, in the beginning, I had nothing to do with the company.

Anthony also discovered something else. Gideon Drew never seemed to grow old, and from this tiny detail, he conceived a ridiculous notion. He believed that Gideon had made some kind of bargain in exchange for immortality. However, there would be a price to pay. Once Gideon had recovered the three things he had lost to Joshua Clanford, the bargain would be complete, and Gideon would have to settle his part of the arrangement.

He now has the first thing: you, a woman who loves him and two children to replace the one he lost.

Now Anthony Clackle told me to do something before he died. He said, 'Pass Cath to Gideon, and it will end.' I didn't know what that meant for a while. I thought he was referring to you, but you were already leaving me, so that didn't make sense. Then I suddenly realised that what Anthony actually meant was I had to give C.A.F. to Gideon, not Cath… and that is what I have now done. The complete shareholding in Clanford And Fox is now his. So the second thing, his stolen wealth, has been returned.

And when you give him the reprinted edition of the book I gave you, legally reinstating him as the correct author of "A Sacrifice of Souls," that will be the last item to be returned. That was also the first thing that was taken from him. So, if I am right, when you give him the book, his purgatory will be over, and the bargain he made all those years ago will be concluded. And the final settlement of his account will become due and payable.

Kind regards,
Blake Thornton

Gideon held up the documents. 'These are all the share certificates for the company,' he said, looking a little stunned, 'and your husband has gone raving mad.'

Catherine was confused. She jumped up out of her chair and ran out of the room. Gideon thought she was upset by Blake's actions. But when Catherine returned a few moments later holding a book, she displayed no sign of distress or annoyance, just the opposite. She stretched out her hand and gave the book to Gideon. 'And that, I believe, is yours...' She smiled, believing she had done something to please him.

'But I still don't quite understand the last part of Blake's letter. What does that all mean about a bargain?'

Gideon glanced up at Catherine with complete and absolute desolation in his eyes. His hand slowly, inexorably, snaked out towards the book. Despite every physical effort to restrain himself from reaching out for it, Gideon could not. His body appeared to be under the control of another otherworldly entity. His right hand edged closer to the tome before eventually grasping it tightly. At that very moment, Gideon's eyes began to glow, their colour changing from crystal blue to a terrifying flaming red. He stood up, his whole body shaking uncontrollably and his eyes much larger and brighter than before. He slowly began to rise up, levitating a few inches from the floor, then suddenly he started to age...

Just as this strange metamorphosis was happening, Max and Claudia came into the room, witnessing what was taking place. They ran over to Catherine, screaming, 'What's happening to Uncle Gideon, Mummy? What's happening?'

Chapter 36
Thursday

There was a knock on the door just after nine o'clock. Blake stumbled down the stairs. He had drunk a lot of booze the night before and was still feeling a bit hazy - he had planned to stay in bed a little longer.

Two policemen were standing at the door, both looking sombre.

'Mr Blake Thornton?' asked the first.

'Yes,' replied Blake.

'I'm Inspector Charlton, and this is Sergeant Wainwright. Can we come in for a moment, sir?'

'Of course, come on through.' Blake made his way into the lounge and pointed at two chairs. 'Please sit down.'

'Would you like to sit down, sir? We have a couple of questions we need to ask,' said Inspector Charlton.

'Oh, right, okay.' Blake sat down.

'I understand you live here with your wife and two children?' asked the inspector.

'I do, or should I say did. She moved out yesterday, in fact. Why?'

'Do you know where she moved to?' asked Sergeant Wainwright, referring to his notebook.

'Yes, just up the road. Clanford House, the big place on…'

'Yes sir, we know where it is,' interrupted the sergeant. Inspector Charlton glanced at Wainwright witheringly. Wainwright looked surprised.

'On her own?' asked Inspector Charlton.'

'To live with another man, if you must know.'

'Do you know who this man was?' asked Sergeant Wainwright.

'Look, where is all this going?' asked Blake, suddenly noticing the use of the past tense.

'There's been an accident,' said Inspector Charlton.

'An accident? What kind of accident? Is somebody injured?'

'I'm afraid I have some very grave news, sir. You see, there was a fire at Clanford House last night, and everybody in the building died. Nobody…' he hesitated on the word, then repeated it.

'Nobody was rescued alive; they are all dead.' The inspector was possibly overstating the situation, but it was best to be precise, even blunt, in his experience. It quickly removed any doubt, ambiguity or misunderstanding that might still be lingering regarding the possibility of survivors.

'Who exactly died?'

'Four people, three of whom we believe to be your wife, Catherine Thornton, and your two children, Max and Claudia Thornton. The fourth person was, we think, the owner Mr Gideon Drew, but that has not been confirmed yet.

Blake said nothing, stunned with disbelief. This wasn't how he had anticipated it would end. He thought Gideon might die; that was always a possibility, but not Catherine, Max, and Claudia. That should not have happened. That can't have happened. It can't be possible. Had he got it completely wrong? It was not supposed to end like this… His mind started to whirl like a windmill, utterly confused by what he was hearing.

'We obviously need to have them formally identified by you if possible, but there is little doubt that it is them. We can't seem to locate any relatives for Mr Drew,' said Sergeant Wainwright, 'but then there is virtually nothing left to identify, except for a wedding ring.'

The inspector glanced at Sergeant Wainwright admonishingly, not overly impressed by his unnecessarily detailed explication.

'Mr Drew appears to have been at the fire's epicentre,' continued the inspector. 'Strangely, it appears he spontaneously burst into flames, which quickly spread to the rest of the house. A large amount of packaging was lying everywhere, which unfortunately didn't help. But there was no evidence of an accelerant being used, so it seems to have been a freak accident. The fire investigation officer has no other explanation as to how it started. Still, we will have his full report in a few days. I am deeply sorry to bring you this news, but…'

Blake interrupted Inspector Charlton. 'I understand what you have to do.' He looked down at the floor, still unable to fully absorb what he had been told.

'How do you know for sure it's Catherine and my children?' asked Blake, still having a problem taking in the devastating news.

'We've spoken to his housekeeper - she lives in the gatehouse... she was quite certain who was in the house at the time.'

'Oh, I see,' replied Blake.

'We need you to identify your family, so if...' said Inspector Charlton. He was trying his best not to intrude further than was necessary into the grief he knew Blake was suffering. 'If you could...'

Blake interrupted. 'When do you want me to come down?' He seemed almost unaware of what was happening, still bewildered by circumstances he could never have imagined possible in his wildest nightmares.

'Tomorrow would be good. I could send a car. Say eleven o'clock – would that be okay?'

'Thank you,' replied Blake, his face still showing no discernible emotion other than shock.

'Do you have anybody that could come around and stay, or would you like me to arrange for somebody to come and stay with you for a...'

'No, that won't be necessary,' replied Blake. 'I have an old friend I can call. He'll come straight over.'

The two officers got up, and Blake showed them out.

It was brief and explicit, yet it didn't sound quite right. Something was missing, but he did not know what. He went over to the drink cabinet in the corner, poured himself a large Jack Daniels and took a large gulp. The impact was almost instantaneous - then the tears he was holding back began to flow.

He poured another large glass, sat down, and began to think back over everything that had happened. Once again, he returned to Prospect Road and all it had predicted, but it had never mentioned this. There was never any fire or deaths, not the last time he had read it. But would it have made any difference if it had? Would he have taken any more notice, he wondered? He could reread it, but what good would that do now? Maybe he should burn it. Perhaps he should have burnt it in the first place. But it was too late to change what had been done, but he would burn it anyway; that would stop it forever. Yes, that is what he would do. It had all started with that manuscript, and now he needed to finish it.

He would take it from the safe and destroy it in the garden. That would end everything... but then everything had ended anyway. He finished his drink, got up, went to the drink cabinet, took out the bottle, and poured himself another bourbon. He needed oblivion right now, and this was the quickest route. One more drink, then he would burn the book.

He took another gulp, and his head began to spin, slowly at first, then a little faster, and then he fell into a state of unconsciousness. When he came round this time, it wasn't to Catherine waking him from a bad dream. He was back sitting at the bottom of some stone steps leading up to what looked like the main door to one of the lecture halls at his old university. Looking around, he realised he must have just fallen down the steps. He struggled to his feet and looked around, trying to familiarise himself with his surroundings.

In the distance, he could see something coming towards him out of the shimmering summer haze. It was indistinct at first, but as the vision drew closer, he could see a girl on a bicycle pedalling frantically towards him.

She pulled up in front of him with a squeal of brakes and a splattering of shingle, smiled, and dropped her bicycle on the ground.

'Are you okay? I saw you fall down the steps.'

'Yes, yes, I'm fine, thank you. I just tripped. Do I know you?'

'Yes, of course you do. You are a silly arse, Thornton. We made love last night. Have you forgotten already? If this is the effect I have on you,' declared Catherine indignantly, 'it's not very complimentary.'

'No, of course not,' replied Blake. 'I'm just a bit dazed.'

'Dazed or dazzled by my beauty?' asked Catherine, playfully twirling around and around.

'Intoxicated by your resplendent intractability,' replied Blake with a grin, his head slowly coming together.

'I'm not sure what that actually means,' said Catherine.

'I'm in love with you, Miss Gayle,' explained Blake. 'That is what it means.'

'Oh, I see. Well, are you coming to the lecture or sodding around here all day, falling down steps?'

'I'm coming to the lecture,' replied Blake.

'Right, good,' said Catherine. She picked up her bicycle and began to cycle away. Looking back, she shouted, 'If you can catch me, Thornton… you can have my body… later.' She turned back and continued riding away.

'Wait!' shouted Blake. 'Wait for me. Please don't leave me behind, Catherine… Not this time… not ever again.'

He hit the play button on the Sony Walkman clipped to his belt, and a Billy Joel song started to play. He smiled, then laughed and jumped onto his bike and pedalled after her as fast as he could.

He caught up with Catherine, and they continued cycling together.

'So, what will you do with your life, Thornton? Once we finish uni?'

'I don't know. Never really thought about it.'

'You're good with words. Maybe… maybe you should work for a newspaper. That could be fun.'

'No, don't fancy that,' replied Blake thoughtfully. 'Not really my thing.'

'I need to know that you're a good proposition,' said Catherine.

'Good proposition?' queried Blake.

'For marriage. I don't want to waste my time.'

'Oh, I see. Hadn't thought quite that far ahead.'

'Well, you should… I have.'

'Oh,' replied Blake.

'What about… What about writing or publishing? That must be fascinating.'

Blake thought about that briefly, and an odd sensation entered his mind. 'No, not publishing. I will never go into that. All those sad stories end tragically, and everybody dies. I couldn't read books like that for a lifetime. No, I will probably go into teaching or maybe accountancy; that's a rewarding career. But publishing? No, I could never do that, not ever…'

The End.

If you enjoyed this book, why not try the next in the Story Teller Pentalogy. Each tale explores a relationship and how it changes.
The first chapter follows…

Sarah is four, and her brother Harry is seven. In their innocence, they discover sex and form a relationship that will last until Harry is thirty-seven.
I found this to be a tender and considered examination of the psychological roots and emotional impact of incest. A compelling read from beginning to end. Lee Siegal, New York Examiner. 2015

Chapter 1. The Prospect of Redemption.
2017. Aftermath and Recrimination

'Carla must have known we wanted to love her and how much you loved her. That's the bit I don't understand and what I find so bloody bewildering.'

There was a sadness in Nigel's voice laden with unfathomable desperation and uncertainty. The palpable liquidity of wretchedness and sorrow sank to the floor like spilt sticky black treacle oozing slowly into every corner of the room. It felt so tactile you could almost touch it, grasp it in your hands.

The inevitable bitter recriminations that had begun to surface were, I suppose, a natural reaction to his mother's unexpected death and his forlorn attempt to understand what had driven her to take her own life.

'Maybe we needed that. Something to obscure the clarity,' replied Tony.

'What, you think we created this fog of confusion,' queried Nigel, slightly puzzled?

'Yes, perhaps we did. Maybe sometimes it is necessary….' Tony paused momentarily and gazed upwards, searching his mind for something. 'I once read something written by a sixteenth-century cardinal. I can't remember which one, but he was talking about the uncertainty of those times. What he said has always stuck in my mind. "*If you remove every vestige of ambiguity in the world, the clarity you have left will always be to your detriment.*" Maybe it was something like this he was referring to.'

'So better not to know everything?' suggested Nigel.

'Yes, some of the time... possibly. It seems to make sense oddly. Carla did know we loved her, but maybe that just wasn't enough,' replied Tony.

'Enough? Enough for what?' rounded Nigel, rage and frustration eating into every syllable.

'To destroy the demons inside her...' replied Tony. 'Was our love for her strong enough to outweigh the hurt and guilt she felt inside? That's what we'll never know, what it felt like for her, what she went through alone, every day, always asking the same question, was it her? Was it something she did?'

'You did love her?' asked Nigel, spoken as a question and a valediction. As if to reassure himself that she had taken something good to the grave.

'Yes, yes, I did once. I loved her for a long time, and sometimes I thought she loved me, but it's not always what it seems. One loves, and one is loved; isn't that the way it is? Perhaps, she just couldn't love anyone anymore. I don't know.' Tony took another sip of his whisky.

'You could have left her then?' suggested Nigel, but more in explication than instruction.

'Like her first husband did? Yes, I could have walked away and caused her more pain, more anguish, but did she deserve that? ... Or I could stay, say nothing, work at it and hope things got better. What I didn't realise was the price I would have to pay. That a tiny, almost imperceptible part of me would die each day until one morning, I woke and realised nothing was left. Every trace of love, desire and longing, every feeling I ever had for her, had gone. Slowly eaten away by years of emptiness and regret, indifference and eventually contempt, utter contempt. Worse still, she had grown to despise me for not leaving. She thought I was there out of pity - and you should always beware of the organically destructive nature of pity. It's the same if you can't forgive someone; eventually, it will destroy you - not the artless recipient of your vicarious empathy.'

'You did stay for over twenty-five years, so maybe she was right?' suggested Nigel hesitantly.

Tony glanced at Nigel, it was a pivotal observation, and Tony needed to think carefully about it before he replied.

'No, it wasn't out of pity; that was the irony. Why should I? I didn't know what happened all those years ago. Sarah didn't tell me anything not until she was nearly twenty-four; then, it was too late to do anything. It had all finished years before. The damage was done. That was when I realised why Carla had been the way she was for such a long time. I thought she was still blaming herself for one thing, but she was thinking about something else altogether. Maybe that's why she grew to despise me because I stayed, and she had to face me every day. That was a constant reminder that no one else was to blame, but that was the absurdity - for nobody was really to blame. It was just an unfortunate combination of circumstances. If they had happened in any other order, the outcome would probably have been completely different - but they didn't.' Tony took another sip of whisky.

'That's a lot of wasted years for you,' mumbled Nigel, looking down into his cup.

'Not really,' replied Tony, 'we all make sacrifices of one kind or another in this life. As my old Dad used to say, you can't get out for nowt. Love is about giving as well as receiving, not necessarily in equal measures, and sometimes that means giving something up. In my case, it took time, but it was worth it. I saw you all grow up, and I had all your love, and I've had Jennie's love for the last twelve years. That's enough. I don't think I missed out on too much. I'm happy with that.'

'But she stole those years and gave you nothing back,' replied Nigel, 'You only get them once, and now they've gone.'

Tony took a sip of his drink - he needed to buy a few more moments before making his reply. He and Nigel had never had this conversation before. He knew he would only have one chance to tell it as it was, and this was it. There would be no going back - no second attempt...

'If she was the thief of time, I was her willing accomplice. Most of us spend large parts of our lives doing something we don't really want to do, but if you're with the person you want to be with, that's the deal you take. For me, that was Carla, and she was all I wanted. Very few of us get to fulfil our dreams and ambitions without some emotional trade-off. The rest of us settle for something slightly less than we always desired or hoped for. But it's good, and it'll do. Occasionally you think of what might have been if you had been dealt a different hand. But in the end, you take what you've been given, grudgingly maybe, but you do take it. Living with someone, anyone, for a long time means embracing a certain amount of compromise and the necessity to make concessions. If we did not, we would all live alone, becoming bitter and resentful.' Tony half-smiled.

'You could still have left her years ago,' questioned Nigel.

'Son, what you have to understand is the rate of attrition was imperceptible. It was like being silently desensitised while I was asleep. I never really noticed what was happening until one day, twenty-five years had passed, and we weren't in love anymore.' Tony stopped briefly and thought about what he had just said. He had never actually said the words before. There had never been anybody he wanted to explain it to, not until now. 'But there were some good times, you know, great days – funny days, days when we were so much in love that I couldn't imagine life without her. Today, I can't imagine what it would be like without her being around, but now it doesn't matter anymore.' Tony paused for a moment to think about what he had said… 'So, it wasn't all bad, being there, watching you and David being born, and watching you grow up. Those were good years. I would have missed much of that had I left. I still think back to the summers when we all used to play cricket in the garden. Harry was about sixteen by then – you were about eight or nine, David was six and Sarah… Sarah was just a teenager…'

Nigel interrupted. 'I remember Harry smashed a ball into Wainthropp's greenhouse next door and broke loads of glass. We all hid in the shed for hours playing cards when old Wainthropp came looking for us. He kept walking up and down his garden waving his stick about and mumbling to himself and wouldn't go back inside.'

'Carla told him we were all in the village doing some shopping,' added Tony, smiling. 'And he believed her even though he was holding the offending cricket ball with my name on it. She told him I'd lost it ages ago, and he still believed her. Very convincing.'

'She was a good liar... even then.' Nigel could never completely let go of the resentment he felt.

'Sarah seemed okay today. It didn't affect her the way I thought it would,' said Tony, adroitly redirecting the conversation away from Nigel's comment.

'Strangely, she enjoys funerals. Always has,' remarked Nigel.

'I find it hard to believe that anybody likes being at a funeral,' replied Tony, a little surprised at Nigel's comment.

'I think Sarah made a special effort for her mother,' replied Nigel sounding almost scornful.

'Does she still hate her,' asked Tony? He knew the answer, but he had to ask anyway. Sarah seldom spoke about her mother to Tony directly, and he chose not to go to places where there were still too many bad memories.

'She was betrayed, Dad. What do you think?'

'She was just an old lady who deserved some redemption at the end,' replied Tony defensively. Perhaps, the memories of happier days had worn away the bitterness he once felt and had managed to keep so carefully hidden for so long. And maybe it was time for a graceful valediction. Tony was not a man to harbour resentment, an admirable trait inherited from his father, a man of robust Northern ways.

'She wasn't always old,' said Nigel, who hadn't inherited his grandfather's magnanimity.

'I'm still afraid for you all,' said Tony with a trepidacious tone that lingered in the words as much as in the content.

'Why? She's gone. Nothing is left, but the memory, and that will fade in time,' replied Nigel abruptly.

'That's the bit I'm afraid of, the memory. I can't do anything about that.'

'You don't have to. We are okay. This is closure for them and me. It ends today, or at least it starts to end.'

'Does it, though?' asked Tony. 'I still think I was partly to blame. I still can't believe I never saw anything. I keep wondering if there was something I missed, a telling glance, a gesture, I don't know. Something I should have seen but may be ignored. You miss so much just because you only see what you want to see, even when it's there, right in front of you, hidden in plain sight.'

'Dad, you were nothing to do with it. You weren't even there for the first five years. That's when it all really started.'

'But why didn't it stop when I married your mother? That's what I don't understand,' replied Tony, reproaching himself and sounding fearfully bewildered.

'Because nothing changed,' said Nigel. 'She allowed it to continue. She never loved Harry or Sarah, and when you married her, all they saw was that she appeared capable of loving somebody, just not them.'

'But I loved Harry and Sarah just like you and David. I never had a favourite or anything like that.'

'Maybe it was something to do with their father?' suggested Nigel. 'Maybe she hated him so much she took it out on them. I don't know.' Tony didn't answer.

Although Tony was aware of Harry and Sarah's father, he had to all intent, played no part in their lives since Tony and Carla were married. Apart, that is, from the occasional Christmas and birthday cards in the early years. Invariably the birthday cards arrived on the wrong day, sometimes even the wrong month. Carla would hide the cards if they came early and produce them on the appropriate dates. Barry had never enquired about their well-being. They, in turn, had tacitly reciprocated by seldom mentioning him except in an oddly estranged third-party context. It was almost as if a mutual agenda of exclusion existed, but it was something he was not a party to. In the early years, Tony had often deliberated over this self-imposed disownment. He often wondered what possible reason their father might have had to sever all contact with them. But as the children grew older and the cards stopped arriving, he gave it less and less thought.

His first instinct was that Barry must have had the same natural feelings for his children as Tony now had for them. And yet, on the evidence available, this apparently was not the case. This was something Tony couldn't comprehend with any degree of clarity. Ironically, it had made the formation of the paternal relationship between them far more natural than he had anticipated. Tony now felt in every respect that he was their father. When he was younger, the concept was alien to his comprehension of lifestyle arrangements. But his views softened, mellowed, and matured - more so than he had thought possible with each passing year. His love for all his children was equal to any man's love for their children.

'We know you loved us. We always knew that, but for Carla, that was the hardest thing of all. The one sense, the one emotion she couldn't handle,' continued Nigel.

'What, me loving my children?' exclaimed Tony, a little surprised and slightly bewildered by this declaration.

'No, not you loving us,' replied Nigel. 'It was Carla coming to terms with how you could love Sarah and Harry the same way you loved us, even though you weren't their father. No matter how she tried, she couldn't do that. Carla couldn't understand that, and I don't think she ever did. She may well have even resented you for being able to love them... us.'

Tony began to consider something he had never really thought about before.

Had he ever really stood back and looked at their relationship objectively? Instead of only considering how he had felt and still felt about all his children – maybe he should have considered how Carla had felt? Had he been too timid in the face of self-possession to see something that had always been there? Had he subconsciously chosen to overlook and ignore it? His love for Carla had always been very intense, despite the paucity of any overt reciprocation on her part. Perhaps this had blinded him over the years. At times, he had even found this predilection to detachment, this ability to encapsulate her emotional relationships in different boxes, to be an attractive quality in Carla.

'Perhaps you're right, but now we'll never know.'

'It doesn't matter anyway,' replied Nigel.

'Hadn't you better go back to bed? Barbara will be wondering where you are,' enquired Tony.

'It's okay. She's fast asleep. Are you sure you don't want anything?' asked Nigel.

'No, son. I have everything I want now....'

'Goodnight, Dad.'

'Goodnight, son.'

Nigel moved his head slightly to one side and ran his left forefinger slowly up and down his neck, thinking over what they had said. 'I love you, Dad.' He smiled as a son does to a father he loves.

'I love you too, son,' replied Tony smiling.

Nigel returned to bed, and Tony resumed looking out the window. The church bells rang out on a warm Saturday morning in late July.

Please send comments to butchmoss@outlook.com or review on amazon books at www.amazon.com
The Tusitala.

If you enjoyed this book, why not try the next in the Story Teller Pentalogy. Each tale explores a relationship and how it changes.

Chapter 1. The Killing Plan.
Part I

2023. For reasons never clearly explained at the inquest, the car in which they were travelling untethered itself from the left-hand carriageway matrix, crossed the electronic central reservation and re-tethered itself to the right-hand carriageway oncoming vehicle matrix. Strangely, no alarms sounded. The sixty-ton SCOMTEL freightliner practically obliterated the vehicle. Rendering it utterly unrecognisable after nine sets of giant wheels had passed over it. Eventually, the freightliner pulled to a halt approximately two hundred yards past the point of collision. At first, the police did not believe the wreckage was a car but something that had fallen from the back of a lorry. However, closer inspection of the debris – coupled with the frantic emergency telephone call from the driver of the freightliner – indicated that something far worse had occurred.

The ferocity of the impact had left no part of the flattened vehicular collage thicker than the width of a finger. This meant there was insufficient body mass to immediately confirm the involvement of people. The tech team could only find scraps of body tissue, blood residue and some tiny fragments of bone. Most of the blood had soaked into the road by the time the emergency services arrived. This could easily have been attributed to a hedgehog or a badger, but it was enough for the forensic team to later confirm from DNA analysis that two people had been involved and who they were. The only item from the car that appeared undamaged by the impact was the tiny plutomarium isotope from the vehicle's power system. Somewhat conspicuously, this was lying in a small pool of quietly bubbling mahogany brown liquid. It glowed with a shimmering shade of pink, a chemical reaction usually triggered by the presence of saltwater.

The road was closed for two days while the forensic investigation team tried to discover how a vehicle could break free of the AMGS (Atlas Matrix Guidance System) and then reattach itself on the wrong side of the road. The many failsafe procedures built into the road and the computerised guidance system integrated into every Protton vehicle's electronic brain made it technically impossible. Nevertheless, it had happened. It was eventually determined at the inquest that it was probably due to an anti-transient system malfunction of an unspecified nature, whatever that was supposed to mean.

Part II
Catherine

It was a late summer's day in 2009. Still warm but soft, delinquent breezes had begun to blow, heralding nature's autumnal transition. A time when unforgiving temperaments had mellowed and were starting to prepare for the equinox that would eventually sweep them, imperceptibly, into the cold depths of winter. However, before those darker days arrived, there would be a period of graceful light and long shadows. Hopefully, these would soften the sharp edges of the harsh reality that was to follow.

The first golden leaves were beginning to fall. Each caught up in a spiralling vortex as if waltzing to Strauss at a Venetian ball in the Doges' Palace before breaking free and wistfully pirouetting to Mother Earth. Occasionally, one or two would find a final breath of wind. And for a few moments, in silent desperation, they would swirl upwards one last time to dance around the gates of Downing Street. Amid the hustle and bustle of daily life, each leaf seemed to believe it was an integral and indispensable part of the proceedings. That was before surrendering to the inevitable and eventually settling onto the cold grey pavement. Finally, it was preparing to shrivel away and turn to dust or be swept away by the council street cleaners.

Sergeant Mackenzie Parish, as he was then, first noticed Catherine on one of these days – their lives would always be marked by such moments. She was part of a delegation of trainee doctors visiting Number Ten to present a petition. They objected to the excessive hours they were forced to work in hospitals during their final years at medical school. They believed this practice jeopardised the fundamental integrity of the job for which they were being trained. Catherine had only been at medical school for just over a year but still felt passionately enough about their grievance to join the committee that had prepared the petition. The fact that she was stunningly beautiful had not been wholly lost on the other committee members. To some degree, they were guilty of co-opting her into assisting them with an established marketing tenet. The media were always slightly more responsive to and supportive of a cause with a visually attractive and articulate spokesperson – and a justifiable complaint. A patronisingly sexist ploy to present an argument, possibly. But doctors live in a world of pragmatism - not a make-believe Disneyland where dreams come true and there is always a happy ending. They needed all the media attention they could muster, and Catherine was the means to that end.

Parish was there on routine security duty when he first noticed her in the crowd of interns chanting and waving placards. She was hard not to see. She was also holding the petition, patiently waiting her turn to present it to the Prime Minister's aide. He eventually came out from Number Ten and up to the railings that now barricaded both ends of Downing Street. The days of handing over a petition, with all the attendant kudos of a photograph in front of the famous black door, were long gone. Catherine had read somewhere that the colour you painted your front door indicated something about you. Black, oddly, was considered to convey the message, 'Stay away! We don't appreciate visitors – Private.'

On the other hand, Red meant you were probably a liberal-minded extrovert, an exhibitionist, al-fresco sex sort of person. Green suggested a traditionalist, staid, conformist; white, organised, religious, neat, and clean, and so on. It was all vacuous rubbish, of course, but it filled a couple of pages in a Sunday colour supplement once a year.

Although she was some ten yards away, her zeal and animated desire to make her point were plain to see. It was this burning desire that first captured Parish's attention. Charming itself into his imagination where it ran wild. When their eyes met, it was just one fleeting glance, but in that split second, he could see the fiery passion in her soul. Something that had been missing from his life for a very long time.

Catherine turned back to speak to the aide from Number Ten, and the moment was gone. She handed over the petition, thanked him with a smile, and press photos were taken. Garrulously walking away with her friends, momentarily exhilarated at having succeeded in her mission. She turned back – the frenzy of the previous moment's elation now abated – and gazed at Parish for the second time. The apocryphal tales of love, at first sight were never further from either of their minds. But in that one fantastic moment, any preconceived cynicism was shattered like an enormous explosion in the brain. She turned around and made her way slowly back through the jostling crowd toward where he stood. It felt like one of those stupid slow-motion moments in a film when the camera was over-cranked and re-run at normal speed. He continued to gaze at her as a stunned gazelle mesmerised in the glare of headlights. The traffic's commotion and noise became muffled and grey and began to fade from his consciousness. He felt his heart pound in his chest as if it were about to burst. This wasn't really happening, he thought. I've been watching too many romcoms. Maybe I should get out more and socialise with ordinary people. All these thoughts raced through his mind when she suddenly stood before him, gazing up interrogatively, without a splinter of shyness.

'I'm Catherine,' she spoke quietly and smiled disarmingly. 'Would you like to come for a drink? We're celebrating.' The lilting quality of her voice seemed to hang listlessly in the air.

I didn't answer immediately. I needed to make sure I hadn't imagined it. My throat had chosen this particular moment to dry up for some inexplicable reason, so I couldn't respond, even if I had wanted to. After a few moments, sufficient moisture returned to my throat, and I was able to reply to what was now a somewhat perplexed Catherine.

'Eh, yes,' I eventually spluttered out, 'but I'm on duty right now. Could it be tonight? I'm off at six.' I suddenly felt like a little boy back at school, explaining to a potential date that I had to stay behind in detention and couldn't walk her home. It all sounded so embarrassingly feeble, and we both knew it.

'Oh! You're a police officer!' she replied coyly. 'I didn't realise.'

'Eh, yes,' I replied a little cautiously. I think my eyes instinctively opened a little wider despite the sunlight. They tended to do that under certain circumstances, this being one of them. Probably has something to do with the brain suddenly demanding more visual information to fully assess how that admission affected someone's demeanour. Body language, expression, eyes…

'Is that a problem?' I asked, suddenly aware of a hint of intractability in her voice. I was unaccustomed to being asked out by an attractive woman, especially one I had never met before. Her precocious suggestion had caught me completely off guard. Catherine had also detected the thin martyred air of remorseful anguish in the tenor of my voice. She later told me she found it quite endearing. It was as if this liaison might suddenly end because of who I was, and all would be lost. Like most women, she was hard-wired with the mysterious ability to extrapolate a meaningful inference from the tiniest gesture or inflection - as far as men were concerned.

'No, not at all, I just didn't realise,' replied Catherine reassuringly. The words were enough to staunch any further loss of confidence I might have felt, and I think she knew that. I had half expected some dry political comment, conditioned as we were to be taunted with all manner of cleverly constructed, politically biased epigrams at these assemblies - but none was forthcoming. 'Aren't you going to arrest me then,' she asked playfully? Her face lit up with contained pleasure as she swivelled playfully on her high heels, her eyes never losing contact with mine.

'Why should I arrest you? I asked. Surprised at the question and unsure how I should reply. 'Have you done something wrong?'

'No,' she replied, 'but I'm sure you could think of something... if you really wanted to.' I smiled; unbelievably, I knew I was already falling in love. We stood there silently for a moment - just looking at each other as if unsure of what should happen next.

'Pen!' she suddenly spluttered, holding out her hand and waving it around jauntily.

I rummaged desperately through my pockets and eventually found a pencil, which I held up, maybe a little over-jubilantly. Catherine smiled kindly, trying not to laugh, took it and scribbled down her telephone number on a scrap of paper she had produced from her jean pocket and handed them back to me. 'Call me when you are...' Catherine paused for what seemed like an interminable amount of time, carefully considering which word to use to close the instruction before eventually settling on 'available.' She uttered the word slowly, letting it drift out of her mouth on a small breath of air - with all the hidden agenda she could marshal into four tiny syllables without sounding slightly demented. Then she smiled again.

I was initially slightly surprised at her manner, but then again, I was not. This was who she was. Catherine reached up on her toes and kissed me gently on the cheek, 'there you go.' Then she turned on her heels and sashayed her way back to her friends, waving goodbye with her hand above her head as she disappeared into the crowd. I didn't move; I couldn't. Somehow, I knew I must remember this moment. Commit every detail to memory, every word, every gesture, and every inflection, for it would never happen again. I called her at six-thirty that night, and we arranged to meet up at a pub near Trafalgar Square, and our life began.

Jade
Part III

2023. Jade had been staying at a friend's house on the other side of Providence near Harlow for a couple of days. Catherine had agreed to pick her up that night as Parish was working late, and she had a few things to do on the way. It was nearly nine o'clock, and darkness had descended when Catherine arrived at Tasha's home.

She was going to toot the horn to alert Jade she had arrived. It was cold outside, and she was warm and cosy inside the car and didn't relish the thought of getting out into the freezing wind, even if only for a few minutes. But noticing how quiet it looked – it was an attractive neighbourhood, with pretty, tall, narrow townhouses and ornate lampposts. The residents would probably not appreciate their peace and tranquillity being rudely interrupted by some inconsiderate stranger sounding a car horn in the street. Not while they were all quietly dozing in front of their holavisions. She reconsidered her decision, slid out of the car, gathered her coat tightly around her to fend off the biting wind, and quickly made the short journey to the front door and rang the bell.

Jade answered the door with a smile - already wearing her coat, scarf, and pink woolly hat. 'Hi, Mum.' She kissed Catherine on the cheek. 'I'm packed and ready to go.' She pointed to her small rucksack by the door. She knew she was not the best timekeeper in the world - but she had obviously made an effort to be ready on time today. It would be a long drive home in the dark.

'Bye, Tash. See yer later,' Jade shouted up the staircase. 'Thanks for everything.'

'Bye, Jade. See you Monday,' came the disembodied reply. Jade smiled, picked up her rucksack and slammed the front door behind her. The wintry night air seemed to have no effect on her.

'Tash is having a bubble bath,' muttered Jade as they walked down the path. 'She'll be hours. She likes to put all those little pink

314

candles around the room, burn incense and play whale music while soaking. I had one earlier... it's very soothing, music, candles and everything....'

'Sounds lovely,' said Catherine, but she did wonder about the whale music. 'I think maybe I'll have a bath when we get back.'

Jade threw her rucksack into the back of the car and flopped down next to Catherine.

'The bath has made me a bit tired, Mum. Is it okay if I go to sleep?'

'Of course, it is. I'll join you in a few minutes anyway,' replied Catherine. Jade pressed a button to lower the back of her seat into the sleeping position and closed her eyes, and Catherine drove away.

Catherine didn't enjoy driving long hours at night, so she, too, would sleep once the car was locked onto the AMGS network. There was nothing further for her to do until they arrived home. She looked across at Jade, now snuggled up into a ball. Already blissfully asleep, her face a serenely calm marble sculpture peeking out from her hood, flawless and untainted by the ravages of time, obligation, or responsibility, with no concept of what fate might await her. The triumphs that she might reach out to touch - the disappointment when they recede just beyond her grasp. You never know what might lie ahead in the years to come. Oh, to be young again. Oh, to be you, thought Catherine. Not a care in the world – a free spirit without... without what, she pondered? I have Parish, I have you, and I have a career. What more could there be? She admonished herself for one fleeting moment of selfish ingratitude - then wondered from where she had conjured those thoughts. Instead, she pushed the corrosive line of harmful indulgence from her mind and deliberated over the unmistakable similarity between father and daughter. It was still a remarkable aspect of human design to assiduously carry forward small, unique traits from parent to child. The same features would always endear and cement families. Nearly everything would change throughout their lives, but certain things would forever remain the same.

Maybe it was time to have another baby. Maybe her hormones were playing games with her mind; she was not getting any younger. Jade would be off to university soon, and then she and

Parish would be alone again. Was it wrong to have another baby to alleviate the pain they would feel when Jade had gone? I will mention it to Parish tomorrow; yes, I will do that. She made another mental note to broach the subject over dinner the following evening and tried to settle down to sleep. But sleep wouldn't come.

Her mind flashed back to the day they first met. She smiled, thinking of the first few weeks of their relationship. Chaotic rotas to juggle just so they could be together. Intense candlelit meals in a quiet bistro or restaurant when neither was hungry. The food was played with but seldom eaten. Sometimes, the waiters would ask if something was wrong with it - but there never was. They were just too immersed in each other to eat. Too involved with each other, talking about anything and everything. And then there were the long nights of lovemaking at Parish's flat. Catherine lived in a shared house with three other girls, which was not ideal for what they had in mind. Sometimes, in the mornings, they would have exotic feasts, figs, guava fruit and eggs benedict or smoked salmon, wild strawberries, and pink champagne. A little decadent, maybe, but an essential respite to allow them to regenerate and replenish their exhausted bodies and prepare them for the labours of the days ahead.

Those deliriously irrational days and nights stretched into weeks and months, then years - but the passion of their frenzied existence had now slowed a little since Jade was born. The three of them had eased into a gently quixotic intermezzo - a pause before the raging storm.....

The Killing Plan.